THE HANGMAN'S REVOLUTION

Other Books by Eoin Colfer

AIRMAN

BENNY AND BABE

BENNY AND OMAR

HALF MOON INVESTIGATIONS

THE SUPERNATURALIST

THE WISH LIST

ARTEMIS FOWL

ARTEMIS FOWL: THE ARCTIC INCIDENT

ARTEMIS FOWL: THE ETERNITY CODE

ARTEMIS FOWL: THE OPAL DECEPTION

ARTEMIS FOWL: THE LOST COLONY

ARTEMIS FOWL: THE TIME PARADOX

ARTEMIS FOWL: THE ATLANTIS COMPLEX

ARTEMIS FOWL: THE LAST GUARDIAN

WARP: THE RELUCTANT ASSASSIN

Graphic Novels

ARTEMIS FOWL: THE GRAPHIC NOVEL

ARTEMIS FOWL: THE ARCTIC INCIDENT: THE GRAPHIC NOVEL

ARTEMIS FOWL: THE ETERNITY CODE: THE GRAPHIC NOVEL

THE SUPERNATURALIST: THE GRAPHIC NOVEL

And for Younger Readers

EOIN COLFER'S LEGEND OF SPUD MURPHY

EOIN COLFER'S LEGEND OF CAPTAIN CROW'S TEETH

EOIN COLFER'S LEGEND OF THE WORST BOY IN THE WORLD

THE HANGMAN'S REVOLUTION

EOIN COLFER

BOOK TWO

HYPERION
LOS ANGELES NEW YORK

First U.S. edition
1 3 5 7 9 10 8 6 4 2
G475-5664-5-14091
Printed in the United States of America

Library of Congress Cataloging-in-Publication Data
Colfer, Eoin.
The hangman's revolution/Eoin Colfer.—First U.S. edition.
pages cm.—(W.A.R.P.; [2])
Summary: FBI agent Chevie Savano escapes into the past to escape the secret police after they kill Charles Smart just as he is telling her of the WARP program, and she and Riley team up to find Colonel Clayton Box before he can launch missles at the capitals of Europe.
ISBN 978-1-4231-6163-9 (hardback)
[1. Time travel—Fiction. 2. Assassins—Fiction. 3. London (England)—History—19th century—Fiction. 4. Great Britain—History—Victoria, 1837–1901—Fiction. 5. Science fiction.] I. Title.
PZ7.C677475Han 2014
[Fic]—dc23 2014001938

Reinforced binding

Visit www.hyperionteens.com

To Dr. William Colfer

THE HANGMAN'S REVOLUTION

What Might Have Been . . .

TOWARD THE END OF THE TWENTIETH CENTURY, Scottish professor Charles Smart succeeded in stabilizing a time tunnel to Victorian London (constructed from exotic matter with negative energy density, duh). Within months the FBI had established the **Witness Anonymous Relocation Program** to stash federal witnesses in the past. When the professor learned that Colonel Box of WARP division was planning to use the wormhole to manipulate governments and regimes, he fled, horrified, into the past, taking his codes with him—a wasted gesture, really, since Colonel Box and his entire unit had disappeared on a mission only days before.

Smart returned to the twenty-first century some years later, but he was far too dead to share his secrets. His arrival had quantum repercussions, which ensnared young FBI consultant Chevron Savano and even younger Riley, a boy from Victorian London who wished to escape the career of assassin mapped out for him by his evil master, the conjurer and murderer for hire Albert Garrick.

Garrick pursued his apprentice to the future and back, but he was ultimately cut adrift in the Smarthole with no means to reassemble his physical person.

More stuff happened, too. High adventure, close calls, and belly laughs—but that's another story (it's quite the story, to be honest) and has no place muddling up this report.

So all's well that ends well for our spirited pair of young adventurers?

For Chevie, not so much, as we will find out.

For Riley, even less so, which will become almost immediately apparent.

Chevie's brief presence in Victorian London caused temporal ripples, which were to have a dire effect on the present. Simply put, Chevron Savano was noticed in the past by the previously mentioned Colonel Box, who had actually set up shop in Victorian London. As a result, the colonel was prompted to have Riley murdered and then move up his world-domination plan by a few days, causing the downfall of major world powers and the emergence of the Boxite Empire. If Chevie had not been noticed, then Box would have stuck to his original Emergence

Day and the catacombs where he made his base would have flooded, foiling his plans forever.

Chevie now lives as a Boxite cadet in a timeline that is not her own. Her mind is rejecting modern-day London and allowing her original memories of time travel adventures and the FBI to bleed through. For cases like Chevie's, Professor Smart predicted two hypothetical outcomes: either the time traveler drowns the visions in antipsychotic drugs so that he/she may live some kind of normal life, or the visions will become so vivid that their discordance with actual events will drive the subject insane.

When we join the story, Chevron Savano's visions are becoming extremely vivid, and if there were antipsychotic drugs handy, they certainly would not be wasted on a mere army cadet.

1 » MOLEY & GOOGOO

If you go back in time and assassinate Rasputin, then there's no need to go back and assassinate Rasputin. So is old Grigori dead, or isn't he?
—Professor Charles Smart

BOXITE YOUTH ACADEMY, PRESENT-DAY LONDON, NEW ALBION, 115 BC (BOXITE CALENDAR)

LONDON TOWN.

Once there had been a magic about the city. Just hearing the name conjured images of Dickens's young trickster Dodger, or of Sherlock Holmes in Baker Street putting his mind to a three-pipe problem, or of any one of a thousand tales of adventure and derring-do that were woven through London's magnificent avenues and shadowy network of backstreets and alleys. For centuries people had journeyed from across the world to England's capital to see where their favorite stories were set, or perhaps to make their fortune, or maybe to simply stand and gaze at the wonders of Trafalgar Square or Big Ben.

Not anymore. Those days of magic were long gone.

For one thing, the tourist industry did not really exist in the Boxite Empire, and for another, Big Ben had been torn down decades ago to make room for a giant statue of the Blessed Colonel, whose stone eyes watched over the city and everyone in it. And Big Ben was not the only landmark dragged under by the Boxites. Brick by brick, the Empire was erasing relics of the past and remaking London in its own image: uniform, imposing, gray, and implacable.

Almost all of the office buildings were constructed out of poured concrete with little in the way of distinguishing marks, just row upon row of dimly lit windows, lidded by half-drawn blinds. As the older London buildings were worn away by acid rain, they were demolished and replaced by utility blocks dropped in place by mega-copters. The blocks were pre-wired and plumbed and just required connection to the main supplies to be fully operational. London's history was being erased on a daily basis.

One such building that had fallen into disrepair and was due to be dynamited in six months' time was the Boxite Youth Academy, the officer school for the Empire's military, where cadets from all over the world came to be indoctrinated in the way of the Blessed Colonel.

Inside this most austere academy no attempt had been made to cater to the comfort or physical well-being of the cadets. Benches were hard stone, and thin mattresses were laid on flat planks. The Spartan model was often cited and weak candidates were not encouraged to play to their strengths but instead traded to one of the Boxite Empire's harsher institutes.

Inside her cubicle, seventeen-year-old Cadet Chevron Savano woke before the morning's reveille siren but kept her eyes closed in order to prepare herself for the day's nightmares.

No, not nightmares, Chevie thought. Though the Blessed Colonel knows I have plenty of those. These are daymares. Waking visions.

Chevie tugged the cot's rough army blanket over her head so that the wall-mounted Boxlights could not even cast a glow on the insides of her eyelids.

What's wrong with me? she wondered. Why do I see things that aren't there?

These visions were interfering catastrophically with her training at the Boxite Youth Academy. Chevie's scores had dipped quite sharply in recent days, so much so that the file clipped to the foot of her bed had an orange card tucked into the folder.

An orange card. A review. The first warning and perhaps her last if she could not make a satisfactory show of herself. The academy rules were sacrosanct. One serious slip, and her place would be offered to the next in line.

And it was a long line. Millions of souls long.

Her review was today, and if it went badly, she could be sold to a Box soldier factory in Dublin—or worse, to the mines in Newcastle as a spade monkey.

Chevie shuddered.

A spade monkey? Surely that would be a fate worse than death.

Chevron could pinpoint exactly when the visions started. It had been six months ago, on the night she'd sleepwalked down to the academy's musty basement and collapsed in a heap of mysterious half-formed clothes: long ropes of drenched, saturated cloth that looped her body like dark serpents. She had been wearing neither nightshirt nor slippers, just this strange material that dissolved into slop as she slowly woke. Then her stomach had convulsed and she'd vomited a strange glowing gel that turned to light particles and drifted away like fireflies.

Light? she remembered thinking.

Am I dying?

Is this death?

But her breath had come in rattling whoops, and Chevie's heart had hammered a testimony to her hold on life.

How did I get here?

Where is here?

Cadet Savano had covered herself with an old dropcloth yanked from a pile of paint cans and she'd stumbled to the top of a wrought iron staircase, her legs as weak as a newborn's.

I am in a basement of some sort, she'd thought.

This is where the Timepod was, dummy, said a voice in her head. *You've come back.*

This voice, which was to become very familiar, made no sense, and so Chevie had ignored it.

Chevie had pounded on the locked door, calling out for help, which arrived eventually in the lumpily muscled shapes of the academy's night watch: two Thundercats, Clover Vallicose and Lunka Witmeyer, secret police attached to the academy. So Chevie was in the academy, at least.

Thundercats? Chevie had thought. She'd giggled and was instantly horrified.

Thundercats? Why would that name make her giggle? A person did not giggle around Thundercats. They were licensed to use necessary and unnecessary force up to, but not exceeding, the infliction of mortal wounds.

How do you exceed mortal wounds? wondered Chevie.

Two days, the Thundercats had told her that night, frowning above their splashback visors. *Two days we've been looking for you, orphan. And you show up in a restricted area. How in the name of the Blessed Colonel did you get down here? And why are you laughing? Do you find us amusing?*

Chevron could only shake her head dumbly. There was nothing in her mind but lingering dreams, confusion, and questions that truncated each other before they were fully born.

How did I . . .

What was that . . .

Riley?

Who?

Why?

It was at that moment the visions—visions that would rip her ordered life apart—began. Before her disbelieving eyes the Thundercats had cracked and split into broken mirror images of themselves. They were replaced by an elderly woman with an unruly cone of hair piled on top of her head.

I knew you'd come, she'd said. *Charles said you would, and Charles Smart is never wrong.*

Then the elderly lady had disappeared, and the Thundercats were reassembled—and Chevie found herself thrashing in their arms, desperate to beat her way free from whatever nightmare she had woken into.

Quietly does it, little bird, Sister Lunka Witmeyer had advised her.

Chevie had trembled like a criminal on the Trafalgar Square public rack.

Who was the elderly woman in her visions? And who was Charles Smart?

These were things she could neither answer nor ask aloud for fear of being judged *unstable* and being shipped off to a school for the hopeless. Chevie's mind teemed with forbidden questions. They kept her awake at night and made her feel dopey all day.

It's a tumor, she thought several times a minute. My brain is eating itself.

And now it was several months later and the visions had cracked the chalice of Chevie's life, which had not exactly been brimming with golden hope to begin with. She was a cadet in a school that bred police, soldiers, and spies for the Boxite army. A hard life of mistrust and interrogation lay ahead of her, if she was lucky. And now it seemed that she would not be lucky. Just like her best friend DeeDee had not been lucky.

• • •

Chevie opened her eyes and, for the time being at least, the world was as her mind stubbornly insisted it should be. No hallucinations. No sharp pain in her temple, which lately had preceded the visions.

I am in the dormitory. Good.

The bunk above her was empty. DeeDee—her friend, counsel, and confederate ever since enrollment—had slept there. They had studied the Boxnet together and practiced their hand-to-hand combat with each other. But DeeDee was gone now, executed for spying, and Chevie herself had been under a pall of suspicion for months.

Chevie was no traitor, and even if she had questions or doubts about Box's Empire she kept them to herself, because the alternatives to living under Box's wing were the wilderness of the Blasted States or the mountain encampments of the barbarian Jax.

No one is happy all the time. The colonel himself was forced to hide in London's catacombs for decades before he emerged with his divine machines.

Suddenly and without the warning of approaching footsteps, the curtain was whipped back, and Chevie's view was obscured by the hulking forms of Thundercats Lunka Witmeyer and Clover Vallicose. Once again Chevie fought the impulse to giggle.

Thundercats? Why would that be funny?

The Thundercats were a special division within the Boxite army. A band of trained specialists who had a fearsome reputation for brutality and thoroughness. They specialized in party security and weeding out traitors. It was unusual that Thundercats would be assigned to the academy, but the director had requested them, claiming it was better to pull weeds than fell trees—meaning that young traitors were easier to kill.

"Box cherish you, Cadet," said Vallicose.

"And you, Sister," Chevie said automatically.

"I cherish you slightly less than Box," said Witmeyer. "But then, I am a mere mortal."

Witmeyer was the comedienne of the two.

Lightheartedness was a personality trait not encouraged by the military, unless it could be put to good use as an interrogation technique or battle distraction. It was said that, when she was stationed in France, Sister Witmeyer told knock-knock jokes even as her helmet wiper raked Jax gore from her splash-back visor.

Chevie swung her legs out of bed, stood at attention, and awaited further instructions. The Thundercats were more than an hour ahead of the posted schedule, but it was not their place to offer an explanation, and hardly her place to ask for one. Today she would not stray even a single degree from protocol. For all she knew, the review had already begun.

"Don't you have something to say to us?" asked Vallicose.

What? wondered Chevie. What am I supposed to say?

Vallicose started off the sentence for her. "Happy . . ."

"Happy Emergence Eve, Sisters," blurted Chevie.

"You had forgotten, perhaps, that on this day in 1899, the Blessed Colonel and his army were making their final preparations to emerge from the catacombs and take back the world?"

"No, Sister, I hadn't forgotten. We owe everything to the Blessed Colonel."

Vallicose scanned Chevie's face, searching for any glint of insubordination, but Chevie kept her eyes front and her back ruler-straight. She was fit, focused, and one of an ethnic minority, a Shawnee Native American: a perfect model for the Boxite army posters that plastered every bus shelter and underground station.

"Hmph," said Vallicose. Perhaps she was impressed, perhaps the opposite. Her grunt was difficult to interpret.

Lunka Witmeyer's words were more straightforward.

"Are you seeing us, sweetie? We haven't transmogrified into little old ladies?"

"I see you both clearly, Sisters," responded Chevie evenly. "I apologize again for that night. It was just a fever."

Vallicose grunted again and followed it with "A fever? Fevers don't shunt a body through steel doors."

They had no way of knowing, none of them, that it was not a fever that had transported Chevie to a sealed basement, but rather a time paradox that had blended the Chevie returning from Victorian London with the Chevie who was a native to this timeline.

Witmeyer snarled behind the high collar of her splashback visor, which she had absolutely no need to wear while on supervision duty inside an academy of unarmed students.

"That night, Savano? That night? But it was more than one night, wasn't it? Seems like every night you're collapsing into a hysterical heap; isn't she, Sister Vallicose?"

Vallicose nodded, and her entire face bulged with suppressed anger. "She called me a *Fed* last Tuesday. What is a *Fed*? Sounds like Jax talk to me."

The French rebels were nicknamed *Jacques*, usually spelled *Jax*.

"I—I don't know," stammered Chevie. "The fever comes and goes. Antibiotics are what I need, that's all."

Suddenly Clover Vallicose was in her face. "Antibiotics? There are soldiers dying for the Blessed Colonel right now. Lying on foreign slag heaps, watching their life's blood splash onto unhallowed rocks, and you think their medicine should be diverted into your worthless veins? Is that what you think, Savano?"

Chevie ground her teeth to keep herself from collapsing. "No, Sister. Of course not. Heroes of the Empire should always take priority. Any one of us cadets would be proud to lay down our lives for them."

Witmeyer laughed, then finger-ticked an imaginary box. "Straight out of the manual, but well remembered under pressure." She nodded at the cadet. "Now get ready, Cadet; the director is waiting."

Chevie shuddered. She could not help it.

Director Waldo Gunn.

A hero of Box's War, awarded the Empire Cross. For thirty years the director had endured working undercover in Provence. Director Gunn was a true believer and a master assassin—who resembled nothing more than a diminutive, kindly grandfather.

Look at the hands, the other cadets whispered as he passed in the corridor. *They are darker than the rest of his skin, stained red by Jax blood.*

Chevie had only seen Director Gunn in person as he strode the academy corridors on Box's business, surrounded by committee members and his personal guard, a phalanx of pistoning legs and swinging arms.

I have never seen his hands.

Forget Director Gunn's hands. Get dressed, Cadet, Chevie told herself. *Your life is at stake.*

Chevie hurriedly zipped up her regulation navy jumpsuit and high boots, tugging on a peaked cap emblazoned with a golden Boxite Youth Academy symbol. She stepped smartly past Vallicose and into the dorm.

The Thundercats marched Chevie Savano down the academy's long corridor, their boots drawing creaks and groans from floorboards that had long since sprung their pegs. The dormitory's other cadets were concealed behind drawn curtains, and the only significant sounds besides boots and boards were the occasional whimper of someone with night terrors and the background drone of Colonel Clayton Box's collected speeches, which were piped through the sound system twenty-four hours a day.

The corridor was a hundred feet long, the length of what had once been four joined but separate terraced houses on Farley Square in Bloomsbury. Through the sash windows Chevie saw the steel edges of the Blessed Colonel's pyramidal mausoleum, and the crimson laser glint from the all-seeing-eye mounted on its peak.

Like Sauron, thought the second Chevie, who was hiding inside the mind of the first one. Traitor Chevie, as she had named the mind disease that was determined to get her killed.

Sauron?

What is a Sauron?

The door to Director Gunn's office was conspicuously plain, in stark contrast to the wall in which it sat. The wall was decorated with a heroic mural depicting the second round of Boxstrike, when the United States, the British Isles, and mainland Europe were brought forcibly under angels' wings. The style was typical of the Empire, with muscled figures in profile, and fans of crepuscular sun rays. The door was a simple wooden panel, adorned with nothing more than faded blue paint.

This door had been Director Gunn's only modification to the building when he took office. A door transported from the guesthouse in France where Waldo Gunn had poached Jax information and personnel for all those years.

How many now dead men have touched that doorknob? wondered Chevie as she paused before knocking.

Witmeyer poked her with a gloved finger. "Are you nervous, sweetie? Is that it?"

Chevie bit her lip and nodded. It was true, she was more nervous than she could remember being. In fact, she was bordering on frantic.

I am at war with myself, she realized. How could a person win that fight?

She flexed her fingers to stop their shaking, then once more reached toward the door.

"Enter, Cadet," came the commanding voice from within.

The director knows I'm here, thought Chevie. It's true what they say: Waldo Gunn has the sight.

Sure, the sight, sneered Traitor Chevie. *Or a camera over the door.*

Chevie curled her fingers into a fist, then stuffed it in her mouth to stifle the sob. They would execute her in the yard if she could not control herself. They would ask for volunteers from the ranks of her own class to shoot her.

Remember DeeDee.

Deirdre Woollen, her dearest friend since first grade, had been hauled out of class, interrogated for two days, and then executed. And all because Deirdre had been discovered unsupervised in the director's study while the war maps were on display.

She was a Jax spy, they'd whispered in the dorms. *Gathering intelligence.*

DeeDee a spy?

Chevie had been shocked.

Shocked because DeeDee was dumber than plankton, Traitor Chevie whispered in her ear. *DeeDee was your friend, but she couldn't gather enough intelligence to spell* c-a-t. *Deirdre Woollen probably got herself turned around while searching for the bathroom, and Gunn shot her for it.*

It was true, Chevie knew, but she couldn't allow herself to think it, in case she talked in her sleep.

Sister Witmeyer knuckled Chevie's skull. "You have been summoned."

Chevie found the courage to grasp the doorknob and turn it, and as she walked into the office, she heard Traitor Chevie in her mind.

You better let me out of here, Cadet, because if you don't, neither of us is leaving this room alive.

Please, thought Chevie. *Please be quiet.*

The director's office was long and narrow with a red carpet stretching down the center like the tongue of some gigantic animal. Director Waldo Gunn was a fan of the art of homodermy—a special type of taxidermy—and the stuffed and preserved corpses of notable academy martyrs lined the walls. Chevie knew that the waxy, rouged cadavers were a testament to the dedication of these graduates, but secretly she thought that she would rather be burned to ashes and forgotten forever than end up as a lifeless sentry in this room. Chevie kept her eyes front and tried not to feel the frosty gaze of the Empire's heroes on her shoulder blades.

The director was seated at his desk, and from ten feet away Chevie could smell the aroma of must and garlic that traveled with him like a personal cloud.

Being a committee member had its privileges, among them smelling however the hell you felt like.

He stinks, said Traitor Chevie. *Somebody power-hose that guy.*

Director Gunn had been tapping a stylus on a Boxnet tablet, and he suddenly stopped, almost as though Chevie had spoken aloud.

Oh no, thought Chevie. Oh no.

Director Gunn seemed elfin behind the large desk, with his too large head and pinhole blue eyes peering out above a faceful of gray beard.

"Did you speak, Cadet Savano?"

The voice was curiously low. For some reason, Chevie had always expected it to be higher.

"No, sir, Director. I don't think so. Not that I know of."

Gunn sighed. "'I don't think so'? 'Not that I know of'? These blurtings of yours are why you stand before me today."

"Exactly, Director," confirmed Witmeyer, who, along with her partner, had followed Chevie inside.

"Umfh, Director," muttered Clover Vallicose.

Chevie started, surprised to find the Thundercats at her shoulders.

Silent assassins.

Gunn leaned back in his antique chair with its turned-down armrests.

"Come closer, Chevron. Stand before me."

Chevie walked forward in a daze, her progress halted by the bang of her thighs on the desk's rim. She noticed her own photograph displayed on the tablet's screen. The director had been reviewing her file.

Gunn sighed again. "You showed such promise, Savano. Such aptitude. . . . But now . . ."

The director set down the pad and intertwined his tiny, hairy fingers in his lap.

Hobbit! shouted Traitor Chevie in her head. *Hobbit. HOBBIT. HOBBIT.*

It was silent, but somehow deafening. Chevie felt a line of sweat trace her brow.

"I am aware, Director, that the past few months have been disappointing . . ."

"Disappointing?" huffed Clover Vallicose. "Catastrophic."

"All of these bewildering outbursts," continued Waldo Gunn. "These strange terms. FBI, what is the FBI?"

"I . . . I don't know, Director."

"And yet you used these letters to describe our academy."

Chevie couldn't even remember this specific outburst, though the letters did seem familiar.

"And in history class you shouted, 'Tell it to Oprah!' What is OPRA? The Oriental People's Republican Army, perhaps?"

Chevie shook her head helplessly. "It's not me, Director. I don't say these things."

"Oh, you say them. The question is why."

"She's a spy," said Vallicose bluntly. "A Jax spy sent to sow confusion."

Chevie flashed back to how DeeDee's face had looked before the bullet struck her. She had seemed a hundred years old.

"I am no spy, Director," she said. "I may be ill. A tumor, maybe, or a virus, but I am no spy. I love the Empire. I would die for the flag."

A huge Empire flag hung on the wall behind Gunn, perhaps the most recognizable image in the world: a gold circle, and inside the circle a 3-D box, the lower rear horizontal and forward right vertical rendered thicker to form a cross.

This is all wrong, thought Traitor Chevie, brain-shuddering at the very sight of the image.

Director Gunn spun the pad absently on the desktop, puffs of mildew rising from his sleeve.

"You love the Empire, Cadet?"

"Absolutely, Director. With my body and soul."

"And do you know the Empire, Savano? Do you realize the sacrifices this empire has demanded of the faithful?"

History questions, thought Chevie. I have a chance.

"I do," she said. "Chapter and verse."

Director Gunn *hmm*ed. Cadet Savano had set herself a challenge.

"What do you know of the Blessed Colonel, Clayton Box?"

An easy one.

"Colonel Box. A god who came among us to scorch sin from the earth."

Gunn waved a testy hand. "Yes, yes, yes. Any child with a cereal box knows this. You are a cadet. What is your *understanding* of the Revolution?"

Chevie frowned; this was a loaded question. Director Gunn was asking for her take on the Revolution. He wanted her to summarize, and *summaries* often included opinions, and *opinions* could get a person killed.

Chevie spoke slowly, taking her time, trying to ignore the hulking Thundercats breathing beast-like in each ear, waiting for the order to pounce.

"The world was in chaos. The empires of man were vast and cruel. Millions of souls perished through ignorance, cruelty, want."

"But more important than the perishing?" said Gunn in a voice that seemed too deep for his miniature frame.

Take it easy, Bilbo, thought Traitor Chevie. *I'm getting there.*

"More important than the dying bodies were the lost souls. People were dying in vast numbers without enlightenment. God decided that He could no longer suffer this, so He appeared on earth in the form of Colonel Box to build a New Albion that would be a shining example of virtue to the world."

"And how did the colonel plan to build this New Albion?"

"He recruited his disciples, the first Thundercats."

Traitor Chevie couldn't swallow this. *It's a spiel. A hoax, a joke. The whole world is being conned. Box was a rogue soldier. I remember the file.*

The effort of keeping these blasphemies inside forced beads of sweat through the skin of Chevie's brow.

"For thirty long years, Colonel Box and his disciples went into the catacombs below London, where they communed with the souls of the faithful and slowly built the colonel's machines. When they returned from the underworld on Emergence Day, Colonel Box ordered his men to launch the first missiles at the Houses of Parliament, Windsor Castle, and the naval port of

Portsmouth. Most of the government and monarchy got their just deserts in less than an hour, and it took little more than a day for Colonel Box to arm his legion of London poor folk and take the capital. Within a month, Britain was completely given over to the colonel. The reign of man was at an end. Colonel Box set the arms factories in Sheffield to building the great ballistic missiles that the colonel had designed, and in under a year, after the second round of Boxstrike, the earth once more belonged to the righteous."

Traitor Chevie brain-snorted. *London poor folk? Criminals, more like.*

Director Gunn nodded; so far, Chevron Savano was on track. "The transition period was not without its hiccups, was it? Some problems are too small to be solved with missiles."

"No, sir. There was opposition. Those who denied the colonel were publicly hanged all along Swingers' Row by . . ."

Chevie's train of thought ground to a halt.

Gunn was on her like a grizzled tomcat on a cornered mouse.

"Publicly hanged by who?"

Chevie could feel the Thundercats shifting at her shoulders.

Who? Who was the hangman?

"Surely you remember, Cadet. After all, the entire war is known as the Hangman's Revolution. A little irreverent, perhaps, but cleansing was essential. The Hangman is one of our most honored saints. Beatified by the colonel himself. His portrait is on the wall in front of you, for heaven's sake."

Listen to this guy, said Traitor Chevie. *He believes his own bull. Box granted sainthood to an executioner. That's like a monster pinning a medal on a troll.*

Chevie gazed at the portrait, hoping for inspiration, and an image flashed in her mind's eye. The wiry man from the painting but holding a tattooist's needle, the cracks in his nails traced with ink. She gave voice to the image without thinking about it.

"The tattooist," she blurted. "Anton Farley the tattooist. He was the hangman."

Gunn jumped to his feet, slamming his palms on his desk.

The director's hands are red! Chevie saw. Red with Jax blood.

"Farley the tattooist!" he roared.

Roared? Really? said blasphemous Chevie. *That's more like a bleat.*

"Shut up!" said real-world Chevie. "Just shut up."

Gunn fixed her with his blazing eyes. "Shut up? You would . . . Do you know who I am?"

"Hobbit!" shouted Chevie. "Hobbit . . . Hobbit . . . HOBBIT!"

The Thundercats moved, each grabbing one of Chevie's shoulders.

I have so had enough of these guys, thought Traitor Chevie, the silent killer, the betrayer.

If the Thundercats had been expecting resistance, they would have fared better; but Cadet Chevron Savano had only proven to be a middling combatant at best. And, in any event, the particular moves she used now had never been taught in the academy.

Chevie took Witmeyer first, spinning under the Thundercat's outstretched arm and jabbing her kidney with four straight fingers. Continuing the pirouette, Chevie bent Vallicose's knee with a powerful kick, then turned back to Witmeyer, who seemed bemused to be in intense pain. Chevie grabbed the warrior nun's splashback visor and yanked it downward until their faces were level.

"Hi," said Chevie, in a tone that was somehow more shocking than the assault, then she punched Witmeyer in the nose. Chevie could never put the Thundercat down with force alone, but pain was distracting Witmeyer, which gave Chevie a chance to snag her weapon and cover Vallicose as the warrior nun reached for the buzz baton on her hip.

"Leave it, Miley," Chevie ordered, flicking off the pistol's safety. Then she nodded to Vallicose. "You too, Gaga."

Inside, Cadet Chevie was wailing in terror.

What?

Did the Traitor teach me to fight?

How else could I have attacked Thundercats?

The Traitor has damned me to hell.

Miley?

Gaga?

Of course the *most* dangerous person in the room had been forgotten, as her brain erroneously assigned him the role of *least* dangerous person in the room. This had been the secret of his success in France. Director Gunn scrabbled onto the desk, hefted his tablet computer, and bashed Chevie across the skull.

Cadet Savano toppled in angular sections, and as unconsciousness drew its slow curtains across her senses, the last thing she heard was Gunn's sarcastic voice.

"My most feared Thundercats laid low by a helpless girl. Perhaps you two are not as formidable as you think, eh, Moley and Googoo?"

Ha, thought Traitor Chevie. *Moley and Googoo? Hobbit be stoopid.*

Then both Chevies were lost in the dark.

2 » POWDERED WIGS & PARASOLS

A guy walks into a bar and says to the barman: "Gimme one whiskey for myself and ten billion for all my possible alternate selves."

—Professor Charles Smart

ORIENT THEATRE, HOLBORN, LONDON, 1899

NOW OUR STORY MIGRATES, FOLLOWING THE curve of Professor Smart's wormhole, emerging in the Victorian Era, where three million souls fuss and sprawl on the banks of the Thames, Fleet, and Lea. Where the sky is black with Machine Age pollution that would choke a Pompeii donkey. Where life is cheap and death is gratis. And if this prose seems overly soused in bleakness, let me remind you that we have not even touched on the great slums, where rendered fat is considered a culinary delicacy and the chief distraction for the legions of red-knuckled, soot-faced orphans is a brisk game of rat-hunt.

But we will not tarry in these quagmires of deprivation, for our tale entices us elsewhere. We follow the riffle of crow tail feathers across the patchwork rooftops of Soho and Mayfair toward Holborn, dipping through the majestic spans of its viaduct and hovering above a chalked sidewalk that proclaims in footstep-smudged capital letters that the grand reopening of the Orient Theatre takes place on this very day. In truth, the phrase *grand reopening* seems a trifle hyperbolic given the dilapidated state of the building beyond, but exaggerated claims are the essence of theater, are they not? The public demands embellishment. Superlatives only, if you please. Sopranos are *incomparable.* Comic turns are invariably *sidesplitting* (only clowns can offer mutilation as an endorsement), and magicians are occasionally *magnificent,* often *incredible,* and without exception *great.*

The Orient Theatre's resident illusionist would consider himself currently *great,* though in truth he is often *astonishing* and on occasion even *amazing.* Indeed, he once idly toyed with the professional moniker the Astonishing Amazini before settling on the more modest title: the Great Savano.

Perhaps the name bongs a gong?

The Great Savano, known as Riley to his handful of friends, lay napping on that afternoon in the steel bathtub that had served as his bed for the past weeks. About six months ago he had inherited the Orient Theatre and the various caches of gold sovereigns that were hidden around or buried under the building. It may seem a lavish bequest for a mere magician's assistant, but the boy had earned it a hundred times over in his fourteen years. Each gas jet in the footlights had cost him a punch around the earhole; every seat represented a night spent shivering in a locked cellar. For the curtains he had paid with ingots of servitude, while the proscenium arch had been bought with the hours he had spent suspended on a painter's scaffold, squinting as he traced the curls of its scrolls with a gilt-dipped brush. He had, essentially, signed the theater's papers with his own blood, while his sweat and tears had served as payment for the main stash of glittering sovereigns beneath the conductor's podium.

Even now, as his wiry frame folded itself into the tub, swathed with waves of his fox-fur magician's cloak, boot heels clanging on the steel vessel, Riley paid in dark dreams for his ownership of the Orient. His old master, Albert Garrick, haunted him, dripping threats into his ear. He never showed his face, mind you; he just whispered ghastly terrorizations. How he would punish Riley, how he was not perished but merely adrift in Professor Smart's damned tunnel, how he would haul himself from the ethereal nothingness and wreak bloody vengeance.

I have time to plan my escape, Riley, my boy. Time is all I have.

Garrick was the devil, thought Riley, as he thrashed and pulled for the surface. And the devil can never be banished so long as one soul fears him.

I fear him, Lord knows I do.

It was not the devil who awaited him in the land of queen and men; it was Bob Winkle, resplendent in his new travel suit.

Bob Winkle, the young grifter whom Riley had rescued from a life of crime in the Old Nichol and set up with a bunk in the Orient. Bob the Beak, as he was known by some, because he had shown quite a knack for winkling information from reluctant sources.

"Yer going to bash a hole in that tub with all the jiggling," was Bob Winkle's comment now. "Kicking like a dangler, you are."

Riley granted himself a moment before engaging. A breath or two to exhale the shade of Garrick and anchor himself in the wide-awake world.

"You plump out that rig well, Bob," he said at last. And it was the truth. Bob cut a fine figure in his newly delivered suit: a jacket of orange tweed with brass glinting on cuffs and waistcoat, legs stuffed into the vases of high boots.

"I resembles a circus monkey," said Bob equably. In Bob's opinion, a circus monkey was a few steps up the ladder from a tenement snakesman on the greasy pole to Newgate Prison.

Riley's hands emerged from folds of fur, and he curled his fingers around the tub's rim. "I've seen a monkey, Bob. Your mug ain't half so appealing."

A josh between young men. Nothing extraordinary on the face of it. No more out of place than a sailor in a gin joint, but for Riley casual jokiness had a newborn quality. His mind was beginning to slough off the tight membrane of Garrick's tyranny, just as Bob had shed his scraps of mortified clothing, his archaeological layers of compacted dirt, and the unhealthy ocher hue that had pasted him since birth. In truth, with some mileage between him and the shadow of Old Nichol, Bob Winkle was flourishing. He had sprouted several inches in the half year since his salvation, and his hair had revealed itself to be wheat yellow. Riley's old frame, on the other hand, stubbornly refused to lengthen, but at least his humor was brightening somewhat—while he was awake, at least.

Bob lent his governor a helping hand. "You don't have to sneak a kip in the tub, boss. We has a bed, you know."

"A specter wouldn't fit sideways on that mattress," said Riley. "I'll hang on to my bath, if you don't mind. You're not exactly wearing a hole in it."

Bob rapped the tub. "I ain't a mackerel, boss. And dirt seals the pores, keeps sickness out of a body."

"And I ain't sneaking a kip. I was up all night rigging the theater, as you know. That was a well-earned snooze."

There were more comfortable places to grab some sleep, Riley knew, but the FBI had stashed him in a tub when Garrick was nipping on his coattails in the future, and he had survived that day, so even though the tub itself had little to do with that undeadness, he clung to it as a symbol.

Sleep in a tub,

Dodge the nub.

The rhyme would never be immortalized in the pages of the *Strand* magazine, but it comforted him nonetheless.

Bob poked Riley's cloak with a finger, feeling the fine chain mail hidden in the lining. "I see you've taken to sporting this in the tub now? Surely that ain't in the bather's handbook."

Riley flexed his legs, testing the cloak's weight. "Onstage, the chain mail can turn aside a blade if one of the tricks goes awry, but I need to wear it easy as pie, like there's not an ounce of strain on my legs. For that casualness I got to practice, Bob. And perhaps if you practiced your card handling with the same dedication, you'd be a sight further along the road to wearing your own cloak."

Bob changed the subject sharpish. "I 'ad a cable from my source."

The source was an investigator friend of Bob's who had been dispatched to Brighton to sniff out Riley's half brother, Tom, who had last been seen in that seaside town.

Riley looked up sharply. "And?"

"Nothing much," said Bob. "'E's poking around, but no joy so far. Waste of tuppence if you ask me. I'm going there now on the afternoon train."

"But you'll miss the grand reopening."

"Can't be helped, boss. You gots your budge; I've got mine."

Riley nodded. Bob would flood the town with Old Nichol muck snipes. If anyone could sniff out hide or hair of a lost man, it was a hungry urchin from the tenements.

"How are the Trips? Is the show set?"

The Trips were Bob's brothers, whom Riley had lodged with a decent widow woman who made sure they got grub and schooling. In their spare time they helped around the theater and ran errands.

"Still set, same as the last time you asked," said Bob. "Mirrors, smoke bombs, flashers, blades, gramophone, curtains loaded. The sack is stuffed with rats, as we used to say back in the Nichol. I sent 'em out with playbills. Paper the whole town they will."

"Excellent," said Riley, taking the dozen or so steps to the small kitchen, where a hot roll and a mug of ale waited for him on the corner table. "I told you, Bob. I ain't drinking no more before nightfall. Chevie would have my scalp."

Bob shrugged, then helped himself to the ale. "Ah, yes, the Injun princess. It wouldn't do to earn Chevron's displeasure, 'er being in the future and all."

Bob Winkle had taken active part in the final act of Riley's struggle with Garrick and so was well-ish versed on the time-traveling shenanigans, though he only knew the half of it and only believed a quarter of that.

"Chevie's gone, Riley," said Bob, then emphasized his pronouncement with an ale belch. "Into the henceforth, or into a hole in the ground. You said it yerself, she's likely to have ear-hole palpitations."

"Smarthole mutations," corrected Riley.

"Whichever, makes no odds. The point being that much as I would love to be reunited with Miss Chevie, seeing as she expressed a wish to walk out with me, it ain't very likely. So live yer life according to yer own needs and not under the shadow of the future."

This was quite the speech; Riley suspected that Bob Winkle missed Chevie almost as much as he did.

"There is nothing wrong with learning lessons, Bob, and adjusting yer behavior according-wise."

Bob finished the beer. "Don't I know it, boss? I ain't attended a single rat fight since we moved here. Nor trawled the Belgravia sewers for posh drain droppings."

"Ah, sewage-dipped posh droppings," said Riley, deadpan. "The pearls of London town."

Bob grinned, revealing a row of ivories that were remarkably white for a tenement graduate. "Hark at the comedian. P'raps we should give you a second spot on the playbill. How's about Charlie Chuckles as a moniker?"

Riley returned his mate's smile and bowed low. "Charles Chuckles, Esquire, at your service."

They both laughed, and then Riley finished his roll, chewing slowly, enjoying the slow dissolve of fresh-baked dough, untainted by the fear of a sudden blow from Garrick.

I ain't afraid, he thought. At this exact moment in the day, I ain't afraid.

Riley felt as though his caged heart had been set free.

"Ahem," said Bob. "When you has finished with the far-off looks and the simpleton smiling, we should be doing a final run-through before I skedaddles."

Riley affected a stern gaze. "You are cognizant of the fact that I am your boss, Master Winkle?"

Bob huffed and descended the three wooden steps to the backstage area. "I ain't even cognizant of the meaning of the word *cognizant*." He paused at the foot of the steps. "And Bob Winkle has a rule: if he don't understand it, then sod it."

Not a bad rule, thought Riley; then he followed his friend into the belly of the theater.

Our theater, he realized, and a jaunty spring introduced itself to his step. It was quite possible that Riley had never even formulated a sentence containing the word *jaunty*, not to mention contemplated becoming a living example of its definition.

Jaunty, thought Riley. Look at me, all jaunty and such. Jaunty Riley.

The stage was modest by the standards of London's famous West End, barely fifteen feet from left to right, twenty if the wing nooks were added in; but Riley was proud of the old girl nonetheless, despite the fact that here he'd been punched, kicked, sliced, etherized, and on one occasion hung from a noose tied to a rafter.

He patted one of the proscenium arch's pillars fondly. "That weren't your fault, eh, girl? You were looking out for me."

Still, the memory made Riley wince. "Tell me, Mr. Winkle, did I ever relate the story of how Garrick says to me one fine morning: 'Riley,' he says. 'How's about we re-create the hanging of Dick Turpin at York? And how's about—' "

Bob groaned. " 'And how's about you be Turpin?' That worn-out tale. I heard that more times than I heard Great Tom a-bonging from St. Paul's."

This, Riley thought, would be the ideal time to check on Bob's studies, while he was chock-full of his own hilariousness.

"Well then, Mr. Winkle, perhaps you would tell me something else? Seven somethings in fact."

The cockiness gushed from Bob's face, and had it been liquid, it would have filled his boots.

"Bob is busy," he said. "Bob has duties."

Riley tugged a slim leather-bound volume from his pants pocket. He had destroyed many of Garrick's possessions, but this handwritten *Guide to Magicks & Illusion* was a priceless inheritance of daily practical use.

Also, it cheered Riley to think that Garrick's ghost would shrivel with horror at the notion of his notebook's being consulted by the one who had banished him from this earth.

"'Chapter one,'" he read. "'Magic of the theatrical kind, being very separate from actual conjuring, has seven basic elements.' Seven, Robert Winkle. Trot them out, if you please."

"Seven," repeated Bob. "You said no testing today, guv, on account of the grand reopening."

"No, I never did. Seven."

"Seven." Bob was currently Riley's assistant, but his dearest wish was to twirl his own wand. However, to do this, he would have to step up his rote learning, and *rote* learning was not Bob's strong suit. He put his fingers to his temples and stared out into the seats, the very picture of a mentalist.

"Well, misdirection is first. The bones in the cemetery know that much."

"Misdirection," said Riley. "We don't want the punters peeping where we don't want them peeping."

"Then the ditch. Dumping what we doesn't need the marks spying, like the Rams do with corpses at Caversham Lock."

"Disposal," corrected Riley. "We ain't a criminal gang dealing in dead bodies, just doves and the like. Next?"

Bob chewed a thumbnail. "I know this, bossman. It's the conceal, ain't it?"

Riley rubbed his hands together until a rose sprouted from the fingertips. "The conceal, or the palm. Hiding an object in an apparently empty hand."

Bob's jaw dropped so far you might think Riley had pulled an elephant from a tulip bulb. "Well, I never seen such smooth finger work. You is wasted, guv. Up on the lawn in Leicester Square you should be, dipping for wallets."

Riley was not about to be distracted by such brazen bootlicking, but he gave himself a moment to smile at his apprentice's efforts nonetheless. "Four to go, Bob, regardless of where I should or should not be."

Bob made a great show of checking an invisible pocket watch.

"Oh Lord, lookee at the time, how she flies," he said. "And I too must fly if I'm to make the Brighton train."

Bob buttoned his new jacket to the neck and pumped Riley's hand.

"Break a leg, O Great Savano. I will cable you from the seaside."

Riley knew that it was pointless to quiz Bob any further. In young Winkle's head, he was already halfway to Brighton.

"Very well, Bob. Off with you. Cable as soon as you have news."

"And that will be right soon, or my name ain't Handsome Bob Winkle."

Handsome Bob?

That was a new one.

And with no more delay, in case Riley would squeeze in

another question, Bob was down the aisle and out the front door, leaving Riley alone in a place where he was determined to forge brand-new memories.

Riley's preparations were interrupted by a clatter coming from the front of the house, tumbling down the center aisle, and mounting the stage itself. It was the stir of men entering the building and being none too genteel about it. These were men who cared not about such things as busted hinges or broken locks. It was in they wanted; and in they were coming, regardless of barriers.

Riley had initially smiled, thinking the Trips were back and famished, but his grin soured when he saw what was barreling down the aisle toward him.

"Rams," he said. "With the king himself at the head of the bunch."

Riley fought his instinct to run and hide. Instead he squared his shoulders, threw back the specially tailored folds of his black fur-trimmed velvet cloak, and bowed dramatically.

"Your Majesty," he said, and confetti showered from the rafters, as though Otto Malarkey and his gang of thugs, bludgers, cads, nobblers, and all-around ne'er-do-wells had been expected.

The Battering Rams were London's premier gang of organized criminals, a title that had previously belonged to the Hooligan Boys, a bunch who had forfeited any claim to the term *organized* when they dynamited the eastern wall of Newgate Prison while the majority of their imprisoned war council was leaning against the other side. It was said that the bluebottles were shoveling Hooligan parts for weeks. The Battering Rams were an altogether cannier bunch. No rowdy, gin-soaked men of the moment, these. No, the Rams were more your seasoned criminals, in it for the long haul. Veterans, most of them, who had been blooded in the Transvaal or China. They appreciated a tidy battle plan, and they were prepared to follow a man with a bit of flair. And in Otto Malarkey they had found a tactical genius who had flair flowing out of his beloved pirate boots.

Otto had never been a pirate as such, but he had smuggled taxables into Whitby under the famous smuggler clergyman Reverend John Pine, who had gifted Otto the boots from his deathbed. Malarkey learned the classics at Reverend Pine's desk. He took strategy from Caesar and politicking from Cicero. For his renowned skill with the sword he had to wait till he was dumped into the island prison of Little Saltee, where he learned the gentleman's art from a fellow inmate. When the Rams' previous king, one of Otto's brothers, perished in an ignoble wrestling match with a mountain gorilla, Otto inherited the Battering Rams' horned crown. He had steered the gang to realms of ill-gotten gains they could never have dreamed of under previous Ram kings. Lately, though, it had to be said, the power had gone a little to Otto's head and his trademark flair had taken a turn for the flamboyant.

He was plowing his own fashion furrow and bringing quite a few of his hardened mates along with him.

So now, when Riley unfurled from his theatrical bow, he

was greeted by a front row half full of snorting, bristling coves who sounded and smelled like the Battering Rams he knew so well. But they looked like dandies from some ancient royal court, resplendent in powdered wigs and rouged cheeks, and in their midst sat Otto Malarkey himself, the most powdered of the lot.

Riley spoke as he straightened. "Good evening, ladies and . . ."

The traditional theater greeting stuck in his gullet when he noticed Otto twirling a lace parasol.

"Ladies . . . and . . ."

Otto waited politely for a moment, then whispered through a funnel of fingers like a prompter from the wings. "Gentlemen. Ladies and gentlemen."

Riley forced a smile but was careful not to laugh. A display of mirth at this juncture could prove fatal. "Gentlemen, of course. Ladies and gentlemen. Apologies, Your High Rammity. I was not expecting an audience at this hour. Perhaps the advertisement chalked on the sidewalk outside was smudged by the passage of feet. The curtain does not rise on the evening's entertainments for another three hours."

Otto Malarkey idly opened and closed his parasol indoors, which was very bad luck. Riley felt a tingling of foreboding in his teeth. Theater folk are devout disciples of Lady Luck.

"I is King Ram, my young conjurer, and a single fig I does not give for what is expected. The world is, as the Bard might say, as I like it. I rolls up how and when I choose. I pay what I fancy if I fancy. I do not look to others; they looks to King Otto for tips and cues. Take this current rigout, for example."

He paused then, almost challenging Riley to giggle, a challenge he wordlessly declined.

"We takes our high fashion cues from nature. The toughest peacock wears its feathers, the tiger revels in its stripes, and so we wear our finery, so that all may see us and know not to cross steel with the fancy boys of the Battering Rams."

During this speech Riley felt his old training rise up from the dusky caverns of his mind and settle over his skull like a shroud. Not the magician's training, though that was some of it; what dictated his actions now was the part of him that had absorbed Garrick's skills in combat and assassination. It could well be that Malarkey simply fancied himself a trot to the theater with his bully chums and death would not be dealt here today, but if the High Rammity did have violence in mind, he would find Riley ready for him.

"Perhaps His Majesty and his esteemed company would enjoy a demonstration of my talents? A preview, if you will."

Malarkey rapped the floorboards with the handle of his parasol. "You is a clever lad, a real dimber-damber. I always said it, Riley—or should I say, the Great Savano—but before we abandon ourselves to the wonders of the Orient, let us take a moment to chat viz your obligation to the Brotherhood."

This was another long and winding statement, and while it meandered along, Riley examined what he now considered the enemy. There were six Rams arranged before him: Malarkey himself—or Golgoth, as he was known in the ring—a giant of a man barely contained by the ruffles of what looked like an opera shirt. He was flanked by Noble and Jeeves, two of his most experienced bludgers, who had manhandled Riley somewhat during their previous encounter, both barely recognizable under bonnets of powdered wig, the effect of which was ruined somewhat by facial scarification and heavy stubble. Beside Jeeves sat a man so colossal he had enough skin for two, and to the right of him sat a Ram so small he might have needed the extra skin. The monster was Otto's little brother, Barnabus, saddled with the nickname "Inhumane" Malarkey in reference to the prosecuting attorney's description of the assault that had earned Barnabus a half stretch in Newgate. The smaller man was Inhumane's constant companion and general dogsbody, Pooley. Inhumane was squeezed into a blue silk frock coat with golden piping that had been tailored for a less robust frame, and Pooley was dressed in the uniform of a Russian Hussar. All were bearing obvious steel, and possibly hidden steel to complement it. All except Farley, the Rams' tattooist, who sat two rows back, clad in his customary dark coat and worn breeches. A writing pad sat upon his knee, and he scribbled while Malarkey talked. It seemed the tattooist had now become the chronicler of King Otto's life and times.

Riley studied the Rams and dispassionately reckoned that he could, with his training, dispatch three before the others took him. Though there was another way he might remove at least one with no resistance. He was skipping ahead to this point in his hastily assembled plan when he registered Otto saying the word *obligation.*

No ordinary word this. It wasn't like saying *pie and sausage.*

Obligation was a big word among the Family. Obligation was taken as serious as cholera.

"Viz my obligation, Your High Rammity?" said Riley, careful not to show fear. "What obligation are you referring to? We ain't in Ram country here in Holborn."

But he knew. He knew in his gut what his obligation was.

Otto did not speak; instead he tugged one lace glove from his giant paw with utmost deliberation, finger by finger, then tapped his own right shoulder.

Riley knew what lay under the silken sleeve. A Ram tattoo similar to the one Farley had inked on his own shoulder six months previous, during a particularly testing escapade that would have puffed out Allan Quatermain himself. Riley's choice at the time had been to either take the ink or be fed to the pigs. Taking the ink had seemed less immediately terminal.

"You is one of us, lad," said Inhumane. "You is Family."

Riley maintained his showman's face, but behind the smile, panic was boiling his fluids.

How could I not have foreseen this? I am a Ram. Everything I do belongs to them.

"Everything of yours is ours," said Malarkey sweetly, as though the king were privy to members' thoughts. "This here building. The swanky velvet seats therein. Tell me, boy, you ain't been spending Ram chink on refurbishings, have you?"

Riley spread his arms. "Just a few knickety-knacks. Here

and there, odds and ends." It was gibberish, but he was stalling for time.

"'Coz that would be a royal decision. Committee at the very least. You should've submitted a request form."

"I didn't know there was such a form, Your High Rammity. I never thought."

This was apparently hilarious.

Pooley drummed his thighs with bone-thin fists. "'E never thought. Hark at him."

"'E never finks," said Inhumane, and he chuckled long and low, with a sound like far-off cannon fire. "That is the problem."

"Brass tacks then, Mr. Malarkey, sir," said Riley. "What's on my account?"

"Brass tacks," said Malarkey. "I like you, boy, which is why I ain't taking this personal. I ain't taking all of this sneaky earning the wrong way. I *could* see it like you been dipping into my pocket. Taking the bread out of my starving little brother's pie hole."

A thought struck Inhumane. "I *am* starving, as it 'appens."

Otto laughed, waving the parasol like a baton. "See? He's starving, is Barnabus. You wanna watch out—he's likely to take a bite out of yer leg. He's partial to tender meat, is Barnabus."

Riley went slightly on the offensive. "So, we're all square at the moment, King Otto?"

Had Riley been famed comic George Robey, the cacophony of laughter following this statement could hardly have been more enthusiastic. With eyes closed, one would have sworn that the Orient was packed to the gods based on volume alone. The mirth shook the men and the men shook the theater until their seats strained their floor bolts.

"All square?" wept King Otto, having taken a pull of brandy from the handle of his parasol. "Dear me, Riley. You is a tonic and no mistake. All square?" He thumped the Rams in range. "Did you ever hear of such a thing? There ain't no *all square* in the Brotherhood, my boy. All square is not a condition we deals in."

Riley felt despair drop over him neat as a butterfly net. "Perhaps you could set me straight, King Otto."

Financial details were too vulgar for royalty to deal with, so Otto delegated. "Farley, spell it out for the Great Savano. Keep it simple. After all, he's only a lad, despite his grand title."

Farley smiled at Riley, the first display of friendly teeth since the Rams had arrived. The conservatively clad tattooist seemed out of place in such rambunctious company. A scrivener among pugilists.

"Here's the bad news, Riley. Once you take the ink, then your life is forfeit to the Rams. You may lease it back at the king's pleasure for a half share of your worldly goods past and present."

"Past worldly goods? How's that to be collected without a time machine?"

Farley looked up from his notebook. "King Otto can hardly be blamed if you once had a fortune then lost it. Fifty percent is due nonetheless."

The High Rammity swigged once more from his parasol flask, then spat into the aisle. "Magnanimous as I am, I waive the past. Present fortunes only."

Riley bowed. "You are too kind."

Otto sat bolt upright. "Sauce? You are giving me sauce? P'raps my terms is too lenient, then? You could be catching a bullet before the magic show. Sixty percent if you insist on lip, O Great Savano."

Catching a bullet, thought Riley. How clever of King Otto to refer to the most anticipated trick in my repertoire: the bullet catch.

Fifty percent, sixty. It made no difference. Riley was to be a slave at Malarkey's pleasure, and he knew it.

"So, to continue," said Farley, "sixty percent of whatever the Orient brings in. If she brings in nothing, then we sell her lock, stock, and we plump the coffers with the proceeds. If the Great Savano makes a go of it, then we seed the crowd with dippers and do a side trade in the three w's."

The three w's: wallets, watches, and nose wipers.

Disaster.

Even if the Orient did well, the pickpockets would drive Johnny Punter away. Riley knew well how this tale played. He would end up working for the rest of his life to pay off some dreamed-up debt while his half brother moved away from him in the world. Best to cut loose before the Rams sniffed out the diverse buried boxes in which Garrick's blood-tainted sovereigns were stashed. He would change his professional moniker and go on the circuit, maybe tart up an old wagon and tour the county fairs.

"You is mine, lad," Otto was saying. "You are my soldier. And I will have my due as sure as old Horatio is on his column in Trafalgar Square. And when this place has been squeezed, I will put you to work for me in the Hidey-Hole, pulling rats from hats."

Oh no, thought Riley. Not me. I've been to the future and back. I've learned a dodge or two. The Great Savano does not enter into servitude for men in powdered wigs.

"As Your Majesty commands," he said, bowing low once more. "But allow me the opportunity to negotiate."

Inhumane stopped mouth breathing long enough to comment. "'Negotiate,' 'e says. Negotiate. We is Rams, lad. Negotiating ain't a condition which . . . the other side . . . of the . . . Rams we be . . ."

It was hopeless; the sentence had gotten away from him, and so Inhumane fell silent, working it out on his fingers, chewing on the phrases.

"I agree with my brother in sentiment if not delivery," said Otto. "No negotiations. It's a question of rules. Rules is like hearts. Once you break them, they stay broke." He waved his parasol in Farley's direction. "Get that, did ye? It was a good one."

The tattooist dipped his nib in an ink bottle, which was perched birdlike in his breast pocket.

"All preserved for future kings," he said, moving his pen across the page in quick scratches.

"Good." Malarkey returned his attention to the stage. "So, negotiating? There will be none."

"Hear my proposal, King Otto," said Riley. "It's for the benefit of the enterprise. Our joint enterprise."

In truth, Riley had less interest in negotiation than Malarkey did. He knew it was fruitless, but appearing to have an interest in a wrangle for terms made it seem as though he had accepted the proposition in general. It was classic misdirection.

Otto stretched his legs and hooked his pirate boots over the stage lip.

"I'm entertained," he said. "I admit it. And so long as I am entertained then I am inclined to listen. So proceed, Riley boy, but take a care to be entertaining."

Riley bowed once more. "As you wish, Your High Rammity," he said, the calmness of his tone belying internal turmoil. Tonight's performance was forfeit; he would use the illusions already set up to spirit himself away from the stage into the bowels of the Orient, where Garrick's treasure was hidden.

Riley walked briskly to the wings and selected one chair from three—the plain wooden model with the secret hinges and elastic cord threaded through the hollow legs and back.

Riley, who was now every inch the Great Savano, tilted the chair onto a single hind leg, spinning it under his hand, reeling in the audience's gaze.

"A theater is not really about walls or dressing rooms or even a stage," he said, his voice slightly singsong, mesmerizing. "It's about seats." The chair spun faster and faster, its legs blurring together. "Seats love their work. They relish the fat, rich posteriors that will descend from on high."

Inhumane frowned, an expression that settled with a certain familiarity onto his features. "This seat is relishing my posterior?"

Riley spun the chair over his head, then brought it crashing down so that it collapsed into segments and splinters. "But when the seats are empty, they simply fall to pieces."

Smashing an old chair, even with such deft manipulation, was not such a great achievement, so no one applauded.

"But when those seats are full . . ."

Riley lowered himself slowly into a seating position until it seemed certain that he would fall.

"When those seats are full . . ."

Riley dipped even lower, but then . . . but then the broken chair began to jitter and fuss, dancing to some unheard music, knitting itself together until, in a rush, it surged upward into wholeness just as Riley descended to meet it.

The chair, magically restored, took Riley's weight with a puff of sawdust.

"When those seats are full, they are money machines," Riley told his audience. Then, on cue, he opened his mouth and rolled out his tongue, revealing the sovereign that lay thereon.

Riley made to snatch it, but then his tongue slid sharpish back inside his mouth, and his teeth clacked shut.

"Gold!" he said, as though nothing lay on his tongue. "You saw it! Bright and shiny gold. He has it. We wants it. So how do we get it?"

Pooley stood on his chair. "Bash 'is bleedin' teeth in, and cut 'is bleedin' tongue out."

These blunt verbals broke the Great Savano's spell somewhat, but Riley recovered well.

"Yes, my stunted friend. We could *cut his bleedin' tongue* out, but then this is the only gold coin Johnny Punter will ever donate to the Rams' coffers."

Malarkey was listening now. Riley was twice as sharp as the average street cove, which made him four times brighter than the glocky duds sitting beside him today.

"Tell me then, my clever boy. How does we get that sov, and others like it?"

"That is the question. A sovereign for a sovereign. We get the sov by making Johnny Punter want to give it to us."

Riley snapped his fingers together, and a flurry of butterflies fluttered from their tips, spiraling in a tight cone up into the penny seats. The audience's mouths dropped open, as did Riley's own, and out rolled the gold-bearing tongue. He whiplashed his own tongue like a jump rope, and the sov leaped into his hand.

"Presto," said Riley, neatly palming the coin from one hand to another, then flicking it through the air. The sovereign spun end over end to land with the soft fat plop of pure gold on flesh in Malarkey's waiting hand.

"Your cut, King Otto," says the magician, all smarmy and professional, finishing the bit with a bow so low, he was eyeballing his own anklebones.

Malarkey closed his fingers around the coin in case the Great Savano would magic it away somehow.

"You puts on a good show, little Ramlet," he said. "But—"

Riley cut him off smoothly, taking back control.

The person in control of the room is in control of the illusion, Garrick had told him. *He decides whether or not magic comes into the world. You must be that person.*

"But my show is not finished," Riley said, projecting to the gods. "And I am improvising to tailor my illusions to Your Majesty. The Great Savano has another point to make, and in a most entertaining fashion."

Malarkey winced. His hair told him something was wrong. Beneath the wig, Otto's famed raven tresses yearned to be free and itched at the roots like they always did when things was a little off-color. Malarkey's *hair-sight* had saved his life on more than one occasion—but Oh Lord, couldn't that junior Ram chappie do the magic act like a topper?—so one more trick, then down to business.

I never gets to go to real theater anymore. It's all knife acts and then screaming.

So he said, "Sharpish, Ramlet. And I better not sniff a whiff of underhand or it's coming out of yer hide."

Riley bowed again, but it seemed to King Otto that all this bowing and scraping was perhaps not as respect-laden as it might be. Another point to dwell on later.

After the trick.

"So we have our customer for the present," said Riley,

bowing slightly. "But what will happen to Johnny Punter if we follow friend Farley's counsel and fill the theater with Family?"

Family. A cozy name for the criminal so-called fraternity.

Riley pulled a handkerchief from inside a wide pocket in his cape and shook it out until it unfurled to the size of a tablecloth.

"That was folded, is all," muttered Inhumane, eager to prove himself a smarty-pants. Then as often happened, his words ran away too fast for his stumbling mouth to keep pace. "Folded is all, and then with the shaking wot . . . under his . . . cloak. Wot's a magician's cloak called now? So, anyways, it gets big, and now youse is all like, oh 'eck, and . . ."

Malarkey poked his brother with his drinks parasol. "I know, brother. Now think yer words inside yer head and let the pup perform."

Riley worked the handkerchief. It was as Inhumane had guessed: simply folded, but not *simply* folded; the pattern of folds was as precise and complicated as an origami dragon, designed to conceal two wires shaped to cover his head and shoulders. Once the wires were perpendicular and the frame assembled, Riley draped the cloth neatly over himself. It assumed his shape and covered him completely. Riley stumbled stiff-legged this way and that, his arms stretched out before him, his eyes peeping through the gauze.

"See?" said Riley. "I am surrounded, confused, and blinded. I am being dipped, poked, jostled, and fleeced. Never again shall I cast my shadow across the Orient Theatre's lobby. I shall away from here and take my gold with me."

This bit of patter was to give him a chance to depress the trapdoor latch with his toe.

"Never shall I return here with my hard-earned chink, thinks old Johnny to himself. For I am a-dripping in nervous sweat and leered at by dodgy-looking coves with black teeth and murder in their beady eyes. And this is what happens to Johnny Punter when he hears Family members sniffing at his collar."

Riley found the latch and pressed it. Now all that he needed to do was make a neat jump to the basement to demonstrate how Johnny Punter would disappear—and to actually disappear.

He wrapped the magician's cloak around himself for the jump, pulling the folds tight to speed his passage through the tight wooden frame, when all of a sudden, and to the great surprise of all present, the usually serene Anton Farley seemed to take issue with his performance.

"No! No!" Farley said, jumping to his feet. "Enough of this tomfoolery. Back away from the trapdoor, or whatever you have there, boy. Come down here with these fools."

Silence.

Stunned silence.

Was Farley issuing commands? Had he just referred to his fellow Rams as *fools*? And didn't he sound more like a spoon-in-the-mouth toff now than a shiv-in-the-sock Ram?

Riddle upon mystery.

In situations like this, Malarkey, due to rank, would be deferred to for first reaction.

"Farley? Is it a brain fever that has seized you? Fools, you say? Fools, is it?"

Farley pulled a pistol of the revolver variety from his ink-sack, waving it casually as though it were an everyday item.

"Fools, cretins, idiots. Take yer pick." The tattooist slapped his own forehead. "Listen to me. *Yer* pick. Take *your* pick. I have been undercover for so long . . . you have no idea. Sometimes I don't know what day of the week it is."

Pooley was sneaking a knife from his boot, so Farley shot him in the heart, barely pausing to draw a bead.

"No loss, that one," said Farley. "No wailing outside Highgate for him."

The gunshot echoed to the rafter, fading with each balcony until it became a whisper of its former self, and Pooley was dead where he sat, life leaving him with the wisp of smoke that drifted from the hole in his chest.

"A revolver," said Malarkey, conversational in his surprise. "I never knew you were in possession of a revolver. American, is it?"

Inhumane began to sob, fat tears collecting in his deep eye sockets before spilling down his cheeks. "I don't understand."

For once, the giant imbecile was not alone in his state of mind. Only one person understood what was going on here, and he was the one with the bullets. Malarkey was struck to petrification, not on account of fear but from sheer disbelief. Otto Malarkey had been a war baby, born on the outskirts of the Balaclava battleground during the Crimean War. Gunfire and cannon shot were his lullaby. So it was not the thunderclap of Farley's revolver that rooted Malarkey to his seat, it was the shock that the tattooist would first call him a fool and then shoot one of his soldiers.

"Farley, man, what are you doing?"

"What am *I* doing?" said Farley. "You're dressed like Elton John in the court of Louis XV, and you're asking me what I'm doing? You've got a powdered wig on, Otto."

Malarkey pawed the wig from his crown. "I had an inkling this was ridiculous. Why do none of you coves tell me true when I asks yer opinions? And what is an Elton John, in the name of God?"

Farley ignored the question, instead speaking into his wrist as though a fairy were concealed within.

"I have them, Colonel. All together, the entire inner circle. And the boy, as a bonus. We won't get another opportunity like this, sir."

He waited a moment, cocking his head as though an unseen specter was whispering in his ear. And this attitude of speaking into his wrist and listening to the air rang a bell in Riley's memory.

I have seen this before, he realized. Or rather, I will see it in the future. Did not Chevie's comrades in the FBI communicate in this fashion?

Before he could fully untie the riddle-knot, Farley received his answer.

"I know all that, sir. But I strongly suggest moving up our

schedule. The FBI sent Savano, and they could send someone else. So either we move or we dismantle the wormhole landing plate in Half Moon Street." He waited again, pacing in the aisle.

"Thank you, sir," he said, then sighed with a relief that seemed to wipe ten years off his age. "You won't regret it, sir."

"Out of his noggin," whispered Malarkey. "The man is talking to the air."

Riley tugged the fitted sheet from his head. Farley was not out of his noggin. Farley was not who he pretended to be. He was acting like a new man. Gone was his deferential demeanor, his air of quiet compassion. Shoulders that had been hunched from long hours of needlework were now ramrod straight. His eyes were bright with new purpose.

No. Not new purpose—revealed purpose.

"You have no idea, *King* Otto," Farley said, leveling the weapon specifically at Malarkey, "how long I have waited for this. All these years I have been listening to your delusional claptrap. Rabbiting on like you were the Chosen One. Well, today, you get to meet your god and find out just how chosen you are." Farley dropped his voice down to his boots in a reasonable impersonation of King Otto. "'Update me price list—there's a decent cove, Farley.' 'Fetch me a pie from Old Lady Numpty—there's a nice monkey, Farley.' 'Do you think I should wear me fleece out on the town, Farley? Only it scratches me shoulders so,'" Farley added a japing lurch to his impression, which was indeed reminiscent of the king with a few toddies in him.

Riley watched all this and thought: I need to make my move while Farley is airing his grudges, otherwise he might remember I'm standing here.

Riley must've thought too loud, because Farley swung the gun around. "You there, time traveler. Trot yourself down here with the rest of the bunch."

Riley knew that to leave the stage on Farley's terms would mean death, so he spoke directly to Malarkey.

"That's a revolver, King Otto. Five bullets left."

Farley snorted. "Clever boy. Five bullets. One each."

But Otto had been shot before on numerous occasions; indeed there was a musket ball lodged in the meat of his thigh that he'd grown quite fond of rubbing when he was in vacant or pensive mood.

"It takes more than one shot to kill a Malarkey, Judas," he said, and his voice carried an undertone of menace, now that the surprise had passed.

This notion did not appear to unduly worry Farley. In fact, he seemed glad the point was made.

"I said we should have killed you straight away," he said. "I wrote a report on the subject."

Malarkey did not fully understand this, but nevertheless he took it as a compliment. "Well, I does be a dangerous creature. Both mind and muscle rolled up in one person, as it were."

"Not you, you rouged cretin. The boy. He is too smart by half."

King Otto leaned forward in his seat, grasping the armrests, ready for action. "It don't take much smarts to count to five, Farley. You ain't gonna get all of us."

Riley, meanwhile, was feeling a shade guilty for mentioning

the bullet count. Farley would be forced to plug the homicidal Rams before turning his barker to the harmless boy-magician.

And it will take three shots to slow Inhumane, I'll warrant.

By that time Malarkey would be at the tattooist's throat, handing Riley the second's grace he needed to jump through the trapdoor.

I'll be gone in a twinkle. The white rabbit ain't got nothing on me.

But Farley was no dullard. Surely the bullet count would have occurred to him.

Surely.

Malarkey rose slowly from his chair, as did his remaining men.

"I'm gonna stuff that Yankee barker down yer gullet, Mr. Farley. And after that, you're bound for a swift burial in a flour sack. Less'n you have more bullets."

Farley laughed, three harsh barks, then reached his long artist's fingers into his ink tote. When they emerged, they were wrapped around the butt of some strange-looking implement—F-shaped, with a thin string of light pointing from its nozzle.

Riley recognized it from his jaunt up the Smarthole.

Machine pistol. Machine pistol.

"Oh, I have more bullets," said Farley, and he pulled the trigger, spraying supersonic death across the stage and auditorium of the Orient Theatre.

3 » CLICK, NOT BOOM

Trying to trace the consequences of time travel is like a monkey with no thumbs trying to reassemble an exploded bomb, at night, wearing clown gloves.

—Professor Charles Smart

LONDON, PRESENT DAY

CHEVIE SAVANO FOUND HERSELF WAKING FOR the second time in a single morning, on this occasion suffering a headache that seemed too big for her skull to contain.

Electric panic coursed through her limbs, but she fought to keep them from spasming.

Play dead, she told herself. *Buy some time.*

Strong fingers gripped her shoulders, and she knew the grip without having to look.

Thundercats.

The Traitor did this, she thought, hating that tiny malignant twist of flesh. The Traitor murdered me.

It was true that Chevie wasn't currently dead, but there could be no doubt that this status would be short-lived.

Short-lived. Ha.

You'll have to update your status to Single and Deceased.

The Traitor again. More jibber-jabber. Update her status? What did that even mean?

So Chevie sat still as a corpse, collecting herself, trying to breach the corona of pain around her head with mind-fingers.

"Charles Smart," she heard a voice say.

It's the hobbit's voice.

Director Gunn.

"She talks about Charles Smart, and here he is in the colonel's letter: Professor Charles Smart. Can you explain that?"

Professor Smart. He was one of the people from her visions. The old lady with the bird's-nest hair had said that Smart was expecting her. Could it be that Smart was a real person?

Someone grunted a negative. One from Clover Vallicose's grunt lexicon.

"It's a mystery, Director," said Lunka Witmeyer from behind Chevie. "But we have an order passed down through the years. Sealed by the holy seal until this very morning."

Vallicose chimed in, her voice throbbing with religious fervor. "An order passed down from the Blessed Colonel Himself. It would be my honor to carry it out immediately."

"No, Sister. Something is afoot here," said the director. "Something outside the scope of my knowledge and influence." Gunn moved things around on his desk. "And I don't like things outside that circle. I like to bring them inside before I deal with them."

Vallicose shuffled. "Are you ignoring the Blessed Colonel's command, Director?"

There was a moment of tense silence in which Chevie believed absolutely that Vallicose would shoot her own superior if his next sentence was blasphemous.

"Of course not, Sister. And I do not appreciate your tone. I would simply prefer to have more information before the . . . sanctions . . . are implemented. This Smart person may have confederates."

"The order is quite specific, Director. It has to be today."

"I know that, Vallicose. I can read. Don't forget who summoned you here."

Waldo Gunn was a powerful man, but even he would have to tread carefully in this unique situation. A time-sensitive order from the colonel could not be ignored, or even deviated from in the slightest. His political adversaries would have him swinging in Hangman's Square by dawn. Waldo Gunn could end up a homodermic installation in his own hall of fame.

Chevie heard Gunn's fingers drumming the desktop. "Very well. We use the girl to confront this man Smart. See how he reacts. There must be some connection between them. Then, when you have established that connection, take ten minutes to interrogate him on-site. I must know if there is a danger to the colonel's empire."

This was shrewd: plant the idea that perhaps the Empire

was at risk. Surely no one could object to his patriotism.

Vallicose grunted again, but it was a respectful, affirmative grunt. Their plan was set.

One of the hands on Chevie's shoulders moved up to her neck and gripped tightly.

"This little one's faking," said Lunka Witmeyer. "She's awake and eavesdropping."

Chevie felt Director Gunn's gaze swivel her way. She *felt* his eyes burn into her forehead, bringing a blush to her cheeks.

"Open your eyes, Cadet Savano," said Waldo Gunn, "and you may yet live through this day."

Chevie did as she was ordered and found herself handcuffed to a chair in front of Director Gunn's desk. It seemed as though the Thundercats weren't taking any more chances with Chevie's newfound combat expertise.

On the desk was a photocopy of a citizen's identity card. The man in the picture was in his seventies, with wild gray hair and a surprised expression. He wore a white lab coat with a selection of pens clipped to the lapels, several of which had leaked blotted ink patterns onto his coat.

He is real, thought Chevie.

"Professor Charles Smart," said Director Gunn, confirming what Chevie somehow knew. "Who works in weapons R and D in the Mayfair facility. We thought Smart was one of our brightest scientists, but now we have compelling evidence that he is in fact a Jax spy."

Chevie kept her face still. Emotion would only serve to damn her.

"Perhaps you are working together," suggested Gunn.

"No, Director," said Chevie. "I have never met this man or communicated with him."

At least I don't think so.

"So you are no Jax spy?"

Chevie straightened her shoulders, in spite of the strong hands bearing down on them. "Of course not, Director. I am a loyal citizen. I love God and Empire, sir."

Gunn nodded, considering her words. "There is one way you can redeem yourself, prove to me that you are not a spy, and perhaps even get approval for a brain scan."

"Anything, Director," said Chevie earnestly. "I'll do anything."

Gunn nodded, seemingly with approval. He opened a desk drawer and withdrew a standard-issue sidearm. He laid it on the table, where it sat, squat, ugly, and black.

"Smart is a Jax spy, and he needs to be executed. I need a true patriot to pull the trigger. Are you a patriot, Cadet Savano?"

Chevie felt her body tense. She wanted to break free from the hands that restrained her and run from the room into some kind of world where teenagers did not have to answer such questions.

Director Waldo Gunn leaned forward so his beard brushed the desktop.

"Well, Cadet Savano, are you a patriot?"

Chevie nodded. "Yes, Director. I am a patriot. The Jax spy must be executed."

She *was* a patriot, wasn't she?

Most of her, anyway.

But not Traitor Chevie.

Traitor Chevie was an anarchist. And which Chevron Savano would have her finger on the trigger when the time came?

So now Cadet Savano rode in a Chariot of Box automobile that purred across central London. It was said that central London had once had a carnival air about it, jammed from one dawn to the next with tourists and revelers. They said that the Ministry of Defense was once a theater where the stars of the stage plied their pretending trade. The Hall of Sanctions had been a huge restaurant that sold steak to anyone who could pay for it; all one had to do was take a seat and place an order. Even foreigners were welcome, they said; even heathens.

DeeDee Woollen had once confided in Chevie that her grandfather's book showed pictures of young people in London dance halls without a care for curfew or modest dress.

DeeDee was always going to get herself in trouble, spreading stories like that.

Shot in the head for describing Grandpa's pictures, said Traitor Chevie. *Seems fair.*

Perhaps London had once been a center of frivolous celebration, but now it was the hub of the Empire. Colonel Box had risen from the catacombs to claim New Albion, so it was fitting that it should serve as the nerve center for the entire Empire's government. The sidewalks were still slick from their dawn scrub, and armies of civil-servant drones hurried along, reflected in the shining flagstones, eager to reach their office cubicles before morning services.

Chevie often wondered what it must have been like to live in a city of diversity, where everything didn't have a gray sheen of sameness.

California. Someday I will watch the sunset from the beach. Even the party can't control the ocean.

Don't bet on it, kiddo. Traitor Chevie again. *They control everything else in this crazy world. Even what you're thinking.*

Clover Vallicose was up front at the wheel. She flicked through a playlist of Boxite tunes on the stereo until she happened on the song "Spy Zodety" by sanctioned musician D Bob Jones. It told the story of American Boxite spy Woody Zodety, who resisted forty-eight hours of Jax torture before he was rescued. The famous golden oldie featured a bridge of screams, which were Zodety's actual howls of pain, lifted from an interrogation-room tape.

Vallicose grunted along with the screams, hammering the steering wheel with her gloved palm.

"I love D Bob," she said, with a tremor in her voice. "God speaks through him." She called over her shoulder. "Did you ever see that video, Sister Witmeyer? The entire forty-eight-hour torture session is on the Boxnet. Zodety never told those Jax animals a thing."

"I saw it, Sister Clover. Inspiring stuff."

Chevie got the feeling that perhaps Witmeyer wasn't as devout as her partner, but she played along for politics' sake.

Witmeyer pressed a button on the armrest, and the

windows darkened until all Chevie could see was her own worried reflection staring back at her through round brown eyes.

"Just *entre nous,*" said Witmeyer, "where did you pick up those combat moves?"

Chevie was surprised to hear the Thundercat using a French phrase. Coming from any other mouth, those two words could be considered traitorous. One of her classmates, a snippy local London girl, had been shipped off to the Dublin factory for describing the gluey canteen soup as an *apéritif.*

Perhaps Sister Witmeyer was slipping a Jax phrase into the conversation in an attempt to trip her up.

Chevie replied. "They were not *moves,* Sister. I panicked and lashed out."

"Believe me, little one, they were moves. I have been in enough fights to know the difference between panic and training."

"I can only apologize, Sister. It won't happen again."

Witmeyer chuckled. "That it won't, little sister. That it won't."

"Little sister"—that's a little ominous, said Traitor Chevie. *I'd watch my back if I were you. Wait a minute. I* am *you, only less stupid.*

Chevie bit her bottom lip in case a whimper should leak out.

The drive to Mayfair would usually take up to thirty minutes during morning rush hour, but service vehicles parted before the luxury sedan's high curved prow as soon as drivers spotted it in their rearview mirrors, and barely ten minutes later Sister Vallicose was parking outside Charles Smart's town house, which was sandwiched between two monolithic apartment blocks.

I know how that house feels, thought Chevie.

"Look at this," said Witmeyer. "An honest-to-goodness house. This Smart person must be something special to merit a house in the city center. I'm living in a cupboard, and this scientist who probably never killed a single person for Box is living it up in a house."

A professor with a house was unusual, as most citizens were squashed into mega-blocks comprised of identical utilitarian apartments with barely enough room to swing a cat—if owning a cat had been legal inside Greater London's boundaries.

"Citizen Smart may have left for work already," said Chevie, hoping for a reprieve.

Witmeyer opened her door. "We called ahead. Though he doesn't know it, Smart is waiting inside for us to come and execute him." She handed Chevie the standard-issue sidearm. "Or should I say for *you* to execute him, Cadet."

Chevie took the gun, and it felt like a cold block of guilt in her hand.

A cold block of guilt, said Traitor Chevie. *This timeline is so moody.*

Chevie was surprised that her legs carried her to Charles Smart's door, but they did—a little shakily, maybe, but they managed to avoid buckling. She curled her fingers into a fist to knock, but before she could, the door was wrenched open and an old man appeared in the doorway.

"Just tell me," said the man in a Scottish accent. "Is he dead?"

Chevie was taken aback. *Dead? Is who dead?*

"Dead? I don't understand, Citizen."

"I get a call from a Thundercat. 'Stay at home,' she tells me. 'Don't go to work.' So is my boy dead? Was he killed in France?"

Felix, whispered Traitor Chevie. *His son's name is Felix.*

"Felix," she said aloud, which was a mistake.

The old man reeled as though struck and clamped his hands to his skull.

"I knew it!" he cried. "I knew it. You're here about Felix. So which is it? Dead or captured?"

Witmeyer bent low, whispering into Chevie's ear. "You know about his son. Curious."

I *don't know about him,* Chevie wanted to protest. *The Traitor knows.*

But this made no sense. How could the Traitor know things that were true yet outside her experience?

Perhaps I have the gift of second sight. Perhaps I am psychic.

There was some hope in this thought. Chevie knew that the Thundercats had a psy-division, and of course it would mean that she was not dying.

"We're not here about your son," said Chevie, touching the old man's elbow. "It's a different matter."

Charles Smart drew several deep breaths, calming himself, coming back to earth from the hell of a parent's grief.

"Felix is safe. Thank God. Oh, thank God. A different matter. What different matter?"

"Maybe we could come inside? Would that be all right?"

Before Smart could answer, Clover Vallicose actually growled and barged past Chevie and Smart into the hallway.

"'Would that be all right?'" she said mockingly. "That's not how we do things, Savano. We don't ask permission."

They sat in Smart's kitchen, which was festooned with laboratory equipment. Circuit boards were piled high on the table, and yards of plastic-coated wiring crisscrossed the floor and ceiling. Banks of switches were screwed to the walls, and conduits were threaded through rough holes in the plaster. Colored bulbs blinked from the frying pan, and a block of glowing orange gel bubbled lazily in the oven like some sedated sea creature. Screwdrivers, hand drills, clippers, and assorted screws littered the drain board, and the sink was half full of greenish mist that seemed reluctant to leave the bowl. Chevie thought she saw a fin momentarily break the mist's surface, but no one else seemed to notice, so she put it down to the Traitor.

"Nice place you have here," said Witmeyer, brushing a few stray capacitors from the table. "Geek chic."

Charles Smart had recovered his composure by this point, and it had occurred to him that if the Thundercats were not here for his son, then they were here for him. He sat facing the visitors, outwardly calm, but inwardly barely in control of the panic that bubbled under his skin. A visit from the goon squad was never a good thing.

"Mrs. Smart died a long time ago, Sister," he said. "Without her, I've let the place go somewhat."

"What is all this clutter?" asked Witmeyer. "Are you building something?"

The way Witmeyer said *building something,* it was clear that Smart should not be building anything.

Smart thought before answering. It was prudent to consider any possible interpretation of what you were about to say when dealing with Thundercats. A slip of the tongue could be the last mistake you ever made.

"I am working on various approved projects in my own spare time. Labor-saving devices, mostly, to aid with the war effort in France and here at home. My latest invention is a hoist that will allow enormous weights to be manipulated by one person. With my hoist, a single Thundercat could clear an entire highway pileup in minutes."

Witmeyer was impressed. "That has definite military applications. I've seen bogged-down tanks cost a unit half a day to pull out of the mud."

Smart clapped his hands. "Exactly! Exactly what I told my supervisor, but he won't approve further funding."

Witmeyer tapped her temple, taking a mental note. "Perhaps I could have a word."

Chevie didn't know how Witmeyer could give this poor man false hope when they were about to shoot him. When *she* was about to shoot him. Suddenly the gun, which had felt like a block of ice in her jacket pocket, seemed to burn into her skin.

Clover Vallicose had no patience for chitchat. "Cadet

Savano seems to know your son. Can you explain that?"

"No," said Professor Smart. "I was waiting for her to explain. Is it true, Cadet? Do you know my boy? Though he's hardly a boy anymore. He's well into his forties by now and still not married. 'Felix,' I said to him. 'You need to lower your standards. You're no oil painting, if you know what I mean. . . .'"

Vallicose thumped the table, scattering fuses and memory boards. "Why do you prattle, Citizen? We are here on the Blessed Colonel's business, and I feel you are not taking us seriously."

Smart paled, and Chevie felt a kinship with the old man. They were both sinking in the same boat.

"Yes, of course," said Smart. "You don't want to hear about my son's romantic problems. Why should you concern yourselves, Sisters?"

"Indeed, we do not."

Smart cleared his throat. "In that case, perhaps we could get to the point of your visit. What exactly has brought you here?"

Vallicose nodded at her partner and grunted.

The grunt translated as: *You take over, partner. Explaining things is your area.*

Witmeyer drew a tin of chewing tobacco from her pocket and took her sweet time bunching a plug and depositing it inside her bottom lip.

"It's like this, Citizen. We have an order, passed down from Colonel Box himself, to terminate your life cycle. He was quite specific about the time and date, but not about the method. That has been left to our discretion."

I am the method, thought Chevie. I am about to become an instrument of death. An assassin who kills on command.

Chevie had always known this day would come. After all, wasn't that what she was being trained for? But now that the day had arrived, she was far from certain that she could be a loyal Boxite and murder this somehow familiar stranger.

Witmeyer gave her bombshell a moment to penetrate, chewing noisily on the tobacco and spitting a long rope of brown juice in the general direction of Smart's sink.

"You shouldn't spit," said Smart absently. "Believe it or not, this is a sterile environment."

The professor did not seem as puzzled as he should rightly have been. There was no slack-jawed disbelief or raging objection. Smart simply muttered to himself and ran his fingertip in complex zigzags across the tabletop.

"I did it, then," he mumbled. "I must have done it. Incredible."

Witmeyer snapped her fingers. "Are you still with us, Professor? Would you care to share what you must have done?"

Smart lifted his head, but his eyes were unfocused. "The only way Colonel Box could know about me would be if we met, or if he knew my work." A thought seemed to slap him across the face. "Oh my God. Oh no. All those missiles, those futuristic missiles. It's my fault. I opened the wormhole. It could only have been me."

Clover Vallicose's tiny reservoir of patience was running out. "Citizen, speak plainly. What missiles? Are you building missiles for the Jax?"

Smart drifted back into the room. "Jax? What? No, of course not. Don't you see?" He waved his arms wildly. "This. All of this. It's my doing. It must be. The only way the colonel could have built such weapons is if I opened the wormhole for him. I enabled this godforsaken empire."

Chevie felt her heart speed up, thumping palpably in her chest.

Yes, said Traitor Chevie. *Yes. This is it. Now we're getting somewhere.*

Smart was on his feet, running both hands through his sparse white hair, smoothing long strands backward across his shining skull. "How would it have gone? I built the machine in another timeline, and Box accessed it. He went back with his team and took over the country. With his knowledge, it would have been child's play. Crazy? Am I crazy? No. It must be." Smart opened the bread bin and pressed a series of buttons on a panel hidden inside. "So, what then? He's emperor of all he surveys. The last thing Box wants is someone coming back and taking it all away from him, so he leaves an order that I am to be killed. But he won't have me executed as a child. He has to wait until the world is his, plus the length of the wormhole, in case he needs an escape route."

Smart rushed around the kitchen, flipping switches on circuit boards that had seemed discarded. His eyes were wild; his hair sprang from his skull in an electric halo no matter how he tried to flatten it.

"Don't you see?" he shouted. "I did this. All of it. And now I must undo it."

Vallicose drew her weapon. "You speak in riddles, spy. Blasphemous riddles at that. Stand still, blast you, and allow our young cadet to carry out her orders."

The kitchen was now humming like a giant refrigerator, and Witmeyer felt the situation slipping away. "Very well, Citizen. You've had your little episode. It's natural, people react in different ways. Now, you tell us in plain English what you are babbling about, and the girl here will kill you quickly. We can't be any fairer than that."

Smart ignored her. "I can still stop Box. Without those missiles, he's nothing."

Vallicose was offended. "Box? Do you speak of the Blessed Colonel as an equal?" She stood suddenly, shunting her chair backward. "On your knees, Citizen. And pray to God for purgatory instead of hell."

Witmeyer rolled her eyes. Here came the fire and brimstone.

"Cadet Savano, this is ridiculous. Do your duty and put an end to the madness."

There is no end to madness, thought Chevie. No end.

"You heard me, Savano. Prove yourself a patriot."

Smart is the key, said Traitor Chevie. *He is the way out.*

"Shut up!" said Chevie, and she pulled her weapon. "Shut up."

Smart behaved as though he were alone, rattling off long equations, throwing switches, and testing the wind with his finger.

"It should work. I have been building it for years. The calculations are sound."

Chevie pointed the gun at him. What choice did she have?

"Stand still," she ordered. "Stop talking."

"Good girl," said Witmeyer. "It will all be over soon."

"Shoot!" said Vallicose. "For Box and Empire, shoot!"

No, said Traitor Chevie. *You know this man. Think. Remember.*

A vision popped into Chevie's head. Smart, but with a monkey arm.

Not now, she begged the Traitor. *Just let me get through this.*

She followed Smart with the barrel. A moving target. "Please, Professor."

Please, Professor what? Stand still and be shot like a good fellow?

"The bridge is constant," said Charles Smart, dialing the knobs on the oven. "I should be in time to stop Box."

"Kill the heathen!" shouted Vallicose. "Kill him!"

Professor Charles Smart, that's his name, not heathen. *And his son Felix. Agent Orange. Remember, Chevron.*

Chevie pointed the gun at her own head. "Get out of me! Leave me!"

"Well now," said Witmeyer, delighted. "This is interesting."

The entire room was vibrating now. Whatever Smart was doing, it was a lot more than making an omelette.

You know this, said Traitor Chevie. *You know exactly what is happening here.*

"Kill the heathen!" shrieked Clover Vallicose.

No. She could not. Chevie could not believe that the Blessed Colonel wanted her to murder old men.

Her head pounded. Hammer blows behind the eyes. The Traitor was exploding.

"No!" she shouted. "I won't kill him! No."

She took the cold steel from her own temple and turned it on Witmeyer. "Raise your hands."

Vallicose pointed a righteous finger at Chevie. "Do you see now? I was right. Was I not right?"

"You were right, Sister, but we had our orders. And she is a mere child."

Witmeyer raised her hands, but in a mocking fashion, wiggling her fingers as though terrified when her features showed she was anything but.

"Don't shoot me, Cadet. I am your friend, truly."

The walls began to flex slightly, and Vallicose had seen more than enough to convince her that something traitorous and possibly heretical was going on here.

"I will kill the professor now," she declared. "We can investigate later."

"As usual," said Witmeyer.

Chevie was confused. Did they not see the gun? Did the Thundercats think themselves immortal?

"Stay where you are!" she ordered, half-wishing the Traitor would take over now and she would become a super soldier. "Leave the professor alone."

Vallicose ignored Chevie completely, moving briskly toward Smart, who had opened the dishwasher and was rearranging the plates inside. With each switched plate, the lighting inside the kitchen changed color.

Witmeyer stood, keeping her hands raised. "You don't

think, Cadet, that we would put a loaded weapon in the hands of a traitor."

They were testing me, thought Chevie. And I failed.

Just to be sure, she aimed the gun at Witmeyer's leg and pulled the trigger. There was no bang, just the hollow *clack* of a hammer on an empty chamber.

Witmeyer sighed. "*Click*, not *boom*. That means, Cadet, that you are out of time."

The walls suddenly began to shake.

"Yes," said Professor Charles Smart. "It's working."

Whatever was working, Vallicose didn't like it. "In the name of the Blessed Colonel, shut this racket off."

Smart crossed his legs and sank into the lotus position. "It can't be shut off. Not now. We are all going on a journey, Sisters. It will be easier if you relax."

"No journey for you, traitor," said Clover Vallicose. She drew her weapon from a hip holster and fired. Smart was hit high in the chest and skittered backward as though dragged from behind. Blood frothed from the jagged wound, saturating his upper body in seconds. There was no doubt in Chevie's mind that this couldn't be anything but a fatal injury.

"You see," said Vallicose. "The Blessed Colonel ordered two people killed today. Smart was one."

And I was the other, Chevie realized. They were always going to kill me.

Vallicose holstered her weapon. "Shoot the child and be done, Sister Lunka. There is something not right with this place."

"I'm just going to reach into my pocket," said Witmeyer, whose hands were still over her head as though she were a prisoner. "And pull out a gun to shoot you with. I sincerely wish this wasn't necessary. But orders is orders, as they say."

If there can ever be a good time for a house to convulse, this was that time. Smart's house shook as though in the grip of an angry giant, sending the occupants bouncing off the walls. Chevie came to rest on top of the dying professor. His blood seemed to draw her closer, like crimson tentacles.

"I'm sorry," she said as the kitchen dissolved around them, revealing that they were no longer in London but some other dimension composed of matter that seemed solid, liquid, and gas, but also somehow aware. Smart space.

"Smart space," said Charles Smart, as if he could hear Chevie's thoughts. "And my name is Smart. Geddit?"

The professor chuckled, blood burbling over his teeth.

There was something familiar about this whole insane situation, but it eluded her still. Tantalizingly close, but not close enough, and she chased it like a seagull feather down Malibu beach on a windy morning.

Relax, said Traitor Chevie. *We're in the tunnel now. My time is coming.*

The Traitor is coming. Great.

Chevie remembered the Thundercats. She rolled off Smart and looked around for them. Witmeyer lay folded almost double, like a discarded coat, wedged into a corner of ceiling that used to be floor, floating away into the smart space. Vallicose stood ramrod straight, her arms overhead like a diver. There were tears on her face, but they were tears of fanatical joy.

"I am ready, Lord!" she cried. "Take me to your arms. I am ready."

It seemed as though the Thundercats were occupied. Chevie should see if there was anything she could do for the dying man.

The professor's breath was ragged and irregular.

"The key," he said, surely his last words. He was pawing at her weakly. No, not pawing, giving her something. A plastic pendant.

"And the table," whispered Smart. "Lie on the table. It will anchor you."

"Okay, Professor. I will lie on the table." It was crazy, but not the craziest order she'd had today, not by a long shot.

His mission accomplished, Smart's eyes rolled back, a long sigh rattled in his gullet, and he was gone.

Again, said Traitor Chevie. *He has died in the wormhole before. Remember?*

And she did remember something. It seemed like a déjà vu or maybe a dream fragment.

Don't worry, said Traitor Chevie. *I'm coming any second now. All will be revealed.*

Chevie clasped the key tight in her fingers, and orange light glowed through her skin, because her skin had become translucent.

Translucent skin. Rarely a positive development.

The table! Chevie threw herself spread-eagled on the metal kitchen table and hoped that whatever the term *anchoring* meant in this situation, it would be good.

She couldn't understand why she wasn't terror-stricken.

I am afraid, yes, but not terrified.

Covered in blood in the midst of some supernatural event—and yet, while she had been shaken to her core a minute earlier, Chevie felt as though she was discovering a core of steel.

That's me. I'm coming.

The Traitor's voice seemed louder now, part of the real world.

No, that was wrong. *She* was part of the Traitor's world.

Take me, God. Take me to your bosom.

That was Clover Vallicose thinking out loud.

You are not rid of us, Chevron Savano. We have a mission.

And there was Witmeyer—not dead, then. Wishful thinking.

The orange glow spread until it filled the space inside and outside Chevie's head.

Perhaps I have shrunk.

A wind howled around her, tossing Chevie like a twig in a hurricane, then the orange light exploded, lifting Chevie and the table on the head of a giant geyser. Maybe liquid, maybe imaginary; but there was no pain, just the balm of helplessness.

Whatever is happening is going to happen, no matter what I do.

She saw Smart fall away below her and felt herself borne far away from everything she knew.

Traitor Chevie tutted. *Isn't there anything familiar about all of this? Haven't you dreamed about orange light?*

It was true. Chevie had woken several times in the past weeks with a quickly evaporating sense of *orangeness*, which had seemed stupid to think about, but maybe wasn't so stupid now.

The geyser was suddenly spent, and Chevie found herself suspended by something in a sea of something, and that was about as well as she would ever be able to describe it.

This could not get any stranger, she thought. A notion that held true for a moment or two, until a second version of herself appeared in front of her. It was definitely her, but different. Harder. More combat miles.

Traitor Chevie, she thought, and the thought carried outside her head.

Her doppelganger reached out, grasping Chevie's skull in both hands.

"I'm gonna open your mind," she said. "It might not hurt."

But it probably will, thought Chevie.

And she was right.

4 » FIZZ, AND IT'S ALL OVER

Time travel causes chaos, and chaos doesn't follow your rules.
That's why it's called chaos, dummy.
—Professor Charles Smart

THE ORIENT THEATRE, HOLBORN, LONDON, 1899

ANTON FARLEY FIRING AT HIS LORD AND BENEfactor with some kind of futuristic multi-shooter? Well, it was more than a brain could comprehend. Meek and mild Farley? Farley the ink man, who was content to be the butt of jokes? Farley the complacent, who bore without complaint the jibes of the Battering Rams, who could often be a cruel bunch, especially when the grog took control of their tongues?

Malarkey had a vague memory of one drunken night in the Hidey-Hole when Pooley had referred to Anton Farley as *that doting simperling with his bag o' colors.*

Malarkey was not certain whether or not the word *simperling* was an actual soldier in the army of the queen's own lingo, but it got the message across. Farley had never so much as batted an eyelid.

It's been simmering, thought the Ram king now. All the slights been festering in his gnarled old heart.

Still, *festering slights* could not explain this sudden display of marksmanship, not to mention the fantastical weapon currently being brandished to devastating effect by the disgruntled tattooist.

In the twinkle of an eye since Farley had set his weapon a-spitting bullets, Jeeves and Noble had been cut down by the deadly hail. Virtually sundered, poor Noble had been.

And yet the gun made no more noise than a hacking consumptive, Malarkey thought now from the shadows of the orchestra pit into which he had flung himself, caring little as to the depth of the hole.

Had it been the pit of Hell itself, I would have taken the leap, he realized.

In truth, he did care now about the pit's depth. Otto would have preferred a sight more depth and a sight more shadow, too.

I am trapped like a fish in a barrel down here. A blind man with a slingshot could nail me.

Malarkey felt a tear gather in one eye. *Imagine. Great King Otto served his papers by a sixty-year-old tattooist. It don't seem right. I always imagined that it would require a legion of bluebottles to drag me under, or perhaps an escaped lion from Regent's Zoo. At the very least a hostile bunch of traitorous cohorts doing for me like Julius Caesar's mates did for 'im. But no. A ruddy ink-jockey.*

It was an ignoble way to go, and Malarkey had always been uncommonly worried about posterity.

Farley can make up any old yarn, he realized. He could swear I died whimpering like a puppy in a sack. He could say Otto Malarkey soiled himself.

Otto's pride urged him to call out to Farley, to offer parlay, but his soldier's sense cautioned him to keep his big trap shut, as it was possible that Farley was not altogether certain as to where his king had disappeared.

Where is my brother? wondered Malarkey, not for a second considering that Barnabus could be dead. Inhumane had once found himself in the path of a Chinese blunderbuss during a skirmish behind an opium den, and the scattershot had only made him angry.

Farley's weapon spoke again, sending a burst of hissing projectiles streaking across the square of light over Malarkey's head.

Who was the tattooist aiming at?

This unspoken question was answered when a thunderous crash was followed by the appearance of a massive forearm over the lip of the orchestra pit. Blood flowed along the arm, collected in the hollow of the man's palm, and was released in four spiraling dribbles between once powerful fingers.

Malarkey watched the viscous liquid pool between his boots, and he realized that any man who allowed this volume of blood to vacate his body would presently be shaking hands with Saint Peter.

Otto Malarkey knew then that the once indomitable Barnabus Malarkey had fought his last battle.

King Otto threw prudence to the wind and howled to the gods.

"Farley. Faaarley!"

A voice floated down from the stalls. Boomy and echoing, descending and condescending.

"Ah, Your Majesty. I was looking for you, as I wish to augment your last tattoo. A few touches of crimson, perhaps."

A narrow beam of red light flitted across the pit mouth. It came to a point against the pit wall, then began a slow jittering descent toward the corner where Otto Malarkey sat shivering in rage and grief.

Barely a minute earlier, Riley had watched the situation deteriorate from ominous to lethal. He had predicted that Farley would be forced to concentrate his efforts on the warrior Rams, and that prediction would have been proven spot on had Farley not been an AS officer with multiple weapons, some from the late twentieth century. He trained his Steyr machine pistol on the Rams while keeping the Colt revolver aimed at Riley.

Hell and damnation, thought Riley. Two barrels.

Even though the mortality rate was high in Victorian London, murder was rare, and guns were scarce among civilians, even the Family. For one villain to be in possession of a brace of firearms was indeed exceptional. Albert Garrick, who had been a lifelong knife man, often said that guns were like mutts: they took feeding and often didn't produce the barks when called upon—unreliable standards of manufacturing and London's damp climate saw to that—but the gleam on Farley's barrels spoke of nightly polishings with love and oil, and Riley would be willing to bet they barked to order.

This time Riley's prediction was dead right. Farley's machine pistol spat a stream of bullets into the throng of Rams, bullets that ripped through flesh and shattered bone. Jeeves and Noble fell in a mist of blood and it was obvious they weren't ever going to be climbing back up again. Otto Malarkey and his brother, two veteran scrappers, dived for whatever cover they reckoned would fox this devastating new weapon. Otto tumbled into the orchestra pit with surprising grace for a big fellow, and Inhumane dived into the aisle, hoping to bash his way out through a wall, which would not be the first or second time wall-bashing had saved his hide. But the Orient walls were solid brick and in good nick to boot. There would be no bashing through to the outside world, even with a noggin as hard as Inhumane Malarkey's.

Riley had barely a moment's grace before Farley, with cold deliberation, spared him a quick glance for aiming purposes and then pulled the Colt's trigger, accompanying his shot with the glib comment:

"Catch this, why don't you, boy?"

He was referring to the famous *bullet catch* that was advertised in chalk on the sidewalk outside.

Farley is a bitter man indeed, thought Riley, if he can waste time jibing when there is killing to be done.

The bullet came at him, and Riley whirled inside his cloak,

folding the layers of chain mail and increasing his chances of survival. The slug hit him in the chest and the impact was terrific, forcing Riley backward several steps. He could not tell if he was actually dying or merely hurt. In any event it was vital that he appear to be a goner so that Farley would point his beadies elsewhere. Riley slumped against the wall, allowing the folds of his cloak to droop apart. He slapped a hand to his chest as though his palm was magical and could somehow stop the crimson blossom spreading across his white shirt.

"Ha!" said Farley. "The Great Savano, my eye."

Riley coughed once, stumbled forward, and then toppled over, and the velvet folds of his cloak welcomed him to blackness.

Chevie Savano was in the time tunnel, she realized now.

The Smarthole, she thought. Thank heaven for that.

Any television-watching kid over the age of ten had heard of the famous Einstein-Rosen bridge, or wormhole, or time tunnel, or whatever the latest sci-fi show chose to call it, but very few people had actually been immersed in one, and of the few that had been inside the tunnel, not one of them had been *relieved* to be so situated.

Until now.

Chevie felt a wave of relief, spreading a balm across a psyche that had been scarred by seventeen years of living in the Boxite Empire.

It doesn't have to be, she realized. None of it.

The consciousness known previously as Traitor Chevie

had punched its way to the surface, and suddenly Chevie remembered it all. Riley, Garrick, Victorian London, and most importantly, Colonel Box.

Clayton Box.

The missing special forces colonel and his team. So that's where they went.

Box was the one who had been pushing the use of the Smarthole as a conduit directly to terrorists' grandfathers.

Stamp out the bloodline, had been Box's advice. *Kill them before they breed.*

Which had prompted Charles Smart to disappear into the past and shut down the program.

Everyone thought Box had gone MIA, but in reality the colonel and his team had gone MIT. They had brought the technology of the future into the past.

It seemed so obvious now that Chevie wondered how it had never occurred to anyone.

Did people really believe that the specs for intercontinental ballistic missiles had been dreamed up by Box the Divine?

Of course they did.

Why wouldn't they?

Chevie had believed it all her life.

It was actually a lot easier to believe than what had actually happened.

Ludicrous.

It's good to be cynical me again, thought Chevie. No more bowing and scraping. From now on . . .

From now on . . . what?

Chevie didn't know. She didn't know for sure where this pod, which Smart had hidden by disguising it as a kitchen, would dump her. And if she did end up in Victorian London, would the Thundercats have traveled back with her?

Thundercats. Now she got it.

Box had named his security police after an old kids' cartoon show.

What a drama queen.

But back to the point. She had no plan and nowhere to go.

Find Riley.

That was a good starting place.

The boy had said his theater was in Holborn. She knew where that was.

Of course all this was provided she didn't emerge on Mars being chased by white apes.

And it was likely that the Thundercats were in this quantum foam with her, but at least they should be disoriented for the first few moments, which would give her a chance to bolt.

Find Riley, and maybe sabotage Box's plot.

That plan was too big. How could she put the kibosh on the rise of an entire world order?

Find Riley, and go from there.

It was a comforting thought: to find someone who would be happy to see her.

A friend.

Imagine that.

• • •

Farley watched Riley fall, which was unfortunate, because Riley would have dearly liked a private moment to raise an elbow to protect his face from impact with the stage floor. With Farley's gaze on him, all he could do was tuck his chin and take the clunk on his forehead. Luckily, Garrick had always praised head butts to high heaven, saying that *God has given us a nice wedge of bone and the means to aim it.* So Riley had years of head-butting training to call on when his head smashed into the trapdoor. Had the trapdoor not been off the latch, he might have split his brainpan. As it was, the bang was severe enough that stars winked around his head as he tumbled through the trapdoor and into the trap room, leaving his cloak heaped on the stage above.

The move had been accomplished smoothly enough that perhaps Farley would be fooled into believing that Riley's cloak had become his shroud and the boy lay dead in its folds. After all, there had been blood.

Pig's blood from a rubber bladder, but blood all the same.

The bladder had been clipped to the back of a ring on the Great Savano's middle finger and, during his bullet-catch act, was supposed to burst for a little blood around his gums. But it served equally well to fake a shot to the chest; the bullet had actually been stopped by the folds of chain mail.

Riley tumbled into the trap room, thumping onto the platform that was spring-loaded and counterweighted to shoot him upward for the show's finale. Fortunately he did not knock against the lever. Heaven knows how Farley would react if Riley resurrected before his eyes.

Actually, even the glockiest of dummies could predict Farley's reaction. He would kill Riley again *toot sweet.*

The commotion of Riley's fall was masked by the rapid clatter of a large man moving quickly in the stalls.

That's Malarkey's brother having a go, thought Riley. Which is my cue to make myself scarce. Down the corridor to the back door and off into the city.

Farley's futuristic gun spoke again, a staccato of dry coughs followed by a crash so big, the theater shook.

Barnabus is no more, Riley realized. The Rams have lost their most fearsome fighter and King Otto has lost his brother.

Riley should have been scurrying down the corridor, a trip he could make blindfolded; but instead he was thinking about Otto, huddled in the orchestra pit, waiting for the bullet to send him the way of his brother.

Go, Riley told himself. *Flee.*

Otto had never done anything for him. Never brought nothing into his life but grief and anxiety.

So why are you still here, Riley? Be off into the city.

But the boy was stricken by a sudden sense of compassion.

That's Chevie's fault, that is. I was never compassionate under Garrick. Unto dust, *Garrick always said.* The only concern you need have about life is to preserve your own and that of your master.

He could follow Garrick's path no more. An attempt must be made to save Otto.

"Blazes and tarnation," swore Riley, and he opened the small hatch that linked the trap room to the orchestra pit.

• • •

Chevie somehow knew that her time in the Smarthole was drawing to an end. Perhaps *time* was the wrong word for her trip, as it could not be measured in minutes or seconds. *Space* didn't work either, as there was no sense of traditional movement. If anything, the experience was closest to a fevered dream that seemed simultaneously totally real and utterly impossible.

Chevie recalled from past experience that when the journey ended, her senses would be addled by what Professor Smart had christened *the Zen Ten.*

Everything is all right and outta sight, Smart had quipped in the famous talk at Columbia University during his U.S. lecture tour. *When those little virtual particles annihilate, a person gets literally plugged into the universe.*

This dazed and confused period had been only quantumjecture at the time, but now Chevie knew for a fact that the Zen Ten existed and it could last a lot longer than ten seconds. In fact, she would have been willing to bet that Smart had only picked the figure ten because it rhymed with Zen and so made for a catchy phrase.

Stay alert, she told herself. *Stay focused.*

Then she was coughed up into the real world and the fugue of time foam smothered her senses.

Chevie began to giggle.

I'm back in a Victorian basement. This is hysterical.

Across the room she saw the Thundercats coalesce and solidify, and this was even more hilarious.

"You two look ridiculous," she said.

Vallicose and Witmeyer did seem a little pathetic at the moment, snuffling on all fours like two large pigs in their knee-length, flesh-colored Thundercoats.

Vallicose smiled broadly, and it did not suit her face.

"We are going to kill you slowly, heathen," she said, which took the good out of the smile. "You are in league with Lucifer."

Chevie knew she should be upset by the idea of a slow death, but the Zen Ten had her in its clown-glove grip. "Lucifer? Is that Lucifer O'Malley from Venice? He owes me ten bucks."

"There, you see?" said Vallicose, pointing and also drooling. "Venice is in Italy, which is near France. She's a Jax spy."

Witmeyer had the good sense to be worried, but her face couldn't show it yet.

"I have an idea. Let's kill her quickly and then move right on to figuring out what is going on here."

Vallicose punched her partner playfully on the shoulder.

"Now now, Lunka. Slow killing, I said."

Witmeyer giggled. "Stop it, Clover. You are such a silly. Quick killing."

Chevie thought she might collapse from the shock at what happened next.

Oh my God. No one is ever going to believe this. Do I *even believe it?*

Vallicose and Witmeyer began tickling each other.

"Slow kill, Lunka."

"No, fast kill."

"Slow, slow. A thousand cuts."

"Clover, one cut across the throat. *Fizz,* and it's all over."

Witmeyer mimed the fizzing blood with wiggling fingers at her neck.

"What is that?"

"It's the blood, fizzing."

"Blood doesn't *fizz,* Lunka."

"If you puncture the jugular. Just a tiny hole."

"Spray. Blood sprays, and it's impossible to get out of a uniform."

I could kill them now, thought Chevie. Two quick kills. I would be saving myself a lot of heartache, and the Blessed Colonel knows that Victorian Londoners are not ready for tickling Thundercats.

But she could never do something like that, no matter which one of her personalities was dominant at the time. And Chevie reminded herself that there was no such thing as a *Blessed Colonel* back here. Just a run-of-the-mill colonel who was about as far from blessed as it was possible to be.

I couldn't kill Smart and I can't kill these two, Chevie realized, and then she added an alarming addendum to that thought. *But they could certainly kill me.*

She stood shakily and checked herself for wormhole mutations. Nothing visible. No dinosaur head or duck feet, but she would scrutinize every square inch later and also have a good root about in her own brain.

Sometimes the changes are not physical.

And with the Zen Ten playing with her mind, it was difficult to know whether or not her neurons were firing on all cylinders.

Concentrate on one thing, she told herself.

Find Riley.

On their last adventure, she had taken the lead, steering the boy through his twenty-first-century experience; now she was the fish out of water, stumbling around in a mud-floored basement. Riley would provide her compass.

The last time I wanted to go home. This time I don't even know if my home exists anymore. And if it does, do I really want to go back there?

Chevie lurched toward the doorway, giggling as she went, deliberately not glancing at the Thundercats, in case she burst out laughing and incapacitated herself.

"Look," she heard Witmeyer say. "The child is escaping. And Smart gave her something, I saw it. A key. It could take us home."

Vallicose reacted to this hilarious news by laughing until her throat was raw, and then she said in a jovial tone, "Don't worry. The Lord will lead us to her, and then we shall kill her slowly and take the key from her godless corpse."

Chevie felt the key warm against her skin and she used the damp brick wall to steady her as she made good her escape.

Find Riley.

Godless corpse? she thought. Hilarious.

Riley peered through the trap-room hatch, and there was Malarkey, huddled in a corner behind a stack of wooden music stands that would provide no more protection than a showgirl's fan. The Ram king wore a strange expression, which Riley realized was a stew of primal rage and utter despair.

Like Jekyll and Hyde at the same time, thought Riley, who was very partial to the Scottish writer Robert Louis Stevenson and counted *Treasure Island* as the finest adventure story he had ever read.

It was odd to see the High Rammity like this. So *human.* Without any of the customary airs or swaggers about him.

This is the real man, Riley thought. This is Otto Malarkey, not King Ram or Golgoth.

A narrow beam of red light drew complicated jitters on the black wall, and as Farley's voice drifted from above, Riley momentarily mused, *The words carry well despite Farley's reedy tones. Madame Orient has fine acoustics, so she does.*

"Ah, Your Majesty," said the tattooist. "I was looking for you, as I wish to augment your last tattoo. A few touches of crimson, perhaps."

A few touches of crimson. It could be the title of a penny dreadful. Once that laser-sighting dot settled on Malarkey, then he was *as dead as Dick,* as the old saying went, referring to the notorious highwayman Dick Turpin. That red dot, which Riley happened to know was called a *laser,* would ensure that a bullet flew true to its mark. And weapons bearing the laser sight did not happen to misfire or explode in the fist with any regularity.

Simply put, Malarkey's goose was not just cooked, but served on a silver platter with all the trimmings.

Riley could not help thinking that were he to let matters take their course, then one of the flies in his ointment would be removed for him. But this was an uncharitable thought, and he dismissed it the moment it popped into his head.

Riley thrust his arms through the hatch space.

"Malarkey! King Otto! This way!"

The Ram seemed not to hear him, mesmerized as he was by the red dot, and so Riley had no choice but to duck through the portal and tap Malarkey's arm.

"This way," he hissed. "Survival lies through here."

Malarkey moved with the speed of a veteran bludger, grasping Riley's shoulders and squeezing as though to crush.

"No, King Otto," grunted the boy. "It's me, Riley. We need to flee this lurk. Farley's run a-muck."

Otto's eyes remembered where he was.

"Farley, that snake."

Riley shook free. "Yes. Farley. Now get a move on or we'll be grinning at the daisy roots. We're all coopered up down here."

Garrick had often tried to beat the slang out of Riley, but in stressful situations it floated to the surface, and it did seem to slice through Malarkey's stupefaction.

"We is rightly coopered 'ere," agreed Malarkey. The red dot was a mere second's jittering away now. "Lead on, Ramlet."

Riley did not need telling a second time, turning on a penny and diving bodily through the trap-room hatch into the welcome arms of velvet shadows. Malarkey swept the music stands aside and followed his subject through the portal, scrabbling across the mud floor to put some distance between himself and the infernal dot.

A stream of lead followed them, plowing a trough in the floor until Farley's line of sight was cut off by the iron frame.

"What ho, Farley!" shouted Malarkey. "Can't you augment my tattoo around corners?"

Riley rolled his eyes. Why must there always be baiting when there was fleeing to be done?

"Down here, Otto," he said urgently. "A shilling will get you ten that Farley ain't reached the bottom of his bag."

Otto huffed, unbuttoning his silken vest, exposing diverse blades and hooks slotted therein. "I ain't opened mine yet, there's the diff. All's I need is a squint of Farley's ugly counting house in that there doorway, and I will deal him the big bounce, even if I have to mount the cart for it, so help me, crisscross."

He don't get it, Riley realized. Otto thinks the odds are even apart from Farley's gun. He thinks we have wrested the upper hand.

"No, King Otto. We must quit this lurk, toot sweet."

Otto chose a baling hook and a glittering dirk from his arsenal. "You quit, boy. Hightail it to the Hidey-Hole and raise the troops. I'm for bloody vengeance."

"Are you cowering like a craven cur, Otto?" came Farley's taunt from above. "Is the great king afraid of his ink man?"

Malarkey's face seemed to glow red in the dark. "Listen how he pokes at me. The cove what murdered poor Barnabus."

Riley felt his own temper rise. "You would do like the Light Brigade, would you? Kill your own self through pig-headedness. Who will avenge Inhumane then?"

But Malarkey was not in the humor for plain logic. The red mist was in his eyes, and he would rather die than retreat.

"Barnabus dead," he said, scraping hook and blade together,

till sparks marked the contact. "Barnabus dead. Barnabus dead."

Barnabus dead, thought Riley. I think His Majesty's brain ain't open for business.

Their situation, though already dire, worsened considerably with the hop-roll of a small metal cylinder through the hatch. On its arrival the cylinder hissed and spun as though it contained a frantic serpent.

"Grenade!" shouted Riley.

But if he had hoped his exclamation would galvanize the king, his hope was in vain, for Malarkey simply glared at the little bomb as if his stare alone could defuse it.

"Blooming hell," said Riley.

Their salvation rested squarely on his shoulders. He would save them, or they would not be saved.

I must assault my king, he thought; and he ducked under Malarkey's weapons, barging Otto's person backward onto the loaded trapdoor platform, allowing his own self to tumble on afterward. Once both sets of limbs were more or less inside the platform's borders, he kicked the lever, activating the power of four compression springs and a three-hundred-pound counterweight. In rehearsal, the resulting force had been enough to catapult Riley ten feet into the air overhead, where he would land on the uppermost chair in a stack; but with Malarkey on the platform, they would be lucky to clear the stage, and only then if one of the Ram king's legs did not foul up the workings.

Perhaps Malarkey's meaty limbs would have snagged in the trapdoor, but Riley was never to find out. The grenade exploded, its force gathering under the platform like the hand of God and accelerating Ram and Ramlet clean through the trapdoor and spinning them downstage, platform in splinters around their ears.

Otto took the brunt of the concussion, as he was closer to the blast, but his trunk was saved from shrapnel by the reinforced platform. However, the platform's planking wrought considerable destruction on Malarkey's flesh when it splintered, shredding his back more comprehensively than any bosun's cat-o'-nine-tails.

Riley was thrown onto his back, legs dangling over the lip, unable to tell whether he was coated with royal blood or his own. His skull hummed like a belfry at one minute past the hour, and his heart seemed to have decided to bust out of his chest.

Otto ain't stirring, he thought, his head being angled toward Malarkey. The king is dead.

But dead the king was not, as evidenced by the flute of blood Otto coughed up on the boards.

Farley's head appeared stage left at the apron, peeping almost comically from the stalls.

He looks like a bird, thought Riley, with his noggin a-wobbling in that manner.

"Ah, both still alive," said Farley. "Excellent. Excellent. This is the best afternoon's fun I have had for a long time." He mounted the steps. "This is what's going to happen, Malarkey. Once I have put an end to your reign, then I return with my squad to the Hidey-Hole and make an offer of employment to the leaderless Rams. Those who take the shilling, as it were, will become part of a new world order. Those who don't will be joining you in whatever hell is reserved for murdering criminals." Farley dipped into his bag and came out with six shells in a circular clip, which he used to fill the revolver's chambers. "Speed loader," he explained. "I had our gunsmith fabricate the thing for me. Do you like it? Little inventions like this are going to help us take over the country."

Farley knelt at Malarkey's side and placed his revolver barrel at the king's temple. "I wish I had more time, Malarkey, because a hanging is what you really deserve. A bullet is too good for you. You ought to be strung up in Trafalgar Square for the whole city to see. Good old-fashioned British justice." He sighed. "But the explosion will bring the constables, so a bullet to the brain will have to do."

It seemed to Riley that his eyes were the only part of him functioning, as per usual. He could see the instrument of his death, but he couldn't do anything about it. One bullet for Malarkey and the second for him.

Tom, he thought, *I never found you. I failed.*

Farley cocked his weapon, amused by Malarkey's total helplessness.

"Look at you, Otto. The mighty Golgoth."

That was surely an end to the gloating. To delay any more would tempt fate.

"Good-bye, Your Majesty," said Farley.

Then something fast erupted from the wings at stage left. A figure attached to a pair of legs that moved so quickly they seemed like blue fans. One of the legs swept upward and kicked Farley in the side of his head. Hard. The tattooist moved backward on his hunkers, like a drunken Cossack, until his momentum took him over the lip of the stage and into the orchestra pit below. Judging by the level of clatter, Riley reckoned that his landing was not a cushy one.

P'raps he fractured half a dozen bones, thought Riley. We can only hope.

The blue-clad legs bent at the knees and Riley's savior knelt before him. The shock of recognition brought the boy's voice box back to life.

"Miss Chevron," he said. "It is yourself in the flesh, come to save me once more."

Chevie's face was pale with concern for her young friend, but she smiled to hide it.

"That's right, kid," she said, running her hands up and down his torso and limbs, feeling for breaks. "Someone has to look out for you. I leave you on your own for a hundred years and look what happens."

Leaving posthaste, everyone agreed, was a good plan. Everyone agreed except Farley, that is, because no one consulted the tattooist; even if they had, a fortune-teller would have been needed to interpret the drool pooling by Farley's cheek.

Farley. The hangman. She had been reading about him all her life.

No. Wrong.

Old Chevie, *whipped Chevie,* had been reading about Farley all her life.

But that Chevie was gone. She was now . . .

Traitor Chevie?

The *real* Chevron Savano. And actually, truth be told, when you got a look at this Farley, he was a little underwhelming.

"*This* guy did the damage? This old guy? He's like, a hundred."

"I would guess sixty," said Riley defensively. "And wiry with it. A drill enthusiast, I'll wager."

Chevie peered into the orchestra pit where Farley was tangled in a heap of music stands. "And anyway, I thought he was a friend of yours, Riley."

"An opinion we shared until recently," said Riley, cocking his head to one side to dislodge a shrill ringing that he suspected was an aftereffect of the explosion. "We really should scram, Chevie. The beaks will be whistling at the door, and p'raps Farley ain't the only Johnny Future in the vicinity."

"Let me just ignore whatever the hell you just said and do this," said Chevie. She lowered herself into the pit and relieved Farley of his bag, then pried the revolver from his hand. "I feel better now," she said, hefting the large weapon. "Less naked."

Riley pointed at her outfit. "You are more or less naked, as usual. That ain't much more than a bathing costume what you're sporting there."

Chevie took a moment to check her outfit, which she hadn't done since tumbling from the Smarthole. Just as her alternate personality had emerged from the time tunnel, so, it seemed, had some of her old clothing. She now wore a strange hybrid outfit with elements of both possible futures. In essence she still wore her Youth Academy navy jumpsuit, but its heavy wool had become spandex, and the golden symbol had morphed to FBI. She had lost the hat when Director Gunn clocked her with the computer tablet.

I look like SuperFed, she thought.

Chevie realized that she was feeling inappropriately buoyant, in light of the dead bodies littering the theater aisle, the stink of cordite, and the fact that she was possibly stranded in the wrong time zone.

But I am me again, and perhaps the future doesn't have to happen. DeeDee doesn't have to die.

"This outfit is like a metaphor for how my brain is," she said, spreading her arms. "I am mostly old Chevie, the one you know. But some of the new girl is still here."

Riley decided that he would quiz Chevie later on the subjects of apparel and metaphors, and Malarkey reacted to all this exposition with a twitch of his head, which, being connected to his torso, set many of his wounds a-pumping blood.

"Dandy," he said, being further from the grave than he looked. "Nuffin' I likes better than a nice metaphor of an afternoon. But while you two are playing bo-peep, I am spilling me life's fluids onto this here stage. So if you wouldn't mind . . ."

Chevie tossed Farley's bag onto the stage and swung herself after it.

"Sorry, Otto. Riley and I haven't seen each other for a while, so we gotta bo-peep it up for a little. And anyway, the last time our paths intersected, your fingers were around my throat, so pardon me if I put you on the bottom of my priority list."

Otto shook a fist at her. "Why is you talking like this? Speak plain, girl."

Riley donned his cloak, then helped Otto to his feet. "Let me interpret, Your Majesty. Chevie ain't all that pushed about yer welfare, on account of you being murdering scum."

Otto leaned over, weighed down by a head that suddenly seemed to be composed of lead.

"The Injun said that, did she?"

"Give or take," said Riley, ducking his own head under Otto's left armpit to support the Ram king.

Chevie propped up Malarkey's right side. "Let's talk politics and allegiances later, shall we? After we put some space between us and this bloodbath. I'd say there were bad people after all of us."

Riley did not comment. He did not, for example, point out that it was Chevie herself who was delaying their escape. He knew from experience that there was nothing his friend from the future liked better than a protracted squabble, and the more inopportune the timing, the louder she argued.

And this ain't the time for a barney.

They dragged, coaxed, and heaved Otto Malarkey's mammoth bulk to the stage door, and lurched outside as one, all exhausted by the effort of moving a frame the size of a dray horse.

"I have a bad case of the pants," Riley declared, gasping for air, his cheek slick with Malarkey's blood. "We can't lug this bruiser far."

Chevie leaned against the wall. "No kidding. What's stage two of the plan?"

Riley thought fast. "We need to get ourselves in lavender, and I mean sharpish. A quiet lurk somewhere, not no penny gaff neither. Bacteria would be the death of King Otto at the mo."

Chevie found that her mind was beginning to wrap itself around Riley's lingo.

"Somewhere nearby while we're at it. This big lug is bleeding all over my FBI super suit."

Riley was being drizzled by a fair deal of blood himself. "It's a good plan, just a deuced shame that I don't know any such place."

Otto gathered his feet and took some of his own weight.

"Fetch a Shoeblack and have him summon a cab. It 'appens that I might know a place that would be just the ticket."

"Someplace unknown to your confederates," said Riley. "The Rams had one rotten apple in the barrel and it may have been contagious, if you know what I mean."

Malarkey hawked and spat a ball of blood to the dusty sidewalk.

"Oh, believe me, Ramlet, there ain't no one who knows about *this* gaff."

Riley steadied King Otto against the brick wall and ran down the alley to Holborn proper, whistling for a Shoeblack boy as he went.

Chevie and Malarkey were left alone. King Otto looked down at the girl through heavily lidded eyes.

"Murdering scum, is it?"

Chevie realized that she was in quite a weak position should Malarkey decide to regain his prodigious strength.

"Well, murdering, at the very least."

Otto closed his eyes. "Fair enough," he said, and he had himself a little rest, leaving Chevie to gaze anxiously down the length of the alley at her disappearing friend.

5 » GREATCOAT & SPLASHBACK

Ouroboros. The snake that eats its own tail—that's the time traveler. Going around in circles, destroying his own past. Crapping out a whole new future. Apologies. Pooping out a whole new future.
—Professor Charles Smart

VICTORIAN LONDON WAS NOT KIND TO VISITORS. It lured them into its soot-stained labyrinth with a vague fairy-tale promise of streets paved with gold, then sucked their coin through the slitted windows of gin houses and opium dens. The Great Oven trod hard on the souls of outsiders with a life of slave labor or destitution with naught at the end of the struggle but an ignoble death, tied to a sleeping bench in the bone house. Every year, thousands of cheery country stock rolled into London as though the land was on a tilt, and every year thousands more were rolled into unmarked paupers' graves, if they were lucky—and pig troughs or furnaces if they were not. While it was true that murder was rare, it wasn't classed as murder if the city did the killing. If a factory swallowed a dozen limbs a week, then that was just the price of employment. If a person's hand was fast enough to grasp a shilling, then it ought to be fast enough to stay out of the grinder. It stood to reason. And anyway, what matter if a few bumpkins went into the earth before their terms? There were always scores more in a shuffling line outside the factories.

For a stranger to English shores come to town off the gangplank, London was a series of local hazards designed to strip Johnny Foreigner naked and toss him on the slag heap without a farthing to his name. The population boom was due in some part to the fact that naval types couldn't afford to quit the place until a boat docked with an empty berth, and there was a long line for those planks. Jack Tars would gladly jump on a deck bound for the dark heart of cannibal country rather than spend another fogbound night in the Great Oven, and often committed some deliberate crime in order to secure a yard of floor space in one of the metropolitan jails, bridewells, or penitentiaries along with forty thousand of their fellow city-dwellers each year.

In London town, a soul was never more than a dozen paces from an open cess ditch or rat-infested garbage heap. And if the streets had ever truly been paved with gold, it would have long since been eroded by the torrents of acidic filth flung from the high balconies that teetered over rookery roads.

In short, London was a grimed blemish on England's fair soil.

Clover Vallicose was having the time of her life.

Half Moon Street, Mayfair, London, 1899,
Ten minutes previously

The Thundercats had wallowed in the Zen Ten for a further minute after Chevie's departure, and then stumbled from the terraced house, supporting each other with meaty arms and blocky shoulders. Lunka Witmeyer's good mood was truncated by a bout of retching that bent her over a water barrel in the yard at the rear of the house on Half Moon Street, on the border of Soho and Mayfair.

Witmeyer had never traveled well on a train, so the time tunnel had a violent effect on her gut.

While her partner endured the cramp daggers in her abdomen, Clover Vallicose straightened her greatcoat and the splashback visor slung below her chin, and then ventured into the alley that ran from the rear of the house to Half Moon Street proper. Everything beyond that yard was strange to the Thundercat and yet strangely familiar, too.

I know this place, she thought. I have studied this place.

And she had, for Half Moon Street had a particular significance in Boxite history. Following the Emergence from London's catacombs, the hangman for Box, Major Anton Farley, had set up his operations headquarters on this very road. In fact, he had occupied the top-floor suite of a hotel that had previously gone by the name Flemings, which overlooked Smart's town house. Farley's first move had been to hang half a dozen of the writers and artists who infested the area and move in his own Box-fearing people.

Clover Vallicose had no qualms about hanging artists who would much rather take up the pen or brush than the rifle in support of an empire that needed them. She herself had once shot a Welsh mime who had constructed a pantomime that could be interpreted as saying that the Thundercats were a bit trigger-happy, even though the wounded man had sworn that all it said was that he was stuck in a well.

Happy days.

And here she was on Half Moon Street, where it all began. And apparently *when* it all began.

Vallicose had spent countless hours poring over microfiche and photographs from the period, fascinated by the Empire's origins, regretting bitterly that she had not been there at the birth of the glorious reign.

And now I am here. Is it possible that God has granted my wish?

There was a lot more pondering to be done on this subject, and a lot more information to be beaten out of people; but that would have to wait, because Clover spotted Chevron Savano running away. Fleeing, Jax scum that she was. And no matter the circumstances, Clover had been given an order from the Blessed Colonel himself.

Kill the spy.

And she could no sooner forget that order than she could forget the existence of Box himself.

She sensed rather than heard her partner approach.

"What's happening, Clove?"

Clove. Lunka rarely used that endearment. Too much

blood had stained the earth under their feet for them to be true friends. That's not to say they wouldn't die for each other. But that was duty.

"Later, Sister. The Jax coward runs from her fate. We must follow."

"Wait," protested Witmeyer, wiping sheaves of her long dark hair between gloved thumb and forefinger. "I need to . . ."

But her partner had engaged in her most annoying habit of leaving in the middle of a discussion. And to make her departure even more irritating, Vallicose tossed a comment back over her shoulder.

"That's why I keep my hair cropped. In this occupation, one never knows when one might need to vomit."

It was always duty first with Clover Vallicose. First and last. Duty was the steel at her core, and it strengthened her resolve to serve Box every minute of every day. Duty helped Vallicose sleep at night, wrapped her in layers of absolution, and dispelled the dark dreams brought on by any remaining scraps of conscience. She was that most dangerous of adversaries: a true believer.

At age six she had been plucked from her orphanage by an army scout who had seen a video of her beating up a boy twice her size for not making the sign of the Box as he passed a portrait of the Blessed Colonel. In the orphanage Clover had shared a sleeping cupboard with eight other kids, whereas in the academy she was given her own cubicle and three square meals a day. Her faith grew even stronger as a result.

The Blessed Colonel had chosen her for something great, she believed. And her belief never faltered through those years in the academy. Through the decade of service in France her belief grew even stronger, and she was promoted from regular army to Thundercat. The most public of secret police.

My time is at hand, she thought every day.

And on this day, perhaps she was right.

If Vallicose was a true believer, then Witmeyer, on the other hand, was an opportunist. To Lunka, the Thundercat badge was a free pass to act as she pleased. Oh, she could quote scripture all day long if it aligned with her chosen course of action; but with Witmeyer the action came first, then the scripture to back it up. Neither Thundercat was naive enough to think the other shared her beliefs or lack thereof, but both knew they could rely on the other in a tight spot, and each knew very well how to turn a tight spot to their own advantage.

The spot they found themselves in on this particular day in 1899 was tighter than most, even for a couple of seasoned Thundercats with buzz batons and automatic sidearms. Witmeyer, normally the optimist, was finding it hard to put her finger on the upside. But Vallicose, usually the truculent grunter, was positively ebullient as they followed Chevie's boot heels across London.

"Oh, praise be," Vallicose gushed. "There is Victory Square, where they dragged out Queen Victoria herself. Swore like a fishwife, apparently. That devil spawn ruled over Albion like a dragon squatting on a tower. They say her blood still stains the cobbles." She elbowed her partner. "Perhaps we will witness that happy day when her neck gets stretched."

Witmeyer walked stiffly, like a drunkard imitating the sober. "Smart's machine sent us into the past, Clove. Is that what you're telling me?"

Ahead, Chevie grabbed a lamppost, swinging herself around a corner onto Piccadilly. Vallicose settled into double-time to keep her prey in view.

"Of course. Smart was conducting illegal experiments, obviously. Savano nearly escaped, but thank heavens we have managed to follow."

Witmeyer matched her partner's pace. "Thank heavens," she said weakly.

The street widened to a thoroughfare, and the Thundercats drew stunned gazes from a bunch of shady loiterers warming the seats of their pants by a brazier.

One character, a pale streak of a man, decided to make a remark. "What ho!" he called. "The oxen have shrugged off their yokes."

Witmeyer channeled her anxiety into an uppercut that drove the man into the brazier, sending coal and sparks tumbling into the street. The remaining vertical loiterers were too shocked to even contemplate reprisals.

Vallicose grunted her approval, a familiar sound that comforted Witmeyer somewhat.

They double-timed on, Vallicose apparently delighted rather than perturbed by the absolute strangeness of their circumstances. Witmeyer found that the best strategy was to bite down on her knuckles and focus on their prey. Once Savano was dead she could deal with her unexpected situation.

"This is Picadilly as it used to be," breathed Vallicose. "I've seen pictures."

Witmeyer was in no mood for a history lesson, being up to her neck in it, so to speak; but Clover seemed on the point of fainting from excitement.

"Piccadilly," said Witmeyer, unimpressed by the entire avenue and the smell of animal doings hanging like a pall over the street.

"You don't understand, Sister," said Vallicose. "After the first round of Boxstrike, Farley used these lampposts to hang any royals or politicians who survived the missiles. This is Swingers' Row, but it was known as Piccadilly."

I don't believe this, thought Witmeyer, biting her knuckles. None of this is happening.

They tailed Chevie from a distance, their trousered legs, flesh-colored greatcoats, and splashback visors drawing double takes from the throngs of office clerks, corner boys, street vendors, and fella-me-lads spilling over the footpaths onto Piccadilly. Dozens of comments were thrown their way, but the Thundercats were forced to bear these insults or risk losing Chevie.

Vallicose and Witmeyer were seasoned trackers, having honed their skills in the poppy fields of Normandy, hunting down shooters from the notorious Jax guerrillas division, Les Invisibles. They could have taken Chevie at their pleasure but held back, timing their swoop to coincide with a break in the crowds. This was not their London, and more attention on their heads was the last thing they wanted.

There was no danger of Savano escaping. Her run was like that of a headless chicken. The girl was dead already but didn't know it.

This would indeed have been the case had not a constable appeared before them on the footpath three turns later, blocking their way.

"Halt!" he said, raising a baton. "I want a word with you two . . . ladies."

As a representative of the era's law keepers, the man was a disgrace. He was unshaven and generally unkempt, with a uniform that seemed to bear the grime of several years upon it and the stink of stale gin on his breath.

Vallicose was loath to slow down, but the only alternative was to incapacitate a policeman in broad daylight on a crowded avenue.

"Is there a problem, brother?" she said testily. "Because much as I respect your office, I have no moments to spare at this particular time."

Witmeyer and Vallicose towered over the scruffy constable, but he appeared not to notice their threatening loom.

"Not a problem as it were . . . eh . . . ladies. I just fancied a closer look at the pair of you. Foreign, is it? From overseas?"

Wordplay, falsehood, and bogus reportage were Lunka's areas of expertise, so a question like this would generally fall to her, but today she was chewing on her fist and rolling her eyes.

"I ain't seen nuffink like you pair in all my born days," continued the officer, now twirling his baton on a rope handle. "Blooming great man-boots up past yer knees. And wot, pray tell, is that rigout around yer neck? Perhaps you is some class of savage, or European? Am I right, ladies?"

Vallicose prodded her partner with an elbow.

Answer the man, said the prod. *Tell him something believable.*

Nothing but puffed air came from Witmeyer's mouth, and she seemed to be following the flight of an invisible bird with her eyes.

"Nevertheless, foreign or no," continued the bluebottle, "I am *intreeegued,* as they say."

The policeman's eyes suddenly fixed on Vallicose's sidearm. "And would that be some class of weapon a-hanging from your belt, madam? If so, I best be confiscating it and doing a thorough search of your person."

Vallicose allowed herself to be briefly amazed that a man wielding nothing more than a wooden stick could be faced with two hulking adversaries loaded down with firearms and still think himself with the advantage. Then she hugged the constable close, as one would a friend, and punched him solidly in the solar plexus.

"No searching today, Citizen," she said quietly, escorting the gasping copper around a corner into the darkness of an alley, where she slid him along a dripping wall into the embrace of creeping damp and shadows.

It was a laughably simple conquest of a foe who barely rated the appellation, but though the maneuver had not cost

Vallicose more than a single grunt of effort, she had paid in another way.

When she stepped back into the light, Chevron Savano had disappeared.

Vallicose swore and thumped her partner's chest.

"Damnation, Sister. Words and such are your forté."

The thump restarted Witmeyer's brain. "*Forté*?" she said. "French, is it? You're spouting French at me?"

Vallicose was shocked at herself. "I apologize, Sister. Such blasphemy is uncalled for, but the girl has gone."

Lunka Witmeyer's marbles were settling quickly. "Not gone, Sister. Out of our sight is all she is, and to disappear so quickly she must have taken the next crossroads."

Vallicose nodded. This was the partner she knew.

"Yes, yes. But left or right is the question."

Witmeyer set off at a run. "Let us cross that road when we come to it."

They came to it quickly and were on the point of splitting up when an explosion sent shudders along the street, and a cloud of thick black smoke drifted out from the eaves of a distant building.

"What are the chances?" said Witmeyer, with her nose pointed in that direction.

"Praise be, it's a sign, Sister," said Vallicose, already planning how she would hurt Chevron Savano.

There was a crowd of gawpers and gawkers assembled by the doors of the Orient Theatre, and the Thundercats shouldered through the throng as though their authority held good in this time. Once past the door, they settled comfortably into their combat routine. Vallicose first and low, Witmeyer upright behind, so any opponent would meet double fire. There was no illumination in the interior, but light flooded from the foyer, daubing a pale glow along the aisle. It was obvious that the explosion had done most of its damage on the stage, which had mushroomed upward in a tangle of planks. There were bodies in the stalls. Gunshot victims, tossed backward by the force of the projectiles that killed them.

Witmeyer placed her fingers in a row of bullet holes in a backrest.

"Either there were a hundred shooters . . ."

"Or we have ourselves automatic fire," completed Vallicose.

A puzzling development for the Thundercats, as they had assumed themselves to be the only ones with such arms.

"Savano?" wondered Vallicose.

"No. She was supervised all the way from her bed and was unarmed. But this must be connected to Smart's machine."

"Smart's *Boxless* machine," said Vallicose.

"Boxless, of course," muttered Witmeyer, the comment a sign that her wits had reasserted themselves; and for once Vallicose was comforted by her partner's acerbic tongue.

They advanced quickly, every sense alert for danger. A huge body in row C proved to be slightly less dead than supposed and begged for water in the name of God. In spite of the fact that God had been invoked, Vallicose shot him in the chest.

"Clover," said Witmeyer, her tone disapproving.

"He was taking the Lord's name in vain."

"I don't mind that you killed the brute," said Witmeyer. "You could have clubbed him. Our supply of bullets is limited. Also, it might have been an idea to question the man. He may have seen Savano."

"Two good points, Sister. From now on, bare hands or blades when possible, and only after interrogation."

"If it's not too much trouble."

A moan emanated from the pit before them, boomified by the space. It echoed to the rafters, and others would have fled in terror, crying *ghost,* but not the Thundercats, who had heard the cries of the injured in eerier settings than this.

The partners chuckled, knowing they were unperturbed where others would not be.

"Remember, Sister, when that Jax butcher charged us with a cleaver?"

"I remember he regretted it," said Witmeyer. And they were silent for a brief moment, savoring the memory.

Another moan rose from the orchestra pit, and the Thundercats crept soundlessly to the lip and peered over. A man lay tangled among the music stands with blood trickling from various minor wounds and one of his arms stretched a little farther than seemed normal.

"It's possible that he will live," said Witmeyer.

"Possible, but unlikely," said Clover Vallicose.

The man had committed no specific crime against Box or Empire that Vallicose was aware of, but she felt certain that a little interrogation would reveal some misdemeanor. And anyway, the first unofficial rule of security policing was that corpses were the worst kind of witness. Dead men do not talk.

Vallicose swung herself down into the pit, landing neatly astride the unfortunate individual who was about to be seriously hurt as a prelude to being mortally injured.

If this man can point us in the traitor's direction, I might kill him without prolonged torture, thought Vallicose charitably.

"Let's be having you, Citizen," she said, hauling the man onto his back by dragging on his dislocated shoulder. The pain must have been unimaginable. The man confirmed this by screaming high and jagged.

Vallicose had a plan. She would ask her questions with her weapon pointed directly at the citizen's head. This was one of her preferred interrogation tactics, but, as she had learned one messy morning in Police Plaza interview room B, best to always make sure the gun's safety is on.

Vallicose checked the safety and then frowned as her eyes drifted to the man's features.

There was something strange about the face.

Clover felt her balance drift away, and her pulse pounded in her ears.

What is it about this person? Something familiar.

The man beneath her coughed and sprayed blood on Vallicose's coat. An action that would have normally earned him an open-handed slap. But Clover did not strike.

Why?

Because there was something about that bloodstained face. Familiar, but more than that. Revered? Was that possible?

Vallicose felt her hands shake.

What is it? Who is this?

Witmeyer's whisper floated down from above.

"Problems, Sister?"

"N—no," stammered Vallicose.

Stammering? she thought. I haven't stammered in decades.

"Well then, the trail grows cold."

The man's nose was thin and hooked. Distinctive. And it slotted into a face in her memory.

It was so dark down here. Like the great pit itself.

"A light, Sister," she called to her partner. "Shine a light."

Witmeyer shifted for a better angle and then flicked the switch of a tiny halogen flashlight attached to her gun barrel. The man's face was illuminated starkly, and Vallicose felt her face slacken with shock.

Farley. The Hangman.

It was him. It was. How many times had she seen the portrait over Director Gunn's desk?

Anton Farley.

Those thin lips, and the slick of gray hair.

This is why I have been sent here, thought Vallicose. God has a plan for His faithful servant.

Vallicose felt the fever of devoted decades rush back to her in a concentrated burst. Overwhelming her. Prayer fragments dribbled from her lips as she cradled the injured man in her arms.

Farley, she thought. I am holding the Hangman. The angel of death.

The angel half-opened his eyes and spoke softly.

"The colonel," he said. "Take me to the colonel."

Vallicose broke down and wept.

6 » HANDS UP, PRINCESS

I knew a guy once who liked to argue about time travel. He liked to line things up, consequences and so forth. This moron thought winning the argument made him right. The wormhole doesn't care about words. What happens, happens.

—Professor Charles Smart

GROSVENOR SQUARE, MAYFAIR, LONDON, 1899

ILEY HAD MANAGED TO ENGAGE A CABBIE with the lure of a shiny sovereign, and soon they were clattering away from Holborn in the back of a covered carriage on their way to Malarkey's secret gaff in Grosvenor Square. Chevie rolled Malarkey onto the bench, draping him with a heavy winter blanket she had pulled from under the seat. In seconds, blood blossoms bloomed on the green wool.

"This is not good," she said to Riley, who was tugging at the curtains covering the carriage's side window.

Malarkey tried to sit up. "Wot? Me hair, is it? They ain't gone and singed me lovely hair."

"Don't throw a fit," said Riley, gently forcing Otto down. "Yer hair is in premium order. Rapunzel would weep with jealousy at the sight of a barnet like yours."

"Thank heaven," said Malarkey, closing his eyes. "Oh, thank heaven. So long as I looks decent, I can bear all else."

"Decent?" said Chevie, taking in Otto's attire. "This is decent?"

"In truth, Chevie, he looks like a strumpet that got shot out of a cannon."

"You is giving me sauce, boy?" muttered Otto. "I is in repose, not deceased. And what's more, I is your regent." He seemed on the point of passing further comment concerning Riley's impudence, when a shadow crossed his brow. "Barnabus." He sighed. "I am alone now. An orphan." A single tear traced the king's wrinkles, rolling back and forth across his cheek, and he lay back without further protest. His breath slowed to a labored rhythm.

Riley and Chevie watched him in silence for a few jouncing seconds, then turned to each other.

"I haven't missed cobblestones much," said Chevie, as the carriage wheels lurched into and out of a rut. "But I have missed you, though I didn't know it."

They embraced warmly until Riley pulled away. "What brings you here, Chevie? Come to save me, have you? And how can one body *not know* they missed another body?"

"It's a long story, kid. Let's just say I haven't been myself lately. But I'm back now."

Riley hugged her again. "And thank heavens for it, Chevie.

You saved our bacon and no mistake. Farley came a-calling with his futuristic blunderbuss and was like to put all of us in the sod. Farley of all people. He was always such a bono Johnny."

Chevie assumed that *bono Johnny* meant *good fellow* and proceeded accordingly. "Yeah, well, that *bono Johnny* has a serious dark side. He's from the future, like me. There's a whole team of them back here getting ready to make their move on the government and royal family."

Riley crossed himself. "On Queen Vic? God save her."

"I don't understand it," said Chevie, rubbing her temples. "They should fail; they were supposed to fail. Those guys are all in their sixties by now. So why did their plan succeed this time?" She grasped Riley's shoulders. "Did Farley say anything before he started shooting? Did he mention anyone?"

Riley thought back. "He mentioned you. I thought it strange at the time."

Chevie's guts twisted. "Me? What did he say, exactly?"

"Something about how the FBI had sent you, so they could send someone else, and it was for the best to move up the schedule."

"Oh no, oh God." Chevie slumped on the bench.

Me. It was me.

Box had moved up his plan because of her. If he hadn't moved up the plan, then the Boxites would have failed for some reason. And so, because of her, the entire Boxite Empire had come into existence. The cult of Box had spread like a virulent weed across Europe and America. How many innocents had died? How many lives had been destroyed by torture and oppression?

Chevie flashed on a slo-mo scene of Deirdre Woollen's head falling away from a smoking gun barrel. Dying on the wet concrete for taking a wrong turn.

DeeDee. Executed. It was too much to bear.

All because of me.

It was ridiculous, Chevie knew, to hold herself responsible for world events. She was a seventeen-year-old kid who had never wanted to go through a time tunnel. Why not blame Charles Smart? Or Albert Garrick? Or Colonel Clayton Box and his lust for power? She was a small cog at most, a low-value domino in a very long chain.

It was ridiculous to hold herself responsible, but Chevie couldn't help it. And the guilt was overwhelming, sending her thought process into spinning turmoil. She felt suddenly nauseated and light-headed, and sagged on the bench, breathing great gulps of air, trying not to be ill.

Riley patted her shoulder. "Come now, Miss Chevron. We've been in rockier waters. A strong drink is all you need. A real grave digger, to settle your nerves."

Chevie's gaze was fixed on the planks below her feet. She watched the green and brown river of cobbles flash past through a gap in the wood.

Riley persisted. "Chevie, no need to pull the shutters up. In case you ain't realized, we're smack bang in the middle of a crisis here. Come on, now. Let's be having the old Chevron, all sauce and vinegar. We could do with that Chevie and no blooming mistake."

Chevie spoke to the planks. "You don't understand, kid.

The future you remember: London full of tourists, the FBI, Queen Elizabeth—that's all gone."

"Not Harry Potter too?" said Riley, horrified.

"Yes, Harry Potter. Everything. Farley and his comrades launch missile strikes on the Houses of Parliament, Portsmouth, and Windsor Castle."

"Queen Vic gets it?"

"No, she gets strung up along Piccadilly."

Riley stared at his hands, which had begun to shake. "Cockneys will never stand for Queen Vic's murder. We love the old Widow of Windsor."

"The people don't get much of a say in it. Colonel Box comes out of the catacombs with his legion armed to the teeth with this sort of weapon." Chevie nudged Farley's bag with her toe.

Riley was puzzled. "A legion of old dogs, though, you said. Even Farley was past his prime. How is these graybeards going to conquer an army?"

This was a very good point, and Riley came up with his own answer.

"The Rams. Farley gathered the top dogs all together in the Orient for a neat assassination. Your Colonel Box is planning to enlist the rest—the roughest, toughest band of godless bully boys in London—to do his dirty work."

It made perfect sense.

"Farley takes out the high command," said Chevie, nodding. "Then Box steps in with his team to take over. Presto, he has a trained army ready to carry out his orders."

They sat in silence, contemplating the impending disaster as they watched over the slumped bulk of Otto Malarkey.

We are the unlikeliest of trios, thought Riley.

And he was right. The ingredients of their particular stew did make for a queer broth: a boy magician, a future police officer, and a Ram king. But there was one other trio in London, freshly formed and moving toward their own haven, which was equally unlikely.

Two Thundercat warrior women and a tattooist.

There was silence inside the covered cab as Riley and Chevie saw violent futures painted in their minds' eyes, and the cacophony of London town beyond their curtained compartment made little impact. They did not notice the gradual ebb of the human tide or even the slight sweetening of the air as the cab jostled from Holborn to the more genteel surroundings of Grosvenor Square. Nothing much registered in their troubled brains until the cabbie rapped a board with the heel of his whip.

"Grosvenor Square," he called. "All ashore."

Grosvenor Square, Chevie thought. Why does that address sound familiar?

They alighted from a cab already rank with the sour smells of their own blood, sweat, and fear into a candy box painting of a square, lined with beautiful terraced town houses set around a private park. There were no prone beggars underfoot transferring their personal filth to the pristine footpaths, nor clusters of belligerent corner boys hawking their tobacco phlegm onto the scrubbed cobbles. It was altogether a smarter area of London, and not the class of address that generally harbored as roughly hewn an oaf as Otto Malarkey.

The Ram king leaned heavily on his rescuers and growled at the cabbie to stay the blazes where he was until they gained entrance to his manor. The cabbie, rightly surmising that there might be hell to pay from this wounded beast if his wishes were not promptly met, did as he was bid and held his pawing horses fast, hoping Nobbie and Daisy did not pick this moment to raise their tails, as this was not the kind of square where a fellow could ride off and leave deposits on the road behind him.

Using the cab as a shield from the eyes of neighbors or patroling bobbies, Malarkey directed the group toward the steps of the only house on the north side that looked like a war had been waged on its façade. The portico had been completely obliterated, except for the stubs of two pillars that stood like elephant's feet on the top step. Not a pane of glass remained in the windows, boarded against the London rain—which fell hard as nails in February—and the masonry was pockmarked with shrapnel gouges that sprayed outward from a shiny new front door, painted a lurid purple. The upper facade was wreathed in painters' drop cloths, supported by a rigging of wooden scaffolding.

Riley poked his head forward from Malarkey's armpit and caught Chevie's eye.

"Charismo's gaff. The militia blew it to smithereens, remember?"

Chevie did remember. In her current timeline—or lifespan, or whatever—they had been held captive at Tibor Charismo's house—this house—mere months ago, in the summer of 1898. She wondered briefly whether it was more likely that she was lying in a psycho ward somewhere and all of this was an elaborate hallucination, or that she was a time-traveling federal agent partnered with a kid magician.

It doesn't matter. I have to play the cards in front of me the best I can.

What else could she do besides lie down and die?

Tempting.

She suddenly remembered her father, who had raised her in their little house on the Malibu bluffs.

Whatta ya gonna do, squirt? Give up? There ain't many Shawnee left, and we need someone to protect us.

That was when she'd been on the point of throwing in her judo lessons after a botched match cost her a tournament.

The memory gave Chevie strength and focus. She put her back into her task and hefted Otto to the top step.

"Come on, kid," she said. "Someone's gotta protect the Shawnee."

There were no spare hands in the group for tugging on a bell pull, so Otto kicked the lurid door several times until it was whipped open by a horrified little man, buttoned up tight from his polished boots to the collar of his glaring white shirt.

"Excuse me!" said the diminutive fellow, voice shrill, face florid. "This is a spanking brand-new door, so it is. Commodore Pierce will have your foot for an ashtray if you do not immediately desist with your infernal drumming and remove your pestilential selves from this respectable threshold. Where do you think you are? A dockside gin hovel?"

The little man was one of those singular individuals who inspire a degree of contentment wherever they appear, in spite of the caustic nature of their verbiage. Had there been such a thing as a happiness meter, the beleaguered gang at the doorstep would have seen their collective mercury rise at the sight of this ruddy-jowled five-footer. A skinnier specimen would be difficult to find outside of the bone shop. He wore a narrow suit of gray tweed with creases sharper than his own scythe of a nose. The man's eyebrows curled imperiously, if such an attitude is possible for mere eyebrows. But these eyebrows were not *mere*—they were splendid and quivering. The face was a handsome miniature; child-sized man features, which confused a body on first look. And the hands that flapped at Malarkey and Co. were disproportionately large and articulate, seeming to play an invisible piano as he spoke.

"You are idiots, is that it?" continued the furious little man. "The idiot complement of three villages, congregated to set about people's fine new front doors. Well, you have *idioted* at the wrong door, idiots. Commodore Pierce may be a denizen of the square, but he is a son of the United States navy, and he will trounce you soundly, so he will."

The *so he will* tagged on to the little man's sentence revealed him to be a native of the Emerald Isle, so not just a little man, but a little Irish man.

Leprechaun, thought Chevie, and immediately felt guilty.

As a Shawnee Native American, she had been on the receiving end of stereotyping often enough not to engage in it.

"Figary," said King Otto wearily.

"Don't you name my name, you scoundrel," said Figary, fingers tapping a polka in the air. "Commodore Pierce will . . ." He paused before the threat materialized and actually looked at Malarkey.

"Commodore? Is it yourself? Or some ghastly doppelganger recently dragged through a tart's dressing room? The latter, please say the latter! And I see you brought the tart with you. Or perhaps this *lady* is some class of circus performer?"

Malarkey coughed. "Enough chatter, you tater muncher. I be . . . I mean, I *am* bleeding, Michael Figary. Help us inside and fetch the maggots."

Figary displayed not one feather of deference. "Maggot fetching, is it? For this, Mick Figary left his mammy's knee. And where is your beautiful Boston brogue, Commodore? You sound like an English back-alley scoundrel with a dirk in his boot and a shadow of ill deeds stretched out behind him, so you do." Figary's eyebrows rose to new heights and arched like the wings of a bird in flight. "It is your house, sir, so of course you may enter, but try not to daub blood on the walls. They are fresh painted, so they are."

Figary ushered them inside with a bow that reeked of insincerity.

Riley grunt-chuckled. "I ain't never seen such a sarcastic bow."

"I like him," said Chevie. "He's funny."

"He referred to you as a circus tart," Malarkey reminded her.

"A simple case of mistaken identity," said Chevie. "Like when he called you Commodore."

"Not a commodore, then," said Figary. "And probably not many more things besides." And with a disappointed cluck, the Irishman disappeared down the scullery stairs, his hard shoes clacking a jig rhythm on the steps.

They carried Malarkey into the kitchen—the same kitchen where Chevie and Riley had almost been dismembered barely six months previously, to ease their passage into a furnace. Riley remembered nothing of the incident, as he had been up to the gills in poisonous narcotics at the time. Chevron Savano's recently resurfaced memories, however, were crystal clear, and she felt a pall of unease as soon as she set a booted foot in the room. It had not been a pleasant afternoon for the pair, and this one was not shaping up to be a gallon of giggles either.

They heaved Otto onto a wooden worktop and peeled the tattered vestiges of his opera shirt from his back.

"Silk," moaned Otto. "The finest silk. I had it imported."

Figary tip-tapped into the room just in time to hear this last comment.

"Imported, is it?" he said, depositing two jars in the porcelain sink. "From where? The Isle of Delusions, perhaps? Or th Peacock Peninsula?"

Malarkey groaned. "Michael Figary. I swear, you're ev more insolent than usual. Are you drunk?"

Figary opened the first quart jar, which was teeming with fat white maggots. "Of course I am drunk. It is evening, is it not? You would have me apply maggots to your repulsive back-flesh in full possession of my wits?"

"You damned brandy shunter," said Malarkey weakly. "Belay that sauce and be about your business."

Figary soaked a cloth in alcohol from the second jar and began to expertly clean King Otto's back.

"Yes, Commodore. I am currently swabbing your wounds. *Swabbing* being a nautical term, much like *belay*. But no need to expound on seafaring lingo to your good self, you being a *commodore*, and all."

Malarkey gritted his teeth. "Etherize me, you niminy-piminy Paddy. I can't suffer no more of yer lip."

Figary rolled up his sleeves, then plunged his arm into the maggot jar, scooping up a handful, which he molded into a poultice and then applied to one of his employer's gaping wounds.

"It seems barbaric, does it not?" Michael Figary commented to the disgusted newcomers. "Smearing maggots on the lacerations? But these little blighters will devour the necrotic tissue and sterilize the healthy. The trick is to get them out before they colonize our commodore's flesh; that would not do at all, for though his title would appear to be bogus, his coin is genuine and pays for Missus Figary's son's brandy. And for that I would patch up all the copper captains in London town, so I would."

"I thank thee for thy loyalty," said Malarkey, wincing as

another maggot dumpling plopped onto his back. "And I will shed light on this bizarre vignette upon regaining consciousness, as I intend to swoon dead away and think on my poor murdered brother." And without another word, Malarkey closed his eyes and descended from the torture of his consciousness to the pain of his dreams.

Figary worked silently and efficiently while his master slumbered, sealing each crevice with maggots, then mummifying the broad back with linen bandages.

"Murdered brother," he said at last, liberally dousing his own hands with disinfectant. "It would appear that the *commodore* and his juvenile japesters have passed a lively afternoon, so it does."

Riley stepped forward. "Perhaps I can explain, sir."

Figary halted his flow with a raised hand. "Oh, in the name of heaven, please forbear. Explanations from children invariably fail to explain, and as I will doubtless be forced to endure the *commodore's* version of the day's happenings when he awakens, I prefer to pass the intervening moments in blissful ignorance, perhaps fortified by a nip of the *craythur*."

Riley felt that Figary's statement could sacrifice half a dozen words without any loss of meaning.

"I understand, sir," he said, which was not entirely true. "Perhaps we could also fortify ourselves?"

Figary pointed vaguely. "Larder," he said. "Washroom. Wardrobe. Have at them, youngsters." He glared pointedly at Chevie. "Most especially the wardrobe for you, mademoiselle. You appear to have neglected to don outerwear. I shall never think on the letters F-B-I from this moment forth without a shudder." And to illustrate, Michael Figary shuddered as though a dram of tar water had slithered down his gullet, then he left Malarkey's guests to their own devices.

"I still like him," said Chevie. "Are you hungry?"

"I was," replied Riley. "But then I thought on the squirming piles of maggots feasting on Otto's rancid flesh. You?"

"I was," said Chevie. "Then I remembered being stuffed into that dumbwaiter the last time I was here, listening to a murdering goon named Barnum talk lovingly to the knife he planned to dismember me with."

Riley grimaced. "Maybe we could shift ourselves to the drawing room. Perhaps have a medicinal drop of the *craythur* or two for our nerves and a catch-up until Otto comes back to the land of the living?"

Chevie draped her arm around her only real friend. "A catch-up, at least. I like your cloak. The Great Savano, eh?"

"Do you approve of the moniker?"

"I am flattered, kid."

"I was considering a savage Injun costume."

"I am less flattered."

"One gin?"

"No."

"Fine. Beer it is."

"No drinking, Riley. We need to be sharp for Moley and GooGoo."

This stopped Riley in his tracks. "Moley and GooGoo? You have not previously mentioned this pair."

Chevie steered him to the door. "Oh, a person needs to be sitting down in a bright room before I fill them in on Moley and GooGoo."

"No time like the present."

This casual remark set Chevie laughing until the tears coursed down her sallow cheeks.

Centuries before these events took place, in 1306, King Ned so detested the impenetrable fogs that regularly settled over the low-lying city that he banned coal fires entirely. It was the interaction of smoke with haze from London's myriad rivers and streams that formed the infamous pea-soupers that held river commerce for ransom more effectively than any army of buccaneers could ever hope to.

But Ned's mortality tripped him the following year, and his decree sailed down the river with no return ticket, and with it the city's brief respite from the damp grip of its indigenous fog, which descended vengefully. Charles Dickens described it like *a soft black drizzle, with flakes of soot in it as big as full-grown snowflakes—gone into mourning, one might imagine, for the death of the sun.*

Clover Vallicose and Lunka Witmeyer were fogbound now, as they grimly trudged to return Anton Farley to their savior and spiritual leader: the blessed Clayton Box, who planned on saving the world from the sins of man.

Vallicose had risen joyfully to this new challenge. Indeed, the Thundercat could not remember ever feeling so utterly righteous in the execution of her duty. The vapors of all niggly concerns and confusions were burned away to reveal the instrument of steel purpose that she had become. It was nothing short of a metamorphosis. The past did not matter, and neither did the future. All that mattered was purpose. Clover barely considered herself human anymore.

I am truly an angel for Box. Plucked from my universe to serve Him.

Because she was *worthy.* That was the only possible reason she had been chosen.

Vallicose carried Farley on one shoulder, easily bearing his weight—joyfully bearing it, in fact. Hoping for discomfort, so that she could offer it up as a personal sacrifice.

Witmeyer forged their path, ranging ahead through the mist that seemed to paw at her face and hands; and where it settled, she swore it hissed and burned like acid. In one respect she had been glad of the fog, for it reduced all persons to ghostly shapes. Everyone loomed and lurched and seemed a monster; therefore there were no monsters, and a couple of Thundercats could move as freely as any other unfortunate with no other choice than to traverse the city on such a befuddled evening. But she quickly forgot this boon and began to resent the sulfurous miasma that reeked of river sewage and coated the tongue and nostrils with bitter resin.

Lunka's faith was not as strong as that of Clover Vallicose. She had always believed that there had indeed been a Colonel Box, who rallied an army to the oldest banner on earth—holy war—and who conquered far-off lands in much the same way the Crusaders had centuries before. Good luck to him, Lunka had thought, and all who sailed with him. Some men sleep better with a cause as their pillow. But Witmeyer's cause had always been her personal well-being, and her credo was as short as it was simple: *Be on the winning side.*

And all her life she had performed enthusiastically for that side, exceeding her masters' expectations, willing to stamp on any who would topple her chosen regime. To the ends of the earth Witmeyer had traveled, wearing the Box symbol on her lapel, indistinguishable from her evangelical teammates on the outside. But behind the splashback visor, Witmeyer liked to think that her eyes were open. She saw the truth. She saw them all for the animals they were.

Be on the winning side.

But here, now, in this time, the winning side had not yet won.

Could their being here change the ordained outcome?

Was it ordained anymore?

It seemed to her now that Cadet Savano's *babblings* were visions of an alternate future.

Could it be that here, in this brave old world, there was something different to be found? Something actually *worth* fighting for?

"Which way?" Witmeyer called back, twisting her mouth to avoid turning her head, though what difference did sight really make down in the dregs of the pea soup?

Vallicose repeated the question to Farley, who was somewhat conscious, and eventually she deciphered his mumblings and passed them forward.

"Keep west. Follow the canal."

The same instructions for the past hour. Simple enough,

one might think; but with the early winter night and a wash of gray fog on the banks, following the canal was accomplished more through sound and smell than sight, for nothing could be seen but the dull hulks of barges and narrow boats that could have been sea monsters if not for the glow of fog lights slung from mast and gunwale. The water itself stank like a field latrine, and what cobbles there were squelched in their housings when trod on, as though the entire basin had become an open sewer.

Follow the canal? Follow the stench is more like it.

There were many things about this version of London that already irritated Witmeyer, but the stink, which ranged in notes from rank to odious, was top of the list.

These are not the glorious beginnings we read about in the academy.

Witmeyer stepped on something that first squeaked and then splattered; and though she had been in worse situations on many occasions, Lunka sensed that she was very close to the end of her tether.

It is the lack of control, she realized. *I have always understood my situation until now. But here, in this malodorous world, I am as ignorant and helpless as a newborn.*

How was a simple soldier supposed to know whom to kill in all this damned fog?

Onward along the canal bank they inched, Witmeyer with her gun arm rigid before her, and Vallicose behind, who had shifted Farley so that she tenderly cradled him in her arms like a babe. They had been walking for hours, first down the alley behind the Orient Theatre and then north away from Holborn, sticking to the alleyways and tumbledown brick mazes off the main avenues, avoiding any unnecessary contact with the locals, though they seemed a dull bunch and difficult to inspire into any sort of action beyond a leer or malformed insult. There was no prettifying on this side of the Great Oven. Goods were not displayed in shop windows but laid out on boards or slabs. The lanes were not washed cobblestone but packed earth with a river of sludge running down the center of each walkway. Men did not sport top hats and tails but flat caps and sackcloth and a mouthful of raw gums or blackened tooth stumps. And the women were not society ladies in buttoned-up bodices and blooming skirts but fishwives with veined forearms and matted nests of hair that would never smell of anything but mackerel.

Night was already dropping down to meet the rising fog, so the Thundercats did not attract as much attention as they might have, but even so, Witmeyer was forced into a fight with a couple of drunks on a fishing jetty. Though perhaps Lunka Witmeyer was not *forced,* perhaps she was glad of the diversion. Certainly the crash of the second man into a tower of crates made her smile for the first time since their jaunt through Smart's tunnel.

They saw the monolithic jumble of King's Cross and St. Pancras, with the streams of hansom cabs seemingly crawling from their brickwork like ants, and they heard the hellish chaos where the city's coaches and chairs butted bumpers and the steam trains *chud-chud*ded into northern and southern terminals, more than five hundred engines each day. Then through the railroad yards they skulked like criminals, past the spider's web of tracks all leading into the shed for old locomotives, to the banks of Regent's Canal, where the air once rang with the music of industry as the engineers worked their locks or wall cranes, but now were home only to the most tenacious of that industry who managed to eke out a subsistence in spite of crushing competition from the railway. Entire families living in a tea cabin, working for a single wage.

West then, to Camden, feeling the cold travel by piggyback on tendrils of fog, worming underneath their greatcoats and down the legs of their high boots. Witmeyer began to forget about more ethereal problems, such as her own loss of control and general dissatisfaction with her faith, and worry instead about freezing to death. She had never felt cold like this in London. The entire setup reminded her of a winter she had spent reeducating radicals in St. Petersburg, with its freezing fog and steam engines.

"To hell with this," she said, stopping level with the ice-frosted cover of a canal boat. "I need a drink or a fight. Or something!"

The morphed shapes of Vallicose and Farley solidified beside her.

"What impedes us, Sister?" asked Clover.

Witmeyer swallowed a scowl. Clover had been here for five minutes, and already she was using words like *impede.* She was loving this. Loving it.

"Impedes us, Sister?" snapped Witmeyer. "Impedes us? Oh, a couple of things. The century we're in, for one thing. Our mission, for another. What happened to eliminating Savano? That order came from on high, after all."

Usually Vallicose had little patience for questions when her single-mindedness was focused on a task, but now she bore her partner's moodiness with a beatific smile, which only served to further enrage Witmeyer.

"This is not a laughing matter, Sister. We are out on the end of a very long limb here. Yes, we have weapons, but not so many bullets. And anyway, my fingers are so cold and swollen, I don't know if I could pull the trigger. And I don't feel well, Clove. Seriously. Since that unholy time tunnel, my insides feel wrong. I think that machine reacted with our bulking steroids."

Vallicose shifted Farley's weight gently. "Don't you see, Lunka? This is the Hangman, before he ascends to that glory. Before the Hangman's Revolution. We have been chosen to stand at his right hand. At the right hand of the Blessed Colonel himself. All other missions are subject to that honor. Where, or indeed *when*, we are does not matter. All that matters is our holy mission, which is to take the Hangman to the colonel, and he is in the Camden Catacombs—every schoolchild knows this. We are so close."

Witmeyer had long known that there was no point in trying to actually communicate with her partner about anything in an honest fashion. Vallicose was simply incapable of thinking outside the party lines. In order to achieve any sort of dialogue, Lunka Witmeyer knew she would have to construct an argument that her partner could understand.

"Of course, Sister. We are honored by this new mission—blessed—but the Holy Hangman is injured and freezing. We must seek food and shelter or we may forever be remembered as the Thundercats who allowed Anton Farley to die of exposure. Perhaps our mission is to simply save his life."

This had to be considered, and Vallicose found her gaze drifting to the cottages on the canal's far bank, their windows aglow with warm, welcoming light. A fire would indeed be a blessing. Even a brief stop would serve to fortify them all.

Vallicose looked down upon the Hangman, Farley, hanging limply in her arms.

Duty is so difficult, she thought. So many opportunities to make mistakes.

She wished that Farley would perk up so she could question him as to their exact orders.

Perhaps I am being tested. This is my personal valley of darkness.

As though he felt her gaze upon his brow, Farley's eyes fluttered open.

"Awup," he mumbled. "Haawuup."

"He speaks," said Vallicose. "My Lord Hangman speaks."

"What does *My Lord Hangman* say?" asked Witmeyer, knowing that the sarcasm would not even register with her partner.

Vallicose cradled Farley's skull gently in one massive hand and drew him close to her ear.

"Yes, Major Farley. Give us your instructions. We exist to serve."

Farley spoke his order, a simple command that Vallicose had uttered herself countless times.

"Well?" said Witmeyer, the single word sending a cloud of iced breath puffing from her lips. "What is the good news?"

Vallicose half-smiled, perplexed. "He says, that is, my Lord Hangman says: *Hands up.*"

Witmeyer did not return the smile, but was instantly on her guard, sweeping her weapon around the canal. She found herself in the gunsight of a sentry standing in what she had thought was a covered punt but she now realized was a rigid inflatable boat with an outboard motor strapped to the stern. The man himself was rendered indistinct by his black uniform and shroud of fog, but the rifle barrel poking from the gloom was perfectly clear.

"Hands up, princess," said the man. "And drop the weapon."

Witmeyer bared her teeth. Now here was a situation she understood.

"What did you call me, little man?"

A *clack* echoed across the flat expanse of water as the man racked the slide on his weapon. "Hands up, that's all you need to worry about."

Witmeyer moved laterally away from her partner, making them separate targets. "Are you ready, Sister?" she called to Vallicose. "Remember what I said about conserving bullets."

But her partner stood stock-still and said to the Hangman, "Put your hands around my neck, my Lord."

When he'd done so, Vallicose raised her hands as ordered. Witmeyer could not remember ever having seen her partner in this position, and in spite of all she had experienced on this most eventful day, it was the sight of Clover Vallicose posed with such supplication that drove home to her that her partner had set them firmly on the road to ruin.

"Now you," said the sentry, and Witmeyer had no choice but to comply, allowing her pistol to dangle by the trigger guard.

The man's teeth must have been exceptionally white, because Witmeyer could have sworn they flashed from the gloom.

"See, princess? That wasn't so hard."

Witmeyer felt fury build like a physical pressure behind her eyes.

Unless that man is the colonel himself, she thought, I am going to injure him before this is all over.

They boarded the rigid inflatable—which should not have existed for another half-century—and the sentry pulled a couple of hoods from under the seat.

Farley saw the hoods and shook his head.

Why bother? the gesture said, and Witmeyer understood the implications. They were to be taken to the nerve center of operations, at which point they would join the revolution effort or they would be executed. Either way, hoods would not be necessary.

7 » MUCKSNIPES & GUTTERFLIES

I have a dog, lovely little guy, eyes like chocolate buttons.
Anyway, this dog, Justin, sits looking at me, nodding his little head,
and you'd swear that he understands every word I say.
Pretty much exactly like you people now.
—Professor Charles Smart

THE CAMDEN CATACOMBS WERE CATACOMBS IN name only, as there were no cobwebbed crypts under their vaulted ceilings. These so-called catacombs had been excavated not as a place of eternal rest for the souls of the departed, but as a crucible of labor for the living. Camden Lock Market had long been a center of commerce, and the arrival of the railway only increased the bustle of man and beast. So much so that the railway company built a series of underground stable yards for their work ponies and even included a pool and a dock for boats coming off Regent's Canal. These yards were constructed hurriedly and on a budget, and so they flooded regularly. After a heavy rain it was not uncommon for lovers strolling the canal to have their romantic vista ruined by the grisly sight of drowned, wide-eyed ponies heaped like sacks on the bank.

This water problem seemed insurmountable, so the railway company was nothing short of thrilled when, in 1884, a retired American colonel with more money than brains made it an extremely generous cash offer for the entire subterranean labyrinth. What this Colonel Box planned to do with the caverns, the railway folk did not give a single fig about, as his pile of money was sufficiently high for the doomed project to miraculously realize a profit.

A champagne reception was thrown for Box in the Savoy, and then the railway folk sent a clerk to bank the tender before it evaporated. As a footnote to the entire affair, the clerk who had been dispatched on his errand with a withering series of threats and insults from Director Rolls-Jameson took the impulsive decision to abscond on a ferry to Europe with a suitcase of pound notes and was never heard from again, though there were rumors that he bought an olive grove on the Côte d'Azur and lived a long and happy life.

Regardless of this embezzlement, the catacombs now belonged to the colonel, and he set his team's engineer the task of flood-proofing the entire underground area, which, contrary to the universal rule of restoration, did not prove as difficult as first supposed. In fact, the entire problem was solved by the construction of a single buttressed, steel-reinforced wall between the catacombs and adjacent sewer network, which had never been equal to the task of conveying Camden sewage and rainwater to the distant Thames.

Once the wall had been scrupulously built to specifications and tested by a winter of torrential rainstorms, Colonel Box and his team of British and American special forces—drawn from Delta Force, Navy SEALs, and SAS Boat Squad, among others—transferred the future gear into their underground lair, satisfied to finally have a base of operations from which to move forward their master plan.

For the next decade and a half, Box and his men labored underground like beavering badgers, stripping down whatever twenty-first-century weaponry had made it through the Smarthole and fabricating facsimiles. There were setbacks, of course, including the mundane shortage of adequate tooling equipment, and an extraordinary takeover attempt by the Spiffy Squires, a gang of what could only be described as river pirates, who, upon hearing some third-hand legend of an Ali Baba's cave of riches underneath Camden Lock, moved their operations from the Thames estuary to the canal and attacked on two fronts: by land and by water. The Spiffy Squires were little more than Oxford dropouts suffering from spoiled-brat syndrome, and they were no match for Box and his aging soldiers, though Box did lose two good men, which made him realize that he would need to eventually bolster his ranks with locals if his operation was to succeed. And so Major Anton Farley was dispatched to infiltrate London's biggest and most organized criminal outfit: the Battering Rams. And when the time came, when all the weapons were ready, then the Rams' war council would be executed and the rest of the gang would be offered a proposition.

That blessed day had finally arrived.

Camden Catacombs, London, 1899

The boatman left the engine in its cover and expertly poled the Zodiac inflatable along the Regent's Canal portside bank, toward the brick-toothed mouths of Camden Bridge's arches. Dark wavelets thumped the rubber floats, urging the inflatable to midstream, but the oarsman compensated unhurriedly with deep mixing swirls of his pole.

A thousand times, thought Witmeyer. He has made this trip a thousand times.

She glanced sideways at her partner, who sat beside her amidships, and was unsurprised to see Vallicose's face shining with a zealot's glow.

Clove thinks herself on the way to Paradise.

Ironic, as the dark canal waters could easily have been the River Styx and their ferryman might have been the legendary Charon, delivering them to the Underworld.

Why not? Is anything impossible now?

Witmeyer shook herself, partly for warmth, but also to dispel the philosophical nature of her thoughts. She had been quite interested in the great thinkers as a younger girl. As a cadet, she had even dated a poet as part of a teen undercover assignment, and she had been upset for hours when she had had to inform on him; but she had learned from that assignment that this was not a world for philosophy. The history shows on the Boxnet assured the faithful that Victorian London was the largest cesspool of human sin and corruption the planet had ever seen. Victorian London apparently made Sodom and Gomorrah look like Girl Scout camps.

I have survived on my instincts thus far and I will survive this trial, too.

The inflatable moved in rhythmic pushes, water hissing on the gunwales, until the bridge yawned over them, greasy stalactites dripping from its arches. They might have been rowing down the gullet of a whale for all the Thundercats could see, but the sentry hauled back on his long oar and guided the small boat toward an indistinct bank of flotsam and decomposing canal garbage. The prow cut cleanly through the soft belly of the bank, and suddenly they had slipped through a shadowed access arch and underneath the bridge itself.

Vallicose could barely contain her excitement.

The mouth of the Catacombs. I can feel the Blessed Colonel's presence.

Of course, she had been here before. On school tours. For Boxites, this place was the equivalent of Bethlehem. This was where the Boxite Empire had been born, in this Spartan underground series of caverns.

A flashlight beam cut through the gloom and pinned the small boat to a white ring of water.

"What have you got there, Rosey?" said a northern English accent from the darkness.

"Farley and a couple of strays," replied their escort.

Rosey? thought Vallicose, doing her *surprised* grunt. Sergeant Woodrow Rosenbaum, born in New Jersey. The Evangelist. *I have his Bible trading card in my locker.*

"Sergeant Rosenbaum," she said with a curt bow of her head. "What an honor to meet the Evangelist. I didn't recognize you in the fog."

"The Evangelist?" said the second man, stepping from the shadows. "What's she talking about, Rosey?"

The second man was all soldier, from crew cut to military-issue boots. The uniform was a strange hybrid of futuristic and Victorian. The flak jacket was definitely not from this century, but the clunky revolver on his belt and the battered top hat perched atop his shaven head anchored him in this time.

Vallicose studied him. "You are Aldridge," she said. "Corporal Sonny Aldridge. Born in Newcastle."

Aldridge raised the barrel of his rifle, which, like him, seemed to be cobbled together from parts.

"That sounds like surveillance information, miss. I don't like people knowing things about me."

"I have your trading card in my collection," said Vallicose. "Every loyal citizen knows this information. It is written on the plinth of your taxidermic installation in the Hall of Heroes."

Aldridge did not lower his weapon. "It is written on the what of my what in the where?"

Farley coughed and propped himself on one elbow. His face was pale in the flashlight beam, but his deep-set eyes sparkled from their recesses.

"Corporal, these people are future folk, and they saved my life. The colonel will want to see them immediately. This could change everything."

Sonny Aldridge grimaced. "Are you sure, Major? The colonel doesn't like surprises."

Farley was adamant. "This is different, Corporal Aldridge. Today's phrase is *lizard king*—now buzz us in. That's an order."

Aldridge shrugged, absolving himself of responsibility. What could he do but follow orders? He pulled a walkie-talkie from his vest, sent two bursts of squawk, and then pressed the *speak* button.

"Aldridge here. Lizard king. I say again, lizard king. Crank the gate. Four coming in."

Behind him on a heavy steel panel, two thick chains shook off their slack, clinking rigid, and sprayed trails of water into the lit circle. The panel jerked straight up into a square frame set in the wall above, and from inside the catacombs tumbled a cacophony of industry, including the buzz of arc lights and weld sparks. The impression was of production and purpose.

"Oh," said Vallicose. "Oh. Oh."

Aldridge waved them past with the antenna of his walkie-talkie, and Sergeant Rosenbaum threaded the Zodiac through the canal gate into the belly of the catacombs.

Witmeyer was a tough woman to impress. After all, she had seen more wonders in the course of her fifteen years as a soldier for Box than most people might see in a dozen lifetimes. At the tender age of eighteen she had been one of the special forces team that had dynamited the Eiffel Tower, possibly the greatest propaganda coup ever achieved in the Jax wars. Before she had reached her third decade, Lunka Witmeyer had spearheaded the campaign to eliminate the unholy elephant from the continents of Africa and Asia. By twenty-three she was co-commander of her own search-and-destroy shuttle in low Earth orbit, hunting down resistance Internet satellites, so Lunka Witmeyer had literally seen the world. But the sights that greeted her wide eyes in those catacombs impressed her mightily—as much if not more than anything she had seen in her varied career. Colonel Box and his men were building an army underground, preparing for the first round of Boxstrike.

The gateway opened into a series of low rooms interconnected by brick arches and lit by a series of arc lights strung along the walls and powered by various portable generators that growled and shuddered in corners like watchdogs. The arches gave the space the feeling of a cathedral, and the impression was one of holy labor. Men worked on weapons, stripping them down or building them up. Witmeyer saw racks of mortar tubes, assault vehicles, grenade launchers, limpet mines, rifles that vaguely resembled AK-47's, pump-action shotguns, and boxes of ammunition. And a cluster of Zodiacs bobbing on the leash at a steel ladder that led to a mini-jetty.

"This is quite an operation," said Witmeyer, thinking that just maybe this was the team to join. Queen Victoria might have manpower on her side, but just one of those mortars could easily destroy an entire barracks, and a man with a single AK-47 plus unlimited bullets could mow down foot soldiers until his barrel overheated.

The working soldiers barely looked up as the boat passed, and Witmeyer saw that many of them were considerably younger than Rosenbaum.

The colonel has been recruiting.

It made sense. It didn't matter how many guns you had if there were no soldiers to fire them. Firepower only worked with a certain amount of manpower.

A pity the colonel didn't wait around until battle drones were invented, thought Witmeyer. He could have single-handedly won the holy war.

It was obvious to her now that if she and Clover had traveled back in time bearing arms, then so too had Colonel Box and his men. There were no divine weapons specifications handed down from on high. Box and Co. were simply time travelers. The *Blessed Colonel* was not so much blessed as lucky.

Witmeyer wondered how this bombshell would affect her partner, and the cruel streak in her looked forward to witnessing Clover's reaction.

She is going to freak the hell out, she thought, not without satisfaction. All this time she has believed her precious colonel to be a god who walks among us, and it turns out that he is no more special than the rest of us.

Except Charles Smart. He'd been special, and Vallicose had shot him.

Rosenbaum threw a rope to a brother soldier, and they tied

it to a dock post. With a jerk of his rifle, he urged his passengers onto the steel jetty. Vallicose refused to relinquish Farley, so she strode along the walkway bearing the Blessed Hangman in her arms.

"I can walk," said Farley irritably. "Put me down."

Vallicose didn't hear; perhaps she was beyond hearing. The Thundercat seemed to have achieved a semi-trancelike state. Her legs moved and her heart pounded, but her mind was consumed by rapture.

I am here, she thought in disbelief. In the Catacombs, during the time of preparation, on my way to meet the Blessed Colonel.

How could any of this be happening were she not *chosen*? Her devotion had willed this event into being. Box had watched her, and this was her reward.

Somewhere in the back of her mind, a small voice squeaked that maybe the Blessed Colonel had all these futuristic weapons because he was from the future, but the zealot in Clover Vallicose had no difficulty ignoring this little voice of reason.

Heads were turning now. These two particular Thundercats attracted enough attention walking through Thundercat headquarters in their own time, but here in Victorian London, under the full blaze of electric light, most of the recently hired soldiers would honestly have been less surprised to see a couple of *crigs*, the mythical crab-pig hybrid monster that, according to legend, roamed the sewer network. Even the men who had time-hopped from the 1980s had never seen specimens quite like these. Vallicose and Witmeyer were both over six feet tall, and each was striking in her own way. Vallicose's skin was porcelain pale, and her green eyes were large and fringed by red eyelashes so long they almost curled back on themselves. Witmeyer was darker, with twin slashes of high cheekbones and a deep cleft in her chin. Her hair fell in dark sheaves around her shoulders and rippled as she walked. Add to these details the fact that both women had been fed steroids and various growth hormones from birth, and you had two beautiful women who could not fit through a doorway without both ducking and turning sideways.

"Look at this, me bully boys," said one soldier, a native of this century. "I don't know whether to kiss 'em or shoot 'em."

Vallicose, who was usually quick to take offense, floated past in a holy cloud, so Witmeyer was forced to deliver the punitive head butt.

"You think about it for a while," she told the unconscious kiss 'em/shoot 'em soldier. A chorus of caws and claps rose about them like circling crows as Witmeyer's summary punishment was met with approval.

Rosenbaum ignored the mini-fracas and kept walking through the first of many arches, some of which had been bolstered with iron scaffolding, as they were already losing integrity due to the vibrations of the machinery below. The strange bunch passed through several large windowless rooms with clusters of soldiers either running drills or laboring over stripped-down war machines. The weapons were curious in that they resembled twenty-first-century equipment, but on closer inspection it became clear that the tooling was a little less refined. They were manufacturing weapons here based on futuristic prototypes.

One room contained a smelter that poured white-hot molten metal from a giant gourd into various molds while smoke was sucked up the funnel of a blackened chimney. The men working the gourd with long-handled gaffs were stripped to the waist, skin blasted black by the enormous heat. Witmeyer found it impossible to look at them and not think of demons in the fires of hell.

This is enough underworld imagery for one day, she told herself. *First the River Styx, and now this.*

The heat warmed their backs as they skirted the smelter, proceeding to a long narrow hallway with a row of smaller arches leading to a single steel door. Vallicose knew these arches well, as she had lingered in this corridor on her visits to the Camden Catacombs. *The Corridor of Power* was the name the guides would give to it; Clover had often pressed her cheek to the brick arches and imagined she felt a thrum from the residual Boxite power that had been absorbed into the stonework.

On the other side of that door, thought Vallicose, and she unconsciously tightened her grip on Farley.

"Put me down, damn you!" said Farley. "You are crushing me."

Vallicose blinked the world into focus. "Oh, apologies, Major Farley. I am a little overwhelmed."

Farley climbed down from her arms. "I will not appear before my commanding officer like a babe in arms."

"Of course, sir. Forgive me. Should I fix . . . ?" She pointed at Farley's left shoulder. "It's hanging a bit low. The sooner it is back in its rightful place, the better."

Farley glared at his shoulder angrily, as though it had betrayed him by allowing itself to become dislocated by his fall into the music stands.

"We have a doctor and two medics here. I hardly think—"

While he was talking, Witmeyer stepped up behind Farley and grasped him by the shoulders. Before he could protest, she squeezed him as though he were an accordion, reattaching the shoulder joint.

"That's a little thing we do," she explained. "Clover distracts, and I perform the field surgery. I amputated a leg with a hatchet once that way."

Fixing Farley's dislocated shoulder actually cheered her up a little, as it was reminiscent of her glory days sweeping through the villages of northern France. Farley was not cheered even a jot. His knees quivered, and he howled in shock and pain.

"What are you doing, Sister?" Vallicose shouted in dismay.

"I thought we were doing a number. You distract, I heal. That's what we always do."

"This is the Hangman!" said Clover. "It is not our place to distract the Hangman."

Witmeyer scowled, which on her face was a terrible expression indeed, and upon seeing it most right-minded people would beat a retreat and hide behind a thick concrete wall, but never Vallicose.

"Forget the war-face, Sister Witmeyer. We are in uncharted waters here. We are on hallowed ground. The old ways are dead."

More's the pity, thought Witmeyer. I preferred it when the Blessed Colonel and the Hangman were symbols of a history we twisted to suit our own purposes.

A confrontation between the Thundercats became inevitable at that moment, and perhaps it would have taken place right then and there had not the steel door been pushed open with such force that it clanged against the wall, sending brick-dust clouds floating from the frame. The door swung three quarters closed, humming like a tuning fork, and shielding the opening from Vallicose's and Witmeyer's view.

"What is that infernal noise?" asked a man's voice. "How many times have I asked for dying men to be kept out of earshot?"

Farley gripped his shoulder tightly to contain the agony. "Sorry, Colonel. We have newcomers here; they don't know the rules."

"Newcomers at my door?" said the colonel, not sounding pleased to hear it. "There are rules for newcomers, but there are rules *about* newcomers too, Major."

"Begging your pardon, sir, but this is different. Extraordinary, in fact. I felt confident that you would wish to interview these two personally."

"Did you indeed?" said the colonel. "And why would that be?"

"They are from the future, Colonel. The new future. The *changed* future."

This news was greeted with a quick intake of breath and a long pause before the door swung open completely, revealing the man whom Farley had referred to as Colonel.

Vallicose genuflected, bowing her head and placing her left hand on the Boxite logo stitched into her greatcoat.

"Hail Colonel Box," she said, launching into the Colonel's Prayer. "Blessed be Clayton. He who labored long in the darkness so that we all may see the Light. Look down on us and forgive us our human frailty. Deliver us from the godless and the sinner. You are our shepherd, our daily inspiration, and our road to Heaven. Hail Colonel Box. Amen."

Witmeyer did not genuflect or bow her head. She wanted to get a good look at this man, who had neglected to mention in the gospel that his weapons cache came from the future and that he was not in fact a god.

So while Box stood enthralled by Vallicose's recitation, Witmeyer studied the colonel from top to toe and committed every detail to memory.

Colonel Clayton Box was a tall man. Six-four or six-five, maybe, with a slick wedge of golden hair that sat atop his crown like a gold brick. The sides of his head were shaved, which should please Vallicose. He looked pretty much like his portraits, but there was an intensity in his features that no paintbrush or camera could ever capture. His eyes seemed uncommonly round and dark, a deep blue with shards of white running through them like lightning bolts. Those eyes stared at Vallicose without blinking, no matter how long Witmeyer watched, making her think that the colonel must be somehow coordinating his blink pattern with hers. Impossible, of course. It was true that the man's face was familiar from a million billboards and banners—familiar, but not identical. Witmeyer thought that the party artists had been a little generous when commissioned to capture the colonel's likeness. The strong points were well drawn, but the colonel's weaker features had all been given a little boost. The jaw, for example, was slung low and jutted forward, which gave Box the look of an orangutan, and the lips were narrow like the slit flaps of a fish's gut, and they moved while Vallicose was talking, as though the colonel was casting a spell on her. Box's skin was slick and pasty from too many years underground, and his mustache, while medium impressive, certainly did not live up to expectations. Especially when one considered that the number-one nursery rhyme taught in New Albion nurseries was "The Colonel's Mustache," which went:

The colonel's mustache
The colonel's mustache
As thick as a brush
And grown in a flash
You may travel the world
Spend a fortune in cash
But you won't see the like
Of the colonel's mustache.

Every child in the Empire knew that rhyme, written by poet laureate Edderick Bulsara, who had also penned such masterpieces as "The Colonel's Flat Cap" and "The Colonel's Pet Cat," which were all as different as chalk and something very like chalk.

If Witmeyer was painfully honest with herself, she had to admit that, what with all the steroids in her regimen, sometimes her own mustache was the like of the colonel's.

But none of this mattered—not the mustache, not the pugnacious jaw or the creepy lips—when the man himself looked you in the eyes. When those deep blue orbs were turned a person's way, that person felt like their soul had been laid bare for all to see. That person knew that somehow Colonel Clayton Box had some form of second sight that saw right through the everyday mask that everyone wore to the secret face beneath. It was terrifying, awe inspiring, and felt never-ending.

Witmeyer found this out while Box studied her for all of two seconds.

"One question," he said in an accent that was mostly neutral, with only a slight hint of a Texas twang. "What do you think of my mustache?"

It's a trap, screamed Witmeyer's intuition. *Whatever you do, don't answer truthfully.*

"Lovely, Colonel," she said. "Very . . . luxuriant."

Box's eyes narrowed. "Hmmm," he said, and then turned to Vallicose. "Same question to you. The mustache. Opinions?"

Vallicose's entire face quivered, but she knew that it would be impossible for her to lie to the Blessed Colonel. "I like the *idea* of your mustache," she said slowly.

"But?" prompted Clayton Box.

"But in reality, it seems a little sparse. It pains me to speak these words, Colonel, but I could never lie to you."

"Hmmm," said Box again. "I respect the truth." He pointed at Witmeyer. "But she lied to me. I will not tolerate falsehood. Shoot her."

This was intended as a test for the newcomers, just a little psychological needling to see how they would react, but the two Thundercats were on the move before the command's echo faded. Both went for Rosenbaum. Witmeyer winded him with a punch to the solar plexus, then snagged his revolver from its holster. Vallicose palmed Woodrow Rosenbaum's head to one side, grabbed a blade from his belt, and then the Thundercats were on each other, blade to neck and barrel to temple.

"We're partners, Clove," said Witmeyer. "We go back."

Vallicose was teary-eyed. "I'm sorry, Lunka, but I have no choice."

Box gave this most entertaining scenario a second, then intervened. "Wait, okay, wait. I thought there was room for only one more in my operation, but with skills like that, I guess I can use two."

Vallicose blinked. "Do you absolve her, Colonel?"

Box frowned, bemused by this level of deference, but also liking it quite a bit.

"I absolve her. Put your weapons down, both of you."

Vallicose obeyed instantly. Witmeyer had to think about it for a moment, then she too lowered her steel.

"If the colonel forgives you, Sister," said Vallicose, "then I can, too."

Witmeyer did not return the favor. She was not in a forgiving mood.

Box glanced back over his own shoulder at the plans and charts that were calling to him. He would schedule an hour to debrief these two later, but for now there were a few tactics that had to be ironed out about the Revolution.

"Put these two under guard until morning," he told Farley. "Then get yourself patched up. I need you in top shape for tomorrow. We have a big day ahead."

"Emergence Day," whispered Vallicose, and she knew then why she had been sent here: to stand by the Blessed Colonel's side as they waged holy war.

Blood will flow, she thought. *The blood of sinners and unbelievers.*

GROSVENOR SQUARE, MAYFAIR, LONDON, 1899

Riley and Chevron slept head to toe on a wide divan in the drawing room while the maggots feasted on Otto Malarkey's flesh. It was possible that there were more urgent matters to attend to than their own exhaustion—in fact, it had only been a few hours since Riley had stolen a catnap in the theater.

Nevertheless, their traumatized minds decided that they had absorbed enough information for one day and shut them both down until dawn. They awoke to find themselves covered in a goose-down quilt. There was a breakfast tray on one of the terribly ostentatious coffee tables, and a slight whiff of brandy in the air, which led them to believe that Figary had something of a soft heart after all.

They passed an hour stripping the breakfast tray down to the last crumb of muffin and catching up on all that had happened since the last time they had almost expired in each other's company. There was a lot to digest on the two sides, and both put forward a summary at the end.

Riley went first. "So what you're telling me, Chevron Savano, is that the entire future has changed just because Farley clapped eyes on you the last time you visited our pungent metropolis. And now everything you hold dear is gone, along with several million murdered innocents, and in its place a dastardly empire of evil that wages holy war with anyone what don't see things its way?"

Chevron swallowed a final chunk of sausage, which, as a fitness fanatic, she would normally never eat, but she had just this morning constructed a new diet rule: *Anything eaten outside your own time zone does not count.*

"That's about it, kid. And what *you're* telling *me* is that you were preparing to open your theater with a magic show featuring you as the Great Savano when a bunch of gangsters arrived to milk you dry, except one of their own turned out to be a future soldier who murdered all the rest?"

Riley nodded. "Hard to credit, ain't it? But that ain't the entirety of it, is it, Chevie? I recall you mentioning two dodgy yokes by the name of Moley and GooGoo?"

Chevie chased the sausage with a swallow of hot chocolate, as she had just decided that the time zone food rule also applied to drinks.

"Moley and GooGoo, also known as Clover Vallicose and Lunka Witmeyer. Two warrior women sent to kill me. They're here now, in this time. Hopefully London will swallow them up, but I doubt it."

"Still," said Riley, "what are they but a couple of gals with guns? Shouldn't be too much of a headache."

"I'm a gal with a gun," Chevie pointed out. "And I would bet money on either of those two against our sleeping king downstairs."

Riley whistled. "Well, that's a new pair of boots altogether. I hope they don't hitch their carriage to the Farley express, or we could be in real trouble."

"You can count on it," said Chevie. "If Colonel Box is somewhere in this time, then Vallicose and Witmeyer will find him."

Riley stripped off his heavy cape and let it fall with a clang to the floor. "Seems to me that our best plan is to keep well out of this row. We can't fight an army."

Chevie's face was suddenly solemn. "I can't do that, Riley. Do you remember I told you that my dad was killed in an accident?"

"I remember, and that's a pain this fellow here knows only too well."

"In this new time stream, Dad doesn't die in a motorcycle accident. A neighbor informs on him for writing songs in his spare time. He was executed by the Thundercats. They said he was a traitor."

"And was he?"

Chevie shrugged. "I don't know. I hope so. They got my best friend, too, just for taking the wrong turn in a hallway."

Riley moved down on the divan so he could drape an arm around his friend. "No one should have those memories in their head. We must try to erase them, or at least make them not true. But there is a more immediate matter that must first be sorted."

Much of Tibor Charismo's guest wardrobe had survived the militia cannon, so Chevie and Riley were also able to change their outfits, which were extremely unsuitable for venturing out and about in Victorian London. Riley's clothes had been shredded, except for his magician's cloak, which, apart from a few tears and scratches, had held together pretty well. And in her workout gear/cadet jumpsuit combo, Chevron might as well have been wearing a sign that read *lunatic trollop* or words to that effect, many of which variations Riley had volunteered until Chevie told him to shut up or she would shoot him.

"I am merely offering the opinion that other coves what don't know you like I do might possibly, and incorrectly, assume that you were a shameless hussy escaped from Bedlam, dressed as you was in vest and long johns."

"Yeah? Well, some *coves what* don't know you might think

you were escaped from the mortuary that I'm about to send you to," countered Chevie feebly.

Riley raised a finger. "That ain't a good argument, pal. Firstly-wise, it don't make a farthing of sense, and second, your pasts and your futures is all mixed up."

"The story of my life," said Chevie. "Yours, too."

Chevie bowed to the pressure and covered up her figure with a silk smoking jacket.

"I'll pick out something for outdoor wear later," she said. "There's a lot to choose from."

It feels nice to have a choice, she decided. I should try to do more of it in the future.

That, Chevie supposed, would depend on the future.

Otto Malarkey roused himself shortly afterward and plodded around the lower floors shouting for his boots, which apparently Figary had spirited away while his master slept, the Irishman being little more than a damn thief—like the rest of his miscreant race, according to Malarkey, who bellowed this and similar insults with such volume that the entire square was made cognizant of his opinions on the subject of his manservant.

Eventually Otto tackled the stairs and stumbled into the drawing room, red in the face from shouting, but otherwise in reasonable order.

"Where are my blasted boots?" he demanded, in a passable American drawl.

Chevie shrugged. "I ain't the boot lady, Otto. You ought to take better care of your stuff."

It took Otto a moment to sort out his identities and figure out who he was supposed to be at this current moment. He was pretty definite that he was in the commodore's home. So therefore, why were the Injun princess and the Ramlet sitting in his drawing room? Were they not part of Otto Malarkey's life? And to rub salt in the wound, why was the girl giving him sauce? Could it be that she actually believed him to be the genteel Commodore Pierce, who sang shanties after dinner over cigars, always censoring the bawdy verses so as not to cause the ladies to blush behind their fans?

"I ain't no commodore, missy," he said, dropping the Yankee affectation. "So you would be wise not to cross swords with me."

Figary entered through the drawing room's mirrored second door, bearing Malarkey's boots in his arms. The enormous high boots were half the size of the diminutive Irish butler.

"Oh, I think the world and its mother is well aware that you *ain't no commodore.* In spite of your non-commodore-ness, Missus Figary's boy here decided to polish up your precious boots for you as a little pick-Jack-up when you awoke. And this is the thanks I get: invectives and accusations."

Malarkey grabbed the boots without a word of thanks. "Invective and accusation is the way of it with me, just as drunken impudence is the way with Missus Figary's only boy, Michael."

Otto sat on a filigreed chair with a velvet cushion and legs in the shape of cornucopias, tugging his boots on over his knees and smiling at the footwear as though each boot was a beloved hound at his feet.

"There we go, lads," he said. "All's right with the world,

eh? So long as we are not parted." Once the boots were settled, Otto gazed sharply at Michael Figary. "And now to matters of import. How does my hair look on this day? They say anxiety affects the follicles."

Figary rolled his eyes. "The hair is magnificent, so it is, Commodore, truly. And now would it be too much trouble to request a little of God's own truth? Missus Figary's boy would like to know who it is that employs him."

"So he would," said Riley, for sport, earning a withering glance from Figary.

"I owe you that, I suppose, though I know you will not get a jot of pleasure from it," said Otto. "God's truth, I will miss being the commodore. It was good old sport playing the toff." Malarkey rubbed his flanks. "Let me begin with the boots. They belonged to my mentor, Reverend John Pine. His favorite pair. He was the smuggler king and gave me my first taste of organized crime. He left me the boots, and I used them to kick a path for my brothers and me to the top of the Battering Rams. And now I am king of the bunch."

Figary's hand rose to cover the horrified *O* of his mouth. "Well, carry me out and bury me decent, I am working for the king of knaves; Otto Malarkey, is it? The big costermonger himself."

Otto shook out his locks. "You have me, Figary. What would Missus Figary think of her boy Michael now? Working as a butler for the high king of low life?"

Figary looked to the heavens as though he could feel the disapproving glare of his dear departed mother.

"I didn't know, Mammy. I never did," he said, then returned his attention to Malarkey. "Do you have any idea how many novenas I will have to say for forgiveness? I'll be praying until Christmas."

The butler crossed the room to a walnut drinks trolley and poured himself a large tumbler of brandy, which he tossed back in two gulps.

"You are a lucky man that I am generally an inebriated coward, for if I ever faced you sober and found my courage, then you would be in for a thrashing, so you would."

"I have no doubt, Michael," said Malarkey.

"Would you care to tell us what's going on, Otto?" asked Chevie. "Why the leprechaun keeps referring to you as *Commodore* might be a good place to start."

"Leprechaun, is it?" said Figary, red dots of fury rising on his cheeks. "So this is the class of visitors I can expect from now on? Urchins and waywards? Having the pick of our finest togs too, I see. Perhaps we should send carriages to the tenement hovels? Just ferry them in to pick us dry."

"I have allowed some latitude because of the circumstances," growled Malarkey. "But you will not insult my guests, Mr. Figary, is that understood?"

Figary searched the pockets of his tweed jacket until he located a small leather-bound notebook with a pencil in the spine. He took it out, licked the pencil, and wrote a note to himself.

"'Otto Malarkey, the ex-smuggler and current crime boss, is an enthusiastic supporter of murder and theft but takes a dim view of people insulting his guests, so he does.'" He shut the notebook with a defiant snap. "Oh, I understand you, sir. You can be sure of that. And if you'll excuse me, I shall repair to my room in order to compose my letter of resignation." He executed his trademark sarcastic bow and strode toward the door.

"I will not be maneuvered, sir," Malarkey called after him. "This little jape only works the once on Otto Malarkey."

Figary did not offer a rejoinder. The only sound from without was the clatter-jig of the butler's hard shoes climbing the stairs to his room.

Otto stood and bellowed. "Off with you then, you peacock! I am King Otto, and I will bend the knee to no damn Irish gin-soak!"

More clattering, fading now.

"Oh, very well, blast you!" shouted Otto, stamping his feet as though ants were heaped beneath them. "Double. I'll give you double chink to stay. You can purchase that village of yours. SO YOU CAN."

Figary's head appeared in the doorway. "A deal, sir. And cheap at twice the price, if I may say so."

Malarkey and Chevie could only stare in wonderment. After all, a mere moment before, Figary's footsteps had echoed from the top story. Riley, on the other hand—and with both hands—drummed up a round of applause.

"Well done, sir. Well done indeed."

Figary bowed, and this time it was real. "Thank you, Master Urchin. Never bet against Michael Figary when there are wooden surfaces and hard soles involved. Sure I can play those stairs like a grand piano."

Malarkey shook his head ruefully. "You will be the death of me, Figary. Tell me one thing, hand on heart now: were you truly ignorant of my real moniker? All this time?"

Michael Figary laughed. "Is there anybody in London town who does not know the great King Otto? I knew you the second I walked into the hallway for my interview. I knew you from your *silhouette,* sir. Missus Figary didn't raise any idiots, so she didn't."

And this was a statement that no one in Grosvenor Square had the gall to poke a hole in.

Malarkey insisted on breakfast before he would continue with his story of the copper commodore. And so Figary, in a matter of seconds it seemed, conjured up a mountain of kippers and eggs, of which Riley accepted a portion even though he had stuffed himself to rotundity not an hour previously.

"This is sheer ambrosia," Riley declared. "Mr. Figary is worth his wages and more besides."

"What a clever urchin," said Figary, patting Riley's head. "May we keep him, Commodore?"

"There is no need to persist with the title," said Otto. "I would not have you lie with every breath."

Figary played his invisible piano, dismissing the objection. "What is a title but a collection of letters or stripes on a sleeve? And at any rate, I think it wise to maintain the illusion, if we are to stay on in Grosvenor Square. The residents are not known for their tolerance of criminals. I refer you to Mr. Charismo, the previous resident of this house, so I do."

Malarkey nodded. This was a wise argument, and in truth he had always liked how the word sounded in Figary's Irish burr.

"Very well, you may address me as Commodore, for appearances' sake."

"My pleasure, Commodore."

Once the master-servant relationship had been bolstered with cash and titles, the morning's exposition could begin in earnest. Otto told his Commodore Pierce tale, bemoaning the fact that Ram kings rarely survived to enjoy a retirement wallowing in their ill-gotten gains, but he intended to buck that trend. So when his associate Tibor Charismo's assets were seized and the demolished Grosvenor Square house went under the hammer for mere pennies, Otto had purchased it under the name Commodore Pierce, a secret alias he had established years previously to salt away his private wealth, mainly stolen Saltee Island diamonds. Perhaps the house had been under something of a shadow at the time of purchase, but with a new facade and the passage of time, someone would pay top guinea for a Grosvenor Square address, and that would go a long way to financing his retirement. Otto's plan was to abdicate from the Hidey-Hole when the house was habitable, take up residence as Commodore Pierce, then turn it over for a profit as soon as possible. After that it was a first-class cabin on the *Campania* all the way to New York City. He even had an American passport run up by the best purveyor of fakements in London.

But then, Otto began visiting the works, dressed as the commodore and spouting such Americanisms as: *Those drains better be done by nightfall or there'll be hell to pay,* and *I am prepared to pay top dollar for premium workmanship.* It was a jolly gas, and Malarkey warmed to the role. And when he'd hired Figary as overseer and general butler, that had sealed the deal. Malarkey loved everything about the commodore; his cavalier mannerisms, how the genteel ladies sneaked peeks at him from behind their fans, the constant warring with Figary. He adored the entirety of the experience, and now that the house was nearing completion, he found himself loath to give it up.

"But give it up I must," he concluded. "For Grosvenor Square ain't more than a brief trot from the Haymarket, and some cracker casing a swell's digs or flying the blue pigeon in the vicinity would be sure to cop a squint of my lovely hair; then it's off to Highgate for old Golgoth."

Figary's piano hands went crazy. "Desist please, Commodore. If you are to be a resident of Grosvenor, then this Cockney double-talk must be knocked on the head, so it must. What are you saying, man? Pigeons and crackers? It's gibberish concocted by criminals."

Riley and Chevie exchanged amused glances. It was incredible to them that King Otto would react to his butler's impertinence with no more than a resigned grimace.

"Betterment of the self is a hard road," said Otto, reading their looks. "And betimes a cove must swallow down what he would ordinarily chuck to the floor and stamp on." He shot Figary a dark glare of foreboding that would have most men leaving town without taking the time to pack a suitcase. "But take heed, Michael Figary, for every man has his breaking point, and when King Otto breaks, he breaks uncommonly violent."

"Tush," said Figary. "Tush, bah, and fiddlesticks, Commodore. King Otto's days are numbered, but thanks to me, Commodore Pierce will enjoy a long retirement in high society."

Chevie felt that, amusing as it was to see Otto Malarkey chastised by his Irish butler, there were probably more important things they could be discussing.

"Maybe we should talk about the Rams, Otto. My guess is that Farley's boss wants to step into your boots."

"The tattooist said as much," said Otto. "He said the Rams would be part of a new world order, those that took the shilling."

Chevie kneaded her knuckles. "The Rams are the key. Box's foot soldiers took the city for him; without the Rams he's nothing. How loyal are your men, Otto?"

Malarkey spat on the carpet, which had Figary back at the brandy decanter. "Loyalty among thieves, is it?" said Otto. "That only exists when there ain't cash involved. As soon as it becomes a transaction, then it's 'the king is dead, long live the king.'"

Chevie stood. "I mean to stop Farley and the whole lot of them. How about you, Malarkey?"

"Farley killed my brother. And for that I'll see him and anyone who stands with him at the bottom of the Thames."

"So we're all of a mind," said Riley. "But how are three hunted individuals to take on an army with weapons like Farley was toting?"

"We need to see the lay of the land," mused Otto. "Find

out which way the Rams are blowing. My boys are greedy coves, yes, but they are also suspicious, and cautious. My Rams need to be approached like actual rams. Real careful-like. One wrong word, and Farley could find himself with a hole in his gullet."

"We need eyes on the inside," said Chevie. "One of us has to go into the Hidey-Hole. And it has to be today. This is Emergence Day. Box attacks today."

"But who?" wondered Riley. "Chevie made a spectacular impression the last time she was here. Farley himself did my ink. And as for you, Your Majesty, even the glockiest duffer in your outfit would point the finger from a mile off."

"The Rams know us all," said Chevie.

Otto Malarkey stroked sheaves of his long hair from root to tip. "Not all of us, they don't."

It took a second for the penny to drop, but when it did the Irish butler actually hooted in surprise and slopped some of his beloved brandy on the rug.

"Me? You want Missus Figary's only son to venture into a den of maniacal thugs and pirates? Michael Figary, raised on buttermilk and scholarly discourse, in amongst the muck snipes and gutterflies, is it? Well, you can blow that idea right out of your head."

"So you can," Chevie added.

She couldn't help herself.

8 » A CLUSTER OF THREE

Things that shouldn't happen do happen. Things that should happen don't. It's a maze in a minefield on a fault line.
—Professor Charles Smart

COLONEL CLAYTON BOX.

The Blessed Colonel.

A god who walked the earth.

But he hadn't always been. Once upon a nonanointed time, there had simply been Clay Box, a kid from Texas who grew up surrounded by men with big guns and women with smaller ones tucked into their purses, because you never knew when the Second Amendment might need to be upheld. Clay's father, Clayton Sr., had taught him to shoot a .22 rifle when he was eight years old, and the boy was shooting a Competition Pro model by the time he was twelve. Pop Box was overjoyed to find that his son had a real passion for sharpshooting. He couldn't have been more wrong. Young Clay did not have a passion for shooting, or anything else for that matter; the reason he was so proficient at putting rounds through the bull's-eye was that he treated the entire procedure as a mathematical equation. He was completely dispassionate, and when he shot, it was almost as if he was watching himself from above, considering the challenge, adjusting his scope, factoring range and wind speed. For Clay, marksmanship was no different than skinning a frog in biology. The important thing was efficiency. Winning a ribbon meant little to young Clay, but losing it because of some lack of efficiency would have infuriated him beyond words.

The only thing or person that Clayton actually loved was his mother, Nancy. He had often asked himself why he felt so strongly about his mother and not about his father or TV, but he could never find an answer that satisfied him. *Perhaps I came from her and so she is part of me, and the closest I can come to loving myself is to love her.*

Clayton had no interest in making friends, but he did accept a young Hispanic neighbor, Luis Chavez, as a companion, as the boy was desperate for a buddy and willing to do whatever Clayton suggested in order to strengthen their bond. He had no way of knowing that Clayton valued him about as much as he did the frogs from biology.

Clayton's suggestions included hiking out to the scrublands with their rifles and shooting at rabbits and buzzards. Real-world shooting helped Clayton refine his technique and adapt to the unexpected. He felt not a shred of remorse for littering the brush with bloody animal corpses. Those creatures had served their purpose, and they meant no more to Clay than drawings of them would.

Clayton Sr. was over the gosh-danged, star-spangled

moon. His boy—HIS BOY, who folks said had a *strangeness* about him—was ripping up tournaments all over the country. He whipped that army brat Jennings Kreuger, and that snot-nosed Ivy Leaguer Holt Whitsun-Bang. The press were all over Whitsun-Bang when he won silver at the nationals; wait till they got a load of his Clay. At the last qualifiers, fourteen-year-old Clayton put a cluster of three in the bull, so tight it looked like a goddamn shamrock.

Clayton allowed his father to be happy, and he practiced smiling in the mirror so his mom would stop asking him what was the matter. And as long as his parents didn't interfere with his development, he could let them stay alive.

It was not strange for Clayton to seriously consider killing people. He thought about it every day. And surely the ultimate point of weapons training was to kill humans. And didn't his father support that by buying him a gun in the first place?

Clayton fired his competition weapon as often as he could over the next few years and trekked out into the wilderness for night shoots with Luis whenever possible. Pretty soon the wild critters presented no challenge and Clay felt himself losing his edge. After placing second in the prestigious Green Creek Shootout, he decided that the stakes would have to be higher.

Luis and Clay spent a couple of weeks picking off neighborhood pets, but that was tiresome, as the bodies had to be removed and buried, an arduous task that was of no benefit to Clay's development, as far as he could see. And so one night, when Clay sent Luis into a garden to fetch the corpse of Laddie the Labrador from old Mrs. Wang's garden, he found himself drawing a bead on his young friend and wondering whether shooting a human would affect him like books and TV said it would. Would he be traumatized, or permanently scarred, even? Clay doubted it, and almost before he knew what he was doing, he thumbed a round into the breech of his rifle, screwed an eye to the night vision sights, and shot Luis from five hundred yards.

Hell of a shot, Clay, he said quietly, impersonating his father. *Hell of a shot.*

He sat and waited for something to happen inside his brain. Hoping that he would feel something. But nothing came. Shooting a human was like shooting a paper target. He knew that now, and so the experience had been worthwhile.

When the police arrived, Clayton was sitting on the bluff, finishing a bag of Oreos he'd brought along as a snack.

The gun went off, he said over and over again, doing the sad face he'd learned from TV police procedurals. *The gun went off.*

And they had believed him, as he knew they would, for he was a clean-cut honors student, and the alternative was too terrible.

Three months later, Clayton was accepted into West Point in New York State. The army was a natural place for a boy like him and, truth be told, relationships had been more strained than usual in the Box house since Luis's shooting, so his father was glad to see him pack his gear.

Two years and this boy will make the Olympic team, the admissions officer told Clay Sr. and Nancy.

Nancy cried because she would miss her son terribly, but also because a part of her was relieved to have Clay and his bag of lethal tricks out of the house. Maybe now the whispers would stop.

Clay felt an unfamiliar jauntiness as he boarded the Greyhound bus for New York. There were big things ahead for him. He was certain of it.

Camden Catacombs, London, 1899

The zealot's smile that had been pasted across Vallicose's face since meeting Clayton Box was shaken a bit by the Blessed Colonel's quarters. In the future, these quarters would be preserved for posterity, but they would not look like this. On the historical tour she would take, this room was undecorated except for a painting based on Michelangelo's *Pietà*. A room that made it abundantly clear that the inhabitant cared not a jot for worldly possessions, and, in fact, Vallicose had modeled her own quarters in the academy's officers' wing on Box's. No embellishments besides a miniature version of the same print. And now she found herself in an underground palace that was more opulent than even the Jax president's residence, which was said to have carpet so deep that small dogs had gotten lost in it, and so much gold leaf that the floors had to be reinforced against the weight. Vallicose had seen a photograph taken with a spy-cam.

It was disgustingly decadent.

But this chamber was sumptuous beyond even the Palais de l'Élysée. Lavish beyond words. The individual pieces could be described, but the combined effect left the visitor overwhelmed. The walls were lined with illuminated tapestries depicting medieval Crusades to the Holy Land. The hard floor was heaped unevenly with Oriental rugs weighed down on the corners with vases veined in gold. Several chandeliers hung from the ceiling, all gleaming with electric light, their crystals casting rainbows on the walls and furniture. The gilded chairs were hand-carved and strewn with velvet cushions. Incense burned from golden pots, making the cavernous chamber with its high arches seem like some form of temple.

Box waved vaguely at the decoration. "All this. The decoration. I'm toying with it. I'm not sure if it's a good fit for me. Gadhafi made it work. And old Saddam. Saddam spent millions on his homes. Billions. And to a lot of cultures, wealth is power. They don't understand modesty, just can't fathom it as a concept." The colonel flicked one of the several dozen tassels in the room. "But if you want the military's loyalty, then you need to appeal to their basic instincts. Traditional values: country, family, self-sacrifice." Box tipped a jade warrior statue with his foot. "This hardly says self-sacrifice, does it?"

Witmeyer kept her face bland, unwilling to respond one way or the other.

"No, Lord Colonel," said Vallicose, eyes respectfully downcast. "It does not."

Box sat on the lip of his desk. "No. It doesn't. I think

humble might be the way to go for appearances' sake. Perhaps with a holy picture."

"The *Pietà*," blurted Vallicose.

Box turned his striking blue eyes on her. "The *Pietà*. Yes. Son and mother together. It doesn't get much more *family values* than that. Well done, soldier."

"Thank you, Lord," said Vallicose.

Box pushed out his lower jaw, then moved it from side to side, as though working out a kink. This was his *thinking* face.

"Lord," he said finally. "You referred to me as *Lord*. That's interesting. I can only surmise that my plan was—will be even more successful than I anticipated."

"The Boxite Empire covers most of the globe, Lord."

"Most?"

"France, Lord. France holds out. And parts of South America."

Box frowned. "That is . . . inefficient. The Boxite Empire, *my* empire, should be more efficient."

"The Thundercats are making headway in Normandy."

"Thundercats?" Box did his version of a smile, which seemed more like a grimace. "Ah yes, my cartoon friends. I found that show mildly amusing. And so I must have appropriated the name for my police. Which branch are you?"

"Sister Witmeyer and I are special agents in security and counterintelligence," said Vallicose.

Box walked around the desk, folded his lanky frame into a chair, and opened a ledger on the leather tabletop.

"Very well, my Thundercat future soldiers. I need you to tell me everything, starting with the history of that striking symbol on your coat."

Vallicose began to talk, slowly at first, but soon the future facts flowed out so fast that Box had trouble writing them all down. When she paused to draw breath, Witmeyer took over. And as the Thundercats filled in the details, Clayton Box experienced a warmth in his chest that he rarely felt.

I am happy, he realized. I am satisfied.

When Vallicose and Witmeyer had finished describing their snapshots of the future, Box looked over what he had written.

"Yes," he said. "Yes, yes. That all sounds most efficient. Most efficient."

Though the Thundercats could not have realized it, this was the highest compliment the colonel could have paid, and in a roundabout way, he was paying it to himself.

Box called Rosenbaum and issued some commands.

"Destroy the landing pad on Half Moon Street. I want things to stay the way they are going to be. No one comes, no one leaves."

"Yes, Colonel. I'll get a squad over there right away."

"And I need death warrants written up, date sensitive, for Professor Charles Smart, who will live on Half Moon Street. And Cadet Chevron Savano, who will be a student in the Boxite Academy, which I will found after the second round of Boxstrike, apparently."

Rosenbaum jotted down the details in a notebook.

"Method of execution?" he asked.

Box waved his hand. "Oh, at the executioner's discretion, but both terminations must take place at Smart's residence."

"Discretionary, Colonel," said Rosenbaum. "Noted."

"I need a picture of the *Pietà* to hang behind my desk, and begin moving all this junk out of here."

Rosenbaum could have pointed out that they were leaving the catacombs the following day, but the colonel was not fond of people questioning his orders.

"Send a cleanup crew to the Orient. I want all those bodies dumped in case they lead back to us at this crucial moment."

"At once, Colonel."

Box pointed at Vallicose's coat. "And I would like this symbol, the Boxite symbol, stitched onto all uniforms."

Rosenbaum nodded. "The dual symbolism is quite clever."

"It is efficient," corrected Box. "It conveys our ethos and loyalties in the minimum amount of strokes." He bent to his ledger and was sketching the Boxite symbol when Farley entered the room, looking a little the worse for wear but a lot less terminal than he had when the Thundercats had found him in the orchestra pit.

"Colonel," he said, "Malarkey's bug is pinging loud and clear. He has run to his Grosvenor Square address. I would wager that Savano is with him. Let me take a small group of men . . ."

The colonel raised his large, bottom-heavy head from the twin waves of his ledger.

"No, Major," he said. "I need you at the Hidey-Hole, to make the offer. The Rams know you. And Grosvenor Square is a privileged area; there will be plenty of police around. We need someone quiet and deadly. Rosenbaum, you are the sneakiest of us. Do you think Malarkey is a man you could kill?"

Woodrow clicked his pen. He was tired of being the secretary; it was not what he had been trained to do. He was trained to kill people without drawing attention to himself, and he hadn't had a mission in months.

He could have answered: *I can kill Malarkey in a heartbeat.*

Or:

I could end his life in a flash.

Or his favorite from the Godfather movies.

Malarkey will be sleeping with the fishes.

But imagery and metaphor would simply confuse the colonel, who prized plain-speaking above all else.

So he said, "Yes, Colonel, I can kill Malarkey."

"Good," said Box. "Do it tomorrow morning."

9 » SO I AM

The thing that nobody ever factors in is personality.
Time is like water: big people make a big splash.
—Professor Charles Smart

THE BATTERING RAMS' HIDEY-HOLE,
ROGUES' WALK, LONDON, 1899

THE DISTANCE IN MILES FROM GROSVENOR Square to the Haymarket was barely a single unit, but measured with a moral ruler, the divide between Otto Malarkey's town residences could fairly be judged as worlds apart. Where Grosvenor Square was the genteel, garden park where lords and dukes were happy to pay in excess of fifty thousand of Her Majesty's guineas for a single dwelling and spend such a fortune on brocaded Louis Seize boudoirs that it would have in fact been more economical to paper every wall with pound notes, the Haymarket thoroughfare was such a concentrated collection of vice and crime that its environs were religiously avoided by all but the most corrupt bluebottles on the beat. If Grosvenor Square might be described as the jewel of the capital, then the Haymarket could be fairly called London town's phony diamond. From a distance it glittered, but at close quarters it became clear that its glitter came not from a precious stone, but from the blade of the dagger coming to slit Johnny Punter's throat.

And this is where they have sent me, thought Michael Figary, as he stepped down from a carriage on the top end of Regent Circus. This is where Missus Figary's only son must go for his master.

The Haymarket rolled out before him in all its tawdry glory. Even at this time of the late morning, with the sun barely rising from the chimney pots, the revelers had begun to shake their musty feathers and make the pilgrimage to the market for their opium pipes, gin jars, and gambling parlors; clustering around these sporting gents, eager to lighten their purses with or without consent, were the shoals of sharp-faced rogues, thieves, and shamsters.

Michael Figary pinched a handkerchief over his nose as he picked his way along the sidewalk, stepping nimbly over fallen troopers in the brandy wars, and skirting the splashes from droppings carelessly deposited by wilted cab horses. The handkerchief was not an effective barrier against the assault on his nostrils, but then, how could a mere square of perfumed lace hope to compete against the odor of a hundred years' unchecked decadence?

On first listen, Figary's instructions had seemed simple: *Gain access to the Hidey-Hole and find the lie of the land viz the Rams' loyalties, then skip smartly to Grosvenor Square with any informations.*

Straightforward it sounded, but this forthrightness crumbled under examination. Firstly, how to gain entrance to the Rams' citadel? How then to remain during a war council? Finally, how to emerge unscathed with a pan full of intelligence to convey to his master?

Michael Figary mulled over these questions as he approached the double doors to the Hidey-Hole, definitely the most notorious den of vice in all of London, and certainly in the top five in Europe. The answer to all his problems was as plain as it had been since he arrived at it in Grosvenor Square: hard cash would open doors for both his casual admittance and hurried exit. Shining sovereigns would buy the nuggets of information he sought. These men were the princes of corruption, and princes of every court had one thing in common: a desire for currency to pay their tailors and romance their ladies. There was not enough money in the world to satisfy princes.

Well, perhaps for one night, thought Figary, feeling the weight of sovereigns in the pockets of a second pair of breeches he wore beneath the outer tweeds, breathing deeply to feel the shift of the pound notes tied to his chest. The commodore had given him over two hundred pounds to spend at his own discretion this evening.

And were I less loyal, or indeed more sober, then I would book a first-class berth on a steamer to Dublin.

But Figary was both loyal and slightly drunk, and he intended to see his mission through. For although Michael Figary affected an Irish Catholic innocence, in actuality he had once been employed by the Dublin crime boss Lord Brass as a *dipper on commission* in the Monto area of Dublin, which bore some resemblance to the Haymarket. In fact, Michael Figary had operated as one of the best pickpockets in the city until he saved enough money to relocate to London, where he reinvented himself as Missus Figary's only son and butler extraordinaire. So Figary was perhaps not as out of place as he pretended; indeed, he was more familiar with the goings-on in this class of place than he cared to admit.

The Hidey-Hole was open for business, and though Figary had never been in this particular establishment, he trotted up the steps with the confidence of an inveterate degenerate.

There were a couple of real beauties guarding the door—beauties in the ironic sense that even their own mothers could not refer to these mugs as beautiful, or even handsome. *Plain* would be stretching it. *Ugly* would be closer to the mark, and *terrifying* would be spot-on.

I suppose that's why they are at the door, thought Figary.

He addressed the men as though answering their question.

"Yes indeed, it is a brisk morning, so it is."

"So it is, what?" asked malevolent bludger number one, who Figary could now see sported a glass eye in the place of his own right eye. A glass eye with a purple skull instead of an iris.

"A brisk morning, so it is."

"It is wot?"

This from malevolent bludger two, who still had both eyes given to him by God and his parents, but was marked as a thug by the scarlet vest that he wore *sans chemise*, despite the much-mentioned briskness of the morning and the mores of common decency. On a more genteel street, a bare-backed man would find himself in prison quick smart.

Figary changed tack.

"It is a good day to make money . . ."

"So it is," said Purple Skull, who was possibly displaying a sense of humor.

"It is *always* a good day for chink," added Scarlet Vest.

Figary slipped them both a sovereign, which was an extortionate entry fee for any gambling den, but it did ensure that he had made two new friends, if not for life, then at least for the length of his visit to the Hidey-Hole—unless their shift finished, or they got drunk, or they got a better offer.

I should have at the very least one half of an hour before they turn on me, thought Figary. It pained the butler to part with a deuce of sovereigns now that his situation was honest and he knew exactly how many hours of toil were required to earn such an amount, and so he lifted a small whiskey flask from Scarlet Vest's sash to compensate himself somewhat and skipped through the doorway into the belly of the beast.

That beast being, of course, a Ram.

The interior of the Hidey-Hole was an extraordinary feat of architecture. Extraordinary in that it did not collapse in on itself despite the fact that most of the building's supports, struts, chimneys, and internal walls had been pulverized to make way for gaming tables, animal pens, food stalls, a hog spit-roast over a sunken brick fire, an entire pub that could have been transported from the Strand, two boxing rings, and a full-sized cannon, which according to Ram legend had been stolen from the militia on a drunken lark and was now marooned with a busted axle on an island of weight-warped planking and scattered cannonball.

"Charming," muttered Figary to himself, his eyes instantly springing leaks from the combination of smoke and alcohol fumes.

It was heading toward midday, and the brethren were emerging from their sleeping spots. There was much passing of wind—the louder the ceremony, the better—to the delight of small groups of dancing girls and serving ladies who drifted from table to table. Rams made their way down to the ground floor by way of rickety stairs, makeshift rope ladders, or even toeholds kicked into the walls. Even Figary, who was not the prude he had pretended to be for his employer, could not help but be a little shocked.

I have never witnessed this concentration of depravity, he thought, and from a man who'd worked the Monto, this was quite the jolting realization.

To the pig, then! became his immediate plan. Because nothing calms the soul of an anxious Celt like his mother's voice, and failing that, a plate of bacon.

Figary walked with feigned swagger to the pig boy and circled the roasting pig, checking the meat from every angle.

"Nice-looking pig, so it is," he said to the young chef who was ladling grease over the carcass.

"I ain't allowed to discuss the pig," said the youth through lips that sheltered but a single pair of widely spaced teeth, which stood forlornly on his bottom gum like the pillars of some long-collapsed bridge.

"No pig talk, it is," said Michael Figary. "Slice me off a plate, and don't spare the crackling."

"Crackling be extra," said the sulky boy.

Figary guessed that the boy had good reasons to sulk, with his dental shortcomings and employment tending pig for the criminal class. He knocked a knuckle against a wooden price list on a pole stuck directly into the floor. "I can read, my boy, so I can. Meat, if you please."

The pig boy commenced butchering with an army knife, and skillful he was too, dropping thin slices directly onto a tin platter.

"You want grease?"

"Grease be extra?" asked Figary innocently.

The boy sucked his teeth and gave Figary a suspicious glare. "Right you be, little man. Grease do be extra."

"Let's have some, then," said Figary, dropping some pennies into the money jar. His daily fare was generally more refined now that he bunked in Grosvenor Square, but every now and then nothing hit the spot like a feed of pork and grease. "Tell me, bucko. Why is pig talk forbidden?"

The young butcher did not answer until Figary added two more pennies to the pot.

"On some occasions the pig do not be pig exactly," he confided.

Figary sniffed the animal's haunch. "But not today?"

"No," said the boy, handing across a heaped plate. "Today be kosher pig. Stole it meself special for the meeting."

Figary's ears pricked up. "What meeting? I didn't hear about any meeting."

The boy shrugged. "'Course not. You ain't no Ram."

Figary sampled a sliver of pork, and it was wonderfully juicy and tender. If he closed his eyes for a moment, he could be in Lord Brass's Monto tavern.

"No, I ain't no Ram. What I am is a guest from the Monto."

The boy's sigh whistled through his teeth. "I has me money. You has yer pig. I ain't allowed to talk about a 'strordinary meeting viz meeting the new king."

"I quite understand, so I do," said Figary, and he sidled away, holding the plate at chest level for everyone to see. For he had found it to be a universal truth in any company that a man who has succeeded in obtaining food is presumed trustworthy and never questioned, except for general rhetoricals about the quality of his meal.

An extraordinary meeting about a new king, eh?

This was momentous news indeed. The appointment of a new Ram king had far-reaching consequences that would affect everyone dwelling in the city, from rookery to Parliament, via docks and train station.

"Nice pile o' pig here, ain't it?" quoth one Ram to Figary. It was plain that this cove was indeed a Ram, for he had gone beyond the call of duty and had the Ram symbol tattooed on his bare chest.

"It is, so it is," replied Figary, stuffing his mouth with pork to prove the point.

The room was filling up now, and Figary felt it would be prudent to find a shadowy spot and observe. He sidled off toward a church pew that was by the wall and piled high with an army's worth of cutlasses and bayonets, and he wiggled himself in at the end. He was far from invisible behind the carelessly stacked pile of glittering blades, but he did not stand out like a cat at a dogfight either. The second advantage of this positioning was the window at his shoulder, which could be hopped through should the need arise.

Now, Michael Figary, hold your whisht and see what you may see, he told himself, wiping his greasy fingers on the sailcloth nailed as a makeshift curtain across the window.

Unlike most spy jobs, where forbearance was the chief virtue required since events tend to roll out slowly even in the greatest adventure, Figary found that his patience was not tested even for a moment. For no sooner had he picked the last of the crackling from between his teeth—with a wooden pick that he carried in his wallet for such occasions—than a focused hubbub heated up by the doorway and spread like a wind across a field of Irish barley.

What ho, something is up, Figary thought. *Make yourself small, Michael.*

Figary hunched down behind the tower of swords, finding himself a triangle of crisscrossed blades to peep through.

The room that had been sluggishly shaking itself awake

for the day's entertainment seemed suddenly to accelerate the procedure, with Rams lining up for access to the ropes, ladders, and rickety stairs that led from the upper levels. A tight bunch of Rams moved with purpose toward the center of the room where, upon a raised dais, sat a large gilded chair. Upon the chair's high backrest hung a ram's fleece, with long curling horns. The Ram king crown. Otto Malarkey's crown.

Figary felt the tension rise with the temperature. Voices were raised and punches were thrown. Around the room swells and silks were taken by the elbow and escorted from the premises, for this was to be a *members only* sort of gathering.

Figary felt that perhaps this would be a good time to leave, but the moment quickly passed, and the butler realized that he was now committed to the mission, whether his mother would have approved of it or not.

Make yourself smaller, Figary told himself. *You are a dormouse, so you are.*

Farley was at the head of the incoming bunch. He separated himself from the crush of Rams pressing him for information and mounted the dais in one bound. This act in itself was mutinous, as the king's square was for him alone and those he invited. The tattooist was taking liberties. But while many men would have been spiked or bludgeoned before they could open their mouths, the Rams had a special affection for Farley, as he had pricked the skin of many of them. A good tattooist was vital for any gang if they preferred to not lose an arm to infection or gangrene, and the amount of arms Farley had lost to a dirty needle could be measured on one hand. So the general muttered consensus was to let the old duffer have his speak; after all, he had been by Malarkey's side when whatever occurred had occurred.

Farley raised his arms for silence. "Rams. Brethren. Your attention, if you please."

On most days some jokester would fire comments into the spaces between sentences, but when Farley asked for silence, that is what he got, and without the usual gradual sputter out. The room fell instantly quiet, except for the insistent crowing of one cockerel, who was given half minute to shut his beak before one of the Rams clocked him with the butt of his knife. At another time the cockerel's surprised final squawk would have raised cheers, but not on this day.

"I know you have all heard the rumors regarding Otto," said Farley. "And I am here to tell you that the good ones are false and the bad ones are true."

This brought on a hubbub of mumbling and many shouted versions of the same question.

"Is King Otto murdered, then?"

"He is," replied Farley, reckoning this could already be true and if it wasn't, then it soon would be.

"You seen him go down, Farley, with yer own peepers?" This from Scarlet Vest, who had obviously abandoned his post at the door.

Farley nodded. "I seen . . . I saw Otto killed. And Inhumane. Noble and Jeeves, too."

If the silence before had been one of anticipation, this new one had a sense of disbelief about it.

Otto, Barnabus. Jeeves and Noble. *All* dead. It was akin to losing the entire royal family in one fell swoop.

"The war council gone. The top table killed. How, in the name of Dastardly Dick Turpin, did this happen, Farley? It would take an army." This from a Ram who for some reason known only to himself wore a paper crown with the word *BAH* scrawled on it in charcoal.

Farley swallowed. This was the crucial moment: wooing the Rams. Buying their loyalties.

"Before I answer your questions, let me show you something." Farley reached into the pocket of his shabby overcoat and drew forth a heavy pouch, and from this pouch he selected one gold sovereign, which he flicked into the air. The coin tumbled and flashed lustrous beams into the eyes of the transfixed Rams. With each spin, it reeled in the Rams more than a thousand entreaties ever could. So by the time the sov fell into greedy fingers, the crowd was halfway converted to Farley's cause, though they did not know what that cause might be.

"All I ask is that you listen to my pitch, and for that alone I will pay ten gold sovereigns to every man jack here from this bag and a dozen like it. Once I have said my piece, you can either sign up and take a slice of the Empire itself, or you can decide to have a go at the new top man. It is purely up to you."

He stood silent then, so that the assembled might chew on his offer. The sovereign was passed around, bitten, spat on, and finally handed to an old Welsh man known as Duds, who was acknowledged as the greatest faker of currency who had ever stamped a lead shilling.

Duds ran a series of tests, which included pinging the coin with a tuning fork, setting it spinning on a table, and giving it a good licking.

"It's a good 'un," he said at last. "Sure as my name is Admiral Nelson."

This drew a fond little chuckle from the Rams, as no one had the faintest idea what Duds's real name was. Each moniker he used was as fake as the monies he passed.

The Rams turned back to Farley with a synchronized swivel of heads worthy of hungry seagulls following the meaty slide of fish guts down a slab.

Tell us, said their ravenous gaze. *Tell us how we may earn the gold.*

Farley saw they were satisfied to let him continue, so he rolled on with the script prepared for him.

"You asked me if Malarkey is dead, and I tell you he is. And how do I come by this information? How am I so certain? I am certain because it was I who pulled the trigger."

"That must have been one hell of a trigger, old man," said Scarlet Vest, who seemed to have appointed himself spokesman.

"It was, and more besides, for it went on to do for the rest of the war council. All with one weapon. And one load."

This was an incredible admission. Here was one of their own stumping up to the murder of the century.

"Whoa, Jameson," said Scarlet Vest, referring to Dr. Jameson's plucky invasion of the Transvaal. "Wot you are telling the brethren is that little old you did the big job on our entire war council, all by your lonesome, with a single barker?"

Farley met Scarlet's eyes and held them until the man dropped his gaze. "That's what I am telling you."

The Rams could keep silent no more. Why, if this were true, then it was the one of the bloodiest coups in the history of the brotherhood. Not since Franz Flowers, also known as the Golem of Warsaw, treated Ram king Albert Spade and his top three bludgers to a Viking funeral by setting Spade's riverboat alight, had such a brazen power grab occurred.

And this had been accomplished by the tattooist? It beggared belief.

Scarlet Vest spoke for the house. "I would like to take me a look-see at this barker, Farley; that's what I would like for a first. And for a second, I would like to pay my respects to King Otto, face-to-face. Because I ain't believing that you put down not one but two Malarkeys."

Farley was unruffled. He had been expecting some back and forth from the Rams. They would learn discipline soon enough, when the colonel held sway.

"Very well, boys. You would like to see my weapon, is that it?"

"For a start," said Scarlet Vest, all puffy with his new spokesman responsibilities.

Farley reached again into his bag. "Well, by all means, let's make a start." He drew out his machine pistol, flicked on the laser sights, and shot Scarlet Vest and one man on either side of him directly. Three dead in half a second, and not a Ram reacted until the deed was done. Farley continued to make his point by transcribing a semicircle of bullet holes in the floor before him.

"I take orders from one man," said Farley, then he pointed his smoking barrel at the fallen Scarlet Vest. "And that ain't him."

The Rams were a little anxious, but not overly upset, as Scarlet and his mates were well-known muck-snipes who would rob a fishwife of her fish and a fish of its wife.

Farley allowed the gun to dangle at his side, but it was clear that it could be easily raised. "Now, hear this, Rams. There is a new army in London: the army of Colonel Box, and we have big plans for this town. If you are with us, then together we will wreak vengeance on all who have wronged us over the years: the police, the army, the jailers, the bailiffs, the politicians, the crown itself. My master, the colonel, will put these magical weapons in your hands and make you invincible. You will reap the spoils of war and be lords in the new country. Those who say no will never leave this building alive. We will set upon them and close their mouths forever. So, the choice is yours: you can be rich as kings, or dead as martyrs. Which is it to be?"

Farley's speech was followed by a ragged cheer, which gathered impetus and spiraled about the room, joined and strengthened by stamping and clapping and even pistol shots. There were no words in the cheer, just a halloo of support for the idea of finally going to war for pure profit. No more queen and country, no more blessed book and holy land. Just honest fighting for honest cash.

Farley caught the mood of the cheer, and he smiled even as the sight of these men turned his stomach.

Once the city is ours, we will recruit from the army and toss every one of these criminals in a deep dark hole.

But he was relieved that his gamble had paid off. The colonel had advised him to take a squad with him into the Hidey-Hole, but he had respectfully disagreed.

I know these men, Colonel. They are donkeys. All I need is a shiny carrot to lure them into our den, and then they will be ours. The squad stays outside.

The colonel had agreed but made one suggestion.

May I suggest a few cracks of the whip also, just to let them see for themselves what we are capable of.

Farley looked down at the three corpses laid out before him like sacrificial offerings at an altar.

The whip has been cracked, Colonel, he thought. You have your army. The Ram is dead.

But Malarkey yet lives, said the voice of doom in his head. *And you killed his brother.*

The Pig Boy was tired of being the pig boy. He had fought his way into the Battering Rams with dreams of strutting down the Haymarket with the other swell bludgers. A fine powder-blue bowler he would purchase, to set off the navy vest and sapphire rings that would be lifted from a toff's gaff in Mayfair or the like. On the night of his acceptance into the brethren, Pig Boy had borne the sting of Farley's needles and watched the blood seep from the Battering Rams tattoo on his shoulder and said to himself: *Now. Now at last things will be different.*

And he had been proven right. Things *were* different. They were blooming worse. Before taking the ink, he could at least tuck away in his own poke whatever he stole. Now a good slice of it had to be forked over to the Rams' treasurer, who was a stickler for every ha'penny.

And he had become the Pig Boy.

One night he had done the butchering, just to demonstrate how handy he was with the knife, and the next thing you know, King Otto had dubbed him official butcher. This was not Pig Boy's dream.

Your name be James or Jimmy or even Jem, he reminded himself. *Not blooming Pig Boy.*

And now. *Now.* Even that tiny measure of favor he had earned as butcher was up in smoke as by all accounts King Otto was feeding the worms, and James Jimmy Jem happened to know that Farley weren't a pig man.

As he ladled grease on the swine, Pig Boy wondered how he could get in with the new chap and secure a promotion from the butchering budge.

Information is currency, he thought to himself. So, does I be knowing something worth selling?

He did not. Here was Farley offering sovs to every Ram in the building, and Pig Boy knew with a gloomy certainty that he would be excluded from the feast, as what could a pig boy bring to the table except pork?

I is in a sort of half-Ram limbo, he thought. Stuck at the pig job, never getting no respect.

Everyone else would pocket the gold, he was certain. Even that little Irish cove hiding over there behind the blades, who were not even a Ram.

Pig Boy chewed on this gristle for a while, and then inspiration struck.

This be a Ram meeting. All civilians were shown the door, 'cept for the dancing girls and lady friends, and yet wee Paddy sits yonder, picking his teeth.

Now would this information be worth a pat on the back? Pig Boy wondered.

Nothing to lose by volunteering it, he decided, and he raised his arm, waving the knife so it glinted in the eyes of old Farley.

"Over here, m'lord," he called. "I gots something to say."

Farley had always despised the monarchy and everything they stood for, so referring to him as *m'lord* was certainly not the way to earn his favor. He squinted across the hall.

Who was it? Who called him *lord*?

The Pig Boy.

"Yes, boy," he said, irritated. "What do you *need* to say?"

This had better be good, he thought. Or I may make another example.

The Pig Boy lowered his knife. "Pardons, yer washup. But this 'strordinary meeting be for brethren, right?"

"That is right, boy," said Farley, his strands of patience already fraying.

"Well," said the boy, pointing his knife into a corner, "he ain't no Ram."

Farley shuffled to the edge of the dais to give himself a better view of the little man hunching down behind the pile of blades. There was something about his silhouette. Something familiar.

"You there," he called. "Step out into the light."

Figary was regretting not slipping away when he had the opportunity. After all, *slipping away* was a skill in which he had years of experience. Top-drawer dippers knew that the getaway was just as important as the dip itself. There wasn't much point in lifting a fat wallet only to stand around waiting for the manacles afterward. This was especially true in Dublin's Monto, where the locals tended to enforce their own street justice and a chap could find himself nursing a stump where his hand used to be, just for the lifting of a few pennies from the wrong pocket.

And now Michael Figary was wishing he had slipped away when the crowds were being ushered from the Hidey-Hole, as this assignment had taken a decidedly dark turn, and the butler had grown quite fond of both being alive and not seeing other people murdered before his eyes.

Michael's dear old mammy had been blessed with a touch of the *sight* and could see danger coming from two counties away, and for the first time Figary knew how that sense of impending danger felt as his stomach churned with a premonition of doom.

This doom turned out to be considerably closer than two

counties as Farley shifted to the side of his stage and called directly to the butler.

"You there," he said. "Step out into the light. Double quick now, before I shoot first and ask questions later."

Figary had no choice but to obey and found himself the focus of every Ram and dancing girl in the Hidey-Hole and, as a lifelong pickpocket, being the center of so much hostile attention made him decidedly nauseated.

"Who are you?" asked Farley. "Why did you not leave with the others?"

"I am quite drunk, so I am," replied Figary truthfully. "I was having a little snooze for myself when the gunfire woke me. Though I did not see who did the shooting. Was there someone injured?"

Figary's accent stirred a memory in Farley. "I know you, don't I?"

Michael Figary's sense of doom intensified and he felt light-headed.

Or perhaps I am sobering up. A horrifying thought.

"You do not know me as such, though I have dropped quite the sheaf of bank notes at your tables over the years. I tend to make wild bets after a snifter or two."

Farley was not swallowing this story. He remembered following Malarkey back to Grosvenor Square one night, with a view to possibly murdering him in his bed. And who had answered the door on that night and spoken in precisely that accent, which had carried clear across the street?

"No. No. I know you." He snapped his fingers. "I have you. The commodore's man. Malarkey's manservant."

The moment he let the words out, Farley knew he should have kept them in, for if this imp was here, then Malarkey must have sent him, which meant that King Otto yet lived and was sending out his tendrils to feel out the lie of the land. If the Rams were allowed to question this man, they might glean information that Farley did not wish to be gleaned, for had he not just now sworn that the king was dead? And if he was lying about that important fact, by extension he was probably lying about the gold.

They will tear me apart, Farley realized and he suddenly wished he had brought a team into the building with him.

Do not panic, Major, he ordered himself. *You have been in tighter spots, and the team waits outside. All it takes is a single burst of squawk on the radio, and you will be surrounded by special forces in seconds.*

But seconds could be too long if this butler person blurted out that Malarkey was alive.

I need to close his mouth immediately and permanently, Farley realized.

"You are a spy!" he said, raising his pistol.

"A spy, is it?" said Figary, highly offended, even though it was true. "A spy on whose behalf?"

Rather than wait for an answer, Figary ducked behind the heap of blades, and this was a wise move to make, as Farley emptied the rest of his clip into the shining steel, setting bayonets and cutlasses a-ringing like church bells and demolishing the casual structure. By the clip's end, Figary crouched shivering and exposed but miraculously unhurt, which was more than could be said for Pig Boy who, in a flash of poetic justice, had suffered a ricochet to the gluteus maximus that would make it difficult for him to sit down for several weeks.

While Farley delved into his belt for a second clip, Figary ripped aside the makeshift canvas curtain, only to find the window boarded up, something he could possibly have taken care of, given half an hour and a hammer. But he had neither tools nor time, and before he could so much as duck down behind the pew, Figary heard an ominous *click* that he somehow knew was the precursor to another spluttering string of *bang-bangs*.

This is it, so it is, he thought. My dear mam always told me bacon was bad for the health.

But salvation—or at least temporary reprieve—was at hand, in the shape of one of the dancing girls.

"Hey there. Major Farley. Mr. Hangman. Is there something you're not telling these fine upstanding gentlemen?"

The accent was American, and the tone was brim-full of impudence, which made it impossible not to search for the speaker.

It was one of the dancing girls. Dark-skinned and pretty and destined to be a true beauty if London did not grind her down. Her eyes were wide and brown, and her bare arms were tanned and muscled. One crooked elbow rested on the militia cannon in a manner that was wild and somehow threatening.

Farley was confused. Did he know this girl? She called him *Hangman,* just as Vallicose had.

He stamped his foot, shutting away these questions and confusions until later in the day, when everyone who should be dead was dead and he could afford such luxuries as ponderings and searching his memories for half-forgotten faces.

"Silence, girl. You have no right to speak in this house."

"That isn't very modern of you," said the girl, and she scraped a long, thin stick along the length of the cannon, which Farley now noticed was pointed directly at the ceiling over his head. The thin stick was a match.

"Ha!" said Farley. "That cannon has lain there for the best part of a year. You don't think it's loaded, do you, wench?"

Wench was not really a twentieth-century word. It wasn't a nineteenth-century word, for that matter, but Farley liked it.

A blue-yellow flame sputtered into life at the matchstick's tip, and suddenly the entire room was interested in how this thing would work out. It really was like the stuff of storybooks: the mean old crook facing off against a bonny lass would be sport enough, but throw a multishot pistol and a cannon into the mix, and you had yourself a potboiler, no mistake.

"I don't know if it's loaded or not," said the girl, tipping the matchstick for a larger flame. "Outside the palace, I would say no. But here, in the company of these dogs, I would guess they keep it loaded for devilment. And I would also guess it's been fired before, and that's why the axle broke."

Farley blinked. This was indeed true. The cannon had

been fired three times since Christmas. The last ball went through the roof and killed a horse clear across the river.

Figary was forgotten now.

Forgotten.

He could have stripped down to his long johns and danced a jig and no one would have bothered him with their attention. What was he compared to a little minx and a cannon?

"I fink Bessie might be loaded," said a Ram with the pelt of a fox tied around his waist.

"Nah," said another. "Bessie ain't been loaded for weeks. And anyway, the powder would be soppier than a Valentine's verse."

"I applaud your metaphor, Mr. Oxendale," said Fox Pelt.

"And I applaud your knowledge of literary devices," said Oxendale, bowing.

Farley lost his cool. He had been holding his temper for years, but now that it was out of the bag, he had trouble stuffing it back in.

"Shut your mouths, fools! I am dealing with a situation here."

"Put down the gun, Major," said the girl. "I have plenty of matchsticks." And to prove her point, she lit a second from the first.

Farley raised his gun, and the girl quickly ducked behind the cannon's broad barrel.

"Step away from the cannon," he ordered.

"And then what?" said the girl mockingly. "You won't shoot me?"

When the girl ducked under the cannon, her hair shifted slightly as it knocked the barrel.

A wig! thought Farley. Of course.

"Savano," he said. "I know you."

In response, Chevron Savano lit a third match, holding it dangerously close to the touch hole.

"Kill her!" shouted Farley. "One hundred sovereigns for the man who brings me her head."

The Rams considered this. The Battering Ram oath did preclude certain female-related activities, specifically the insulting of a member's mother and the murdering, without severe provocation, of a female, but gold was gold and this dancing girl was fiddling around with a cannon, which could certainly be considered provocation.

There was a ragged roar as several Rams decided to hell with the oath and rushed the cannon, leaving Chevie no choice but to light the cannon's fuse. Those who were rushing reared back, and those who had not rushed hunkered down; and it was just as well, for, without so much as a heartbeat's delay, the cannon proved itself to be indeed loaded by firing its fifty-pound missile at a steep angle into the Hidey-Hole's ceiling, which decided that this was the final straw of abuse and collapsed concentrically, from the breach outward.

The noise sequence, though expected, was still astounding. It began with a metallic *vuuuumppp* as the ball traveled the length of the barrel. That was followed by a concussive roar, like the crash of a thousand waves on a shoreline of tin and glass, as the cannon hawked its ball into the air. Much of the ceiling was turned to dust by the impact on the way up, and the last remaining wooden beam was blown to splinters as the ball, having completed its arc, whistled to earth once more, bringing a rain of slate, timber, steel, and stone in its wake.

For those inside the Hidey-Hole, the experience was akin to being in an erupting volcano. Devastation rained down from above as they stumbled in circles, clutching their bleeding ears.

Chevie thought, *I never really respected cannonballs till now.*

And:

I really hope Farley is dead, so he will never hang a single soul.

And:

I think this wig looked pretty good until it got blown off.

She had no such luck re her second thought of Farley being dead. She picked through the wreckage and found him merely unconscious with a gash on the forehead from some shrapnel or other and thought, *Well, at least he is having a bad day.*

It did occur to Chevie that were she to finish Farley off now, then she could possibly avert all the public hangings he would get up to; but she was herself, after all, and no cold-blooded murderer, so she contented herself with stealing his weapons bag and radio.

"You are losing a lot of gear today, Major," she said, patting his cheek. "If you keep going like this, you'll end up fighting your great revolution with stern words and tattoo needles."

Though the jeers flowed easily from her mouth, a part of Chevie was appalled that she could speak in this fashion to Major Anton Farley, the Blessed Hangman.

Don't think that way, she told herself. The queen will not hang, my dad will not be executed, and neither will DeeDee.

After all, there were four of them now, and they had two satchels of weapons.

What could go wrong?

On the other side of the room, Figary had sunk to his hunkers and was thinking,

Forgive me, Mammy. But you can't leave toffee apples in a jug and expect a child not to eat them.

Which was something that had been weighing on his mind since childhood.

Someone grabbed his lapels and yanked him to his feet. He looked, and it was Miss Savano.

"Otto sent me as backup, in case you needed it."

Figary's heart swelled with sudden affection for his employer, quite forgetting that it was Malarkey who had sent him on this insane errand in the first instance.

"The commodore. He is a saint, so he is."

Chevie noticed several black-clad men entering quietly through the front doors.

Special forces, she thought. Missus Figary's son is not the only one with backup, so he isn't.

"I think we should leave," she said.

Figary nodded. "Agreed. I could do with a drink, so I could."

Chevie handed the stolen bag to Figary. "Hold this. I need both hands free in case someone gets in our way."

Figary hung the bag on his shoulder. "I will guard it, if

not with my life, then at least until someone threatens my life."

Luckily, as the section of wall beside them had disappeared, there was nothing to impede their hurried exit. They climbed through the rubble and found plenty to impede them on the other side of the wall.

Inspecting the hole were two soldiers dressed in black capes that covered all but the stubby barrels of their automatic weapons.

"Hands up," said the first soldier, and Chevie got the impression that the man was hoping they would not comply.

"You need to make it back to Grosvenor Square," she whispered to Figary from the side of her mouth. "Otto needs to know the plan."

Figary understood that Miss Chevie was about to have a go at these big burly soldiers, and he whispered to her that this was a very bad idea and they should bide their time, but he was whispering to the air, as Chevie had already made her move.

The soldiers had been caught by surprise, with their weapons still hidden beneath their short capes. There was an actual drill that Colonel Box had devised whereby soldiers could practice getting the flaps of their capes out of the way with maximum efficiency. It was a simple duo of movements. First both hands were thrust down and out, *shooting the cuffs,* as it was known; then the elbows were lifted sharply, as if to break the noses of tall attackers, thus flipping back the cape's wings and leaving the hands perfectly positioned to grasp the heretofore concealed weapon. This maneuver took one-point-five seconds, but Chevie covered the ground between her and the soldiers in one-point-three seconds—and she would have done it faster had her voluminous skirt not caused a bit of drag.

"Run!" she shouted at Figary, who stood frozen in surprise. "Go."

"How dare you?" shouted Figary, breaking his freeze. "Missus Figary did not raise her boy to leave girleens in danger."

Then two more soldiers came through the hole and joined the scuffle and Chevie disappeared under the pile of men so quickly that her wig stayed in the air for a moment after her. At this point Figary remembered a Shakespeare quote his mother had often trotted out: *Discretion is the better part of valor.*

And what is a good quality for a butler, Michael Figary, he asked himself, *if not discretion?*

And he clutched Farley's bag tight to his chest and vamoosed down the avenue toward a line of cabs on the Haymarket.

10 » TELL-TALE FUTURE SLUGS

The old maxim that every action has a reaction is true, but when you start messing with time travel, that reaction could take place in a whole different universe.
—Professor Charles Smart

GROSVENOR SQUARE, MAYFAIR, LONDON, 1899

WOODROW ROSENBAUM WAS THE YOUNGEST soldier in Colonel Box's original unit that had time-jumped back from twentieth-century London. At the time, Rosenbaum had been pretty anxious to get the hell out of Dodge, so to speak, because he had been way down the debt hole with a couple of London shylocks, with no reasonable hope of climbing out, short of robbing a bank. And now he was in deep again with Victorian bookmakers, specifically the Ram king, Otto Malarkey. So this assignment suited him very well indeed. Two birds with one stone, as it were. He was carrying out his orders and wiping clean his debt. Not that it mattered in the long term, because Malarkey had lost his crown; but Rosenbaum did not want the details of his gambling problem getting back to the colonel, who considered gambling a horribly inefficient use of currency.

Rosenbaum was the colonel's go-to guy when it came to up-close assassinations. Box still liked to take the long shots himself and then send a cleaner in to dig out the slugs, but for knife work there was no one better than Woodrow Rosenbaum. And knife work did not require a cleanup team, as there were no tell-tale future slugs left in the body; so the corpses could be left where they fell if necessary, though the colonel usually preferred them to be rolled into the river, just in case a zealous inspector traced them back to the catacombs. In this case, it didn't really matter, as there would be plenty of bodies popping up all over London, and one more would not make much difference.

Emergence Day, that's what those two Thundercats called it. Today is Emergence Day.

Providing Farley managed to recruit the Rams. If not, they might not be emerging from the catacombs for a while yet.

Grosvenor Square was a picture this time of morning, with the sun in a clear sky shining down on its clean cobbles and tended park. Rosenbaum ran his fingers over the twin knife hilts in his belt and thought: I don't care what the begrudgers say, a sunny day puts everyone in a better mood.

"Fine morning, is it not?" he said to a pretty flower girl.

"A good day for it," he said to a bobby, who saluted him with a wave of his club.

The bobby did not suspect him of nefarious intention, and why would he? Rosenbaum was dressed up like a common worker, and there were plenty of those swarming over the scaffold that was clamped to Malarkey's secret digs.

Secret, that is, unless an electronic bug has been planted in the precious boots that once belonged to your mentor.

Rosenbaum chuckled. *You will never know how we found you, Otto. You will never even have time to wonder.*

There was a pile of builder's equipment and wares by the front steps. Ducking behind it and then under a drop cloth, Rosenbaum was lost from view in less than a second. In twenty more seconds, he had drawn a flat blade and was working on the latch of an upstairs window. In five more, he was inside Malarkey's house.

He padded across the thick rugs, thinking, *Knock, knock, Commodore. I've come to cancel my debt.*

Riley had fallen asleep on the rug in front of the drawing-room fire, wrapped in his weighted magician's cloak. In fairness to the lad, he was a mere fourteen-year-old boy, and one that had seen more than his fair share of trauma over the past day, and so his body was certainly owed a spot of recuperation. But in the negative column, it had to be said that he had volunteered to stand watch while Malarkey slept, etherized through the worst of the lacerations from his wounds, as Chevie kept watch over Michael Figary. Were Riley an army conscript, this nap would have seen his back against the pocked firing-squad wall. He had not intended to fall asleep, but the warmth of the fire and the sun through the window had proved too much for his weary eyes, so he had shut them for a moment and rolled from his lookout spot on the windowsill onto the soft, deep rug.

Riley smiled in his sleep as the Irish butler entered his dream and muttered the words, "So I am." But then Figary's small frame stretched like pulled taffy and changed into someone else entirely. Someone Riley knew too well, as he dreamed of him most nights.

Riley my boy, said Albert Garrick. *You let me down, son. You betrayed your master. And I will have my revenge.*

And Albert Garrick had loomed over him, raising the very blade he had used to murder Jack the Ripper himself and said, *Slowly I will do it, lad. Slowly, so you feel every stroke.*

Riley bolted awake, shooting up as though electrified, and was amazed to find a man with a knife looming over him.

"G—Garrick?" he stammered. "You ain't real. You ain't here."

It was this surprised awakening that saved his life. Rosenbaum had been poised above him, blade raised for murder, when the boy shot up and startled him back a step or two.

No problem, thought Rosenbaum. A second's delay, is all.

A second was all Riley needed to come fully awake, as he was accustomed to getting his bearings lightning fast. He had never known when Garrick would need him or when he would commence to beating him for no apparent reason. And Riley had often fantasized about the occasion when he would be driven over the edge and finally decide to fight back. He'd planned for this moment so many times that he had choreographed his assault, and it was this strategy, or kata, that he unleashed now on Rosenbaum.

Step one was to twirl in his magician's cloak so that it fanned out to form a black saucer and conceal his exact position. When his attacker lunged, Riley dropped to the ground, leaving Rosenbaum with an armful of cloak, and giving Riley the chance to roll across the room into a patch of breathing space.

In the penny dreadfuls and adventure novels that Riley loved to read, there came a point in every story where the hero would face off against a cold-blooded murderer. They would trade barbs as they fought, and often the battle of wits seemed more important than the clash of steel. But this wasn't the way in real combat. Professionals did not talk when there was killing to be done. They went about their business.

And such was the way of this fight. Rosenbaum was not one of your flamboyant Jack-the-Ripper types; he was a knife fighter who had been told whom to stick his knife into.

Rosenbaum tossed the cape aside and pulled the second knife from his belt, spreading his arms wide to cover both exits to the room. Of course, Riley could choose a window; but they were twelve feet tall and would take time to open, and time was something this boy didn't have. It was important for Rosenbaum to stick him quick, so he couldn't alert Malarkey.

Rosenbaum's mistake was the assumption that the boy would attempt to flee. Then again, how could he have known that Riley had been trained in more martial arts than Rosenbaum had ever heard of?

Riley faked left, and Rosenbaum threw knife number one. It did not spin like a circus thrower's; it flew like a silver streak toward its target, which was not where it was supposed to be, so the knife buried itself in a portrait of Otto—a copy of Martorell's *Saint George Killing the Dragon*, in which Malarkey's own head and nimbus of silky hair replaced Saint George's face and helmet.

Rosenbaum put the dodge down to fluke. After all, what boy could move that quickly, unless by accident? At any rate, he had another knife. Plenty for the job.

Riley's dodge was no fluke; it was step two in his kata when fighting a knife thrower: put some momentum behind a feint, then yank the body backward as if a string controlled it.

Step three was attack, and in this, placement of the feet was the most important element. There were several improvisations that could be made depending on the exact opponent, as long as the feet were in the correct position and the balance was right. Riley took two quick steps forward, leading with his left, bent low, then grabbed the meat of Rosenbaum's inner thigh and squeezed as hard as he could, causing the soldier to put all his energy into holding in a shrill scream. Rosenbaum was not entirely successful in this, and a keening squeal leaked out; for, after all, the inner thigh is a favorite pain center of many attacking disciplines. Rosenbaum drove his second blade straight down to where Riley's head should be, but of course Riley had stepped back, and the soldier's momentum drove the knife tip through the rug and into the floorboards below.

My head is awfully exposed here, thought Rosenbaum, and he was right about that; and the fact that he was fighting a boy meant his head was at the perfect height for Riley to drive his knee upward and catch Rosenbaum under the chin, which he did with all the force he could muster—and after years of imagining just this situation, that was quite an amount of force.

Unfortunately for Rosenbaum, his tongue had been lolling out slightly as he bent over, and when his teeth clacked together, he bit off a good chunk of meat before reeling backward toward the doorway he had come in.

The odds in this particular fight were evening now, as Riley plucked Rosenbaum's second knife from the floor and, judging by how he palmed it between hands, Rosenbaum reckoned the blasted boy knew how to handle a blade. Rosenbaum realized that if he were to bet on this fight, as he had on so many, his cash would be on the boy to win.

But I know something he doesn't, thought Rosenbaum.

And this something was that Rosenbaum always brought a gun on a job. It was against orders, and he'd never had to use it, but Rosenbaum had always reckoned that if it came to it, he could dig the slug out himself and burn the body.

I will burn this whole blasted house down, he thought, and he reached to the small holster at the back of his belt. The holster was there, and the extra magazine, but no gun.

No gun. Had he dropped it?

Rosenbaum spun around to find a small man standing in the doorway, holding the pistol between thumb and forefinger.

"You, my dear intruder fellow," said the little man in a singsong lilt, "have been dipped by the best pickpocket who ever lifted a wallet. You should be honored, so you should."

"What?" shouted Rosenbaum, utterly confused now. This job, which had seemed so simple, had somehow become a twisting nightmare. "What?"

Rosenbaum probably would have shouted *What?* at least one more time, so utterly turned about was he, but Riley picked up one of the iron firedogs from beside the hearth and clocked him hard just behind the right ear. And so the soldier reeled to the window through which he had entered and fell straight out.

"Nicely done, that, boy," said Figary. "Some tea now, I think."

Riley rushed to the window just in time to see Rosenbaum crawl from a pile of planking and take himself shakily off.

"You should forbear from speechifying during a crisis," Riley said to Figary. "What was all that guff about pickpockets and intruder fellows?"

"That was what we call *blather,*" said Figary. "Very useful for distracting a body so that someone else can brain him."

"Why could you not simply shoot the cove?" said Riley.

Figary passed over the gun. "Shoot him? Oh no. Missus Figary's boy abhors committing violent acts."

"But you are not averse to watching them?" Riley pointed out.

"Indeed not. In this particular case, the advantages are twofold. Firstly, my own life is saved, and thank you very much, sir. And secondly, the sin is not on my conscience, so it isn't."

Riley thought he should change the subject of discussion before Figary disappeared down a theological rabbit hole.

"What news of the Rams?" he asked. "Did you see your guardian angel?"

Figary's face fell as he thought on the girl he had abandoned to her fate.

"We should wake the commodore," he said.

11 » THE BLOOMING STINKPIPES

I often think I should just abandon the whole thing. I really do. Time travel could be a gift to humanity. Whoever controls it could do some real good for mankind. But you have to ask yourself, with humanity's track record, is that likely?

—Professor Charles Smart

IT IS A UNIVERSALLY ACCEPTED MAXIM THAT MAKING water in the area where a person drinks water is generally a bad idea, as the waters get muddled, and that person could end up drinking the water he *prepared* earlier, which is never good for the health. Just ask the tens of thousands of Londoners wiped out by cholera.

Until the late 1860s, London sewers fed directly into the Thames, which also provided the city's clouded drinking water, a fact that accounted for more fatalities over the years than war or fire. But there were worse things than being dead, as the rhyme went:

I took a stroll through London town
The smell it near to knocked me down

There ain't no pill nor tot to drink
Can help escape the world's great stink

The Great Stink was how the entire world referred to the London stench that floated up from the sewers and hung in a cloud over the city.

Eventually Queen Vic cried foul and commanded her engineers to fix the blooming stinkpipes, or words to that effect, and so three hundred million bricks were baked to build over eighty miles of tunnels to intercept the effluvium rushing into the Thames.

LONDON SEWERS, 1899

"Efficient sewers was good for the population in general, my little Ramlet," said Otto Malarkey to Riley. "But it was bad news for those of us on the toshing budge."

Riley was impressed by his regent. "You was a tosher, King Otto?"

"Indeed I was, my boy," said Malarkey. "Times were hard in the Malarkey family, so my brothers and I put together a three-man team and down we went into the great underworld. Time was, a man could walk into the tunnels from the Thames's bank, but with the new sewers came new securities, huge gates over the tunnel mouths. If a man was caught in a flush without a handy manhole, he would be flattened like a Shrove Tuesday pancake up against those gates."

They were skirting Regent's Park toward a particular manhole through which Malarkey was certain the colonel's own hidey-hole could be accessed.

"There's money in manure," said Malarkey, quoting the tosher's maxim. "Folks throw away the queerest things, or lose 'em. Either way, they ends up buried in filth, waiting for some tosher to wash 'em off. My brothers and I ran a nice little business, carved out a network for ourselves in central London, where the fattest pickings lie. I found a silver candelabrum once, and I have often wondered how that fit down a flush toilet. Perhaps it was a murder weapon, eh?"

Riley forced himself to listen to Malarkey's tale as an effort to distract his mind from Chevie's predicament. His dear mate was in the clutches of this Colonel Box cove who was in lavender in the sepulchral catacombs below Camden, like some class of subterranean Professor Moriarty. Figary had filled them in on Farley's speech to the Rams, so they knew how time sensitive their mission was. Box had to be stopped today, and Chevie rescued, if she was still . . .

No. I will not even think it.

It was a stroke of amazing fortune that Otto had worked the Camden sewers years previously as a tosher, also known as a stinkpipe magpie. Malarkey knew only too well how those particular sewers flooded regularly and had always overflowed into the railway catacombs until an American colonel had bought them outright and built a waterproof wall that could withstand the regular floodings and the massive flushes.

And if a cove could demolish that wall at the exact time a flush is due, Malarkey had told Riley and Figary, *then Colonel Box and his fine soldiers would find themselves chest-high in floaters and rats.*

It was a loose plan at best, with a million what-ifs floating around it, but it meant that Chevie could possibly be rescued in the chaos, and for that reason alone, Riley's heart and soul were behind it.

What about me? Figary had asked. *I too wish to serve, so I do.*

Stay here, Malarkey told him. *When the deed is done, I will send for you. You are my eyes in London town, Michael. And I will need to know how our sabotage has been received by the Rams.*

They found their manhole and lingered in the environs all innocent and such until the path was clear of all those taking their daily constitutional. Malarkey pulled a strange tool from his satchel that put Riley in mind of a metal animal claw.

"One time in the Bailey, the justice says, he says that my brother was soft in the noggin," said Malarkey, inserting the tool's prongs in corresponding holes in the manhole. "And yet he made up this manhole jemmy from a few old cutoffs. I've never seen the better of it for popping biscuits."

Malarkey put his weight on the handle, and up swung the manhole like a clamshell.

"Down you go, lad," said Malarkey.

Riley had endured many trials and survived many tribulations, and yet he felt a crippling fear now at the thought of descending into the Stygian darkness, into the embrace of damp and reeking fingers. The terror sat like a deadweight on his shoulders. A chain-mail cloak of fear.

"Me? I should go first?"

Malarkey spoke through gritted teeth. "Look sharp, lad. This biscuit ain't holding itself open."

I should be off with myself. What care I for kings and kingdoms? thought Riley, and he was ashamed of his own survival instincts. *Chevie needs me to squirrel down this hole. If I don't, then the whole entire plan is doomed.*

Riley gathered his courage and swung his legs into the manhole. His toes found a slick rung and wiggled full onto it.

"Cripes alive, kiddo," said Malarkey, his voice shaking slightly with strain. "Shift yerself. There ain't nothing to fear in darkness."

This, Riley knew, was patently untrue. Albert Garrick waited for him inside the folds of a shadow, and someday Riley would voluntarily wander into the wrong one. It was simply a matter of when.

Not today. Please not today.

Down he climbed, inch by inch, clanking as he went, fingers wrapped in death grips on the sweating, bubbled metal rungs, shoulders scraping the brickwork.

Tight, he thought. This is so very tight.

And the fear rose in him again, but he swallowed it down, thinking, *You are the Great Savano. Darkness is a magician's friend.*

This notion was helpful, and soon Riley heard a squelch as his feet touched the sewer floor.

Don't think about that noise, he told himself. Or the ungodly stench. Just remember that Chevie needs you to be brave.

It wasn't really fair to take issue with the smell. After all, he had climbed of his own volition into a sewer tunnel and that was where the smell belonged. He was the interloper here.

He sensed the space opening up around him, and heard the gurgle stretch out, an invisible ribbon in the darkness.

I still draw breath, he thought. Though I would prefer not to.

Malarkey made a big job of his climb. Grunting and cursing the ladder for a useless stretch of iron, fit only for children and dwarfs. Riley could feel the heat of him filling the chamber, and he stepped aside just as King Otto thumped down beside him.

"I ain't missed this one jot," he said, fumbling in his haversack for a lantern and matches. "A person ain't human down here, or perhaps human is all he is. Ain't no room for put-ons or graces down in the pit."

Malarkey struck up the lamp, casting a cone of sickly light ahead of them down the sewer tunnel. Dark furred things squeaked their alarm and skittered from the light. They seemed to Riley too big to be rats.

"What moves, King Otto?" he asked. "What squeaks?"

Otto laughed. "They is rats, right enough, but they seem bigger. You is suffering from what they calls *tunnel vision.* Everything nasty seems enlarged to gargantuan proportions." Otto squinted ahead into the darkness. "Except that one. He is indeed a giant."

Riley gazed down the tunnel with its weeping walls and dripping stalactites. A monster rat sat on his hind paws bang in the center of the sewage stream, his teeth like candle flames.

He will move, thought Riley. Surely he will quit his post.

But no, King Rat stood his ground, whiskers twitching in the lamplight.

"That one's a sentry," whispered Otto. "He's giving us fair warning."

Riley whispered back. "Ain't he afraid?"

"What? Of the likes of you and me? Ask yerself: which of us is more suited to this environment? Which of us can summon a million of his pals with a couple of squeaks?"

"So, what do we do? Quit altogether?"

Malarkey pushed Riley ahead of him. "No, we walks slowly by and don't look him in his milky beadies, and hopefully Mr. Rat will grant us safe passage. And anyway, it ain't the rats you got to fret about in the stinkpipe."

Riley decided he would circle around to that last statement shortly, but for now his mind was bent to the task of not doing the Hoxton Shuffle, so named for the involuntary gesticulations of one particularly energetic inmate of Hoxton House lunatic asylum.

Stay calm, he told himself. *You are on a mission. You have seen worse things than an oversized rat.*

This was true, but thinking on those worse things made Riley believe that they might be concealed in the shadows, shifting themselves to avoid the lantern beam.

They went to both sides of the rat, following the path of the sewage that parted at his paws, with the exception of the solids that lumped and piled around his midriff in an eerie facsimile of a sentry's box. The rat twitched a mite at their passage but otherwise paid them no mind.

"What ho," breathed Malarkey. "King Rat does not sniff a threat."

The sewer tunnel curved gently, and the pale light picked out edges and grooves in the stonework. Several areas of the ceiling had collapsed inward, exposing dark earth above that writhed with roots and worms. In some places blessed light penetrated from above, and Riley welcomed its warmth on his face even though its presence meant the tunnel was not sound.

"Onward, boy," Otto urged him when he dawdled. "Ain't no time now for moon-facing. We got destruction to wreak."

Earlier, in the house on Grosvenor Square, it had seemed so sensible to formulate a plan. To map out their movements in a logical way so that their actions would have predictable outcomes. But now, buried in this tunnel of horrors, it seemed impossible that any plan could bend this grimness to their own design.

Malarkey turned the light on Riley's face. "You've caught yerself a dose of the morbs. Feels like the tunnel is closing in, don't it? Feels like nothing is going to work out?"

Riley nodded. He didn't want to look a total weeping willow before his king, so it was better to nod than speak.

"Yep, the morbs," said Otto. "Barnabus used to get 'em something awful down here. Big fellow like him afraid of a few rats. He said it weren't the darkness what did him in, it was the no light." Malarkey shrugged. "Never understood that myself."

Riley remembered something that he considered urgent

enough for immediate speech. "Your Highness, you said it weren't the rats I had to fret about in the stinkpipe. What, then? What should I fret about?"

"Why, everything, Ramlet," cried the king jovially. "Every-blooming-thing conspires against a man in this unnatural excavation. The sludge beneath your boots is teeming with cholera. The bricks have got edges what will flay you quicker than a meat-man's hatchet, and if you don't bleed to death, then a speck of diseased mortar in the bloodstream will see you bottle-green by day's end. There are invisible devils in the tunnels, too. If we happens across a cloud of chokey gas, then king and subject will be for the big sleep together. And of course there's the pump house."

Riley felt so sick with fear at this point that he decided he might as well hear about the pump house. "The pump house?"

"Well, say Her Majesty's engineers sign off on a flush while we are *sub-terra*. There won't be no warning, as we ain't supposed to be down here."

"But that's the whole point of our plan, ain't it, Your Majesty? We passed chink to the pump-house Johnny? No flush till you say so."

"We passed chink to *one* of the pump-house Johnnies," said Malarkey. "But I find that any plan which involves a combination of public servants, timing, and machinery has a top-notch chance of spectacular failure."

Riley reckoned that if he hadn't had a case of the morbs previously, then he definitely had one now.

On they walked, squelching and splashing, hearing their

own footsteps echo down the tunnel as though ghosts walked ahead of them. The sewer floor was mostly curved at a uniform sweep, except where it buckled like a giant serpent or split to allow nature through in the form of earth humps or tree roots. Malarkey's lamp splashed pale light on the bricks so that they seemed yellow and ocher, and not the burnt orange that they probably were. Some stretches seemed more ill-used than others, with collapsed walls and brick-melt left in the aftermath of a great acidic deluge from the evening "rush hour" or a good post-Christmas flushing.

"Oh," said Malarkey brightly. "I clean forgot to mention the creepy-crawlies what seem to flourish in this sepulchral stinkhole."

Riley felt the morbs settle on his brow. "Please, Your Majesty. I got enough on my plate."

"Well, you won't want nuffink on your plate when you gets an earhole full of these nasties."

Riley did not object further, as it was obvious the particulars of these creatures were coming his way.

"Of course you've got your regular insectoids, only magnified by a nourishing diet of dung, which is like caviar and champagne to cock-a-roaches and beetles. I seen a beetle down here one time take on a rat, and the rat would've bested a dog."

This was so ridiculous that Riley relaxed a little.

"That's awful," said Riley, but he must have somehow, in a slump of his shoulders perhaps, revealed a slight lessening in anxiety, which spurred His Majesty to describe greater horrors.

"And you may perhaps notice a glow betimes in a dark corner."

"Please, King Otto, tell me not."

"Scorpions," continued Malarkey, relishing the word. "Luminous scorpions. They got acid in their sting. Melt a man down in a minute or three. I seen a cow once done in by sewer scorpions. Nothing left but horns and a tail."

Riley swallowed. Surely that was the worst of it. Surely.

"But the absolute worst is the . . ." Malarkey said sotto voce, ". . . crigs."

"Crigs!" exclaimed Riley, earning himself a cuff around the ear from his regent.

"Never say it aloud. . . . Crigs . . . is like the devil. Speaking their name aloud summons 'em."

Riley mouthed the cursed creatures' moniker, followed by: "What are they?"

Malarkey took great delight in telling him. "They is a godless creature, half crab, half pig."

Ten feet up, Riley would have slapped his knee and scoffed. *Crab-pigs? That ain't even bordering on possible.*

But down here.

In a tunnel.

Riley had seen strange things in a tunnel, things that would make these crigs seem like the very epitome of everyday.

There was an important question that needed asking. "These . . . creatures. Are they pig size or crab size?"

"Pony-sized," said Malarkey. "At the very least."

• • •

Malarkey navigated the turns with confidence, and as they neared Regent's Canal, the flow rose to Riley's knees, and he had to pick his steps carefully to avoid a dunking. Malarkey caught him by the collar once when a brick shifted under his weight.

"Whoops there, Ramlet," he said. "This is one place where a small drop leads to the big drop, so to speak. If you do happen to submerge, shut yer gob and snort air out yer nose till you finds yer feet, to keep the cholera at bay."

"Is that an effective preventative?" Riley asked.

"Dunno rightly," admitted Otto. "Sounds logical, dunnit?" He glanced sharply at Riley. "I ain't a doctor, you know. Here I is, saving your life and whatnot, and all I get for me troubles is sauce. Quit with yer questions, boy, and keep yer mind on yer feet." Malarkey kicked one foot out in front of him, raising a scythe of water in the pool of light. "Now, look—you made me forget me grammars. Listen to me, spouting *yer* in the stead of *your.* That was three *yers* in a single breath. Figary would have a fit."

"So he would," said Riley, daring to insert a joke at this juncture. It was a risk that paid off, and the two of them shared a chuckle as far as the next junction, which brought them to a wide stone abutment, built not from brick but a pale molded stone, reinforced with steel rods.

"I would feel reasonably confident that we have arrived at our destination," said Malarkey, as he rapped the dam. "Reinforced concrete supporting the arch. Sets underwater, you know. Ingenious. For most coves it would be a shame to destroy something like this, but luckily for us I have always taken a perverse pleasure in tearing down structures what have been meticulously erected by others. Some call it a character failing, I call it a leadership quality, for what were Alexander the Great or Richard the Lionheart but mighty destroyers?" He held out a hand toward Riley. "Chisel and mallet, if you please. I shall take the first crack at this barricade."

Riley found the chisel in his satchel, beside the detonators, which were sealed in waxed paper.

"Your High Rammity," he said, passing them over with some ceremony, which pleased Malarkey.

Malarkey smiled, stretching his door-knocker beard and mustache. "Thank you, loyal subject. Very soon the throne will be mine once more." His gaze drifted for a moment, doubtless thinking about the very same fleece-draped throne, then he was back to business. He set the lantern down on a half-crumbled plinth, dislodging a curious rat, then instructed Riley to set out their stock of candles.

"Not in a pentagram, mind," he warned. "We got enough odds against us as things stand."

Riley found nooks for his candles, careful not to graze his skin on the sweating bricks, and while he cupped matchsticks against the tunnel draft, Malarkey plied the concrete wall with his chisel, which he had covered with a cloth both to avoid sparks and keep the noise down as much as possible.

"Barnabus!" he grunted as he worked. "Barnabus."

It struck Riley that Malarkey had volunteered for first crack. That implied that second crack would be his.

And there ain't no magic trick I can employ to pulverize concrete that I have not had the opportunity to tamper with.

"A light, a light!" shouted Malarkey. "My kingdom for a light. Shine it here, Ramlet."

Riley grabbed the lantern and elevated it to the limit of his reach. Already Malarkey had cleared a potato-sized hole.

"This wall ain't so very tough," he said. "In fact, it's rotted to putty in some spots. Milady Sewer can have that effect on even the stoniest heart. Methinks this entire construction would bust into clay on its lonesome in a few flushes' time."

"Wonderful!" cried Riley. "A couple of jiffies and you will be clean through, and we can climb us a nice ladder back to the sun."

"Barnabus!" said Malarkey in a strange grunt-speak combination.

But not as strange a combination as the accursed crigs, thought Riley, keeping his eyes peeled for creatures that he would swear to not believing in.

Malarkey made such good progress with his assault on the concrete, and so intent was he on the job, that he did indeed break through the wall in a jiffy or two. Ten at the most.

Otto threw the mallet and chisel from him. "What say thee now, Master Wall? Come between Malarkey and his vengeance, shall thee?"

That is quite the bundle of *thees,* thought Riley. Would

Missus Figary's son approve of this verbal jaunt into the past? And following this, he thought: Those tools may rest where they lie, for never will my hand scrabble around on this fetid riverbed.

Malarkey rested palms on knees for a moment, then spat. "Your turn, lad."

Though he was the junior, Riley was entrusted with the explosives work. After all he was a magician, trained by the West End's best, well-versed in the handling and manipulation of potions and volatiles, powder bombs, flash bangs, and other such delicates. What Chevie had given him from Farley's bag was ahead of its time viz its effectiveness, but the principles were the same. She had gone through the contents with them earlier that day.

Plug the hole with the plastic, screw in a detonator, and then get far away. When the time comes we will set her off by radio.

A radio bomb, thought Riley. That probably ain't what Mr. Marconi had in mind when he created all that fuss a while back with his radio Morse code.

Riley put down the lamp and reached into his bag for the small block of plastic explosive.

More powerful than a barrel of dynamite and safer to tote around than nitroglycerin.

He rolled the *plastique* between his palms until he had a sausage of destruction roughly the same size as the hole in the wall.

The Sausage of Destruction. *A good name for a penny dreadful.*

Riley's eye was good, and the sausage fit neatly into Malarkey's groove, blending in perfectly with the concrete. With a jot of fortune, it would not be noticed on the other side.

"Presto!" he said, but Malarkey was not impressed.

"It don't look like no great caboodle," he sniffed. "A single cigar for all that wall? Don't seem possible."

"You saw what old man Farley did with a future gun," argued Riley.

"Hmmm," hmmmed Malarkey. "I seen something, right enough, but I ain't swallowing that future twaddle without a good chew."

"The proof is in the sausage, King Otto," said Riley, pleased with his little joke.

Otto liked that one too, and his laughter echoed down the tunnel, fading as it turned the corner. But another noise was riding the tunnel, a series of regular splashings.

Footsteps.

"Crigs!" shouted Riley.

"Or sewer cannibals," said Malarkey.

"Sewer cannibals!" hissed Riley. "You never mentioned those previous."

"I reckoned you had enough on yer plate with the crigs."

They stood still as statues, both hoping the splashes would take another turning and pass them by, but the exact opposite occurred. The splashes grew louder and more numerous.

"Six troops," judged Malarkey. "And they knows where they is going."

Again, thought Riley. How do they find us? Does the colonel have powers like they say?

"Well," said Otto, "we ain't gonna just illuminate ourselves all polite. Candles, boy."

Candles. Of course. Riley stepped as quietly as he could through the murky water, tipping each candle from its perch. They landed in the sewage with a plop and hiss. Malarkey closed the shutters on the lantern.

"Now, boy, hold on to my belt and wade, I tell you. Do not lift those feet unless we are eyeballed."

Riley did as he was told, wrapping his fingers around Otto's belt and following his regent, both dredging their boots through the mud, feeling the slow slush of sewage around their ankles, and the soft knock of semisolids against their shins. And even though their lives were in danger, he found a small space in his mind to be disgusted.

I will never smell right again, he thought.

He must have shivered, for Malarkey whispered back to him.

"You is probably fretting over your hair. Don't be. The fetid air is surprisingly nourishing for a cove's locks."

"Excellent news," Riley whispered back. "I am much comforted."

Riley felt Malarkey tense, and reckoned his sarcasm had been detected.

"I will box your ears later," said King Otto.

Riley almost looked forward to it, for getting his ears

boxed would mean surviving their sewer jaunt, which at the moment was far from a sure bet.

Malarkey steered them with the flow downstream, a mite from the great concrete abutment and into a bricked nook with a lower vaulted ceiling that brushed Riley's crown as he followed Malarkey in. They huddled together inside the pitch-black corner, a whirlpool of filth swirling down a minor sinkhole between their feet.

Malarkey was forced to bend low so his door-knocker beard brushed Riley's ear.

"I wants you to know, lad," he whispered, "as you've been a decent cove to me recently, that there will be no surrendering should it come to it. Otto Malarkey ain't fleeing *tail out* for the pleasure of a bullet to the brain pan. If we are rumbled, then I is going to bestow the Order of the Boot on these future coves, if that's what they be. You blend in with the larger floaters and make yer way clear."

Riley could not help but be a little indignant at the very notion that he could blend with the larger floaters.

"What?"

"Sorry," said Malarkey contritely. "I meant to say, make *your* way clear. Don't squeal to Figary."

"But . . ."

"Shhh, now, lad. We are as the dead."

Darkness hung over them like a blanket and in consequence, sounds appeared amplified. They heard with crystal clarity the gurgle and hiss of water flowing past their hiding place. They heard the occasional distant cluster of squeaks as a huddle of rats clicked past on their claws. And they heard the inexorable approach of trained men. There were no shouts or barging splashes, just slight rhythmic sluicing of the underground river of waste.

They are approaching from both ends of the tunnel, thought Riley. A pincer movement.

As they huddled in their corner, slowly the light revealed itself, brightening by a single shade the darkness upstream. Perhaps there was a breach in the arches, or perhaps a manhole had been left open. Either way, Riley was glad of the light, as it had come to symbolize life to him, even though he realized that they would be visible to their pursuers should they think to search the niche.

The waiting was almost unbearable. More than once the notion popped into Riley's mind that it would be better to abandon all caution and run hell for leather to their manhole. At least then the cursed wait would be over.

I had thought that never again in this life would I be as afraid as I was with Garrick, but now that familiar dread has returned to my gut.

And then a peculiar thing happened in that dank hellhole: Riley's fear evaporated.

I cannot possibly survive yet another brush with old Jack the Reaper, he realized. Soon I will be at the Pearlies, with my dear mum waiting there for me.

This notion made him smile, a smile he quickly extinguished in case his teeth might glow.

Just because a fellow doesn't fear the big drop no more, doesn't mean he welcomes it.

Now, instead of fear ruling his thoughts, Riley's natural intelligence rose to the surface.

I will not be blending with the larger floaters, he thought. I will be fighting beside my king.

And these soldiers might be surprised at how well he could fight; after all, Riley had been trained in the martial arts by his erstwhile master: Albert Garrick.

Otto Malarkey will realize my worth before I go, he vowed silently.

The men drew nearer from both sides, until they congregated in a dark huddle directly in front of the niche. Malarkey and Riley held their breaths, tensing themselves for battle, but black as the tunnel was, their nook was blacker. Shadows upon shadows, folded in velvet layers. Even a bat would pass them by. They could not be seen from beyond spitting distance, and the first one to venture inside that radius would pay the price for it.

Or so a reasonable person would think.

Then came a familiar voice from the bunch.

"You there, crouching in your nook. We can see you clear as day."

Farley. The murdering tattooist.

Bluff. It must be.

Malarkey's fingers gripped Riley's shoulder and it was clear he thought the same.

Bluff. They got nothing but front.

The voice spoke again, flat and mocking. "Yes, that's right, Otto. You two boys hug each other tight, and perhaps we'll just go away."

Malarkey removed his hand, and Riley knew what was next. The king was a tosher, and he fancied his chances in a tunnel.

Farley's voice floated from the shadows. "I see you, Malarkey, reaching into your pocket all sneaky. What have you got in there? A blade? Some old one-shot piece? Or even my gun, which is almost out of bullets?"

This was no bluff. The traitor could see their every move. "You two are literally up that creek everyone keeps talking about. Would you like to see how far up the creek you are?"

He snapped his fingers and all at once a dozen focused red beams sprang from the darkness.

The devil's eyes, Malarkey had called them. Where they went, death followed.

The beams sought out the hiding pair and painted their faces and chests.

"You know what the lasers are, right, Otto?" called Farley. "You've seen one before, when I put down your animal of a brother. So come on out, and we'll go talk to the *Blessed* Colonel. We only want to talk."

The shadowy mass shuddered as the men laughed. No one believed this.

"Very well, that's not the whole truth," admitted Farley. "We only want to talk . . . first."

Riley felt Otto squat low, and he knew this was not the bended knee of submission, but the crouch of a wild cat gathering itself to pounce.

Sorry, Your Majesty, thought Riley, reaching into his vest packets for some paper twists. *This time I go first.*

Riley stepped high onto Otto's horizontal back, then threw himself up and out, directly into the path of a dozen crisscrossing laser beams.

12 » THUNDERBOLT

The common wisdom is that a person traveling in time should not touch anything or interact with anyone, but what if someone touches and interacts with you?
—Professor Charles Smart

London Sewers, 1899

LUNKA WITMEYER APPEARED ONE HUNDRED PERCENT ready for action as she stood beside Major Farley in the sewer water, but internally she was experiencing something of a professional crisis. There were several contributory factors, the main one being the time tunnel trip itself. This was a pretty *beyond the call of duty* kind of experience, and yet Clover Vallicose was acting as though they had done nothing more extraordinary than take the wrong exit from the highway. It was all very *meant to be* as far as Clover was concerned. Destiny sucked them back in time a century or so and dumped them in musty catacombs that were shrinking Witmeyer's sinus cavities to pinholes and demoting her, as a woman, to a second-class citizen. Witmeyer did not like being a second-class citizen, and she was smart enough to see the irony in the fact that she was resenting the treatment that she herself had dished out to others for so long.

The tracker in Malarkey's boot tells us he is in the adjacent sewers, which is too close for comfort. Do you think you can handle a local gangster? Box had asked her.

This was language Witmeyer could understand.

And a hundred more like him, she had said confidently.

No need for hyperbole, Sister Witmeyer. Answer plainly and there can be no misunderstandings. In my opinion, bluster and exaggeration lead to crossed wires, which is . . .

Let me guess, Witmeyer had thought. *Inefficient.*

Inefficient, Clayton Box had said.

And even worse than being lectured by Box was the fact that apparently Clover had become Box's right-hand woman, while she herself was trolling the sewers, hunting for strays.

You go with Major Farley, Clover had told her (ordered her, in fact) thirty minutes ago. *I can't leave the Blessed Colonel at this delicate point in the operation.*

The Blessed Colonel, indeed.

Box was like any other man. He liked having his ego stroked, and as long as Clover kept filling his head with tales of how venerated he would be in the future, she would be guaranteed a place at the Blessed Colonel's side.

And though Witmeyer was obeying Clover's order, her heart wasn't in the work; she was only doing it on the off chance that she would get to stamp on this Malarkey's face and put the smile back on her own. But even this hope of a little lighthearted entertainment was snatched from her by Box's addendum to Clover's command: *Oh, and Witmeyer, bring him back here alive, if possible. Otto Malarkey has been plotting against me, and I need to know what he has set in motion.*

In her current mood, Lunka Witmeyer half felt like joining Malarkey in his plot, whatever that might prove to be. It was likely that there was in fact no mysterious plot, and this so-called King Otto was simply a common thug sniffing around the peripheries of the group he once controlled, searching for a way back in. This entire mission was a fool's errand, and a Thundercat's time should not be wasted on it.

I am not being appreciated, she realized now, up to her knees in human and animal slop. *I might as well not even be here.*

The resentment and bitterness choking Witmeyer's heart were new emotions to her. In many ways Witmeyer's social development had been drastically stunted by her career choice, in that her mode of interaction with others was usually violent and intimidating. In matters of the heart she was very much an adolescent. At this precise moment, more than a century outside her comfort zone, standing in a torrent of filth with people who openly despised her, Witmeyer was confused and lonely, which made her very receptive to the emotion that was about to break over her in a tidal wave of endorphins.

On both sides of her, the colonel's soldiers were having a fine time watching Malarkey and his boy through their night vision goggles, and strobing them with their laser sights.

"You know what the lasers are, right, Otto?" called Farley.

"You've seen one before, when I put down your animal of a brother. So come on out, and we'll go talk to the *Blessed* Colonel. We only want to talk."

The men laughed, and Witmeyer got the feeling they were laughing at her as well as Malarkey.

Paranoid. I'm getting paranoid.

"Very well, that's not the whole truth," said Farley. "We only want to talk . . . first."

Lame, thought Witmeyer. All this stupid posturing.

I too used to love posturing, she realized. But the good has gone out of it without Clover by my side with her big serious face on.

Things happened quickly then, but later, when Witmeyer thought about it, she could pluck single frozen moments from that afternoon and study them for hours.

The boy leaped into the air. High, like an animal. A cat, maybe, or a bird, flinging his hands in front of him.

"Alley-oop," said a soldier, drawing a mocking cheer from his mates, but the cheering turned to howls of shock and pain as light blossomed from the boy's fingers. Two white fireballs filled the entire chamber, completely overloading the night vision goggles, momentarily blinding the soldiers—but not Witmeyer, whose helmet visor had thirty extra years of technology in it, including a *flare-guard* coating.

Ha, she thought. Clever child with his magician's tricks. *Not clever enough, boy.*

Her finger was on the trigger when the man, Malarkey, rose from his hiding place, seeming to fill her entire field of vision. Up and up he went, until he seemed too large for the space.

Suddenly Witmeyer's gun felt like deadweight in her hands.

How could her pathetic weapon have any effect on such a magnificent creature?

Magnificent?

Had she just thought that?

But this man *was* magnificent. There was no other word for him. Those shoulders like bridge bulwarks, a chest like a furnace door, a fan of hair that spread like a halo as he moved, and eyes that made Lunka feel transparent when they looked at her.

"Oh," said Witmeyer, feeling awe in the face of another human being for the first time in her life.

This is a man, she thought. This is a specimen.

Time seemed to slow down as Malarkey launched himself from a crumbled plinth and sailed over her head into the jumble of blinded men. Down they went like toy soldiers, and Malarkey gleefully laid into them, wreaking havoc with his anvil fists, square teeth, and wide forehead, which broke Farley's nose with a sickening crunch.

I should shoot him, Witmeyer realized. But the thought hung weightlessly in the maelstrom of her emotions and was swept away.

Malarkey made the most of his momentary advantage, then hightailed it after his young companion around the sweeping tunnel bend.

Witmeyer was instantly dismayed.

He is leaving. My magnificent man.

"After them, you idiots!" she ordered the moaning soldiers, throwing kicks left and right. "And remember your orders: take him alive. Take them both alive. But especially King Otto."

King Otto.

Now there was a man worthy of the title.

Every culture has a raft of poets and playwrights who will declare in heartfelt and varied terms that everyone has a true love just waiting to be found. Several million verses have been written in many thousand languages to support this thesis. As is often the case, these romantic writers are all wrong. While most people do have many potential true loves, there are those individuals who are so unique that no one could reasonably be expected to love them. Just below that level of super-weirdness, there is a small group of extreme individuals who find it impossible to connect to anyone not on their wavelength. These individuals rarely meet and so generally live their lives alone, but occasionally these alphas do cross paths, and when that happens, the attraction is instant, mutual, and irresistible.

The Chinese have a saying: *Love itself is calm; turbulence arrives from extraordinary individuals.*

Turbulence is beyond true love.

Italians call this phenomenon *catching the thunderbolt.*

Almost incredibly, in the reeking depths of a London sewer, during the magnesium light of Riley's flash bombs, both Witmeyer and Malarkey caught the thunderbolt right between the eyes.

• • •

Malarkey sloshed down the tunnel, feeling that he was running away from what he wanted to race toward.

That incredible woman.

Who was she?

Where had she come from?

In the second of magnesium flare, her image had been burned onto his retinas and remained there even now.

Those haughty eyes.

The high slashes of cheekbones.

How she held her weapon with easy comfort.

And her hair. Good God, the hair.

Malarkey was perfectly aware that his own hair was fabulous, due to his many and varied conditioning rituals, including sleeping in an inverted position and weekly snake venom soakings, but this girl's hair made his seem like damp straw in comparison. Even in the bowels of a sewer, she boasted the dark flowing locks of a princess.

What is happening to me? Should I not be consumed with my desire for revenge? he wondered, even as his hands quested along the tunnel walls and his legs churned the water.

Could he be at last experiencing one of the gentler passions that for so long had been denied him?

She had something. A glimmer. A fire.

"Come on, sir," Riley panted from half a dozen steps ahead. "We need to get to the ladder."

The boy was right, the ladder was where they needed to

be; but they needed to be there *now*. Anything *post* now was too late. That ladder was a thirty-rung hand-over-hand climb, and it would take a monkey ten seconds to scale it.

They didn't have ten seconds and they were not monkeys, and Riley's stunt with the flashers had bought them five seconds at most. Already the dreaded crimson beams were jittering on the walls.

"Halt, or I shoot," came a call from behind.

"Damn you, Otto," came another. Farley's voice, but strained with pain.

Nothing from the girl. Malarkey had been perversely hoping that she would call his name before shooting.

Then it came, three sweet words from the darkness: "King Otto, please."

King Otto. Please.

Malarkey smiled even as he labored forward. Strange how this brief phrase could delight him so, even in a time of such crisis.

The boy went under and Otto almost followed, but he righted himself by lurching into the wall and bearing the impact. He searched underwater with one hand until he located Riley's collar and yanked him from the murky depths. Riley was snorting furiously from his nose as he broke the surface.

"Good lad," said Malarkey. "Good."

But the seconds this tumble had cost were seconds that they did not have, and now it was a certainty that they would not reach the ladder, not to mention actually scale the rungs.

"Rats," said Riley, between snorts.

"You said it, Ramlet," agreed Malarkey, hauling them both forward.

"Stop!" From behind. "Last warning!"

Malarkey saw red dots dancing a firefly jig on his arm. "Rats and curses and damnation," he said with feeling, though was it possible that some small part of him wanted to be captured, just to see what would happen?

The same thing what happened to dear old Barnabus, his sensible side interjected.

"No," said Riley, and he pointed toward the ladder. "Rats."

Malarkey was a veteran member of the criminal fraternity and so had made a lifelong habit of working in the shadows. In consequence, his night vision was excellent, and he could see both Riley's point and that which he pointed at.

"Aha," he said with some satisfaction. Interesting. Time for some new combatants in this dark war.

Farley has his red-eyed demons and so too does Otto Malarkey.

"Come and get me, princess," he called over his shoulder. "I will not bite you."

He threw his head back and laughed.

It is all a game, he realized. And I am the master of this game.

Otto Malarkey dragged his thighs through the sewage, bearing Riley aloft as if he were nothing more significant weight-wise than a Gladstone bag.

Up ahead, behind his lumped ramparts and crenellations, sat King Rat, eyes a-gleaming, whiskers twitching with mild curiosity.

"You ain't about to be liking this, Yer Washup," said Malarkey to the rodent, testing the tunnel wall with his fingertips and finding the vibration he expected. And as every tosher worth his canary knew, vibrating walls had more poison behind them than the skin of a plague blister; steer well clear of vibration in the underworld, as no good ever came of a tremble.

No steering clear this time, thought Otto.

"Come out, my beauties," he called, and he threw all his weight and prodigious strength behind a charge directly at the center of the humming wall, knocking out a chunk of masonry and revealing a furred darkness behind. And to incite the necessary frenzy, he put his boot to the belly of King Rat himself, sending him skimming along the stream, chittering his indignation.

We are under attack, he doubtless squeaked. *To arms, brethren. To arms.*

The rats erupted from the hole in a wave of claws and teeth, their squeals of outrage sounding eerily like human baby squeals. They flowed like a shoal of fish in a tight funnel that crashed over the heads and shoulders of Box's men, drawing horrified screams from even the hardiest soldier.

"Hey ho," said Malarkey, his momentum carrying him past the rat stream, and as he was hefting Riley, the boy was also clear.

Riley hung suspended from his regent's grasp, watching from his upside-down position as their pursuers made a lightning transition from hunters to hunted. They began firing their weapons, sending bullets ricocheting from the walls and ironworks, but their efforts were futile. They may as well have been shooting the wind. The rats seemed to flow around their gunfire and latch on to their presumed enemies with tooth and claw. It was a sight that matched anything Riley had previously witnessed for pure horror, made all the more ghastly by the gloom and darkness, which left the brain free to shade in its own details.

The sounds, thought Riley. The sounds of nightmare.

Flesh being torn by sharp teeth and muffled screams.

They dare not open their mouths, he realized.

And suddenly Riley was on an upward arc, swinging toward the top section of the ladder into a shaft of blessed light.

"Grab on, boy!" shouted Malarkey.

And grab on Riley did, as though not just his life but the fate of his soul depended on it. He threaded his arms and legs through the rungs, pressing his cheek to the cold steel, taking a second to gather his faculties before attempting to climb to safety.

Below him in the sewer, a black river of vermin writhed past, bearing Box's troops along like logs in a flood. They screamed now, their resolution not to open their mouths having been trumped by terror, and Riley felt a ray of pity in his cloud of revulsion. These were men, after all, and no man deserved to die in such a horrible manner.

Otto Malarkey laughed aloud as they avoided the grim stripping of their bones by mere inches.

"I spent some time in the circus, lad," he said, his mood positively ebullient. "As a catch-man on the trapeze, I was stationed mostly. Observe."

Anchored only by the tips of his toes, Malarkey swung his torso downward, thrusting both arms deep into the deadly tide of red eyes and vicious teeth. He closed one eye as his hands scrabbled among the tails and fur, as though searching for the shining shilling in a lucky dip.

"Gotcha," he grunted after a moment, and he hauled his hands out of the rat river, each bearing a prize. Farley and the future lady. The ladder creaked under the extra weight, and several bolts popped from their holes. Malarkey's muscles were stretched tight as piano wires and his eyes bulged from the effort.

Farley's nose was busted flat to his face and his eyes were wild.

"Otto, please," he said, desperately, knowing there was surely nothing he could say to extricate him from this particular circle of hell. "I can help you."

"You can help me," said Otto calmly. "You can help me live with myself, knowing I have avenged dear Barnabus."

And as he was not essentially a cruel man, Malarkey delayed proceedings no further and simply dropped Farley into the furred pit of certain death, where he was instantly subsumed by the ripple of tails and shadows.

Without another glance at his brother's killer, Otto switched his attention to the lady.

Malarkey took her in a two-handed grip by the collar of her strangely-cut greatcoat, and she in turn gripped his forearms.

They hung like that wordlessly for a moment, and then the lady twisted one hand free and reached for her sidearm.

Plucky, thought Otto. A true revolveress.

"I ain't going to drop you, lady," he said even as the gun swung toward him. "We can go down for the big tumble together."

The future soldier took a bead on Otto's forehead. The gun spoke of death, but her eyes told another story.

"I am Otto, at your service," he said, trying not to let the strain of bearing this magnificent creature's weight show on his face.

"King Otto," she said, and then she shook her head slightly, sending the red sunset rays flickering along the length of her hair.

I'll be damned, thought Otto. I'll be damned if she ain't feeling this strange feeling too.

"I am Lunka Witmeyer," said the Amazon. "Thundercat."

"Thundercat," said Otto. "I do not doubt it."

Malarkey made a decision then to finally use the muscles built by his years on the French catch trapeze to bring a moment's happiness to his turbulent life.

And so, with the malodorous gas from sewerage bubbles rising, and with the rustle and squeak of rat stampede gushing around Witmeyer's boots, Otto strained and huffed, heaving Lunka Witmeyer slowly higher, inching her toward him, pulling her into the light.

It is more beautiful she gets, he realized. Her eyes are like to drill holes in my heart.

Witmeyer knew what was coming. Three times in her life men had attempted to kiss her. One was dead from trauma, one from shock, and the third survived but walked with a limp.

She felt herself tense, but not from the usual revulsion. She was suddenly nervous, anxious. She half wished to be dropped and half wished to never be let go.

For his part, Malarkey, who had kissed a hundred lassies, suddenly wondered if he should practice the mechanics on someone else first. What if his technique failed to impress? What if he kissed this girl once and never again? Should he not be reveling in his righteous vengeance? Was this new obsession disrespectful to the memory of Barnabus?

Riley called from above. "In the name of heaven, will you kiss or quarrel? I am for quitting this blasted hellhole."

Impudence indeed, but it did the trick.

It's now or never, thought Otto.

Now, now! thought Witmeyer.

And so Ram kissed Thundercat, and suddenly neither bed of roses nor mountain slope could compare with Her Majesty's sewer for romance. In fact, from this moment on, Otto Malarkey could never so much as sniff a chamber pot without a faraway look creeping into his eyes.

Forever they kissed—or perhaps it was merely five seconds. At any rate, the sinews in Otto's tree-trunk arms began to sing, and Malarkey was forced to deposit his sewer-catch on the tunnel floor, now that the carnivorous tide of rodents had passed.

"Remember me, Lunka," he said softly as he swung himself upward and quickly scaled the ladder.

Witmeyer watched this man disappear into the sun—or so it seemed from her vantage—and long after he had gone she called after him.

"I will remember you, King Otto."

And it never occurred to her then or later that she should have shot him.

On the street, Otto lay on his back, tears of pain running down his cheeks, holding his agonized biceps.

"Do you think the angel saw?"

Riley stood over him, nonplussed. "Saw which, my king? The crybaby tears, or the puppy-dog weakness in your limbs?"

"Either."

"She saw neither," said Riley. "The angel was blinded by your . . . majesty."

Malarkey smiled and breathed deep of the fetid air. "Good. Very good. How looks my hair?"

Riley remembered once hearing Chevron Savano use an adjective most sarcastically.

"Awesome," he said. "Totally awesome."

"Excellent, Ramlet. Excellent." He raised one hand. "Now, help your king to his feet. It is the least you can do. And don't think that my brain is too addled to have registered that crybaby comment. Puppy-dog weakness, was it? *Quelle sauce*, as the French would say."

Riley reached out a helping hand and had managed to heft his regent half to his feet when a thought struck him and he dropped King Otto to the cobbles.

I have lost my bag.

This was of import not because of the little bag itself, a mere market-stall satchel, but because of the bag's contents. For in Riley's bag were the detonators, which were now doubtless in the gullet of some rat.

And without the detonators, the plastique was nothing more than a lump of malleable material.

Their great plan—to flood the Camden Catacombs and use the rising waters as cover to rescue Chevie—was sunk.

And their sack of woe was not yet full.

Six Ram foot soldiers appeared from behind the Regent's Park trees where they had been skulking and surrounded their erstwhile king and his page.

"'Evening, Otto," said one, training his rifle on Malarkey's forehead. "We are what you might call a rear guard."

Otto closed his eyes.

"Rats," he said.

It is traditional for fictional antagonists to indulge in a lengthy confrontation toward the climax of their adventure. The villain of the piece will invariably reveal the nuances of his plan, thus arming the heroes with the information needed to foil the plot when they inevitably escape mere seconds before they are due to be executed in some overcomplicated fashion.

This being real life, Malarkey and Riley were not treated

to a face-to-face with Colonel Box; instead they were roughly tossed into a cell in the rear of the catacomb labyrinth that was little more than a cave with bars. The floor was compacted mud over stone, and the walls were slick and uneven.

Witmeyer, who usually enjoyed needling captives, was strangely quiet. She stood wordlessly at the bars, simply staring at Otto Malarkey, taking in every inch of him from hair to toe.

It seemed as though she would say something, or do something. In fact, she took a step forward and opened her mouth, but the moment was shattered when the soldier Aldridge tapped her shoulder.

"The colonel wants a report before we set off," said Corporal Aldridge. "He is a little upset about Farley being dead, and so forth. And you are to double-time it down to the main assembly, where the troops are mustered."

Witmeyer did not respond; she simply stood staring at Otto. She was bewitched, under the spell of a new emotion that she could not fathom, having nothing to relate it to. She found it difficult to form thoughts or sentences, and Witmeyer did not enjoy this helplessness, as quick-wittedness had long been a forte of hers. And yet, she could not shake this warm feeling that had no place in the heart of a Thundercat.

And it seemed as though this magnificent man felt the same. He approached the bars and stood there, hunched beneath the cell's low ceiling, and his eyes looked directly at her and also, somehow, somewhere distant.

"Lunka," he said softly, "we did not part after all."

"No," she said. "We did not part."

What happened next, Aldridge brought upon himself. For just as it is true that a sleepwalker should never be awakened in case he reacts violently, neither should those on either end of a thunderbolt be disturbed in mid-gaze.

"Did you hear me?" he said, tapping Witmeyer's shoulder. "Let's go, lady. Double-time."

Witmeyer's reaction was pure instinct, and it was over before her conscious mind had time to catch up. She reached up and grabbed Aldridge's fingers, twisting them until they cracked; then she caught him by the armpit and heaved him high over her shoulder and into the cell bars. That was probably enough to knock the unfortunate soldier unconscious, but just in case, she slammed Aldridge onto the floor and punched him once in the forehead. If he hadn't been out before, he was out now. Far out.

"Outstanding," said Malarkey. "What sublime form, eh, Ramlet?"

"Quite," said Riley, wincing on Aldridge's behalf.

"Oops," said Witmeyer as her brain realized what she had done. "Oh."

Malarkey wrapped his fingers around the bars. "'Oops, oh.' Such poetry."

Riley thought that the two adults had lost their minds, but he was wise enough to keep this notion to himself, as he had no wish to end up like the crushed man on the floor.

"Has the lady switched sides, then?" he asked the mooning Malarkey. "Are we safe to make a break for it?"

His question went unanswered, and so Riley reckoned

to take a chance on it, as doubtless someone would come to check the chamber soon. He rolled up the leg of his trousers and began to pick at what looked like the flesh of his calf, but it was not flesh—it was a layer of glue, which soon came away from the skin in a flap. Beneath the glue, a burglar's key sat pressed into the skin of his leg.

"Come on now," he said, plucking strands of glue from the key's single tooth. "Don't let old Riley down today."

The key was one of Riley's favorite bettys. A midsize pick that could open anything from manacles to a basic safe. It took a measure of jiggling, but soon the cell door swung open before them. Otto stooped to grab a handful of Aldridge's shirt, then casually tossed him to the rear of the cell. Now nothing stood between Lunka and Otto.

Lunka, thought Riley. I shall not be voicing my opinion on that particular name.

Malarkey took Witmeyer's hand in his, and the hands were much the same size.

"Tell me, woman. Are you with us now?"

Witmeyer felt like she was in a dream, and in this dream she was an entirely different person, who didn't crack skulls unless she felt like it—or the owners of the skulls were blocking her view of Otto Malarkey.

"I am with you, King Otto," she said.

"I could listen to you call me *King* forever," said Otto. "And it makes me want to be king again."

"I want that too," said Witmeyer. "You should take back what is rightfully yours. I will fight at your side."

Otto drew her close. "Together we could take on the world."

"Together," agreed Lunka, and they kissed once more.

Riley thought he would choke in this love cloud.

"When you two have done with the cooing," he said, picking up Aldridge's bowler hat and dragging the coat off his back, "we should quit this lurk before the scoundrel colonel has pennies on all our eyes."

Malarkey broke contact for a moment. "Just a sec, lad. Be right with you, but when you get older you'll understand that a man must coo while he can." And he shook out his hair and went back in for another kiss, leaving Riley to stand there, shifting on his feet like a fellow with a bad dose of worm itch.

13 » EMERGENCE DAY

Sometimes I feel like people aren't listening to me. I spend ninety minutes up here talking about the dangers of time travel, advising you to stay the hell away from time travel, and the first question I get is "Do you think time travel will be available commercially?" Then again, I spend every waking hour bent over quantum equations, so I guess I don't listen to me, either.

—Professor Charles Smart

THE SAVIOR OF THE WORLD.

Clay Junior.

Colonel Box.

But he hadn't always been a colonel. That only came after his administration of what used to be quaintly called a "wet work" team, as if the only discomfiting fact about working in that unit was getting water in your boots.

In the early 1980s, Sergeant Clayton Box was part of Operation Bright Star, training with Egyptian forces in the Sinai. He made such an impression with his accurate forecasting of terrorist attacks that he was drafted into a newly minted

CIA–Green Beret team that was tasked with counterinsurgence in El Salvador. While there, Box drew up a model that diagrammed terrorist groups and could be applied anywhere in the world—except Scandinavia, where people thought differently. This model was called the Box Parallelogram and was the gold standard for understanding terrorist groups for decades.

Box really could not understand what all the fuss was about. He simply put himself in the insurgent leader's shoes, imagined himself a little less intelligent than he was, then ran his unit as efficiently as it was possible with his diminished IQ. The results were astounding. Box could predict where rebels would strike. He could predict who was likely to be recruited and where they would be approached, and most important, he could predict with reasonable accuracy which foot soldiers would rise to the top. The CIA liked that last bit. They liked it a lot, and embarked on a series of apparently baffling hits on low-level targets, which, according to Box, were the equivalent of time-traveling assassinations.

Box liked it, too. The system was efficient.

Time-traveling assassinations. The Box Parallelogram earned him his colonel's wings, and it was whispered in the halls of power that he was being groomed for brigadier general before forty. Almost unheard of.

Box's phrase *time-traveling assassinations* was catchy and it hung around Command Headquarters; and when the Charles Smart project seemed like it might actually be science fact instead of science fiction, Box was called in for a chat.

Tell me, Colonel, a man in a plain black uniform asked him. *How could the Box Parallelogram be made more efficient?*

And he had answered. *The only way to make my paradigm more efficient would be if my team could actually travel in time.*

And just like that, he was transferred to London, leading the WARP detail, and he quickly realized the potential of the time tunnel. Box's superiors thought that the tunnel could occasionally be appropriated for black ops, but Colonel Box was thinking much bigger. The U.S.–U.K. alliance could be theoretically reverse-engineered to become a global empire.

It would be the most efficient use of the wormhole.

The tipping point came for Box when he returned from a babysitting mission in Victorian London to find that his beloved mother had been run over and killed by a drunk driver. Box was intensely upset by this and, after a quick Internet study, he realized that if he paid a visit to a certain baker in Victorian London, then that baker's son would never emigrate to America, and the son's great-grandson would not run over his mother in Texas.

And so, on his next jaunt, Box planned to take time out for a side mission. But, in order to get his tracker log changed, he had no choice but to confide in a technical operator, and the operator passed the log on to the man in the black uniform. Box was called in for another chat and warned off his planned side-op. He was told that the quantum tunnel would be used for the occasional approved target and nothing more.

Box was aghast. Such rampant inefficiency. It was akin to

owning an AK-47 and using it once a year to shoot pigeons.

His mother would be saved, he decided. And the tunnel would be used to maximum efficiency.

Colonel Box applied his own parallelogram to the members of his squad, and over the following weeks recruited his own troops to his cause. They would return to the past; they would build an empire. It would be a great machine, run with total efficiency. And while they were there, Box would visit a certain baker.

Box and his men assembled as much technology and information as would fit in a Timepod, and they jumped back to Victorian London, ostensibly to change out agents. When they failed to return, the WARP program assumed that Clayton Box and his team had been compromised or torn apart by the tunnel, when actually they had moved into the catacombs and set about building their empire.

It has been a long road, thought Box now as he stood before his army, assembled in the great hall, eager for blood and battle. *But the length of the road is irrelevant. My empire will be the most efficient this world has ever seen.*

The only flaw in the plan had become apparent when he visited the house in Clapham where the baker was supposed to have lived and discovered that the records had been mistaken. The man did not live there and never had.

No matter, he had thought. *When I am emperor and automobiles become commonplace, I shall make drunk driving punishable by death. And in that way Mother will eventually be saved.*

CAMDEN CATACOMBS, 1899

Box surveyed his two hundred troops. They were ready, finally. After years for some and decades for others, their weapons were fabricated, their bullets were milled and loaded. How could simple rifles and cannon hope to prevail against trained soldiers in body armor wielding automatic weapons, grenades, and mortar? And once the country was theirs, the munitions factories would be handed new specifications for intercontinental ballistic missiles. Europe's days were numbered.

Boxstrike.

Box liked the sound of that.

In fact, Box liked everything Vallicose had told him about the future. He had always planned to incorporate religion to some extent, as all the great dictators had, but Vallicose had shown him the way. He must go beyond what he had ever planned and take his lead from the pharaohs by becoming a god himself.

A new gospel is being written.

If Box had had a sense of humor he might have smiled, but he was aware that his occasional foray into bonhomie usually resulted in awkwardness all around. He had tried to be friends with Farley, engaging him in casual conversation as he had seen the other men do, but it had never worked. If anything, it had driven them further apart.

And now Farley is dead, which is very inconvenient, but the schedule is set, and so we must forge ahead.

Spread out on a table before him were the operations maps

marked with strike sites and access points. Box folded the maps and, with one step of his long legs, he mounted the table and raised his arms for silence. He was an imposing figure in his black uniform with the newly stitched Boxite crest in gold on the breast, and the group of bristling men fell instantly silent.

Box took a moment to look them over and thought, Look at them, waiting for the traditional pep talk, as though that will increase or decrease their odds of survival. It is ridiculous. The only three words that should be necessary are *Follow the plan.* And yet I must urge them to victory. I must appeal to their basic humanity so that they can pretend they fight for a cause and not cold hard cash.

"The day has come, my warriors." He began speaking through a futuristic megaphone on a strap around his neck, his amplified voice booming through the arches. "Today we take the first step toward a better world."

He paused, waiting for the guttural cheers that his behavioral studies assured him would follow, and they did.

So predictable, he thought. So malleable.

"This country has become aimless and godless. Once we were great, but now we bow down to every foreigner with gold in his fist. There are heathens walking our streets, taking our positions of employment, conversing openly with our women, and I say: No more!"

Now they will say *No more!*, Box predicted.

And they did. Shouted it, in fact. Most boisterously.

"For those among you who have joined us from the

Battering Rams, welcome, brothers! I know you have many questions. Where do our new comrades come from? For that matter, where do these fabulous weapons come from? Let me answer those questions for you. Our weapons are heaven-sent." Box spread his arms like wings—a position he had learned from watching videos of Stalin and Jim Morrison—and he held the pose for a full minute before once again taking up the megaphone. "We are avenging angels, and we ask you to bear arms with us and guarantee your place in heaven. Will you join us?"

The roar was deafening and entirely affirmative. Box was a little relieved, as he had thought the heaven-sent bit might be over the top; but no, the men had swallowed it. And they would swallow much more besides if what Vallicose had told him about the future was true. It felt premature to declare himself a god to these men, as many of them had known him for decades and knew just how human he was; but later, when the country was his, he could begin to build the legend.

"Our enemies wait for us," continued Box. "They are corrupt men, grown fat on the fruits of our labor, and the time has come to knock them from their perches."

This statement was carefully crafted and contained five of the top fifteen words calculated to incite bloodlust in insurgents: *enemies, corrupt, fat, labor,* and *perch*. Number one on the list was *God* and number two *avenge,* which Box had already ticked off the list.

"After our Emergence, things will never be the same again. Tomorrow the sun rises on a new day."

More buzz words, more cheering. In truth, Box was growing a little bored, so he decided to skip a few paragraphs and go directly to the fireworks.

"There are those who would stand in our way," said the colonel. "Would you the faithful care to see what will happen to these unbelievers?"

His soldiers, reliably bloodthirsty, pumped their fists in the air.

Box called over his shoulder. "Sister Vallicose, bring forth the heretic."

Vallicose emerged right on cue, dragging behind her a limp Chevron Savano.

Box had no interest in public execution in itself, but he did acknowledge the potency of human sacrifice as a form of blessing on a campaign or even a structure. There were legends from ancient Japan about *hitobashira,* or the practice of sacrificing a *human pillar,* in which innocents were buried alive at the base of new temples to protect the buildings against attacks from either nature or enemies. And in Homeric legend, Agamemnon was willing to sacrifice his own daughter, Iphigenia, to ensure that the gods would look favorably on his armies during the Trojan War. As for the Aztecs, those guys sacrificed eighty thousand prisoners in four days when consecrating the Great Pyramid of Tenochtitlan. Eighty thousand in four days! That was one labor-intensive ceremony.

When Savano was executed, the men would not realize that they were cheering on a ritualistic pagan sacrifice, but the sight would touch a primal nerve buried deep in their race memories and spur them on to greater acts of valor.

Idiots, thought Box then. Predictable pawns. They have as little control over their reactions as animals.

Savano had been drugged in order to keep her from whining pathetically and perhaps awakening sympathy in the newcomers. There were always a few squeamish weaklings without the stomach for what needed to be done.

This day we will lay open the entire country's vital arteries, thought Box. And our endeavors must be baptized in blood.

He pointed a rigid finger at the drooping Savano.

"This is our enemy!" he said. "A spirit from hell come to thwart our holy mission."

Box allowed his eyes to flare and his voice to shake with emotion.

"Oh, she may seem innocent, brothers. But is that not how the devil always appears?" He turned to Chevron. "Would you deny it, she-devil? Would you deny that the lord of lies himself sent you to spoil God's plans?"

Chevie, of course, could not deny anything in her state. Box could have accused her of shooting Abraham Lincoln without fear of contradiction.

Even a child could see the girl is drugged, thought Box. And yet these drones are prepared to believe that she is a devil's minion who refuses to defend herself.

"And there you have it, brothers. Her silence condemns her. String the demoness up, Sister Vallicose."

Vallicose dragged Chevie through ranks of Rams and soldiers, and most stood aside but some leaned in to poke her with gun barrels, and others spat.

Pigs, thought Box. They are necessary pigs.

Mother would hate them, he realized, and he was suddenly glad that his beloved mother would never know about this stage of his plan.

It certainly will not be reported in the history books, he decided.

Vallicose reached the other end of the cavernous chamber and mounted a steep ramp that led to a wooden frame. Behind the frame, a block of plastic explosive was attached directly to the wall. It was pretty obvious that being secured to the frame would not be a safe situation in the event somebody detonated the explosives. Vallicose cuffed Chevie to the structure, then left her hanging there. Chevie was so out of it that she would probably have stayed put without restraints.

There were a few murmurs from the Rams now, as this entire ritual was beginning to seem unnecessarily cruel, so Box decided to step up the rhetoric.

"And now, brothers," he said, "an example of my power." He pulled a radio transmitter from his pocket. "When I press this red button, the wall will disintegrate. No cannonball is necessary, no dynamite. Just a slab of the holy paste. No need to be afraid, brothers. We are perfectly safe, as the charge is shaped to blow outward. If heaven wants this witch girl to be punished, then God will allow a small portion of the explosion to consume her. If she is innocent, then the force of the explosion will be borne by the structure. Either way, once this wall comes down, the war has begun; and we will man our vehicles, stream through the hole, and sweep though the city to our assigned target. And nothing will stand in our way."

Box was reasonably confident that his *once more unto the breach* speech would be effective, as he had spent hours in front of his mirror practicing expressions and general body language that he had copied from the great dictators of history.

"Press the button!" shouted a voice.

"Press it!" said another, and soon the call was taken up as a chant and it reverberated to the very ceiling.

There was a counter-call, too—hard to hear at first, because it was only one voice, but the voice was loud and persistent. And it was singing. One verse over and over.

"We stabs 'em,

We fights 'em,

Cripples 'em,

Bites 'em."

The men were looking around, searching for the singer who would deflate this powerful moment. Box knew immediately who it must be, and he also knew that this interference must be handled very delicately. The singing continued, and if Box wasn't mistaken, some of the men were joining in—perhaps unconsciously, but in any event, other voices lent volume to the man's words. And just as a corridor had opened through the men for Vallicose and Savano, now space cleared around Malarkey, for of course it was he striding toward the dais, cock of the walk, as though he were the regent in this place.

"No rules for our mayhem," he sang.

"You pay us, we slay 'em.

If you're in a corner,

With welshers or scams.

Pay us a visit,

The Battering Rams."

The last word was sung on a high note, showcasing Malarkey's very melodious tenor voice, and the man had the nerve to take a bow for his performance as many of his men applauded instinctively. Otto would never have his own revue in the West End, but he knew how to play to a room.

Malarkey stood and shook out his magnificent mane. Less a ram's and more a lion's. Most men would have followed their instincts and shot the so-called king where he stood, but Clayton Box did not have *instincts* as such; he had cauterized those nerves as a child, as impulse decisions were rash by nature and often flawed. What he did have was a very efficient thought process that flicked through options and possibilities at lightning speed, his jaw seesawing as he thought.

Box quickly decided that simply killing Malarkey in front of his men would make King Otto a martyr and sow the seeds of dissent at this crucial time. No, now that Malarkey had bought himself some credit with his Rams by behaving with the braggadocio that this type of thug had an inexplicable respect for, the only way to wipe his slate clean was to replace that image with an equally strong one, but in the negative column. Malarkey must be thoroughly humiliated. And then killed.

Box's jaw returned to center as he reached his decision.

I have just the person to inflict that humiliation.

Otto Malarkey's face was a mask of disappointment.

"Is this what we have come to, my bully boys?" he asked. "Skulking in the sewers?"

"Pah!" said a Ram, who habitually sported a hairpiece of badger pelt. "You is just hyperbolating, Malarkey. This ain't no sewer."

"Ah, Peeble, but there you do be in the wrong, old fellow," said Otto. "I know it be a sewer and let me tell you for why."

It had to be said, Otto had charisma, and the troops clustered around him to hear his argument.

"I know it be a sewer," said Otto again, "for I see a rat." He hitched a thumb at the man Peeble. "And I see a floater." Now his thumb swung toward Box.

A fine joke it was, and this could not be denied. Laughter echoed through the hall, and even Box, as a lifelong student of human behavior, could not help but be grudgingly enthralled by this man who seemed to eschew logical behavior at all costs. Box had to admit, if only to himself, that Malarkey's joke had deflated the pre-battle tension most effectively. Tension that he himself had painstakingly escalated.

But what could he possibly do now? The man was doomed, surely.

The colonel noticed some of his own men moving away from their units toward Malarkey, and he caught their eyes and shook his head.

Stay back, the shake said. *But be ready.*

"And now I finds me fine bully boys throwing their lot in with those as would murder Queen Vic, God bless her. Those as would trample on what we all fought for on foreign swamp and desert."

Peeble, still smarting over the rat remark, took up the argument. "That much is true, Otto; we fought overseas for rich men. Now we fights for ourselves and each other. The spoils will be ours alone."

"That is your right," said Otto magnanimously. "All's you got to do is pick a champeen. You know the rules. The Rams fight for whoever wears the fleece. And that would be me."

"We ain't Rams no more," said Peeble sulkily.

Otto whipped his own ruffled shirt over his head and flung it at Peeble, landing it neatly on the man's head.

"You is Rams until I say you ain't Rams, runt. Now step outta my radius, Peeble, less you want me to mistake you for a challenger." Otto flexed his muscles. "So, will you coves honor yer vow? Or will you disgrace yerselves entirely?"

Box stepped down from his platform. "Mr. Malarkey, King Otto. I am the one you seek, but your own rules prevent me from challenging. I am not a Ram, after all."

Otto rubbed his great hands. "Easy fixed, Yankee-doodle. King's prerogative, don't you know. I offers a one-time-only deal. All challenges accepted. All comers flattened without prejudice."

Thank you, Otto, thought Box. *You have sprung my trap.*

He was almost disappointed at how easy it had been, even

though he was impatient to blow the wall and unleash his army of God on queen and Parliament.

"Very well, Malarkey. All comers, you say? Then you will fight my proxy, Sister Vallicose."

An excited murmur spread around the hall. Malarkey to fight a woman in an official challenge? It was not proper. But how could he refuse? *All comers* had been his very words.

"Sister Vallicose? You would have a lady fight your battles for you, Colonel?"

Box waved away his questions. "All comers means all comers, King Otto. Quick as you can, Sister. I have a button to press."

Vallicose entered the fighting circle and stripped off her greatcoat, revealing a torso almost as muscled as Otto's own. And while Malarkey may have had a slight edge size-wise, Vallicose was bred for war. If Otto was a bear, then Clover Vallicose was a panther. And Vallicose owned a singular advantage in that she genuinely believed she was fighting for God. Her eyes were bright and her hands shook not with fear, but from rapture.

"You will die because the Blessed Colonel wishes it," she said calmly to Otto.

"I cannot grapple this one," Malarkey objected. "She ain't right in the noggin. This ain't our way."

Box did not bother to respond, and there was not a man in the room so noble that he did not want these two beasts to clash—except Otto, of course—and his opinion hardly mattered now, not when there was bloody entertainment to be had.

And as a bonus, thought Box, with the dry satisfaction of a chess master who has outmaneuvered a tricky opponent, what better way to ready my men for war than with a gladiatorial contest followed by an execution?

Vallicose stretched out her neck and cracked her knuckles. "Are you prepared for hell, heathen?"

This was a rhetorical question, but if Malarkey were to respond, he would admit to being far from ready. He understood suddenly the ramifications of this contest. Even if he battered this warrior woman, he would lose face with the Rams, for fighting a female for the crown was one of the embargoes he himself had introduced (fighting females at other times could not always be avoided). And if he lost to Vallicose, then he was dead anyway. It was a hopeless situation.

Vallicose punched straight out from her shoulder, and Malarkey barely managed to step wide of the blow.

Close. Very close. Otto felt the hiss from the attack as Vallicose's fist sailed past his ear.

"Ooooooh," said the soldiers, and:

"Zounds."

"What ho."

"A sov on the lady."

Perhaps the situation is not hopeless after all, he thought. There is, mayhap, a solution. A painful solution.

Vallicose was a little overcommitted to the blow and a step off balance, and so Malarkey prodded her shoulder with a single finger, sending her tripping forward.

"Careful, girlie," he said. "This is a genuine fight yer in now."

Vallicose snorted and shook herself like a bull, then she threw back an elbow that would have nearly decapitated Malarkey if he hadn't slapped it away with his palm.

"I'll give you that one, too," said Malarkey. "Another man would be for punishing you, but I is a gent. A commodore, if you must know."

Yes, Malarkey was laying on the glib, but he knew a man only got so many blocks and dodges with a scrapper of this caliber; Vallicose's skill was clear from her speed and carriage.

If I wakes up tomorrow, I will be waking up stiff and sore, Otto thought ruefully.

Malarkey avoided a couple more swings without once attempting to land a blow himself, but his luck ran out on the fifth assault, when Vallicose caught him with a vicious straight-fingered jab to the kidneys—there wasn't a creature on the planet who could shrug that off with a grin. All Malarkey could do was pray that his insides were not ruptured and drop into a genuflection, giving Vallicose the perfect opportunity to follow her jab with a powerhouse sock to the jaw. Most souls would have left the body at this point, and even the great Golgoth was put flat on his back minus a tooth. He took himself a long moment to let the stars clear, then he climbed slowly to his feet.

"A little advice, sister," he said, his head hanging to his chest, blood dripping from his lips. "Punch from the stomach. I know that sounds like gibberish, but it's sound counsel."

Vallicose danced around him. She could smell victory. This was a fine sample of the holy carnage to come this day.

"I hope you have made your peace, heathen," she said, and she threw out a kick that Otto managed to knock aside with his wrist.

The mood of the crowd was a strange one. The Rams had wanted Malarkey nobbled and no mistake, but now damned if Otto wasn't holding on to his principles in spite of the wrath being visited upon his person. He would not return fire on a woman for the crown.

Again and again Vallicose struck, and Malarkey either dodged the blow or did not. And when he did not the savagery took its toll, and it was clear that the Ram king could not endure much more trauma.

"Not bad," he commented after one punch landed square on his ear, which must have stung like the devil's brand. "From the stomach, see?"

Box was perplexed. Why would the man sacrifice himself so? Men generally gave up their own lives for one of two reasons: love, or principle. And Box found it difficult to believe that this glorified thug loved anyone enough to lay down his life. And as for principles? They were a tool, useful for justifying extreme behavior, and it was inconceivable that Malarkey would allow his own murder in the name of principle. And yet, here it was happening before him.

Unless.

Unless he was not willing to see himself murdered, but injured only.

Why? Why would he?

Of course, of course.

Box actually slapped his own forehead.

Distraction.

Box felt the cold shudder of understanding pass through him, and his eyes lifted to the ramp; he was relieved to see nothing. But then there was a movement.

There.

There was the boy, Riley, stealing toward his companion. This entire episode was a ruse.

"Get the boy!" he shouted into the mass of soldiers surrounding the brawl. "Stop him."

But no one responded. One shout was much the same as another in this chamber of heaving humanity and violence.

Box grabbed the megaphone and pulled the trigger.

"Stop him, you idiots! Stop the boy."

It took a moment for the message to filter through, and by this time Riley was out the door at the rear of the chamber, having abandoned his creep toward Chevie.

Box quickly revised his instruction. "To arms!" he shouted. "Positions, everyone. The Revolution begins in one minute. Forget the boy. Forget Malarkey."

Perhaps it was part of the ruse to divide Box's troops, to dilute their effectiveness. There was no need for coping strategies to deal with these interlopers. Their eventual deaths would simply be absorbed into the general massacre.

In the heart of the ruckus, Malarkey grinned.

"Ha," he said, and from his bent-over position he punched

Vallicose once above the right knee, which turned her entire leg to rubber and collapsed her on the spot.

"Count yerself fortunate that I am pressed for time," he said, then ducked into the crowd, sparing one second to kick the man Peeble square in the rear end, lifting him to his tippy-toes.

"There you go, rat," he said, dearly wishing he could linger and watch that lippy oaf Peeble writhe in the particular agony brought on by a spot-on bum kick, but this day was not won by a long shot. Otto plucked his trampled shirt from underfoot, sighing at the scuffs mashed into its silk, then slipped through the busy throngs, following Riley's footsteps toward the underground dock where dear Lunka was waiting in something called an amphibious craft.

Box had a sudden premonition that the cogs of his finely tooled machination were spinning apart, and he was surprised that his ordered brain would even accommodate such things as premonitions.

A premonition is simply a considered consequence. A possible consequence.

Nothing had changed, he decided. The Revolution was inevitable.

Can it fail? he wondered, scanning his mind for concrete stumbling blocks.

No, he decided. Malarkey and Savano are but two loose cannons in a forest of automatic barrels. They will shortly be dead, and I will chastise myself for such inefficiency of thought.

He held aloft the radio detonator.

I will wait forty more seconds for my artillery to mount their vehicles, then blow the wall.

First the queen would die, and then the politicians.

How could the past prevail against the future? Impossible.

Box counted down, visualizing his soldiers loading up, checking each other's equipment, and so forth. Seeing in his mind's eye Malarkey despairing the loss of his men and the utter failure of his plan.

Someone will casually shoot him as they pass, Box felt certain.

Forty, said the voice in his head.

A pity some of his men would miss the execution, but sometimes strokes must be sacrificed for the good of the greater plan.

Time to change the world, thought Box. And he pressed the button.

Something exploded, but it wasn't the wall. It was close, whatever it was, but it most definitely was not the wall, which remained resolutely intact. Box's mind did not initially connect his pressing of the red button with the nearby explosion.

It is much more likely that the detonator is faulty and there has been some coincidental weapons malfunction in another chamber.

Then he heard the water and realized.

We are under attack.

If there was one thing all good magicians knew, it was how to be invisible. Or more accurately, *practically* invisible. Riley was not, in fact, wearing a cap at the moment, but even if he had been, it would be woven from Irish tweed and not the magical translucent threads of Athena's cap of invisibility. Riley could clearly be seen when someone was looking directly at him. When they were not—if there was a distraction, for example—then he was practically invisible when he wished to be so.

When Witmeyer led Riley and Malarkey from their cell to the underground dock, they had passed the arch leading to the assembly room and overheard Box's big troop rallying speech and seen Chevie dragged from the back room. A makeshift plan had been hurriedly cobbled together. There were three strands. Witmeyer would steal an amphibious vehicle. Malarkey would distract the crowds with a challenge, and Riley would steal the detonator.

Yes. Riley's target had been the detonator—and Chevie, too, if he could manage it—but the detonator came first, or she would be blown to smithereens where she hung.

All three objectives were achieved. Malarkey took his licking in the name of queen and country. Witmeyer did not even need to steal the amphibian, as the keys were tossed to her by a trooper. And Riley crept with infinite patience across the chamber's back wall and up the ramp, blending with the shadows until he managed to slide the receiver and detonator from the shaped charge and tuck them into his pocket. And according to the first rule of magic, which was misdirection, he retreated down the ramp with his body in the attitude of one going forward, so if spotted he would appear to be heading toward Chevie and not sliding past her.

Standing there mere inches from his unconscious friend, Riley realized that the animal Box had etherized her and so it would be impossible to rescue her at this juncture. All he could do was tuck his skeleton key into her fist in case she should wake up. To see her in such a helpless dangle caused Riley to flinch in shock, and it was this reflexive jerk that caught Box's eye.

Riley realized that he had been detected, and he abandoned his stealth on the spot. He spun and ran for the doorway, hearing Box's amplified voice rise above the general commotion.

"Stop him, you idiots! Stop the boy."

Riley ran, thinking, *Chevron, oh Chevie. I have abandoned you.* And also, *No. I have deferred your death, for Box would be blowing you to hell presently were it not for me.*

He raced on, wondering what time it was precisely.

Surely five. Surely.

And after five, how many minutes' grace before Otto's bribe to the pump-house master was down the drain?

It did him no good to think about that now, for there were men on his heels, men with longer legs than his.

Men were in his path, too. Ahead was an entire wedge-shaped squadron, double-timing it toward a yellow square painted on the ground. The squad leader was kneeling to examine a mortar tube and he registered Riley half a second before Riley's foot took him in the teeth, scattering them like bowling pins. The leader's gaping mouth acted as a boost, allowing Riley to step up and then launch himself over the heads of several confused foot soldiers. Riley could not help but laugh aloud at the unlikeliness of it all, and the giddiness of rushing adrenaline and danger converging from all quarters.

How many stars would need to align for this fantastical plan to succeed?

A galaxy of stars, surely.

Impossible, surely.

For a moment Riley saw himself as though from above as he flew through the air. He saw himself extended from fingertip to tiptoe, his head thrown back, lips stretched in a smile; and his eyes sparkled, dashed if they didn't, and he wondered was this a true vision or wishful thinking. Then a shock rattled his frame as he hit the ground, and he was back in his own head and running like the devil was on his trail. And if this was not precisely the case, then surely these men were the devil's minions, for their intention was to set the whole country on the road to hell.

"To hell with all of *you*," he called breathlessly, then, like a player in a stage farce, he was dodging through rows of characters all top-heavy with muscle and body armor. "The devil will turn on his own."

It occurred to Riley that most of these men were making no attempt to stop him, no more than they would to swat a fly buzzing around their beer. Their missions were set, ingrained in their muscles from countless dry runs; and they followed them as they would a well-worn path.

What do they care about a running boy, Riley realized, when soon the entire capital would be fleeing from their guns?

But he was not ignored entirely. There was a determined

posse dogging his footsteps, and Riley could imagine their grins as they herded their quarry deeper into the catacombs, where he would soon be dead-ended.

Perhaps not, thought Riley. Perhaps one chance in a million is enough.

A shot buzzed past his ear and burrowed into the wall, reminding Riley that he was clear of the soldiers now and could be fired upon, so he darted right into a low tunnel with a curved ceiling of bedrock, and water flowing in rivulets down the walls.

More shots cracked the stone at his feet and overhead, and Riley realized that the men were not aiming at his person. They were cat-and-mousing him for sport. He felt his breath burning in his chest and his heartbeat pounding in his ears.

I must be close, he thought. Please, God.

The tunnel opened to a larger chamber, which was half-full of crates that lay open, spilling straw from their bellies. Three walls were dark stone, but one was white and smooth.

Here, thought Riley. Here.

The light in this outlying chamber was low with just one orange blister on the ceiling casting a sunset glow on the pale wall, but it was enough if a person knew what he sought, which Riley did.

Smack bang in the center was an off-color ring with a telltale cone of drill dust on the floor below.

Riley thrust his hand into his pocket, wrapping his fingers around the detonator and radio receiver therein.

Perhaps I am too far away, he thought, and he offered up a quick prayer that it was not so.

No time for daintiness with men on his tail, so Riley poked the detonator into the plastique and twisted once.

If that ain't it, then it ain't it, and I keep running until fate throws me a bone.

But he knew that there would be no bone from fate. All his bones had been tossed already.

"That's far enough, boyo," said the head man in the posse group. "I got royals to kill."

Riley did not stop or even slow. Either Box would press the button or he wouldn't.

Riley ducked into the tunnel at the other end of the chamber and kept his feet a-racing.

"Press it!" he shouted aloud, as if he had gallons of breath to spare for yelling useless instructions. "Press it, Box!"

And, in the distant war chamber, Box did press the red button, sending a radio signal not to his own shaped charge as he expected, but to the cylinder of plastique that Riley and Malarkey had previously planted from the sewer side. The explosives blew a cart-sized hole in the reinforced wall, skewering the soldiers on Riley's tail with steel rods, or braining them with lumps of concrete. And that would have been the whole of it had not Malarkey dropped a small fortune on the Camden pump-house manager earlier in the day to flush the sewers at five of the clock precisely. And not just the regular flush—the manager was to open the stopcocks to their limits and take himself off to the Bull and Bear Tavern for a night in his cups. The manager objected that this would near to empty the canal, and Malarkey assured him that it would do no such thing and added a fistful of sovereigns to his asking price.

I guess it won't do no such thing, the manager had said, swiping the coins into his poke. *And now that I comes to ponder it, I have a premonition of a mighty thirst coming on me about the teatime mark.*

And even though the clocks had struck five a few minutes previously, there was still more than ample sewer flush water coming down the pipes to fill Box's catacombs fuller than the manager's stomach would be by closing time.

The reinforced wall had previously deflected the flood and flush torrents from invading the catacombs, but now, with the wall ruptured, the long-thwarted waters were finally allowed ingress, and they roared inside with all the eagerness of the Greek armies entering Troy.

Riley ran on, laughing. It was bordering on the incredible that Box should have scuppered his own plan, but there it was. First, pride; and then the fall.

And if I don't lift up my own two feet, the water will scupper my plans for future breathing, too.

The blister lights overhead crackled and popped as the water invaded their electrics, and when the explosion noise cleared from his ear passages, Riley could hear shouts and roars of panicked men as they hurriedly abandoned their dreams of carnage and sought to save their own skins.

All will be forgotten now save survival.

Riley would have dearly loved to have the luxury of thinking about his own survival, but concerns about Chevie's fate prevented him from concentrating solely on his own.

Perhaps she has freed herself with my skeleton key.

It depended on the strength of the ether Box had administered. Chevie could already be loose in the catacombs.

I pray that it is so, thought Riley. I hope and pray.

Riley was fleet of foot, but even youth cannot outrun the flow of water, especially when it has pressure behind it. Soon enough there was water at his ankles and then fizzing around his knees, and with the water came the rank smell of sewer that Riley now knew well but would never become accustomed to. Riley took to coughing while he ran, which was not a good blend of activities; and soon his run slowed until his cough played out, and he thought that one more hacking session like that would surely sink him.

Then, mercifully, the levels dropped as the claustrophobic tunnel widened to the expanse of loading bay and dock, which was crowded with soldiers attempting to make good their escape. These attempts were hampered by the fact that all the craft that had been seaworthy had been sunk except one, and Witmeyer stood on the prow fighting off any who would board. Otto Malarkey stood behind her, shaking his head in admiration, the Thunderbolt holding full sway over his emotions.

"Otto," called Riley, "Chevie is still in there. We must find her."

Malarkey caught Riley's outstretched hand and swung him onto the deck of the amphibious craft.

"Ramlet. I am glad to see you. And chivalrous as I surely

am, I would most times be overjoyed to add to mine own legend and search out the Injun maiden, but . . ."

Malarkey did not finish his sentence but instead cupped a hand over his ear and cocked his head to listen. Riley did likewise and soon heard a sound that grew loud enough to blot out the industry of men. The noise became huge and overpowering, stomping on the other senses, rendering insignificant their input.

It was the sound of a howling torrent approaching at great speed.

"Miss Chevron is upstream," shouted Malarkey over the din. "And unless we be suicidal fish, we ain't going upstream."

Around them, men hurled themselves into the canal and swam for safety through the open bridge gateway. Futuristic weapons that had been so clickety-clack were now little more than deadweights to drag a man to the canal bed, and so were discarded without hesitation.

The Revolution was over.

Men swam for their very lives.

Witmeyer smiled at the magnificent man in her life.

"Shall I cast off, King Otto?"

Malarkey watched the wall of water approach and felt the spray on his face and bore witness to its might as crates and craft were tumbled in its depths. He now knew how it must have felt for Pharaoh's soldiers when they saw the Red Sea bearing down on them.

"Yes, my love," he said. "Time for us to be away."

Riley knelt on the amphibian's deck.

Oh, Chevie, he thought, guilt racking his frame like lashes from a cat-'o-nine-tails. *I have deserted you.*

And then Witmeyer was behind the wheel and was pulling the amphibian in a tight circle and aiming it like an arrow at the bridge gateway.

Riley took a moment to stop worrying about Chevie so he could fear for himself as behind them the water spread across the dock, sweeping support columns aside like straw and collapsing the entire structure.

I did not realize there was this much water in all of London, he thought.

"Faster!" he shouted at the top of his lungs, as though he could possibly make himself heard in the flood. "Faster!"

And then the wave came down with all the force of a Titan of legend.

14 » THANK YOU, TECUMSEH

I think I told you about my dog, Justin. Well anyway, it's possible that Justin wasn't even supposed to be a dog. Maybe he was supposed to be a pig-crab hybrid. A crig or a prab, something like that. My point being that time travelers can mess up everything right down to the molecular level. Things we take for granted, like butterflies or bananas, could seem like abominations to someone from another time stream.

—Professor Charles Smart

THE WATER WAS RISING. A FLOOD OF BIBLICAL proportions had come to wash away a new ark crewed by violent men whose hearts were avaricious and whose intentions were bloody, and though Colonel Box's chamber door had been constructed with a seal as a precaution against normal flooding, it would inevitably submit to the weight of water.

Box entered his chamber of opulence with Vallicose close on his heels, and in Vallicose's fist was a handful of Chevron Savano's hair. Connected to that hair was Chevie's scalp, and connected to the scalp was her entire head, and so on.

Vallicose tossed Chevie into a corner like a sack of meat and walked a tight circle around the edges of an Arabian rug. Confusion was twisting her features into a mask of deep wrinkles and squints.

"I don't understand," she said, and then again, "I don't understand."

Box dragged two pre-packed steamer trunks from behind a tapestry and did eeny-meeny on them, deciding which he should take.

"I have considered this," he said absently. "Trunk A is my priority. Gold and weapons. Why am I dithering now? Indecisiveness is the ultimate inefficiency." He dragged one of the trunks around in front of his desk. "Sister Vallicose, we will carry this between us. I have a hidey-hole, if you will forgive the expression, which we can repair to."

Vallicose's face fell like melting wax. "I don't understand, Lord. This is Emergence Day. What about Boxstrike?"

Box patiently explained. "That particular plan has been compromised. It is pointless to waste valuable time bemoaning its failure. I have other plans that have already been set in motion. Backup plans—you have heard the phrase, no doubt. It is regrettable that we must move on; believe me, I am as frustrated as you that this tactic was unsuccessful, but the water is rising and we must be away."

Vallicose could not abandon the beliefs of a lifetime so easily. "Yes, I see, Lord, but Boxstrike is more than an idea. It is your divine plan to save the world." She wrung her fingers.

"It's in the Bible. The Rosenbaum's Gospel. We can't just walk away from the gospel."

Chevie was slowly getting her senses back, and she could see that Vallicose was losing her grasp on reality.

That's the problem with being a zealot, she thought. Eventually you have to deal with being wrong.

And eventually everyone is wrong.

Chevie had no sympathy for Vallicose. It might sound callous, but the Thundercat deserved every shred of anguish that the destruction of her belief system was bringing to her. After all, she had used that belief system to justify all the pain and suffering she had inflicted on countless others for twenty years or more, and now she would have to face the fact that she was simply a monster and not an agent of a new god.

That was all very well, and Chevie could allow herself a scintilla of satisfaction, but the water was seeping under the door and sloshing across the floor. And she was far from being one hundred percent.

Those rugs will be ruined, thought Chevie. And also I will be dead.

So perhaps it might be better to indulge in the smugness re: Vallicose later, when a million gallons of sewer water weren't swilling around outside the door.

And it may be a sealed door, she thought, but it isn't a submarine hatch.

She would wait for her moment, then make her move, as she had been taught in her original life as an FBI consultant. In her second life, training as a Boxite cadet, there hadn't been so much emphasis on survival. Just killing.

Wait for my moment? Chevie thought, rising slowly to her hunkers. *Wake up, girl. The moment is here and now. There will never be a better moment.*

It was true, Box was occupied with his lecture, and Vallicose was more or less wailing her frustrations. There were no eyes on her.

They think I am still under, she realized.

Chevie searched around for a weapon, and her eye landed on a vase that lay on a velvet cushion, barely three feet away. Not the ideal weapon, but it would have to do. Chevie reached out and tiptoed her fingers over the cushion to the vase. They crept over the lip and into the vessel's interior. There was something inside, something dry and grainy.

No time for an ugh *moment. This is life or death.*

Chevie made a spearhead with her fingers and wiggled them deep into the vase.

Now. Move now.

Vallicose and Box were still talking. Box was calm and pragmatic, but Vallicose was right on that thin line between emotional and hysterical.

Chevie was already rising when Vallicose turned toward her.

"And Savano," she said, "she remembers another future where there is no Empire of Box. Is that . . ."

Possible, she was about to say. Maybe, or *probable.* In any event, Vallicose never managed to finish her question, because Chevie's hand swiped her across the jaw. Possibly not a serious problem for a soldier, being swiped across the jaw, but Chevie's hand was clad in the armor of a heavy clay vase.

The vase clunked on impact and then shattered, releasing plumes of gray dust into the air, dropping from Chevie's hand in sections.

"Mother!" cried Box.

Mother? thought Chevie. Oh, God. His mother's ashes were in that vase.

Vallicose stumbled backward against a silk-covered ottoman, which caught her awkwardly behind the legs, sending her sprawling into a cluster of Roman columns. Chevie was after her like a cat, pouncing on Vallicose, winding her with a knee to the solar plexus. In a flash she had unclipped the Thundercat's buzz baton and sidearm, and then, making sure to break bodily contact, she touched the baton to Vallicose's bare wrist, sending fifty thousand volts coursing through the fallen woman's frame, knocking her unconscious.

Chevie swung around, expecting Box to be looming over her, but he wasn't. Colonel Box was sitting at his desk where the bulk of the dust had fallen, sweeping it into a pile, and there were tears on his cheeks.

This development was as much a surprise to Box as it was to Chevie, because though she could not possibly have known it, this was the first time since infancy that Box had cried, or even felt remotely saddened—or for that matter, emotional in any way. Emotions were simply a waste of time, and the only feeling Box had ever permitted himself was a slight smug satisfaction when each step of his grand plan had been ticked off the list. He had promised himself to feel some measure of genuine happiness when the throne of England was his, but now it seemed that would have to be deferred until Savano and her ridiculous band were dealt with.

But to have his mother's ashes scattered like this . . . Used as a weapon against him. How could Box have foreseen that, even with all of his calculations? Such an act was so random, so barbaric.

But why do I care? he asked himself. This pile of ash is not my mother.

But he *did* care, and the tears rolled down his cheeks, and he swore that he would kill Savano with his bare hands with savage glee.

Box tidied the ashes into a square, shaping the edges with his index finger, gathering his mother, and then stood, expecting to find Savano dangling from Vallicose's fist, awaiting her fate, possibly with a final impudent quip on her lips. But he was disappointed (another new emotion) to find that the girl had somehow vanquished his new bodyguard and had him covered with a pistol.

"Oh, for heaven's sake," he said, testily. "In every single calculation I have made since your unlikely arrival here, you have been long dead at this point. The odds against your surviving are so overwhelming that it would be better for you, Cadet Savano, if you just lay down and died right now."

Chevie was inclined to disagree. "I think my odds are pretty good, Box. Better than yours. And another thing. Don't call me *Cadet*. I am Special Agent Savano of the FBI. Remember those people? You were attached to them once upon a time."

Box sniffed. "Once upon a time that shall never come to pass."

The door had three panels, and now the bottom section surrendered its integrity, totally mulched by the acidity and force of the sewerage. The water level rose a foot in ten seconds, tugging at Chevie's legs. She needed to leave.

"I am going to go now, Box. And you are going to stay here with your lapdog."

Box seemed not to notice the gun. "That is incorrect. You are not leaving here alive, Savano. You defiled my mother's ashes."

"Gun," said Chevie, wiggling the barrel. "See? Gun."

Box made his thinking face, sticking out his jaw and chewing on the problem.

"I would have liked longer to ponder this situation," he admitted. "But a leader must be adaptable in that we have several fall-back positions, several alternate options, as it were."

This is insane, thought Chevie. I am not going to argue against insanity.

Huge pounding noises came down the corridor and broke against the door. The high shrieking of tortured metal rose in discordant counterpoint to the bass rumblings of tumbling masonry. It sounded as though a wailing dinosaur was crouched on the roof, battering the walls.

Maybe the tunnel is amplifying the sound, thought Chevie, but she didn't believe it.

This is all happening. It's not a nightmare.

Of all the incredible situations that Chevie could recall enduring in either timeline, surely this was the most bizarre: trapped with a fifth gospel saint in an underground lair while sewer slurry threatened to engulf the building.

And there were other factors that she didn't have time to mentally list. Beyond bizarre.

Chevie and Box came to simultaneous decisions.

"Take off your belt," said Chevie. "I'm just going to shoot you in the leg."

"Pass me the gun," said Box. "I must kill you posthaste and make good my tactical retreat."

"Excuse me?" said Chevie, incredulous.

"Pardon?" said Box.

"Okay," said Chevie. "Whatever. I'm shooting you in the leg. Do whatever you like. Dance a jig. But my advice is to take off your belt for a tourniquet and stand completely still."

The water level rose, knocking over the Roman pillars, lifting the ottoman from its stubby legs.

Too much talking, thought Chevie. I need to get out of this death trap. Riley could be in trouble.

Box seemed a little amused by Chevie's threat. "What I don't understand, Cadet Savano, is why you would want to stop me? What was so wonderful about our shared future? The entire world was an inefficient shambles."

Chevie felt an anger build inside her, and she allowed it to erupt through her words. "What about *your* world, Box? I was there. I saw it. Most of the planet is enslaved. You bombed half of Europe. Your secret police murdered millions, including my father."

"So shoot me," said Box. "With one bullet you will save the world from my empire, but you will doom it to World Wars I and II, as well as the many other conflicts I am certain there have been since I left the future. Is that really better than my empire? Are you willing to make that choice? Especially since you will never know the effect of your decision, as I have had the time pod in Half Moon Street destroyed."

The water was icy against Chevie's thighs, but she shuddered mostly from the realization that she was stuck in the past forever.

"Vallicose told me that under my regime apartheid never even developed in South Africa," Box continued, calmly swishing the water with his fingers.

Chevie was incredulous. "Because *you* enslaved the entire country."

"Exactly," said Box. "So much more efficient. Now give me the gun; you can't shoot me."

"I can't kill you," said Chevie. "But I can shoot you."

"So why haven't you?"

Yes. Why hadn't she? The water was rising. Riley needed her. Why was she having this conversation?

"You were speaking," she said weakly, just to give some answer.

"And you were waiting until I had finished? Really?"

He was right. It sounded ridiculous.

Box's eyes were suddenly crafty. "You cannot shoot me, *Cadet,* because I am your savior."

"Don't call me Cadet!" But just as Traitor Chevie had once struggled to be free inside Cadet Chevie's head, now the cadet was stirring in her subconscious.

"You are a cadet. My cadet. And I am your Blessed Colonel. For your entire life you have prayed to me. You have listened to my recorded speeches. Vallicose told me all about our future together."

Chevie backed up a step. "No. That future is dead. Look around you."

Box chuckled coldly; it sounded like the ratcheting of a shotgun slide. "Dead? Cadet, really. Do you think that I put all my egg grenades in one basket? No. This is a setback. Boxstrike is destined to occur. You have merely delayed my emergence."

"All the more reason to shoot you," said Chevie, already knowing what Box would say next.

"So why don't you?" Box spread his arms wide. "Go ahead. Pull the trigger and damn yourself to hell."

Suddenly Chevie's gun felt so heavy.

He is a man. An evil man. You know this.

"Shoot your savior, your religion. You cannot."

Chevie pulled the trigger, but the bullet flew wide, blasting a chunk from the brickwork. Box did not even flinch.

"Your own faith protects me," he said, raising his eyes to heaven. "I am a new god. Shoot!"

Chevie felt a surge from her subconscious as the old Chevie, the scared, cowed cadet, fought to be free.

No. I will not be that person ever again.

She fired again. This time hitting a cushion, which exploded in a whump of feathers. Box was unscathed.

"It is a sign," he said, eyes bright. "I am in your blood, Cadet Savano. I am in your soul. Would you be one who murders her savior? Would you be Judas?"

No, Lord, said the voice in Chevie's head. Her own voice.

"Fire your weapon, Cadet!" thundered Box.

"I will not be that cadet ever again!" Chevie shouted and pulled the trigger for the third time, the bullet fizzing harmlessly into the water around her thighs.

"Three times you have denied me," said Box advancing through the torrent. "But you can deny me no more. I am Clayton Box. Your lord and savior. The savior of the world."

Chevie backed away, hefting the gun in two hands, but still it seemed so heavy.

"Your body betrays you, Cadet. It will not allow you to shoot me. You cannot harm me, because I am your life and the light of the world. No one gets to heaven but through me. On your knees and beg forgiveness."

Chevie felt water lap at the small of her back.

"I will never kneel. Never."

But Old Chevie dragged at her heart. *Kneel. Oh, please kneel. Remember DeeDee.*

DeeDee. Executed.

"Damn you!" screamed Chevie in a last burst of resistance, and pulled the trigger. The shot was a mile wide, shattering the glass on a framed world map.

I can't shoot the Blessed Colonel, Chevie realized. Savior of the world. It is not in me.

In me.

In which *me?*

Who am I now?

I am fighting myself, Chevie realized. And one of me is losing. It's the Traitor.

"On your knees, sinner!" shouted Box. He could have taken the gun easily, but he did not even try. "On your knees. My will be done."

Chevie felt her eyes blur. *It is the Blessed Colonel. I am in His presence. I have sinned.*

Box was mere steps from her, and he seemed to radiate light. His tall frame filled Chevie's mind and vision.

I have defied the colonel. God forgive me.

Chevie felt her knees bend and tears of frustration and sorrow flowed down her cheeks.

Do not kneel. Do. Not. Kneel.

Shoot. Kill him.

But she was sinking down, and the water swirled around her waist, then her chest, hugging her like a mother. As she dropped, her gun hand came up in a last-gasp defiance of Cadet Savano, who was in control now.

"At last she has seen the light," said Box, raising his eyes to heaven. "The vessel of the Lord shall not be martyred this day."

He pressed his chest against the gun barrel. "For the faithful are forever bound to me in this life or any other life and they shall not harm me."

"My Lord," mumbled Chevie. "My Lord Colonel."

Box met her eyes. "There is no tomorrow but the one I bring forth unto the world. And those who would conspire against me must give up their secrets before giving up their lives."

My dad, realized Chevie. He is talking about my dad.

But still she could not pull the trigger, and it was almost a relief when Box took the pistol from her trembling fingers.

It's out of my hands now, she thought. I'll just stay here on my knees, and very soon the waters will close over me.

"Praise God. There is rejoicing in heaven when the prodigal son returns to the fold."

I bet there is no rejoicing on earth, said Traitor Chevie, who was on the way back to her cage.

"Sadly, here on earth," confirmed Box, as though he had heard the thought, "in this valley of tears, the prodigal son or daughter must be severely chastised as an example to others."

Yep, said Traitor Chevie. *Severely chastised. That's what you get for showing mercy.*

Box took hold of Chevie's collar and stalked across the chamber, dragging her facedown through the rising waters. She did not struggle or thrash and would probably have allowed herself to drown had not the colonel dumped her on his own desk, which had been floating until her weight pinned it down. Chevie lay on her back, feet dangling in the water, coughing rancid water from her lungs, salt tears on her cheeks.

Box dangled the gun by its trigger guard and held it out to his side.

"You. Dispatch this sinner to her just reward. I must gather my mother."

He was talking to Vallicose, who was half-conscious now, recovering from her shocking, and had picked herself up from the pile of columns.

"Yes, Lord. Of course, Lord."

Vallicose took the gun, but not with the enthusiasm she generally exhibited when handling weapons.

"I am sorry, Lord."

"Sorry for allowing yourself to be incapacitated, I imagine, for putting my life in danger."

"Yes," said Vallicose. "But mostly for . . ."

Box scooped handfuls of ash into the urn's broken base. "Mostly for what, soldier?"

"For losing faith, Lord. I was beginning to doubt."

"Doubt? You doubted me?"

"Yes, Lord. Nothing is as we were told. Even this room is so vulgar. I had never even seen you pray, so I doubted you until right now, when I saw the divine spirit through you. It was blinding. I beg forgiveness."

Box wiped the last specks of ash from his fingers. He had been saving his moment of anger for Savano, but he found himself suddenly furious with this insufferable idiot Vallicose. He had thought it mildly amusing that she consistently credited God with stratagems that he himself had planned out over months and sometimes years.

"Divinity is a tool," he snapped, cradling the ashes in his arms. "Religion is a tonic for the troops."

Vallicose was confused. "No, Lord. *You* are God, surely."

Box turned on his disciple. "Clayton Box is nobody's god. I am the prime instrument. All the great dictators, with few exceptions, have armed themselves with religion. It is convenient to do so. I have never spoken with the voice of God. I simply came from the future, like you. Are you so zealous that you cannot see the evidence? No God, just science."

"So you don't believe in yourself?"

Box angled his large head. "Do you really think, Vallicose, that, if there is a God, He wishes my master plan to succeed? *God* wishes us to obliterate an entire class of people? God approves of our intention to wipe out whole cities?"

"But those are foreigners. They are heathens."

"Jesus would be a foreigner here, Vallicose. And Moses. Even Saint Paul. All foreigners. People will always follow a leader with God on his side, and so I decided to have God on my side. And from what you tell me, I decided to *be* God. Are you so dense that you cannot understand that?"

Vallicose was crumbling from the inside out. Her surroundings were completely forgotten.

"I followed you all my life. The things I have done in your name . . ."

"Exactly my point," said Box. "Sheep will run straight over a cliff if they believe."

Vallicose's legs could barely hold her up. "I was blind."

Box nodded pointedly at the gun. "But now you can see, soldier. You can see to shoot."

Vallicose looked at the gun in her hand as though she did

not know what it was. In fact, she didn't seem certain what her hand was.

"Shoot?"

"Yes. Shoot the child."

"But God . . ."

The walls shook as successive surges battered them and several sections tumbled inward, allowing the floodwater to gush through the hole. Rat heads bobbed past the busted masonry as the rodents swam for dry land.

Box realized that time was dangerously short.

"But God? But God?" he said, wading toward the door. "Forget God, soldier. God is just the next rank up from general." He took one hand from the vase remnant and jerked a thumb at Chevie. "Now, shoot the girl. Your new *god* commands it. Fall back to the airship hangar in the docklands and bring my trunk."

Two words smacked Vallicose in the face like physical blows. And they were not *airship hangar,* as might have been expected in the 1890s, when such things were rare.

Forget God?

"Forget God?" she said, raising the gun. "Blasphemy."

"Blasphemy is a tool," said Box, not turning back. "Just like God is a tool."

"God is a tool?" Vallicose said, reduced to repeating what she heard. It seemed as though her limbs belonged to somebody else and her skull was too small for her brain. She felt somehow numb and hypersensitive at the same time.

Everything I have ever believed is a lie. Everything I built my life around.

Wait. Not everything.

Not God. I may have been tricked, but not by God—by a man. Perhaps that is why I have been sent here.

Box realized that he had not heard a shot, and he turned back to Vallicose. There was no anger on his almost simian features, just mild disappointment.

"Don't be a child, soldier. You have been to war. Religion is just a weapon in our arsenal. A very big stick."

Vallicose shot him in the heart, and the colonel died so quickly that he never even got to change his expression. All his body did was jettison the tension it had been carrying around for decades and topple slowly forward into the rushing waters, which bore him into Vallicose's waiting arms.

She wept tears of shock and confusion as she gathered him close. "Colonel, O Lord Colonel. God told me to do it. God is not a tool. We are the tools."

Box didn't hear. He was beyond listening. Clayton Box was simply beyond, and his great projected empire would never materialize.

Vallicose wept, her entire body shaking, and her mind snapped under the weight of what she had done. She pulled the colonel tight to her chest, shooting warning looks at the rats who rode the flotsam.

"You shall not have Him," she called, using the last of her bullets on the rodents. "He is mine." She wiped streaks of Box's hair from his brow. "Don't worry, Lord. I am here to protect you. Nothing will happen."

She searched for an island in the chamber and her eyes

settled on the desk, which was slowly spinning, half afloat, semi-anchored by Savano's weight.

This is all her fault, Vallicose thought unreasonably, and she reached out with one arm, pushing Chevie into the floodwater. The current welcomed her into its load of detritus and she was borne swiftly to the door, where her head knocked against the last remaining panel.

Vallicose climbed onto the desktop, dragging Box's body with her, and their combined weight anchoring the table for an extra moment. She settled him across her knees and waited underneath the newly installed painting of Michelangelo's *Pietà* for God's cleansing flood to wash over them both, eager for the Lord to assure her that she had acted according to His will.

Chevie heard the gunshots boom against the curved ceiling, but she was beyond any act of self-preservation. Her mind was packed tight with the struggle between two warring personalities.

Who was she now?

Cadet Chevron, or Special Agent Chevron? Just when it seemed quite possible that she would never emerge from the cocoon of this struggle, she was unceremoniously dumped into the water, and the shock took her a fraction closer to consciousness. But it wasn't quite sufficient and she was a second away from inhaling a pint of cloudy water, which would have been the end, when her forehead crashed into an obstacle and the sharp pain brought an automatic reflex action from the FBI consultant in her.

Chevie floundered for a moment and then jerked herself upright, a hair's breadth from panic, and took a huge gasp of air. The water tugged at her like a fat eel wrapped around her torso, flipping her over and dragging her legs and torso underneath the door's busted central section. Only a ridge of her skull jammed against the top panel kept her in the chamber.

The last thing Chevie saw in Box's apartment was the dead colonel cradled in Vallicose's arms in an eerie echo of the *Pietà* copy hanging behind them. Then the door crumbled entirely and Chevron Savano was pulled along the corridor.

He is dead, she thought. I am free.

And she felt the grip of Cadet Savano lift from her mind. She still had the memories, but they were less potent.

Anyway, time to consider all of that later, when she wasn't drowning in a catacomb and so forth.

There were just inches of air at the curve of the ceiling, and Chevie rode the space, tiptoes and fingers skidding along the brickwork, breathing as much as possible, enlarging her lungs for the final breath, which had to come soon and last until she cleared the catacombs entirely. He legs were buffeted by underwater missiles borne along by the sewer flush. Hundreds of rats swam past frantically, a few taking refuge on her head until she swiped them off.

But no bodies, Chevie thought. I haven't seen any bodies.

Which was a comfort, because in spite of what these men had intended to do with their fantastic weapons, Chevie had no wish to see them murdered. The flush should have given them time to swim out.

Most of them, at any rate.

Her job now was to escape this claustrophobic place, find the rest of her team, and make sure they got away safely.

The corridor split in two, and Chevie took the left branch—or rather, was taken down the left branch—she didn't have any choice in the matter and it was a pity she didn't, because it was the wrong branch to take. The right-hand tunnel led into the underground dock and from there, underneath Camden Bridge and dry land. The left-hand branch led into the smelting room, which had a lower ceiling and was already full.

Imagine the horror, the sheer terror, of being suddenly completely underwater with the only sensory inputs being the frantic scrabble of rats and water pressure. Chevie slid into the foundry and the current changed from linear to swirling, and things began to bump against her.

Bodies, she realized, one twitch away from screaming underwater just for a quick death, but then she opened her eyes and saw a tunnel of light.

A tunnel of light?

But no, it wasn't the afterlife. Some distance away, a pale cylinder of light cut six feet down into the water before raggedly fading into the gloom.

That must be a chimney! thought Chevie, and she pulled out of the current she was in, striking hard for the twenty-foot shaft that allowed machine smoke out of the catacombs.

She willed herself not to panic, even though the odds were stacked sky-high against her actually surviving this ordeal.

And even if I do survive, what then?

Amazingly, this was the first time Chevie's own future had occurred to her beyond dealing with Clayton Box.

This is not the right moment to make a life-changing decision, she thought as she squinted through the murk, fixing on the blades of light cutting through the water.

Actually, it was the perfect time to think about something for half a minute, to distract herself from her situation and keep panic locked up in her mind.

The first fact to accept was that she could never go back to the twenty-first century. She could feel the Timekey lying on her breastbone, but the landing pad had been dismantled and destroyed, so now the pendant was nothing more than a complex ornament.

Chevie was surprised to find that she didn't really care about the future. All she wanted to do was lie down somewhere dry and go to sleep for a long while.

And a medal from Queen Victoria would be nice. And a decent cup of coffee.

Dryness and sleep, she decided, were the priorities. Queen Vic would have to wait a few days.

She reached the chimney, thrust herself inside, and was mightily relieved to find a tube of air leading twenty feet up to the surface. The shaft was soot-blackened and rose steeply, but not vertically, so she had a fighting chance.

Chevie shared the chimney with hundreds of rats, who trotted easily along the shaft. At another time she would have been disgusted and repulsed by their spiky wet fur and pink tails, but on this day she was almost relieved that the rats were taking the same route.

These guys know what they're doing.

All the same, Chevie had no desire to get nipped and pick up a dose of some Victorian plague, so she placed her hands carefully and tried not to flinch when the rats clambered over her forearms, careless in their desperation.

On a good day, with sunshine and breezes, a twenty-foot climb with plenty of toeholds would not have inconvenienced Chevie much—in fact, her pulse probably would not have risen much above sixty—but now, with her uniform sopping wet and death all around, it seemed to Chevie that this sloping shaft could be the straw that not only broke the camel's back, but its will to survive, too.

The chimney's surface was treacherous for a climber. The bricks were coated with soot and oil, which had been slickened by the rats' claws as they hurried to the surface. Chevie dug her fingers into the spaces between bricks and pulled herself upward inch by painful inch. She could see her hands now and was not surprised to find her knuckles bloodied from the climb. She lifted her face toward the sky and thought that the pale disk of evening light was the most beautiful thing she had ever seen.

I will survive this, she thought. I will swim in the ocean again. In clean, sparkling water.

Which was a lofty ambition indeed, given her current surroundings.

She was halfway there now, and the world had reduced itself to this struggle. What came before and after the climb did not matter. It was very simple: go on, or die. So she dug in her fingers and toes, dragging herself along, watching her blood seep out from cracks in her skin's sooty coating.

There were too many rats now—a bubbling carpet of claws and teeth—and so Chevie began sweeping them off with her forearms, clearing a path for herself. The chimney narrowed as it rose, and Chevie fought back panic when it occurred to her that she might not be able to squeeze through the opening.

I will fit, she resolved. Cadet Chevie may not have had the resolve for this fight, but she is gone now. Forever.

But her mind was all Special Agent now. The cadet had been losing coherence from the moment she saw Box's body. The Boxite Empire would never come to pass.

But what will happen to the world? Chevie wondered, thinking as loudly as she could to shut out the squeaks, chitters, and claw-clicking rat sounds. What new horror will rise up?

Would it be as she learned in history class? Or would it be worse?

Chevie could see now that the opening to the outside world was small, but not too small to wriggle through. She also noticed for the first time that there was a grille on the chimney mouth.

Of course there is, she thought. I should have foreseen this and dived for a tool.

But she could never have dived into the black waters where God only knew what was waiting to snag her pale limbs.

Chevie freed one hand and tried the grille. Locked, naturally. Why did she even bother hoping anymore, when nothing ever seemed to go her way?

Except all those times you survived virtually unsurvivable situations.

Chevie hunched her shoulder to her ear, then rammed the grille until it lifted to the extent a securing chain would allow. There was a gap large enough for a few rats, but not even a human arm.

"Hello!" she called through the bars. "Is there anyone there?"

No one answered and no one came to investigate. She was alone.

It was beyond infuriating to be so close to freedom that she could literally taste it. Chevie laced her fingers into the grille and lay flat on the stones.

Just a moment to rest and think.

She allowed the rats to flow over her and envied them their size, which let them squeeze out through the bars. Her toe jiggled a loose brick in its housing and it was this stroke of luck that probably saved her life.

Chevie inched backward until her eyes were level with the loose brick. She cleared away loose mortar with one stiff finger, digging in as far as she could, huffing the dust into her face; then she wiggled the brick from side to side until the wall gave it up. It slid out with a noise like a crypt opening.

She hefted the brick in one hand, climbed a few feet until she could dig her foot into the new hole for stability, and took a swing at the lock that secured the chain. She put all of her strength into the blow but missed, braining an unfortunate rat and splitting the brick down the middle, sending sharp chunks tumbling down the shaft.

One more time, she thought, and: Sorry, Ratty.

Chevie drew back her arm, tightened her core, then swung with the last burst of energy in her beleaguered body, grunting like a Viking swinging his ax. She flattened the old lock into the wall. The mechanism crumpled and popped, and the body separated entirely from the shackle, allowing the end links to swing freely.

"Ha!" she crowed. "Thank you, Tecumseh."

The moment the name *Tecumseh* fell from her lips, Chevie began to cry. Firstly because *Thank you, Tecumseh* was one of the phrases her dad used when anything went his way.

The spirit of the great Shawnee warrior, Tecumseh, watches over us, he had explained.

When Chevie's mind conjured the phrase, she remembered the last time he had used the words. It was on the morning his Harley's gas tank had exploded on the Pacific Coast Highway. His bike had been reluctant to start the first couple of times, and when the engine had caught on the third try, he had looked to the sky and shouted, *Thank you, Tecumseh,* and they had both laughed.

Better for him to die while doing something he loved than while being tied up in a Thundercat chair. At least she had spared him that.

Chevie dropped the brick stub down the shaft and pushed open the grille with her head and shoulders. Suddenly her entire body seemed heavier than a stone statue; she felt that if the open air had been one more inch away, she could not have made it. She wiggled from the chimney mouth and flopped onto the blessed surface.

"Thank you, Tecumseh," she mumbled, watching the last few rats scamper down the canal bank. "Thank you."

She would have been content to lie there on the cold hard clay, ignoring the stares of passersby and dock workers. But for one thing, no one was looking at her—they were all staring at the strange futuristic vehicle that was barreling across Camden Bridge.

And for another thing, there was a strange futuristic vehicle on Camden Bridge.

It would seem that Boxstrike had not been completely averted just yet.

Clover Vallicose sat on Box's desk with the corpse of her Lord draped across her knees, and she cried. She bawled for the loss of her master and her faith, for how stupid she had been to believe in Clayton Box. This was how it always ended; every time she had trusted someone, that person had eventually proven himself unworthy. Her parents had been secretly writing poetry, forcing her to inform on them. Her trusted partner, Lunka Witmeyer, seemed to have freed that gorilla Otto. The Hangman had gotten his bones stripped bare by rats, and now the Blessed Colonel himself had proven to be a hollow vessel.

It was too much for her mind to process; that she could have been so wrong for so long. Clover had believed with all her heart that she had been chosen to stand at her Blessed Colonel's side during the first round of Boxstrike, but it seemed as though she would die with him in this cavern. There would be no Boxstrike to cleanse the British Empire of the covetous men who sat on the polished benches of Parliament. Man would continue to damn the world to an eternity in hell. Their only real chance at salvation lay dead in her lap, and he was not worthy. He had never been worthy.

He had never been.

The notion struck Vallicose like a bolt from the heavens.

Box had never been worthy.

He had never believed as she had believed with every atom in her body, with every beat of her heart.

I believe.

Vallicose realized with a jolt that she herself was a true believer.

I am worthy.

But this was hubris. This was the pride that would damn her.

No. This is why I was chosen. To make sure Boxstrike takes place. I *am the sword of God.* I *am the angel of death. Godstrike!*

As soon as the notion struck her, it seemed to fit. She felt the rightness of it, and her head swam with glorious images of herself at the head of an army.

An army of God.

Whether she lived or died did not matter, for she would live forever in the sight of God and all her sins would be forgiven.

But how to proceed without weapons or army?

Vallicose rolled Box's corpse from her lap and stood on the desk.

Perhaps she did not have an army, but there was one weapon that had not been lost to the flood. One rather large weapon.

Vallicose turned to the newly hung *Pietà* and ripped it down, revealing a steel door in the wall. Vallicose leaped into the water and ducked to punch in the code on the submerged mechanical keypad. Box had shared the combination with her earlier in the day.

Zero six zero two, he'd told her. Revelation chapter six verse two:

I looked, and behold, a white horse, and he who sat on it had a bow; and a crown was given to him, and he went out conquering and to conquer.

Vallicose opened the door with a little more effort than it had cost Box earlier and swam through the gap. Inside was a spiral staircase leading up, and she climbed it just as she had earlier that day, following Box's footsteps.

This is my white horse, he had said. *A secret project that two of my engineers have been working on for ten years.*

At the last bend of the staircase was a large storage shed with reinforced walls and no door.

I will ride my white horse to the very seat of government and blow those graven idols from their hiding place, he had declared, *and you shall ride beside me.*

Just like the first time she had seen it, Vallicose stared at Box's white horse, awestruck.

It was neither a horse nor white, but for blowing graven idols from their hiding places, it would do quite nicely.

It could not be said that Chevie did not believe what she was seeing. After all, she had witnessed some strange things in her short life/lives, including a tunnel composed of quantum foam, a man who could change his face at will, and a gang boss sporting powdered wig and rouge. But despite all her visual experiences, she was still dumbstruck by the sight of an armored tank rumbling across Camden Bridge, which could barely bear its gross tonnage.

But if Chevie was dumbstruck, the Londoners compensated for her silence with a rising chorus of screams and howls, forming a corridor of panic that followed the tank's thundering route, first through the marketplace and then across the groaning bridge. Chevie heard shouts of *Dragon!* and even *Martian!* as the locals tried desperately to assess the metal monstrosity that had burst through the brick wall of a storage warehouse and was now crushing the cobblestones beneath its mighty metal treads.

The turret swung in a wide arc, like the head of a drunken man, and the 120-mm gun barrel knocked a cab horse unconscious and almost ripped the carriage itself in half. Onward the tank powered down Camden High Street, dragging stalls into its maw and spitting out twisted wreckage in its wake.

Your average Londoner is a plucky bloke, and several locals pelted the tank with fruit and vegetables from market stalls. One youngster even lifted a few steaks from a meat cart and lobbed them into the tank's tread mechanism in an effort to clog it up. The effects of this action were twofold: for one, the steak was instantly minced, and for two, the enterprising youngster had his ears boxed by the butcher.

(On a side note, there is evidence that this minced meat was later collected and fried by a German immigrant who many credit as inventing the hamburger.)

Chevie shook her head in an attempt to dislodge the fog of exhaustion that deadened her thoughts and sapped her brain, and she set herself to chasing after the tank, without any plan other than to keep the steel behemoth in sight.

She followed the canal to the bridge and from there onto Camden High Street, which in the space of the minute or so since the tank had appeared had become a scene of panic and bedlam. The population had abandoned any efforts to hinder or communicate with the tank and were hell-bent on evacuating the area as fleetly as possible. Chevie struggled against the flow of human exodus as people flooded down Camden High Street, ran down the banks of Regent's Canal and, in some more hysterical cases, threw themselves from the low bridge into the canal itself.

Chevie abandoned the footpath and ran directly down the road itself, dodging the occasional cab that bolted for the suburbs. The panic increased a notch when the tank's gun barrel spat flame and steel at a wagon that had been abandoned in the road, reducing it to a set of splinter-topped wheels. Amazingly, the pair of horses hitched to the wheels were for the most part unscathed, except for the tail of one, which burst into flames like a straw torch. The horse ambled to a nearby rain barrel and extinguished its tail therein.

I like that horse, thought Chevie. He doesn't scare easily.

Chevie ran in the tank's wake, knowing that she could not hope to catch the armored vehicle unless it stopped, a fact she was more than a little glad of, as she had no idea what she would do in the event she closed the distance between them.

I have no weapons, she realized. And I don't think they will open the hatch if I knock politely. So it probably makes sense to hang back until a plan occurs to me.

Hanging back was in itself something of a plan, but even this fell apart when Chevie found herself suddenly flying through the air and rapidly gaining on the tank.

Now I can fly, she thought. I wish I had known this earlier. It would have been handy in the catacombs.

Vallicose was in the grip of rapture like she had never known. A potent combination of religious fervor and what the ancient Celtic warriors dubbed the *warp spasm*, a particularly frenzied form of red mist that has been known to actually alter physical features. Indeed, Clover Vallicose was barely recognizable now as she piloted the sixty-ton tank along Gower Street. Her features were twisted in an expression very similar to hatred but which was actually a rare look of sheer bliss. If Vallicose were indeed to awaken on the following morning, she would find four of her facial muscles stiff from use after years of dormancy. Not that thoughts of the next day mattered one fig to Vallicose.

She gave no thought to surviving her holy mission; in fact, a large part of her would prefer to die gloriously so that she could all the sooner claim her eternal reward.

Through the narrow viewing port, Vallicose saw a gray slot of street in the dying winter light. She was, of course, familiar with the standard gears and pedals of an armored vehicle, but this tank was rigged for a crew of four, and only the autoloader slung to her left allowed her to fire while she navigated. Aiming, however, was out of the question and could only be accomplished when the tank was stationary. For now she would have to be satisfied with shooting at whatever lay directly in the tank's path. But not for much longer. Already the clock face of Big Ben was in sight, the tower of which cast a shadow over the Houses of Parliament. Her ultimate target.

The internal temperature rose quickly as the engine conducted heat through the entire structure, and Vallicose felt as though she were inside an oven. She smiled in the face of such adversity, for her reward would be all the more deserved. In her delirium she heard the voice of God telling her to fight on, and in the clouds of flame and smoke from the tank's exploding shells she saw His face, smiling and encouraging her to do His work.

"I am coming, Lord," she said through gritted teeth. "I am coming home."

Chevie realized almost immediately that she was not in fact flying but suspended four feet above the ground, held aloft by an iron grip on her belt. It was disconcerting enough to rattle and thump along the side of a vehicle of some sort, but not knowing whether this was a rescue or an assassination attempt made her helpless swinging all the more distressing.

Should I twist free? she wondered. Or trust the owner of that iron grip?

Twisting free would be the best option, Chevie decided, as she could count on one finger the amount of true friends she had in this timeline.

So she planted her feet against the olive green side panel of the vehicle and push/twisted with every ounce of the meager energy left to her after the sewer spelunking expedition.

As she twisted away, the gripper pulled her in, and the combination of forces resulted in Chevron's body transcribing a wide arc so that she collided briefly with the head of the blinkered horse with its tail in a water barrel before being yanked back into the flat bed of the vehicle, where she landed on Thundercat Lunka Witmeyer.

"Horse!" shouted Chevie. "Horse!"

The two went down in a tangle of limbs, rolling into the amphibian's bow, and the combination of vibration and hullabaloo from all sides made it impossible for Chevie to assess her situation. The only shred of information that she could pluck from the jumbled cacophony of sensory input was that she was in a clinch with the hated Witmeyer who had terrorized her so effectively in the academy.

I am not that person anymore, she thought, then said it aloud. "I am not that person anymore!"

She followed the exclamation with several lightning punches, reasoning that she was low on strength, so best to aim for the soft spots. Chevie put two further strikes into Witmeyer's throat and was just about to deliver the killer third, when someone dragged her off.

"No!" she screamed, kicking out at the Thundercat. "Let me finish!"

She was not permitted to finish. Instead, a pair of massive arms came from behind and folded her firmly in their embrace until her vision settled, and Riley appeared in front of her.

"Chevron, oh Chevie," he said, tearfully. "You have a knack for survival, so you do."

Chevie was not prepared to let down her guard just yet. "'So you do'? You sound like Missus Figary's boy."

Riley embraced as much of his friend as he could around the huge arms that were still holding her.

"I need to incapacitate Witmeyer," Chevie whispered urgently.

"No," said Riley. "She's driving."

Riley filled Chevie in on recent events while Witmeyer coughed and spluttered her way to her feet, and then to the steering wheel of their anachronistic transport.

"It goes on water and land," said Riley, delighted in spite of the fact that they were for all intents and purposes in a war-zone. "We were pushed down the canal by the flood, but Lunka managed to drive us onto the bank."

"Lunka?" said Chevie. "It's Lunka now?"

"You smell to high heaven," said Riley happily. "Been toshing, have you?"

Chevie was not mollified by familiarity. "Maybe. While you guys have been cozying up with my mortal enemies."

"She came a-cooing on King Otto," explained Riley.

Malarkey opened his arms, for they were the ones that held Chevie, and he pushed her onto a bench. "Tell me now, Injun, is you gonna row in, or act out? If'n it's number two, then I shall brain you without delay, but if you gives me your pledge that we stand on the same bank of the river, so to speak, then spit and shake and let's be finishing this revolution for once and for all."

A long speech under the circumstances, but Otto had always been overly fond of the sound of his own voice, and Chevie understood the gist despite the unfamiliar terms.

Spit and shake? She did not fancy that.

"Just shake, Otto, okay? A big mouth like yours makes a lot of spit, and I've had enough disgusting liquid for one day."

Otto grunted and shook, and during the shake both shakers were coincidentally thinking along identical lines.

Once this is all over, we two need to have a talk about respect.

"Hmph," said Otto.

"Yep," said Chevie.

And then all minds and eyes were trained on the tank bashing its way ever closer to Westminster.

In a world of jaded repetitions there are very few firsts, but on this day London was witnessing the inaugural trip of a motorized armored vehicle on its avenues, and as a postscript there was a horseless boat-cart trailing behind in the tank's wake of crushed stone and metal.

This was the worst time of day to drive even a buggy into the city, with the offices discharging a glut of workers into the streets, and the taverns taking in what they could, and the remainder spilling onto the sidewalks, which were already three-deep with worthy professors and flighty scholars from the Bloomsbury academies and universities. Street traders marked their pitches with coarse halloos and hollers, endeavoring to make themselves heard above the clank and clamor of wagon, carriage, and cart.

"Where is he going?" wondered Chevie aloud. "He can't escape in a tank."

Witmeyer pointed toward Westminster.

"He isn't trying to escape. Box has a mission."

There was a shortwave radio on the dash, and its speaker crackled into life.

"Lunka? Is that you behind me?"

Witmeyer grabbed the handset. "Clove? Clover. It's over. The army has been destroyed. Tell Box to stand down."

The speaker crackled with what might have been bitter laughter. "The colonel was weak and mortal. Very mortal. Mine is the mission now. The Lord guides my hand."

Witmeyer pounded the dash. "We were lied to, Clover. All these years we were working for men, not God. It's time to make our own decisions."

Vallicose did not speak for a moment; then: "You are no longer on the side of the angels, Lunka Witmeyer. You speak with the forked tongue of the devil, and I will not listen to another word."

The radio went dead and up ahead, the tank's large caliber gun fired an explosive round into the locked wheels of a knot of carriages, blowing them apart like kindling, flooding the street with a wave of panic. And as panic is never organized, the road was soon rendered utterly impassable by a jam of carriages and tangled harnesses.

Utterly impassable, that is, for an indigenous Victorian vehicle, but a twentieth-century tank would make light work of such obstructions. Vallicose opened the throttle wide and powered into the melee, rising on the backs of coach and livestock, its massive weight forging its own elevated road. It was an incredible sight to see and one that shocked even those from another time.

"I seen a lot of strange things in me time, being a gentleman adventurer," said Malarkey. "But I ain't never seen nothing like that. Can we follow?"

"No," said Chevie. "We cannot."

Witmeyer seemed determined to pursue her partner across the highway of trampled vehicles, but at the last second she balked and swung a sharp right onto the Strand with its multicolored awnings, distinctive brick arches, and colonnades. If anything the traffic was denser on the Strand, leaving the pilot no choice but to avail of the first exit, which took the amphibian craft down a steep lane to the banks of the Thames itself, with its inviting expanse of black river and silvery swirls of seawater.

Inviting in the sense that, compared to the packed street above, it was uncluttered by vehicles.

Malarkey guessed what his beloved was thinking.

"Onward," quoth he. "You are my Aphrodite and I shall be your Poseidon."

"I have no idea what you are saying, my king," said Witmeyer. "But I love how you say it."

"All day," said Riley to Chevie. "All day it has been just like this."

All conversation, both romantic and mocking, ceased as the amphibious craft plunged down the embankment, crashed through a railing, decimated a stack of barrels, and shot like an arrow into the Thames. The prow dipped sharply before the buoyancy packs forced it back the way it came with alarming velocity. The passengers were rolled about like marbles in a bowl and came to rest in a single multilimbed, squirming heap in the bilges.

Otto was the first to speak. "Oh, my Lord," he breathed. "Oh, my sweet Jehovah."

For one of the embankment barrels had landed on deck, and the stencil on the cask said BRANDY.

He disentangled himself from the heap and crawled to the gunwale, peering over the side.

"Lordy lord," he said. "It's all going on today, and no mistake."

Chevie was next out of the pile. "What now, Otto? More brandy?"

"Don't I wish?" said Otto, pointing to a craft fifty feet off their stern. "Nah, it ain't brandy, girl. It's that boat."

"We're on a river, Malarkey. Boats are to be expected."

"I will grant you that, saucy. Boats are indeed to be

expected in this the busiest port in the civilized world. But most of 'em do not have *HMVS Boadicea* writ down their flanks."

"'Boadicea'?" said Chevie. "Why is that name familiar?"

"Boadicea," said Riley, crawling from under Witmeyer's meaty thigh. "The warrior queen. Merciless and deadly."

"That's okay," said Chevie. "We aren't the bad guys."

A cannonball whistled overhead, hammering the dock wall behind them, sending chunks of masonry spinning into the air.

"Speak for yourself," said Malarkey, then he helped Lunka Witmeyer to her feet so she could pilot them away from the approaching flatiron gunship.

"*Cannon to the front of me,*" he sang airily.

"*Cannons to the rear.*

I may as well be whistling.

It does no good to fear."

Witmeyer turned to Chevie and her eyes were bright. "Is he not wonderful?" she asked her fellow female. "Look at that hair."

We are all going to die, thought Chevie. Very soon.

Vallicose was on the wrong side of the river. A bunch of drunk sailors had mounted an assault on the tank and had, incredibly enough, managed to jam her viewing port with a wooden leg. By the time she had managed to knock the thing out of the slot, she found herself crashing through the boundary turnstiles of Waterloo Bridge, which had long been known as the Bridge of Sighs because of its granite span's sordid association with the leaps of desolate lovers. It was possible that, traveling at the speed that it was, the tank would not have been able to make the turn, but the front fender whacked into a recessed stone niche, which nudged the vehicle back on course.

Vallicose was not unduly concerned to have swung wide of her target—after all, God was on her side and Big Ben stood up like a beacon and she would simply take the first crossing back over the river.

A bluebottle ran alongside, beating the armored plating with his club and tooting on his whistle, raising an alarm that had already spread across half of London, and Vallicose had to admire the man.

He is fighting for queen and country, she thought. Which is valiant enough, but I can trump him. I am fighting for the souls of this nation.

She accelerated across the bridge's level path and powered along the riverbank. It was true that God was on her side, but He would expect her to prove herself.

God rained fiery sulfur on Sodom and Gomorra, and now I shall do the same to London.

She saw a group of militia ahead, desperately trying to set up a cannon post directly in her path.

Convenient, she thought. Directly in my path is the only target I can hit right now.

She almost casually blew the ordnance and its operators into the river.

Ten shells left, she noted. More than enough.

• • •

The amphibian craft was under fire from the gunboat, though not in any serious danger because the flatiron, much like Vallicose's tank, was restricted to firing straight ahead. Its single twelve-inch gun could be hydraulically elevated, but was without port or starboard maneuverability, which meant that to aim the gun it was necessary to aim the entire boat.

The river was dotted with civilian craft, and yet the Royal Navy boys were reckless with their bombardment, capsizing one pleasure yacht and sinking a fuel barge outright.

"What ho!" said Malarkey, slipping his arm around the pilot's waist. "There's coal for the fishies."

Chevie was inclined to take things more seriously. For Malarkey the Boxite Empire was all a bit hypothetical; but Chevie knew that even with Box dead, his plan for the world could still come to pass. All it took was one maniac with futuristic knowledge, and that described Vallicose pretty exactly.

"Help me," she called to Riley, and they staggered to the stern and the weapons' locker that ran along the gunwale. They heaved back the watertight cover and feasted their eyes on the hardware inside.

"A drainpipe!" said Riley, pointing to one piece of kit. "What good is a blooming drainpipe? Are we s'posed to *rain* the enemy to death?"

Chevie lifted the pipe from its foam housing.

"Two things, pal. One: don't let Figary hear you say *s'pose.* The word is *suppose.*"

"And two?" asked Riley.

"Two," said Chevie, "this is no ordinary piece of pipe."

• • •

Vallicose swung onto Westminster Bridge, and having learned from her earlier overenthusiasm, took the corner gently, not losing control for even a second. The tank's caterpillar tracks bit into the stone, throwing up twin wakes of sparks and chips. The flat road became something of a racetrack as carriages, cyclists, pedestrians, and even an automobile made all possible speed to the Westminster bank in an attempt to remove themselves from the path of this metal dragon that spat death and moved in a cloud of thunder.

Vallicose felt a surge of familiar satisfaction at the terror that the Thundercats' shock-and-awe tactics often inspired. She picked up the microphone of the radio that would connect her to the other Box vehicle.

"Lunka, do you remember the Cannes assault? When we firebombed the film festival? Those damned artists didn't know what hit them."

Witmeyer answered immediately. "Of course I remember, Clove. And that was fun, but this is different. We have to live here now, and Box is dead, his army scattered."

"Box was a fraud," snapped Vallicose. "He was not the man I thought he was. Colonel Box thought only of his own plans."

"Bail out, Clove. Just jump off the bridge, and Otto can scoop you up."

This was such a preposterous suggestion that Vallicose laughed. "Otto will *scoop me up*? Otto is your man, I suppose." She shook her head. "Let me tell you something, Sister

Witmeyer. This is the last thing I will ever say to you: men are weak and they will disappoint you."

Far below her ex-partner, on the amphibian's deck, Witmeyer looked up into the face of King Otto Malarkey and thought: *Not this one. And if he does, I will feed him his own entrails.*

Malarkey caught the look and thought: *See how the lady loves you, Otto. Never in a million years would she harm you.*

The Houses of Parliament lay tantalizingly close on the Middlesex bank of the Thames.

Within firing range?

Possibly.

Vallicose couldn't know for sure, but seeing as the bridge was completely plugged by panicking civilians and their abandoned vehicles, and militia struggling with their artillery, it seemed likely that she would need to launch her assault from farther back than she would like. Even though this tank was not a twenty-first century transplant, surely it had a range of a thousand feet, which would be double what was needed.

The militia sent a salvo her way from a Gatling repeater, and the bullets pinged off the tank's hide, doing little more than scratching the paintwork. Even so, Vallicose resented the pinging, as she was trying to concentrate. She climbed into the turret and cranked the gun forty-five degrees left, thirty-five degrees elevation. No time for graphs and charts; her best guess would have to do.

"Fire in the hole," she said to no one in particular and palmed the red button.

The turret shuddered, then shot out its first missile.

Vallicose saw it pass over the palace wherein sat the Houses of Parliament, if not the politicians themselves, who were no doubt fleeing at this very moment.

No matter, thought Vallicose. The building is the thing. The symbol of British rule.

Her next thought was: Too high. Too high.

But she revised her opinion when the missile struck Elizabeth Tower, commonly known as Big Ben, and whipped the top off neatly from clock face up.

Vallicose crowed with delight.

Five degrees lower.

Another thump, which made the entire bridge shake, and this shot was dead-on, arcing over the militia and into the belly of the central lobby, firing up a cloud of smoke and flame.

Vallicose fancied she heard screaming.

That's nothing, she thought. Wait until their flabby limbs are licked by the flames of hell.

She reloaded. *Two more should do it, and then I shall drive my engine into the heart of the flames.*

After the next shot, the bridge shook a little more than expected, and Vallicose found her tank listing to one side.

Curious, she thought. That is not supposed to happen.

The flatiron gunboat had found itself hopelessly entangled in a farrago of river traffic and had even taken on the sailors from the ruptured coal barge, who proceeded to engage in spirited fisticuffs with the salty boys who had sunk them.

"Serves those careless coves right," said Malarkey, who could not recall having so fine a time. "Firing on the river like that. Blatantly irresponsible, that were."

Witmeyer eased the throttle into neutral, then hit reverse for a single pulse to bring the amphibian to a gradual halt parallel to Westminster Bridge.

Chevie, an agent trained to protect the innocent, was horrified at what she saw.

"She's firing on civilians," she said.

"They're not all civilians," noted Witmeyer.

In response, Chevie locked a small missile into the drainpipe and took aim along the barrel.

"Are you standing behind me?" she asked Riley.

"That I am," confirmed the boy. "Safe behind you."

"Then move," advised Chevie. "With this particular drainpipe, behind is nearly as dangerous as in front."

Chevie had only fired an RPG once before, during maneuvers near Quantico. And she didn't get a chance to use one a second time—at least not on this day—because a bullet fired from the deck of the *Boadicea* hit Chevie in the right shoulder. The ball had little steam behind it and did not even penetrate to the bone, but the damage was more than adequate to knock her to the deck.

Riley dropped to her side. "Chevie!" he said, his face suddenly white with worry for his friend. "Chevie, say you ain't dead."

Chevie coughed so much the bullet popped from its shallow hole.

"I ain't dead," she confirmed. "But I ain't firing rockets either. Witmeyer, you need to do it."

Witmeyer did not turn from her post at the wheel. "I have gone as far as I can," she said. "I will not kill you, but neither will I kill Clover. She has saved me many times."

"Then you must do it, buddy," said Chevie weakly. "You can sight along my shoulder."

"Me?" said Riley. "I ain't never fired no cannon."

Chevie's eyes were narrow with pain. "Please. I can't let the Empire win. I can't."

"Then neither can I," said Riley. "I can point a pipe, surely."

As he spoke, Riley pulled a string of magician's handkerchiefs from his vest and tied off Chevie's wound, which he was relieved to note was not bleeding too freely.

"Okay, good," said Chevie. "I'll talk you through it."

Riley lifted his friend from the deck, gently draping her across the gunwale.

"That's right," she said. "Now lay the launcher across my shoulder. My *good* shoulder."

Now I've got a bad shoulder, she thought. I'm too young to have a bad shoulder.

Riley picked up the launcher gently, as though it might explode in his hands, and laid the green metal on Chevie's shoulder.

"Move in close, pal," she said. "Get as much pipe on either end as you can."

Riley knelt behind Chevie so that his right cheek touched her left ear.

"Now take aim through the crosshairs. You see them?"

Riley closed one eye and sighted through the other, angling the launcher until he was satisfied.

"Now take a breath, hold it, and squeeze the trigger."

Riley felt a nervous sweat coat his face, transferring itself to Chevie's ear. Suddenly he noticed the amphibian's roll and pitch, and from all around came hubbub, ballyhoo, and distraction.

"Squeeze the trigger" *ain't as simple as it sounds.*

"I ain't sure about this, Chevie. What if I am a duffer at this game?"

"Just squeeze," said Chevie softly. "That's all you can do."

Riley held his breath and squeezed the launcher's trigger, sending an RPG streaking toward Westminster Bridge.

Which was a pity, because he was aiming for the tank.

The grenade knocked quite a dent in the bridge and the tank shuddered and settled in the cracked road surface. But cracked was all it was, not ruptured or riven. Quite sound, in fact.

"Pah," said Malarkey. "You ain't studied explosives at all, have you? You youngsters thinks you is so bang up to the elephant and yet you fires a squib at a metal bridge from an angle. *Trajectory.* There's a new word for you, Ramlet."

"The boat is shaky," said Riley, and no one could deny it.

"You ain't hitting that tank from here without a mortar. And even with a mortar, it would be a shot in a million, isn't that right, my darling?"

"I suppose that is right," said Witmeyer, but without the usual sparkle when conversing with her king, something Otto immediately picked up on. He draped an arm across her shoulders, which were suddenly tense.

"Oh, forgive me, big lummox that I am. That is your partner up yonder, and here I am discussing her explosive dismemberment."

"Couldn't we just go, Otto?" asked Witmeyer.

Overhead, the cannon fired another round into the belly of Westminster.

"No, my sweet," said Otto. "I may be the master villain in this town, but I ain't a bad man. Them are, in the main, innocent Jacks and Jills up there. And we shall truly be the high honorable regals in the Great Oven if'n we are the ones that slay the dragon."

Witmeyer hung her head. "Very well, Otto. Tell the boy."

Malarkey switched his caring face to his business one. "How many bang-bangs we got left?"

Riley looked in the trunk. A single missile lay cushioned in foam.

"Just the one," he said, twisting it into the nozzle as he'd seen Chevie do. "Will it be enough?"

Malarkey scratched his beard. "I suppose we is about to find that out, ain't we?"

He spent a minute considering, then issued his instruction as though it was a royal decree.

"The bridge is metal, except for the piers, which are stone. Aim for this end of the pier."

The tank was directly over the sixth pier, which at low

tide stood exposed like a spindly horse leg that could not possibly support the weight plunked on top of it.

Let's hope not, thought Chevie.

"Take the shot, Riley," she said. "I trust you."

I don't even trust me own self, thought Riley. As far as he could figure, if he did not knock that metal beast from its perch, then all manner of catastrophe would descend on his beloved country, the most immediate being the destruction of Parliament and all the toffs debating therein.

Though if they're still debating with all this racket going on, then they're a dimmer bunch than I thought.

"Shoot, Riley," said Chevie. "Quick, before she reloads."

Fingers crossed, thought Riley and he pulled the trigger for the second time.

Vallicose felt the second RPG hit and wondered, Could that be the end for me?

Was it possible that God had deserted her at the last moment?

No. Not possible.

This is my revolution, she thought inside the cauldron of the tank's hellish heat. The Blessed Thundercat, they will call me. The faithful shall be named Clovites. And a clover shall be my symbol.

Perhaps it was a little premature to be considering symbols; better wait till the job was done.

The tank was listing severely, so a little recalculation was necessary in order to ensure maximum destruction of the old regime.

Lower the barrel twenty degrees, thought Vallicose happily. *Maybe a smidge left. Five degrees.*

There was a nice little fire raging in Parliament now. Vallicose could imagine the right honorables suddenly praying to a god they had ignored for decades.

It is too late, my fine fellows, she thought, loading the tube. She began to whistle the tune for "The Colonel's Mustache" before stopping herself with a barked laugh.

That song is dead. Schoolchildren will sing songs about me.

A thought struck her and she was instantly sad.

Oh dear. I shall never be able to kill the queen now. Shame.

Still, she was reasonably sure the emancipated citizens would lynch Victoria in the street.

And that would have to do.

Malarkey shaded his eyes against the nonexistent glare while he studied the fissure the RPG had put in the near side of the stone strut.

"You botched it, Ramlet. You shoot like a . . ."

Chevie was not in the mood for stereotyping. "Like a what, Otto?"

Witmeyer found herself in exactly the same mood. "Yes, he shoots like a what, darling?"

Malarkey had not gotten to be king for so long by being slow on the uptake. "Like a novice, my sweet. Like a total novice."

Chevie pulled the launcher from her shoulder one-handed

and lowered it into the Thames to make sure no one else figured out how to use it.

Riley was despondent. "Well, believe it or not, those were my first times firing a rocket."

Malarkey punched him playfully. "I do believe it, Ramlet. I have not a problem in the world believing it."

Riley was staring up at the fissure, which was jagged and cavernous, as though the troll who lived under this particular bridge had taken a humongous bite out of the stone. But although the bite had penetrated almost to the very surface, it seemed as though the metal frame would hold.

"Well, that's that then," said Witmeyer, sounding a little relieved. "Even if we could fly, it would be too late. We should remove ourselves before the entire empire descends."

Malarkey nodded. "The militia will finish her off eventually."

"Eventually is too late," said Chevie through gritted teeth. "We are so close. So close. After everything we have been through."

Chevie could not shake the feeling that somehow, even though the soldiers had been scattered and the weapons washed into the Thames, the Revolution would still catch fire. Perhaps the destruction of their government would be enough to inspire the city's malcontents.

If Vallicose were allowed to fire one more shell . . .

As if on cue, the tank shuddered, and from its long barrel blasted another shell. It arced over the barricade of carriages, cannon, and clotted humanity, and disappeared into the belly of the Palace of Westminster, where God only knew how much damage it was causing.

And as Chevie watched the shell's progress, Riley watched the bridge.

"Look," he said. "The troll is hungry."

Vallicose pressed the fire button and felt the recoil force the tank deeper into the fissure. If the tank had been square on its treads, the dampers and suspension would have absorbed most of the recoil; but this tank was off-kilter and, truth be told, the grease monkey who had worked on the suspension probably hadn't excelled in mechanic school. The recoil shock was transmitted through the tank and into the bridge, forcing the fissure open about a foot, which was just enough to shear off the chunk of bridge on which sixty percent of the tank's weight rested. It happened so slowly that Vallicose had time to change gears and attempt to seesaw the tank from the widening fissure, but it happened too quickly for her to succeed. A rough pyramid of stone and iron twisted away from the bridge and plunged into the river below. The tank teetered for a long moment, its right track spinning in the air, but gravity was gravity and would not be confounded, and so, with a shudder and shrug, the tank tipped over and fell, groaning and shrieking all the way down.

For Vallicose the fall seemed interminable, and despite the ferocious buffeting and the screams issuing from her mouth, she found the time for some last thoughts.

This is a tight spot, she thought. It will be interesting to see how God extricates me from this one. Whatever happens, it will be the stuff of legend. *Sister Vallicose,* they will say, *the risen phoenix.*

A rhyme occurred to her, to the tune of "The Colonel's Mustache":

Gone in a flash
Gone in a flash
The Westminster Bridge
Was nothing but trash
But Vallicose brave
Had not breathed her last
Like the phoenix she flew
Up from the ash

Vallicose was not sure about rhyming *trash* with *flash*. Was the word *trash* popular in nineteenth-century London?

The truth was that Vallicose was occupying her brain with all this poetry and nonsense because she was distracting herself from a certainty that had suddenly nailed itself to the inside of her mind.

And though she had only a few seconds left to live, the thought grew louder and roared in her ears until she had no option but to scream it aloud.

"I was wrong!" she howled as the black river rushed up hard, as unforgiving as metal.

"I was wroooooong!"

• • •

Witmeyer followed the tank's creak, yaw, and tumble.

"It's only fifty feet or so. Clove might survive."

Chevie, Riley, and Malarkey slid each other a triangle of glances that spoke volumes.

She ain't surviving that, said the looks, and: *Fifty feet? Who taught you to measure?*

It was just within the realm of possibility that Vallicose might survive—if she was strapped into her seat and generously padded with teddy bears. Unfortunately for her, the huge chunk of masonry from the bridge had trapped a little air, and it stayed afloat long enough for the tank to land on top of it and blow itself to a million pieces of metal and bone.

The explosion was awesome in the biblical sense, which Vallicose might have liked if only she had held on to her faith in that final moment. It seemed that all of London recoiled from the detonation—from the swarms on the bridge to the river itself. Chevie swore she saw the pasty riverbed just before she ducked to avoid shrapnel that included granite chips, twisted rivets, and the skeleton of a small creature that seemed to be half-crab, half-pig.

Riley too saw the skeleton as it skimmed the gunwale, snapped its claws on the way past—an effect of its velocity, surely—then disappeared over the starboard bow.

I shall never speak of that, he decided.

In a comical line the amphibian's crew peeped over the gunwale to witness a boiling mushroom of smoke with snakes of flame in its fat stem.

For a long moment after the terrific sustained commotion

of shell, cannonball, and explosion, there seemed to be a noise vacuum into which even the birdsong and wavelets tumbled. Life proceeded silently, as if everyday sounds had faded to insignificance.

Then Lunka Witmeyer spoke.

"Well," she said. "I don't think there's any point in combing the wreckage."

And the sounds of the world came rushing back. From above, the shrieks and howls of the injured, and the horns and sirens of the water brigades. And from behind, the chug of engines and the shouts of authoritative voices through speaking-trumpets.

"Halt!" said the voices. And, "Heave to, there." And, "Prepare to be boarded."

Malarkey turned to see a ragtag flotilla of Her Majesty's naval vessels, penny steamers, and flat barges bearing down on their position.

"So much for thank-yous. I was expecting a medal."

Witmeyer linked arms with him. "This way is better, Otto. This way is mysterious."

Malarkey smiled. "Already, you know me so well."

He clambered onto the wheelhouse and played to the citizens hanging over the railings.

"Fear not, my people. The danger is past. Look upon my works, ye mighty, and despair, for the Ram has slain the dragon." He raised a stiff finger and projected to the heavens. "Remember that your queen could not save you—a king was needed."

Otto bowed low and spoke sotto voce under his armpit to Witmeyer, who stood at the wheel. "That is your cue to motor us out of here, my love. Leave 'em breathless."

From where she lay on the deck, Chevie thought that Malarkey probably would have risen to kingship in any age. And if not kingship, definitely reality-TV star.

Witmeyer toggled the gear lever into drive, then easily threaded the amphibian through the fleet of steam and sail vessels. Though scores of wide eyes stared at them and dozens of gaping jaws flapped their way, Witmeyer acknowledged not a single one, while Otto took bow after bow.

Riley cozied up beside Chevie, trying to cushion her from the worst of the boat's jostling.

"We have done it, Chevie," he said. "We have changed the world back to how it should be."

Chevie huffed. "Not all the way back, kid. There's a hole in Westminster Bridge that wasn't supposed to be there. And half of London has seen a tank."

Riley held her close. "At least Box is gone, eh?"

Chevie's smile would not have looked out of place on a wolf.

"Yes. At least Box is gone."

So perhaps her father would live, or at least die better. Same for DeeDee.

Once the amphibian had cleared the other craft and the flotsam from the explosions, Witmeyer opened the throttle wide and powered the amphibian across the silver-red sunset waves of the Thames. Within seconds, all that could be seen of the amphibian from Westminster was the twin arcs of its wake.

15 » BEAUTIFUL & DANGEROUS

In the end there is no end, especially where time travel is concerned. As soon as you start thinking everything's resolved, a whole lot of ramifications come down the wormhole. By the way, I know you people are calling my wormhole the Smarthole. That isn't very complimentary where I come from.
—Professor Charles Smart

THE ORIENT THEATRE, HOLBORN, LONDON, 1899

OTTO MALARKEY LOUNGED IN A SEAT IN THE Orient Theatre, silent for an uncommonly long period. The first reason for his silence was fitting, as the last time he had been in the Orient he had witnessed the slaughter of his own brother and a band of his bully chums besides. Also, he had been considerably bashed about his own self. For these pains he was certainly due a ruminative moment. But his second reason was a little churlish, considering all that had happened.

"You had to sink the boat?" he finally said, nailing Chevie

with a baleful eye. "That wonderful craft. King of the seas, I could have been."

Chevie was in quite a bit of pain, despite the thimble of laudanum Riley had prescribed before he sealed the wound with a single stitch. She guessed rightly that the boy had often been forced to clean up the battle wounds of his old master. And being in such pain, she was not in the mood for any of Malarkey's guff. "You are king of the city, which should be enough for you. And anyway, you saw what those weapons could do, Otto. You saw it up close."

Chevie sat on the lip of the stage with her back to the drawn velvet curtain, picking at the doorstop sandwich Riley had prepared for her.

Carbohydrates haven't been invented yet, she thought, so this doesn't count. Also, I have been shot.

She had, however, refused the tankard of ale Riley had offered and was instead drinking a mug of sour water that she doubted had been filtered through Scottish Highland rock.

More likely it was filtered through a filthy drainpipe, she thought, and then: I am not having much luck with water in this century.

"Bah," said Otto. "You have a mouth on you, girl. And you are one step away from royal disfavor. But I will make allowances on account of the scratch on yer shoulder."

It had taken no time at all to lose the navy pursuit boats, and Otto had casually suggested that he knew a quiet dock in Limehouse where a cove might stick a boat he didn't want investigated. Chevie could do little about the Limehouse berth,

but she could certainly lob a couple of grenades into the weapons locker after they disembarked, just to make sure that the amphibian was not adapted by Otto's boys for river piracy. Malarkey was still sulking about this, or more accurately, he had saved up the sulk until Lunka Witmeyer was out of earshot, and now that the ex-Thundercat was picking out some new duds from the Orient's wardrobe room, Malarkey was letting fly at Chevie.

"It is a sin to destroy a thing of such grace and beauty," he proclaimed. "And that boat were beautiful, no doubt about it. And dangerous with it."

Chevie swallowed a corner of sandwich. "Oh, yeah. Beautiful and dangerous. They're going to carve that on your headstone. *Here lies Otto Malarkey, killed by something beautiful and dangerous.*"

And speaking of beautiful and dangerous, the curtain opened in a series of swishes, revealing Lunka Witmeyer center stage. She was wearing a tan twill riding skirt, which would mark her as possibly American but nothing more out of the ordinary than that, and boots that buttoned to her knees. A red tapestry jacket and white ruffle-necked blouse completed the outfit. All in all, she looked quite striking.

"What do you think?" she asked.

Chevie glanced over her shoulder. "I think you should light a candle in that dressing room. Your outfit looks like you picked it out in the dark."

It was clear that Chevie wasn't about to forgive Witmeyer yet for her past transgressions.

"You better shut your entire face or I might forget you're injured," warned Witmeyer.

Chevie laughed. "Any time, Thundercat."

Malarkey vaulted onstage and lifted Witmeyer's hand, twirling her under his arm.

"Lord, oh Lord," he said. "You is a picture, and no mistake."

Malarkey had sent a boy with a list of errands to Figary, and the Irish butler, who had picked this moment to arrive at the theater, overheard Malarkey's *picture* comment.

"A picture, is it?" he said, incorrectly assuming that the commodore was teasing this Amazonian warrior woman. Figary was not a cruel man, but like most Gaels he had trouble holding in a jibe, however cutting.

"A picture painted by a one-eyed, drunken monkey . . ." he said. But as the words were tumbling from his mouth, Figary registered the diverse cooing and fluttering that were passing between the commodore and this strange lady, and he decided he should change tack before his mouth got him killed as his dear old ma had always predicted it would.

". . . which is exactly what I said last week to a man with a gallery on the Strand," said Figary smoothly. "This, on the other hand, is a picture of physical perfection, so it is."

He needn't have bothered. Witmeyer and Malarkey were deaf and blind to anything besides each other.

Riley emerged from the wings with a platter of bread, cheese, and meats.

"I usually don't allow foodstuffs on the stage. For one, it's

bad luck, and for two, I have to sweep the stage meself. Both star and skivvy, that's me."

Malarkey surfaced from the sea of love. "Riley, boy, you have done a fine job with the wardrobe. Miss Witmeyer is a stunner, is she not?"

Riley nodded but kept his mouth shut. Chevie could not keep quiet.

"She has certainly stunned me a few times," she said.

Riley offered her a wedge of cheese. "Why don't you stuff that in your trap? It would be healthy for both of us."

Figary walked down the central aisle. "Commodore, it is so good to see you vertical and breathing."

"It takes more than an army to kill me," said Malarkey. "Now, as to your mission. Is it safe for me to be abroad? Are the bluebottles on my tail? What is the talk of the town?"

"Why, *you* are the talk of then entire city," replied Figary. "Your heroic river battle. They are saying King Otto slayed the dragon. They are saying King Otto sent the demon back to hell. King Otto saved the Empire."

Otto nodded, satisfied. "That is no more than the truth of it, I suppose. Anything further?"

"Tea shirts," said Figary.

Chevie frowned. "T-shirts?"

Riley sat beside her on the stage. "Tea shirts. A kind of very starched formal shirt, worn by waiters in the Savoy tearooms and such."

Figary continued his transmission of the news. "A fellow is printing your portrait on tea shirts, selling them all over the

West End. A lovely likeness it is, Commodore; captures your locks perfect, so it does."

"Tea shirts, is it?" said Malarkey. "What an idea."

"You deserve it, Otto," gushed Witmeyer, and it was probably her first *gush*. "You are a hero."

"Chevie should have a tea shirt," said Riley. "She was the one who actually did the deed and not just the speechifying."

This reminded Figary of the speech. "Ah, yes, the famous oration. Also printed on the tea shirts." He coughed dramatically. "'Look upon my works, ye mighty, and despair.' Quoting Shelley, Commodore. Very nice use of irony."

"Irony?" said Malarkey. "No irony whatsoever, Figary. I wanted the government coves to take a good look and remember who saved the city."

"Anyway, Commodore, to answer your initial question: you are no fugitive, sir. I think if the law laid a finger on you, the people would rise up in revolution."

Chevie flinched. She did not like the word *revolution.*

"And what of my wayward men?" asked Malarkey. This was the important question. Civilians could refer to him as King Otto till Judgment Day, but without the Rams behind him, he was no more a king than the dozens of King Henrys locked up in London's asylums.

Figary's hands became more animated, flapping like a magician's doves. "Your men, Commodore. Those fools—forgive me, but those idiots saw the error of their ways. I paid the Hidey-Hole a visit, and there they were, like a bunch of rats sopping from the catacombs. Touching my hem, they were. Begging for my favor. *My* favor, if you please, after the same buckos tried to run me out of the place on the occasion of my previous visit. You need to hop a cab over there posthaste, Commodore. They are polishing your throne, so they are."

Malarkey puffed and preened. "Well, that is indeed good news, though those gulpy dupes don't deserve me."

Witmeyer had a suggestion. "Perhaps we should string up a few, make an example."

"Ah no, my dear, though I am tempted, but now is the time for mercy. Have I not slain the dragon? That is example enough. Let us forgive and forget old quarrels and step into the future together."

"Nicely said, Commodore. And nicely put. This young lady is having a positive influence."

"This is your new mistress, Figary. Mademoiselle Witmeyer, from the future. Show her to the carriage, would you?"

"It would be my pleasure," said Figary. He bowed to Witmeyer, then extended his elbow toward her so that she might link it. Witmeyer, who was familiar with this move only as an offensive jab, presumed she was being attacked and had the butler pinned on the floor faster than he could say *so it would.*

"Do not hurt him, my dear," said Malarkey. "He does a bang-up roast on the Sabbath. And he can get bloodstains out of anything."

Malarkey held out his hand to Riley for a shake. "Considering all the shenanigans we have endured together, Ramlet,

I am inclined to let you operate without taxation but with protection."

Riley clenched Otto's massive paw and shook it with heartfelt thanks and relief.

"Thanks, Your Majesty. I feels as though I could hug you."

Malarkey frowned. "I is the Ram king, lad. And I only hug my queen. Any attempts to embrace me will be firmly rebuffed."

Chevie winked at the Ram king. "He has protection. The best thing you can do is leave us alone."

"I will stay away until I am needed," conceded the Ram king. "But if you *do* have need, send a runner to Figary in Grosvenor Square and I will fly to your sides. King Otto is never too busy for his friends."

This was a good offer indeed from Malarkey, and even Chevie had to almost not scowl.

"We are still not friends, Otto," she said. "But I am less inclined to knock your block off."

"Good enough, girl," said Otto. "For one day only, I shall tolerate your sauce."

"Keep that one out of my way," Chevie added, nodding at Witmeyer, who was straightening Figary's coat. "And sleep with one eye open."

Malarkey sighed. "So that I may gaze upon her?"

"No, so that you may watch your throne. Your sweetheart has a dark past."

"That all be in the future, as it were."

Figary was recovering from his brief ordeal. "Manhandling,

is it? Missus Figary's boy did not risk his life crossing the channel to get himself manhandled, so he didn't."

Lunka Witmeyer actually apologized. First gushing, now apologizing. "I am sorry, strange little fairy man. I see now that you were attempting to be courteous. I am not accustomed to courtesy in my line of work."

Figary thought rightly that it would be wise to accept this ham-handed apology. "Think nothing of it. And what line of work would that be, madam?"

Witmeyer shrugged. "Oh, the usual. Murder, intimidation, some torture. But I usually delegate that."

"I understand completely, so I do," said Figary with a straight face. "Torture is so cruel."

"No, it's the mess. I don't mind the cruelty."

Figary knew then that he would have to tread very carefully with his master's new lady love, or Missus Figary's son could wake up dead some morning. He recalled a fortune-telling gypsy at Puck Fair warning him that he would meet a dark stranger at some unspecified point; he had laughed.

But now that I think on it, did not an owl hoot as Madam Tea Leaf made the prediction?

There *had* been an owl, and as any devotee of the psychic knew, and owl's hoot during a reading was the spirit world's seal of approval.

This is the dark stranger.

She wasn't really dark, but she was standing in the shadows a bit, and that would do.

"Madam," he said. "I am about to extend my elbow toward

you so that I may escort you to the carriage outside the theater."

"Extend away," said Witmeyer, who found this little man amusing, like a puppy, or a suspect listing imaginative reasons why he should not be interrogated. Her favorite had come from a suspected poet. He had admitted that he wrote poetry, but he claimed that his online reviews were so bad he could not technically be called a poet.

Another funny little man, just like this one.

Witmeyer laid a hand on the offered elbow and allowed herself to be escorted down the center aisle. She did not say good-bye to Savano or the boy Riley. There was only one person she cared about, and he was going to be by her side till the day he died. One way or another.

Malarkey took one long look around the theater, his gaze lingering on the spot where his brother Barnabus had fallen. It was some consolation that Farley had died horribly—but not much of one, if he was honest with himself.

"And here am I falling in love in the same week that my brother was murdered," he said, and then pensively, "Look upon my works, ye mighty, and despair."

"We don't none of us control our own hearts, King Otto," said Riley.

Malarkey thought on this and decided that it was indeed true. "We do not, boy," he said. "But we must follow them. And I must follow mine."

He bowed deeply. "Remember, friends. Otto Malarkey is no more than a whistle away."

And he walked swiftly after his beloved so that he might hold the carriage door for her—and ensure she did not kill Figary in response to some sudden movement.

Riley and Chevie sat on the stage, morosely finishing the last morsels of food. The first reason for their moroseness they shared, but in the second, they were direct opposites. The first reason was mutual post-traumatic depression, now that their adrenaline levels were dipping. As for the second, Riley believed that his pal Chevie would soon sling her hook off homeward, whereas Chevie knew this to be impossible, even if the phrase concerning hook-slinging was not in her vocabulary. Not yet, at any rate.

I could be learning a lot of new phrases, she thought.

"You'll be off now," said Riley eventually. "I understand for why you're leaving, pal, but I am sad nonetheless. I have plenty of room here for you. Your own chamber, and so forth; plus, I am making inquiries viz a flush toilet, which a future gal like yourself would no doubt appreciate."

Chevie dipped a hand under her shirt and pulled out the Timekey, which was, amazingly enough, still intact.

"Takes a bashing but keeps on flashing," she said. "But the port has been destroyed. There's no way home for me. I am afraid you're stuck with me."

"I am truly sorry, Chevie, on the one hand," said Riley. "But on the other I am glad to have my dearest friend under my roof. *Our* roof, I should say. We are partners now."

Chevie stuffed the pendant back inside her clothing. "I

appreciate that, Riley. But if this is our home, you need to get someone working on that flush toilet. And indoors, if you don't mind."

"Indoors?" said Riley. "This ain't the Savoy, Chevie." He thought for a minute. "I need a beautiful assistant. How would you feel about that?"

"I could do gun tricks, maybe," said Chevie. "And take on all comers for money."

Riley leaned in close, as though someone might hear. "No need. We have money. It's blood money and there's no denying it, but maybe we can wash it clean again by putting it to decent purposes, eh?"

Chevie meant to smile, to assure Riley that she would stick with him and help out in the theater, do whatever was needed, but she could not escape a sad conclusion.

"I will never know for sure how my father died, or my friend DeeDee. Or even if they died at all."

Here was something they did not share. Riley knew exactly how his parents had died: throats slit by the blade of Albert Garrick.

"Betimes, Chevie, the knowing of things ain't no help regarding peace of mind. Knowing things ain't no boon at all, if you ask me."

Footsteps echoed from the Orient's cozy foyer, and soon a figure caught up with the footsteps and revealed itself to be Bob Winkle. He ran flat out down the aisle, barely stopping before the orchestra pit.

"Ha!" he said, pointing at Chevie. "Injun princess, they are saying all over town, and I just knew it was Miss Chevron back with us again. Bob, says I to meself, there's only one lady who could send a dragon into the Thames with no return ticket—Miss Chevie Savano, I says. And I was right."

The youth was breathless and excited. "I just hopped off the Brighton train to find the whole of the city in an uproar." Bob stopped and sniffed the air. "What is that ungodly stink, boss? Is the drains playing up again?"

Riley grimaced. "That's we two, I am afraid. We was engaged in a bit of toshing."

This didn't seem to surprise Bob one whit. "Yep, toshing will do that to a body. Carbolic is the only thing for it, and you may as well burn your garments."

Chevie didn't like the sound of that. Her strange hybrid suit was all she had left from her future. She had even worn it under the dancing girl disguise. Burning her clothes would be like an admission of defeat.

"I will soak my clothes for a few days," she said. "I am fond of this suit."

"We will ask Figary for advice," said Riley. "I bet he can get the whiff out of anything."

"So he can," said Chevie, and they both smiled, marveling that Figary was such a character that simply repeating his catchphrase could cheer a body up. Even Bob Winkle showed his teeth, though he had never met Missus Figary's boy.

"Anyway," said Bob once his breath came back, "I ain't a-running because of all that's been happening around here. I am running because I have news."

"News?" asked Riley, jumping from the lip of the stage and rushing to Winkle's side. "What news?"

"News viz your brother, Tom."

Riley stepped back. This could be the very best of news, or the very worst, and he thought on his recent declaration that knowing things weren't no boon at all.

But I have to know, he thought.

"You found Tom in Brighton?"

"I found Tom's trail in Brighton," Bob corrected him. "A trail wide as Blackfriars Road, it was. Your boy Tom is quite the character."

Riley's heart beat hard in his chest. "Is? *Is* quite the character. So he's alive, then, and living in Brighton?"

"Yes to the first and not to the second. Tom is alive, but his misadventures have led him here to London. No more than a few miles from where we stand."

Riley felt weak, light-headed. "London. We must be away from here and visit him. But first, new duds, Chevie. We can't have my brother clapping eyes on us in this state. Or clapping nose on us, for that matter. I cannot believe that my own Christian name can finally be revealed. Perhaps I am an Albert, or a George. I fancy Oliver, so I do."

Chevie was watching Bob, and she saw in his face that the news was not yet fully transmitted.

"What else, Bob? There's more, right?"

Bob swallowed, a little nervous to be delivering the bad news, though Riley was a good employer who had never been anything but kind. Still, sometimes the messenger was blamed for the message.

"There is more, Riley. Visiting Tom is not such a walk in the park as a fellow might think."

Riley was bubbling with his excitement, so Bob's tone did not penetrate.

"Of course it is. I know we don't look our spiffing best at the moment, but half an hour in the tub and a lick of the soap will sort us out right as rain."

"It ain't that, pal. Tom ain't just any old where."

"London. You said he's in London."

"In London, right enough. In the most reviled pile o' stones we has in the city, leaning on its leeward shoulder again' the Old Bill Bailey itself."

Riley knew exactly the building that Bob was circling and trying not to utter.

"Newgate?" he said, the excited rouge in his cheeks fading fast. "Tom is in Newgate Prison?"

"He's in a debtor's cell."

Debtors. The most hated species in London. Lower in the law's eyes than smugglers or highwaymen.

"He ain't to be stretched in the morning, is he?" Riley asked Bob Winkle.

"Nah, he ain't hanging tomorrow," said Bob the Beak. "They ain't stretching him till Thursday."

This was indeed devastating news, and it bent Riley in two like a gut punch.

"An attorney," said Riley, when he had recovered himself somewhat. "We need the best attorney in London."

"That would be Sir James Maccabee, the man defrauded by your brother. The case is done and dusted beyond appeal, Riley. I hate to be the one bearing this foul parcel."

Riley's eyes were wide, and he waved his arms around like a man in pitch-blackness searching for a familiar surface.

Chevie felt her post-traumatic depression disappear. She had a new mission now.

"We need to break him out," she said. "Pack your bag of tricks and let's get a move on. I need to see this Newgate before I can put a plan together."

Riley looked at his future friend up on the stage with the light behind her, a true heroic figure that would give a body hope.

"You would help me in this matter?"

"Of course. We are a team."

"A team. Of course."

Chevie hopped off the stage. "We already took down an entire empire this week. What chance does a prison have?"

Riley thought that his friend was underestimating her opponent, as usual. Newgate Prison was a veritable fortress that foiled escape attempts every day of the year and swallowed criminals as effectively as a monstrous hungry beast. Liberating Tom would be the very devil of a job; but Riley thought it best not to deflate his partner, for they would need any good spirits they could find.

"That prison has no chance at all," he said, bolstering his

words with a steel he did not truly feel. "Newgate will open its doors to the two of us, and Tom will be restored to me."

Bob Winkle had no intention of being left out. "Count me in that number, Riley. Without you, I would still be smoking wallpaper in the Old Nichol."

"Three, then, there are three of us. Together we cannot fail."

"We cannot fail," agreed Bob.

"Failing not allowed," said Chevie.

It seemed to Chevie that all this repetition of the word *fail* would surely ensure that failure would take place, so she attempted to put a positive spin on the situation by raising her hand for a group high five.

The other two simply stared puzzled at her elevated hand.

"Come on, team," she said. "Don't leave me hanging."

Which was, perhaps, a bad choice of words in the circumstances, so Chevie tried again.

"Here we go again, boys. Off on another adventure. This time busting Riley's brother out of prison. There will be danger; there will be spills and thrills. There will be knives and there will be guns and there will be people saying stupid things at the worst possible time."

"Probably me!" said Bob cheerfully.

"So we need a motto, something to keep us going when the odds are against us."

"Like *the wind beneath our wings*?" asked Riley.

"No, not like that. And thanks for putting that song in my head, by the way."

She put her hand out and the others knew enough to cover her hand with theirs.

"Here's to not getting killed," she said, and then together they chorused:

"Not getting killed."

It was the best they could hope for, given the circumstances.